Instant Karma

PRAISE FOR *INSTANT KARMA*

Story-telling is a gift, and David Michie imaginatively creates interconnected pictures of lives and situations that we all recognise to bring about an understanding of karma, and through these stories we learn how a recognition of this can help us live better lives. He sets up the characters and contexts very swiftly and skillfully, all with their own particular and recognizable realities to deal with. Human drama and romantic comedy are combined with Buddhist wisdom, science and philosophy into an inspirational and joyful read that is a life lesson.

We learn that we can change our lives, and the lives of others, if we can live with a more awakened awareness of karma—of the cause and effect of our actions.

Instant Karma is optimistic, funny, provocative and transforming. It deserves to find a wide audience—"may all sentient beings find Happiness". There is no more important message.

—Duncan Baird, Publisher

David Michie weaves together a gripping tale of the magic and mysteries of the complex workings of karma. Witty, wise, and thoroughly enjoyable. I couldn't put it down.

—Vicki Mackenzie, author of *Cave in the Snow* and *Reincarnation, The Boy Lama*

Instant Karma is an astute story with an amusing, life-changing plot about the consequences of our actions. The bold, unique subject matter, featuring the teachings of a Buddhist guru and a literal application of the idea of instant karma, makes this novel stand out from the crowd. While Instant Karma does show both the positive and negative impacts of societal change, the book's focus on kindness and hope is refreshing.

—*Publishers Weekly* reviewer for The BookLife Prize

Also by David Michie

Fiction

The Dalai Lama's Cat Series

The Dalai Lama's Cat

The Dalai Lama's Cat and The Art of Purring

The Dalai Lama's Cat and The Power of Meow

The Dalai Lama's Cat and The Four Paws of Spiritual Success

The Dalai Lama's Cat: Awaken the Kitten Within

Matt Lester Spiritual Thrillers

The Magician of Lhasa

The Secret Mantra

Other Fiction

The Queen's Corgi

The Astral Traveler's Handbook & Other Tales

Nonfiction

Buddhism for Busy People: Finding Happiness in an Uncertain World

Hurry Up and Meditate:
Your Starter Kit for Inner Peace and Better Health

Enlightenment to Go:
Shantideva and the Power of Compassion to Transform Your Life

Mindfulness is Better than Chocolate

Buddhism for Pet Lovers:
Supporting our Closest Companions through Life and Death

Instant Karma

THE DAY IT HAPPENED

A LAMA TASHI NOVEL

David Michie

CONCH

Conch Books

First published in 2022

CONCH

Conch Books, an imprint of Mosaic Reputation Management (Pty) Ltd

Cover design: Sue Campbell Book Design
Author photo: Janmarie Michie

Cataloguing-in-Publication details are available from the National Library of Australia www.trove.nla.gov.au
ISBN 978-0-6488665-8-9 (Hardcover)
ISBN 978-0-6488665-6-5 (Paperback)
ISBN 978-0-6488665-7-2 (e-book)

HOMAGE

With heartfelt gratitude to my precious gurus:
Les Sheehy, extraordinary source of inspiration and wisdom;
Geshe Acharya Thubten Loden, peerless master and
embodiment of the Dharma;
Zasep Tulku Rinpoche, precious Vajra Acharya and yogi.

Guru is Buddha, Guru is Dharma, Guru is Sangha,
Guru is the source of all happiness.
To all gurus I prostrate, make offerings and go for refuge.

May this book carry waves of inspiration from my own gurus
To the hearts and minds of countless living beings.

May all beings have happiness and the true causes of happiness.
May all beings be free from suffering and
the true causes of suffering;
May all beings never be parted from the happiness that is
without suffering, the great joy of nirvana liberation;
May all beings abide in peace and equanimity, their minds free
from attachment and aversion, and free from indifference.

All truth passes through three stages.
First, it is ridiculed.
Second, it is violently opposed.
Third, it is accepted as being self-evident.

—ARTHUR SCHOPENHAUER (Philosopher, 1788—1860)

Prologue

The Day Before
Omni, Colorado

NO ONE COULD REMEMBER WHEN THE GURU CAME TO LIVE AT THE top of the mountain. Some distance out of the small but picturesque town of Omni, his home was little more than a summer shack. He had no phone, TV or radio. He subsisted on an austere diet of vegetables and who knows what, from the modest stipend he earned teaching meditation. He drank no alcohol, nor was he ever seen buying the kind of tasty indulgences that most people found necessary for a feeling of contentment. A man of indeterminate age who looked fifty-something but may well have been older, he was a being of few needs. But if asked who was the happiest person they knew, the good townsfolk of Omni—and even the not-so-good ones—would immediately and unanimously have answered: "Lama Tashi."

Although his home was secluded, not far from Rocky Mountain National Park, the guru was no recluse. He held weekly classes at the Lone Pine Meditation Center. A few times a month he'd come into town to collect his frugal provisions. Guiding a shopping cart round the grocery store, when he encountered another person he always made eye contact, nodded in acknowledgement, and smiled. And at such moments, a remarkable thing happened. The person meeting his eyes would melt.

It didn't matter what state of mind they were in. Whether they were hurrying or weary or diligently working their way through their shopping list. When they encountered Lama Tashi they experienced a sudden jolt.

9

An unexpected and powerful reminder about who and what they truly were. It was hard to put this experience into words. How, with a single glance, they came to recognize an important truth about themselves. It was as if this man effortlessly saw beyond the appearance they usually took themselves to be, and reflected back a more panoramic reality. Whatever trials they may be facing, whatever the constraints that so preoccupied them became like mere froth on the ocean surface—ephemeral and inconsequential compared to the boundless reality below. And so benevolent was Lama Tashi's expression, so wholehearted his acceptance that they'd feel an up-welling of joy. In his warm, brown eyes was all the reassurance they needed that, beneath the surface, all was well.

Such was the effect of Lama Tashi's presence that, even in the early days, he was never on the receiving end of the apprehension which members of small communities often felt about outsiders. Lama Tashi had Asian features, wore red robes and never made any pretense that while living in their world he was self-evidently not of it. But he was never shunned for being different. On the contrary, he was actively sought out.

Pauline Taylor, who lived with a menagerie of rescue animals on the outskirts of town, kept an eye out for Lama Tashi's ancient, lime-green Volvo on the road into town, leaving home at the most opportune moment to engineer an encounter with him. Tears welling in her eyes, she told anyone who cared to listen that she had never felt such unconditional love as the time she'd first bumped into Lama Tashi in the Household Detergents aisle.

Professor Hawke, retired from Princeton, who refused to slum it intellectually with just about everyone, used to collar Lama Tashi any time he saw him, insisting he join him for coffee at The Good Roast, and demand answers to arcane questions of quantum mechanics.

Even Margarita Moore, whose staunch views on anyone who wasn't Born Again, heterosexual, and a vigorous supporter of the Second Amendment were well known, was once seen *holding hands* with Lama Tashi outside her church, ardently agreeing that there is only one ultimate reality, and if we wish to experience it, first we must let go of our tightly-held view of self. In that moment, what the guru said seemed—even to her—to be so overwhelmingly obvious that she couldn't possibly disagree.

Within hours, as the impact of his presence began to dissipate, she slid back into her habitual convictions. But at the time what an extraordinary vision it had been to behold!

So popular was Lama Tashi around town that people joked how an endorsement by the guru on the mountain would guarantee electoral success. When someone had questioned if he might himself consider running for office his face had crinkled, silvering goatee wobbled, and he had belly-laughed with appreciative gusto, as if the suggestion was deliberately and hilariously idiotic. Which in a kind of way it was. But in another kind of way, wasn't.

The idea of having Lama Tashi as their representative in City Hall or Congress or even—why the heck not?—the Senate, was an idea that once suggested refused to go away. From time to time someone would ask him, "Would you consider being our Mayor, Lama Tashi?" Or "Would you run for Congress?" And he always replied in the same, cryptic manner. Meeting his questioner in the eye with a warmly encouraging expression he would say, "You are asking the wrong question, my friend. It is important to ask a useful question if we wish to receive a useful answer."

While Lama Tashi was no hermit, he didn't dawdle when he came to town, nor did he frequent the coffee shops or restaurants unless practically dragged there by the likes of Professor Hawke. As a result, no one had much idea about the practices that had given rise to his particular presence, that seemingly magical aura he emanated wherever he went. Over the years, on the few occasions he had been asked what he believed, he answered in a way designed to benefit the person asking, using words offering that most precious of all gifts: hope.

To Kathy Branton, a young woman who concealed an abused childhood beneath a prickly exterior, he said simply that he believed in loving-kindness. Had anyone else mouthed such a saccharine sentiment, Kathy would have bristled. But so unfeigned was the guru's presence, so unreserved the compassion in his eyes, that she came away feeling curiously uplifted.

Asked by Maria Flavio, a lapsed and very guilty Catholic, he had pointed upwards to where the spring sky was a vaulted sweep of pure blue from one horizon to the other. "We are like this," he told her. "Perfectly clear. No matter what clouds pass through, or how long they remain, they have no power to taint our true nature. *That* always remains pristine and radiant."

As Maria had walked away from the encounter she felt a sublime lightness, as if a burden she had been unwittingly carrying around on her shoulders for her whole life had been suddenly and unexpectedly removed.

Sometimes, Lama Tashi didn't use words at all. Beckoned by Darius Styles, Gwen and Angelo's teenage son who suffered from cerebral palsy, Lama Tashi stepped over to where the boy was slumped in his wheelchair in dappled sunshine outside a convenience store, waiting for his mother. Physically, Darius's body was misshapen but there was little wrong with his mind. He had seen Lama Tashi around town before, in his distinctive robes.

As the guru approached, Darius asked a question in sounds the lama couldn't possibly unravel—at least, not by way of hearing. But it didn't matter. Lama Tashi reached out, taking him by his right hand, and looked into his eyes.

To begin with Darius was awkwardly self-conscious, and not simply on account of being in the presence of a stranger wearing strange clothes. Being more sensitive than most to non-verbal communication, there was something about the simple goodness of the guru he found, at first, almost too much to bear.

But after a while, Darius looked up to meet his gaze. And when he did, it wasn't long before he was smiling also. Still holding onto the lama with his own right hand, he shifted himself in his chair so that with his left he was able to reach up and, with the tips of his fingers, touch his heart.

Lama Tashi nodded.

It had been one of the very few unchaperoned exchanges Darius had had in his life. And the most meaningful.

In such ways, Lama Tashi's constant offering to the people among whom he lived, was his gift of hope. Hope to inspire insight and self-acceptance. Hope to create positive change.

JUST AS HE DEFIED THE USUAL CONVENTIONS OF BELIEF, THERE WAS similar ambiguity about why he had chosen to be part of their particular community. To participants at the Lone Pine Meditation Center he would say that he was there to help them experience the true nature of their own minds. To Tom and Tina Jackson, his Vulture Peak Drive neighbors, he explained that his cabin was an ideal place to meditate.

The only being to whom he revealed more of the truth was his cabin companion, a Siamese cat named Shanti. Like so much else in Lama Tashi's life, Shanti hadn't arrived through any deliberate act on his part and instead had spontaneously appeared. One day she simply stepped through the open window when he was meditating and curled up next to him. She never chose to leave.

From time to time Lama Tashi reached out to where Shanti was basking in the summer sun on his windowsill. Or, in the evenings, to where she might be toasting herself in front of the fire.

"Ah yes, this is the most beautiful place to wait, isn't it, my dear Shanti?" he stroked her luxuriant tummy. "The most perfect place to bide our time."

What, exactly, they were biding their time for was not a subject on which he elaborated. Nor did she much care, so long as he continued biding it with her. *And* stroking her tummy, of course.

The afternoon before that most extraordinary of days, Lama Tashi set off in the direction of his neighbor's house. Living at the furthest end of Vulture Peak Drive, somewhat higher than the Jacksons' residence, meant that when he'd first moved in he had become quite familiar with the Jacksons, from a distance, some weeks before they had actually met. Tom, tall, broad-shouldered and ramrod straight carried an air of invincibility about him, looking every inch the recently retired, high-ranking military man. Tina, trim, vivacious and plucky, was always on the go. When she wasn't creating extravagant floral arrangements for weddings, baptisms or other milestones in the community, she was tending to her plants. In particular, she took great joy from the gorgeous salvia blossoms that flourished in the hanging baskets which ranged along the full length of their balcony.

The Jacksons were the kind of people whom other friends from the forces constantly dropped in to see. Their home was Party Central. During those early years there had seldom been a weekend night when their balcony—overlooking the same panoramic vista as Lama Tashi's modest porch—wasn't filled with former comrades and their spouses, with much back-thumping, shoulder-pounding conviviality among the men.

Unflagging entertainment along the mountain didn't disrupt the lama's routine. The occasional few stray bars of music, or laughter that carried on the night breeze was never enough to keep him from sleeping—he was usually in bed by 9 pm. And when he woke for his first meditation session of the day at 3 am, surveying the pristine tranquility of the moonlit valley, it was as if he was the only person in the world.

Over the decades, the socializing next door had fallen away, Tom had begun to stoop and Tina slowed down. There was no escaping the aging process, not that ageing alone accounted for the changes that had come over Tom—and, as a consequence, Tina. There was a more troubling reason why the former Colonel would spend so many solitary hours on the balcony staring into the night, a tumbler of bourbon beside him.

Something he had been able to rationalize, suppress, or ignore through most of his working life was taking advantage of the stillness of his retirement to emerge from its basement trunk and slide into waking consciousness. Something that had only ever revealed itself before in his worst nightmares would creep out at unexpected moments—and once glimpsed, devour all of his attention. Horrific, sickening, misery-inducing, it was something he found hard enough to admit to himself let alone anyone else.

Lama Tashi had seen it clearly the very first time they'd met. That occasion had been a couple of months after his arrival, wheeling his trash can to the end of the road for the weekly collection. Tom had just transported the Jackson's own can on the back of a macho-looking pick-up truck. Turning to find his new neighbor approaching, he had instinctively assumed his unassailable, military man pose.

When Lama Tashi met Tom's clear blue eyes, he immediately saw what was in his heart—and his expression was filled with compassion.

Abashed, Tom hadn't known how to respond. Never had he found himself so completely transparent, especially with regards to that worst of all horrors. He was so successful at hiding it, he doubted that anyone even suspected it was there. Now, caught unawares by a man of self-evident virtue, he didn't know how to react. He certainly wasn't prepared for the rush of benevolence from Lama Tashi's heart, which made him feel both awkwardly self-conscious and utterly unworthy. So he had retreated behind a veil of elaborate courtesy, insisting on giving Lama Tashi a ride back to his house, talking all the way about the city's garbage collection policy.

From the next week on, Tom always stopped by to collect his neighbor's trash can and return it to him, once emptied, later in the day. After the worst winter snowfalls, he'd clear away the snow on Vulture Peak Drive, not only to his own front door, but to the lama's too.

Had he been asked to explain himself, Tom would have drawn himself up and spoken about the importance of being a good neighbor. But it went very much deeper than that. Once, when repairing his own stone fence Tom had, without prompting, spent a week repairing Lama Tashi's. And when the lama had gone on a two month visit to the Himalayas, to reconnect with his elderly guru, his colleagues and family, he had returned to find his cabin newly and securely insulated, protecting him from the worst of the arctic winter freeze as well as the summer heat.

Lama Tashi always expressed his heartfelt appreciation for his neighbor's kindness, although both he and Tom knew that it wasn't his gratitude that Tom yearned for. It was instead something he had so far been unable to bring himself to express.

Lama Tashi had tried to reach out to him over the months, then years. There had been exchanges when he'd as good as physically yanked Tom away from the mesmerizing specter. The irony didn't escape the lama that it was the man who lived closest to him, who did more than most in practical ways to support him, and who was in the direst need of his guidance, who was also the most impervious to his efforts.

Enough! Understanding the unprecedented, seismic shift about to occur, Lama Tashi knew that Tom was about to have the best chance he ever would to be rid of the monster that was slowly crushing the life out of him. Past encouragement had failed. Time to change tack.

Lama Tashi knocked three times on the Jackson's front door. It was a while before the lock turned and Tom was standing in the doorway. Once again, there was the same meeting of eyes. The same recognition in Lama

Tashi's expression as he reflected, with deep concern, how pervasive the darkness in Tom had become.

Tom showed him through the hallway, a light-filled room with a high, windowed ceiling, in the center of which stood a large table. In former times the table would have been dominated by one of Tina's sweeping floral arrangements, a festival of vibrant blossoms and verdant greenery. Today, it stood bare, a great, empty, highly-polished slab. Tom led him to the lounge which opened onto the balcony, the room which had once been the epicenter of the Jackson's social whirl. Its walls were bedecked with photographs of battleships, striker aircraft and, mounted in pride of place, a pair of Enfield muskets from the Civil War. In a far corner stood an upright piano, never played. The balcony outside was open and strangely stark, denuded of the once-lush hanging gardens of Babylon, as Tom had ironically referred to his wife's creations.

"I've come to ask if you would do me a favor," began Lama Tashi, once they were sitting. "I may be needed elsewhere from tomorrow, for a few days. I wonder if you could please visit the cabin, and if I'm not there, feed Shanti?"

Tom nodded. "Of course."

For a few minutes they discussed details of timing, where Shanti's food was stored, and her preference for variety. Her water, and the means by which she came and went from the cabin. Then talk turned to general chit chat about the early warmth of spring this year and its effect on the black bears who were coming out of hibernation earlier than usual.

The small talk ran its course. There was an awkward silence. It was now or never.

Lama Tashi turned, gazing toward the balcony where Tom sat alone, night after night. "I see you in the evenings," he said.

Tom followed his eyes as if joining him to study the diminished version of himself, slumped in his chair.

"I like a bourbon," he observed, tilting his head in the direction of his bar in the corner of the room, showcasing a row of spirit bottles lined up in regimental precision against a mirrored wall.

Lama Tashi surveyed the many bottles. "Alcohol," he nodded, sagely. "Sometimes, I think, the effect is like meditating."

Tom's eyebrows twitched sharply upwards. "How d'you get that?"

"It doesn't change a thing," he explained. "But it may change the way you feel about a thing. Temporarily."

Tom knew exactly what Lama Tashi was up to, trying again to lever open that particular door. He made no reply, looking instead at the floor with an avoidance that had become reflexive.

"It helps you sleep, yes?" the lama attempted.

Tom didn't say anything for a long while before grunting, "Anesthetic."

Lama Tashi nodded. "Pain relief."

"You're probably going to tell me I should meditate instead," Tom flashed a look of open defiance. "But sitting still for hours isn't my bag. I'm a man of action."

They were on the same page now. The subject of Tom's pain acknowledged along with his recalcitrance. And only because of his heartfelt compassion, Lama Tashi did the last thing Tom expected. While Tom studied him through blue eyes so light they were almost vacant of color, Lama Tashi reflected back an altogether different reality.

Gone was the benevolent acceptance with which Tom was familiar and instead was power in a gaze the likes of which he had never felt before. More intimidating than the most threatening he'd encountered in the military. More ominous because it confronted him with the reality he'd spent decades trying his utmost to avoid: the torment of his own mind. An unfathomable horror to which he'd been witness decades earlier and from which there was no escape. A to-the-bone dread which had become his all-consuming preoccupation. In his neighbor's eyes, this was all reflected back to him with an objectivity that conveyed an urgent and powerful warning. No longer could he avoid the appalling recognition that however deeply troubled he felt right now, it was as nothing compared to what lay ahead if something didn't change.

What would he do when there was no balcony to sit on, no bourbon to anesthetize? After he died when his mind, instinctively drawn to the horror, became completely absorbed in it? Unfettered from a body, without anchor to a place where he could return for even temporary relief, he was confronted not so much by some Hieronymus Bosch nightmare as by his own future. Was this not the very definition of hell—the relentless experience of intense pain without cessation? One he may have glimpsed and tried to discount before but which was reflected inescapably in the overwhelming wrathfulness of Lama Tashi's gaze.

"I agree that action is needed," Lama Tashi said after a while, in what felt like from a different lifetime.

Deeply disconcerted, Tom saw his neighbor's expression segue back to its usual tranquil demeanor. Never had he guessed that the mild-mannered guru possessed such core-shaking power. With a shudder, he recognized why Lama Tashi had always shown him such compassion—not only because of what tormented him now, but because of what he understood lay ahead. It was going to get even worse.

Lama Tashi knew that he had Tom's undivided attention. "Nothing in the future is decided," he said, speaking directly to his thoughts. "It is up to you to create the causes for the effects that you wish to experience. *You* create your own reality."

There was a lengthy pause while Tom absorbed what had just happened. Staring at him he asked, "What are you suggesting?"

LATER, BEFORE GOING TO BED, LAMA TASHI STOOD OUTSIDE HIS HOME looking into the darkness—the space which, for his neighbor, was a theatre of horror. The source of baleful specters that came to torment Tom, that held him transfixed by dread, yet somehow compelled to return night after night, bourbon in hand.

Lama Tashi's own experience could hardly be more different. To him the hours of darkness were a time of wonder, when dazzling brightness and activity subsided to reveal more subtle realities which pointed to a wondrous purpose. The gurgling stream beyond the lip of the mountain, the source of the verdant pastures that surrounded them, became audible only when the noises of the day dissolved and the constant promise of life could be heard flowing sweet as a lullaby. Up above, the moon and stars hidden until after nightfall, spangling the sky in cosmic patterns miraculous with possibilities.

From this vast, interdependent spaciousness all things would arise, abide and pass. Ceaseless in motion, for him the ephemeral dance of the elements was an ever-present reminder of transience. For if nothing was permanent, then everything was possible. The only certainty was change.

Shanti appeared at the cottage window and meowed, rubbing the side of her head luxuriantly against the frame. Lama Tashi picked her up, gently holding her to him so that the two of them were sharing their warmth as they gazed into the bountiful night.

"Yes, my dear, all must change," he said. "The only question is: how?"

Wake up and smell the coffee!

Friday
8:00 am (Eastern Standard Time)
6:00 am (Mountain Standard Time)
5:00 am (Pacific Standard Time)

Mind is the forerunner of all actions.
All deeds are led by mind, created by mind.
If one speaks or acts with a corrupt mind, suffering follows,
As the wheel follows the hoof of an ox pulling a cart.

Mind is the forerunner of all actions.
All deeds are led by mind, created by mind.
If one speaks or acts with a serene mind, happiness follows,
As surely as one's shadow.

—THE BUDDHA (5th century BCE)

I

Wall Street, New York City

AMY ROBBINS DROPPED A COIN IN THE HOMELESS MAN'S CAP. AS she did most Fridays. The same guy sat in the same shop entrance, wild and unkempt, cheeks raw from exposure.

"God bless!" he said today, as he always did when her coin clinked against others in the cap.

"You too," she murmured.

A short distance along the pavement was the coffee shop. On a Friday she'd come in early to buy a cappuccino as a reward for surviving another week in the city. A modest reward maybe, but on her junior analyst's salary she had to be careful.

There were three people ahead of her in the line at Brew Ha. Behind the espresso machine, Jordan caught her eye with a grin and raised his eyebrows.

She nodded, smiling.

Over the months he'd got to know her order so that by the time she'd paid, her cappuccino was right there on the counter, complete with her name spelled out in the foam. The first time it had happened she'd been thrilled, and not only because tall, rangy Jordan had evidently remembered her name. It was also the first time she'd felt acknowledged as a regular. Someone from around here. A person with as much right to call herself a New Yorker as anyone else.

Up till then, she always felt like the proverbial country mouse. Her pretty face, bright-eyed perkiness and neat figure might have opened doors back home in Aubrey, Texas, but she'd felt like an imposter even trying to make a life for herself here. There had been times she wondered why she kept on at it—the grungy apartment, the daily commute, the low pay. Except that she was driven by a greater purpose. Like countless others before her, she'd hoped that by simply being here she would discover a way to bring her deepest wishes into reality.

Until then, Brew Ha was her sanctuary, her feel-good place. For as long as it took to drink her cappuccino, every Friday she would reflect nostalgically on the good things back home in Aubrey, like Mr. Deal and the horses she used to care for at Bluegrass Horse Sanctuary, especially her beloved Flash, who she'd ridden since childhood. She'd also remind herself why she was here.

Friends back home had always been complimentary about how she'd styled her bedroom in a way that was contemporary and chic, even if they didn't have the language to describe what she'd done or how it made them feel. She had the right eye, they'd say. She knew how to put things together. Which was why she'd set her heart on getting into interior design someday, once she'd got to understand how things worked in New York City and found the confidence to bring her dreams to life.

On weekends Amy would walk round her new Brooklyn neighborhood and pause outside some of the buildings and wonder about what it might be like to live there. One in particular, the spectacular art-deco Woodrow Wilson building was her all-time favorite. She was so drawn to it she'd even walked into its gracious, marble lobby and marveled at its landscaped gardens. Apartments in the building started out at half a million plus, with two bedrooms costing at least double that. She'd have to be a trader at Sharma Funds before she could even think of earning enough.

Just one person away from the counter that particular morning, Amy felt a vibration in her coat pocket. Taking her phone out, she opened her messages. And was so astonished by what she found that she didn't even realize she'd moved to the front of the line. Both Jordan and the girl on the register had to call out her name, in unison, to bring her back to the here and now.

When she looked up, she was wearing an expression of bewildered exhilaration.

2

Omni, Colorado

MARGARITA OPENED THE PASSENGER DOOR AND CAREFULLY PLACED the cardboard tray containing two, large Americanos on the seat. Single origin from Huila, Columbia, the coffee was Bob's favorite. A bonus to accompany her early return.

She'd been scheduled to fly home from New York later today, but the week's meetings had gone so well that she'd decided to return yesterday afternoon, spending last night at her sister's in Denver before getting up early. She hadn't told Bob, wanting to give him a surprise. Both of them had been working long hours of late. Being the end of the week, perhaps they could take this opportunity to push back? Go somewhere scenic for lunch and take the rest of the day off to do whatever—she had a few ideas.

Closing the passenger door, she stepped round the front of the SUV to the driver's side, smiling as she recalled the last time she'd stopped for coffee. Just like now, she'd got home earlier in the day, arriving home with Bob's favorite single origin coffee. Whether it was her recent absence, or the coffee, or a combination of the two she couldn't say, but the effect on her husband had been unexpectedly arousing. Delightfully so.

Over twenty-five years of marriage the fire of their passion for one another had inevitably receded to something more like a muted glow. But that early-morning coffee run had had the same effect as throwing fuel on the embers, provoking an entirely unexpected blaze of desire that had seen them using several surfaces of their home in ways they hadn't since they'd first dated. It was a good thing that Gabby had moved to college earlier this year!

Margarita couldn't help wondering if her arrival home today would unleash the same vigorous exuberance. Flicking down the driver's visor, she checked her appearance in the mirror, always at its most merciless this time in the morning. She ran her hands through her short cropped dark hair, her gaze resting briefly on her bronzed cheeks before inspecting the mascara which focused attention on what Bob had always told her were her most alluring feature—her vivacious Latina eyes. Her complexion may have faded and lines deepened through menopause, and she was sometimes despairing of the unstoppable changes that had come over her. But sexual attraction had turned out to be a most curious thing, the spark of desire was evidently capable of being re-ignited even given the reality of thinning skin and sagging breasts. Physicality, it seemed, was only part of it. Snapping the visor mirror shut, Margarita pondered for a while on how this particular life force, one she had imagined consigned to her past, was capable of making such a sudden and welcome late-life resurgence.

Not that she pondered for very long.

Opening the driver's door to step inside, the most familiar figure caught her eye. He was quite some distance away—a couple of hundred yards down the street at the top of an outdoor staircase. But even if he had been twice the distance, even if he hadn't been wearing the jungle green jacket they had bought in Costa Rica last year, she would have recognized him in an instant. What on earth was he doing stepping out the door of the apartment above Paige Turner Books? And so early in the morning?

The questions were still forming in her mind when a figure appeared behind him. As he turned back, Margarita could make out the pink of a bathrobe. A woman's hands around his shoulders. He was kissing her— and not in the manner of a cordial farewell. The intimacy of their embrace was unmistakable. Moments later, he was stepping back inside, shutting the door quickly.

Behind the steering wheel, Margarita was too shocked to move.

3

Dan Kavana, America's most loved African American TV anchor, had been fast asleep when his phone rang. Grabbing it from the bedside table, through force of habit he tried switching off the alarm. Before realizing it wasn't an alarm, but an incoming call. From the Head of News. *And* he should have been up an hour ago.

He sat in bed, clearing his throat

"Where are you now?" His boss, Nick Nalder, never wasted time on pleasantries.

"About to leave." Which usually he would have been. "What's up?"

"Contagious bacteria."

Jolted, Dan tugged off the sheets and got out of bed. Nothing like the threat of a contagion to boost ratings. The more dire the better. "Where?" he asked, getting to the bathroom and switching on the light.

"New York. Times Square outlet of Golden Drumsticks."

Golden Drumsticks was the biggest fast food chain in USA. And Times Square as close to the nation's bullseye as you could get.

"How contagious?"

Nalder was already talking to someone else in the newsroom, as was his habit. Dan wondered if what he was saying was meant for him or being directed elsewhere.

"Just get here quick as you can," Nalder told him. "There's a lot of weird shit going down today."

Dan had no idea how he'd disabled his alarm. But he'd have to rush

27

through his ablutions in record time. His wife, Tammy, was away addressing an African American Women in Business conference. Which meant Maddie was his responsibility today. Their twenty-three-year-old daughter had had her neck broken in a car accident two years ago, rendering her quadriplegic. She had always been a slow starter in the mornings. Just getting her out of bed and to the bathroom could be a half hour job.

He quickly began shaving, pressing the dial button to Maddie's lead care-giver, Jacinda. She didn't pick up. Nor did care-givers two or three on the list. Dan left messages as he scrambled through his morning routine. He tip-toed into Maddie's room which, at her own insistence, was the darkest and quietest in the house. He could barely make out her face against the pillow, but he heard her breathing, slow and regular. No indication that she even sensed his presence.

"Little bird," he mouthed his nickname for her, soundlessly, through force of habit.

Shutting her door behind him, hurrying down the passage, he grabbed his phone and keys and headed for where the chauffeured limo would be waiting for him in the driveway.

He felt terrible leaving his own, disabled daughter alone in an empty house. He'd never done it before—and if he'd woken in time, or if there wasn't a major, breaking news story, he wouldn't be doing it now. Taking care of Maddie at home was a commitment Tammy and he had made after the accident and one they'd always kept.

Until now.

4

G RACE ARLINGHAM CLOSED THE FRONT DOOR OF HER COTTAGE
and made her way gingerly across the tiled veranda. She gripped the railing tightly as she took the five steps down to the front path. Pausing at the bottom, with her right hand she adjusted the scarf covering her bald head. A gesture that had become habitual over the past six months.

In the early weeks after losing her hair she used to wonder when she'd be able to get rid of the scarf. At what point the wisps gathered about her scalp would grow back to her familiar lustrous mop. She had, after all, been through this before. The diagnosis. The treatment. The slow emergence from a time when she was, first and foremost, a cancer patient, back to the daily reality of life as a piano teacher in Montpelier. Even if it was a reality that, in some indefinable way, had shifted key.

Since the last two scans, however, Grace had been trying to let go of all expectations. About her hair. About anything. When thoughts about the future arose from habit—when to start her students on their exam pieces? Where the family would do Thanksgiving this year?—she'd quickly smudge them out. Chances were, she wouldn't have any students in five months' time. She would be lucky to make it to Thanksgiving.

Dr. Roberts had shown her the PET scan images. During her last appointment, at her request, he'd flipped the large screen on his desktop, come to sit next to her, and gently explained the significance of the black shadows blooming with such sinister fecundity in her abdomen. Already familiar with the jargon of cancer, she didn't need him to define terms like "metastasize" and "Stage 4." And when he'd talked about the option of palliative care, she knew that she had embarked on a journey from which there was no return. She'd fought the good fight the first time around. She'd had several clear years. At sixty-two, she'd hoped to witness the changing of many more seasons in her beautiful, Vermont forests, but she had already learned that longevity was not a privilege extended to everyone.

If it had only been about her she could have coped. But it wasn't. There were others who relied on her completely. That, more than anything, made her unbearably sad. For their sake she tried to conceal her emotions. Not that she always succeeded. There were times when she would have to retreat to her bedroom, close the door and weep silent tears. She would lie there, heartsore at how their world was going to change when she was no longer at home to love them.

She could feel them watching her from the window at this moment. Turning, she waved.

She didn't need a stick, but she walked slowly. All the more so being apprehensive about what lay ahead.

Reaching the front gate of the white, picket fence running across the front of her property, she halted. Something in the birdbath, a couple of yards away, caught her eye. Stepping closer she saw that a bee had fallen in. Flailing desperately in the water, it was sending ripples across the surface as it fought for its life.

Bending to pick up a fallen leaf, Grace stepped closer. After a couple of tries, she managed to scoop the leaf under the tiny body of the frantic insect and lift it to a nearby stone where there was a broad surface on which it could rest and dry out. As she did this, she repeated the phrase she'd once read that seemed to sum up everything that really mattered in a few words. A saying which, over the years, she had made her own: "May all beings be free from suffering."

Grace paused for a few moments to watch the bee, silently willing it to recover. She had learned to focus during such moments. The little things, she had come to learn, were actually the big things. For a while the tiny black and gold body remained motionless—there was no telling how long it had been struggling in the water. How exhausted it had become in its existential battle.

After what felt like quite some time, the bee flicked one wing, then another. Which was encouraging. Then it was hunching up, seeming to wipe its head with its front legs. Completely engrossed, Grace followed the bee's movements with heartfelt relief. And happy anticipation. If past rescues were anything to go by, the bee's movements were a prelude to what she most wanted to see happen. And sure enough, after a few further moments of head washing and leg twitching, the bee extended its wings a few times, before walking slowly in a circle—and taking off. Grace watched it curve upwards from the stone, gaining height, before disappearing from view as it zig-zagged round the side of the house. She returned to the front gate, with a contented smile.

For a few moments she had been relieved of the burden of her self.

Now she was waiting at the medical center. She'd had the scan, as scheduled, early that morning. Then there had been the blood test. Before she'd gone to the cafeteria for a hot chocolate while the radiologist studied and transferred the results to her doctor. Her appointment with Dr. Roberts was supposed to have been half an hour ago.

He was usually punctual. Some oncologists, she knew, treated their patients as if they had all the time in the world, an irony which never escaped her. A cruelty too. The worst part of having a scan was the wait that followed. "Scanxiety" she'd heard it accurately described.

Sitting outside Dr. Robert's consulting room, she was experiencing plenty of that. Her doctor's previous patient had left more than half an hour earlier. Expecting his door to open at any moment and to be ushered in, instead, Dr. Roberts' secretary had stood up behind her desk, crossed the waiting room towards her and perched on a nearby chair.

"Dr. Roberts will see you as soon as he can, Mrs. Arlingham," she spoke in a sympathetic voice. "He got your scan. He just wanted to speak to the radiologist before he sees you."

"Okay," Grace swallowed.

"He'll be as quick as he can." The nurse smiled.

Dr. Roberts had never felt the need to consult the radiologist before, thought Grace, uneasily. What could that possibly mean?

5

Ten days earlier
Lone Pine Meditation Center
Omni, Colorado

"WHY DOESN'T *EVERYONE* BELIEVE IN KARMA?"
The question came at the end of Lama Tashi's regular Tuesday night class. The person asking it wasn't naive. In the front row, where she had sat through years of such teachings, Megan Mitchell was one of Lama Tashi's most dedicated students. Late thirties and a mother of two, her bright blue eyes and red apple cheeks conveying a nature that was both nurturing as well as inquisitive, having heard him explain karma once again, the law of cause and effect seemed so obvious to her, and so vitally important, that the question simply burst from her lips.

Lama Tashi glanced about the students gathered in the candle-lit room as his students perched on their meditation cushions. They were glad Megan had asked the question. With the right prompting, Rinpoche (pronounced rin-posh-eh)—a term meaning "precious" sometimes bestowed on teachers—could take a while to provide an answer, drawing on personal anecdotes as well as historical ones, along with a variety of scriptural references. In the meantime, they would continue to enjoy simply being in his presence. The real reason they kept returning through the weeks. The months. The years.

The fact was that with Lama Tashi in the room, they would find themselves absorbed into a feeling of oceanic calm. Drawn to a state that was both profoundly peaceful and deeply reassuring, one which seemed to arise quite naturally when he coaxed them out of their habitual perspective to a wider one free from incessant mental chatter.

Lama Tashi took all of this in before he gestured to everyone, the trace of a mischievous smile on his face, "Why don't you have a try answering Megan's question?"

An evening breeze rippled through the room, scattering the steady wisps of rising incense and sending dozens of butter lamps at the feet of the Buddha statue wavering in their brass bowls.

Bob, in his buttoned-collar shirt and middle-aged, preppy clothes, cleared his throat before saying, "It's just not our culture in the West, to believe in karma," he offered. "We have some idea about what it is. We use the word in conversation. But we don't act like karma really exists."

"True," Lama Tashi was nodding, holding his eye momentarily in such a way that Bob wondered if he knew about him. Bob had no doubt that Rinpoche was clairvoyant—a natural consequence of having a clear mind. Whether or not he'd tuned into his particular situation, however, and what his thoughts were about it, was not something he'd contemplated. Nor did he wish to. He made a big effort to avoid allowing any thoughts of Paige Turner Books, his lover Beth, or Beth's apartment above Paige Turner Books, to enter his thoughts whenever he was in the guru's presence.

"Even in societies where karma has been accepted for millennia," Lama Tashi countered, "most people don't act in accordance with the law of cause and effect."

Chantelle, another front row student, shot a side-wise glance at Megan. "Maybe because it's such a big burden, you know, to accept that everything you experience is the result of causes you created. When things go wrong, it's much easier to blame circumstances, or someone else, for your unhappiness."

"Good answer," nodded Lama Tashi.

It was evident from his expression, however, that there was another, specific reply he wanted. They were missing something. And as he observed their mental gymnastics, he seemed amused that this particular answer escaped them.

For a while they studiously avoided his gaze.

"A *simple* reason," he coaxed.

Still receiving no reply after another pause, he eventually put them out of their misery.

"People don't believe in karma because it's not instant," he said. "If cause was followed immediately by effect, there would be no question, no doubt."

A wave of recognition passed, palpably through the room. And along with it, a surge of energy as his students exchanged glances, imagining the possibility he had just offered, of a time and place in which effects followed instantly on the heels of causes. A sudden playful burst of creative possibilities swept through the meditation room.

"Imagine if karma went instant one day?" suggested Anton, a cameraman and digital artist whose long, black hair, combed into a pony tail, contrasted sharply with the palest of faces. "How crazy would that be?"

Several in the group burst out laughing. It was as though Lama Tashi had unbottled a mischievous spirit. Chantelle and Megan raised hands to their mouths with glee.

"Once people worked out what was happening," said Megan. "The effect would be revolutionary."

Lama Tashi tilted his head in acknowledgement. "Pretty crazy," he agreed. "Initially, instant happiness for some. Disaster for others. Great volatility as every person came to discover that there is no effect without a previously-created cause. This is karma, is it not?"

As his students nodded he prompted, "A definition of karma please?"

In certain ways, in the ways that mattered, Rinpoche was old school. He expected his students to commit key principles and definitions to memory, so that when he asked a question as he did now, one in which he had drilled them, they would reply without hesitation and in unison:

"The law of cause and effect."

"And what are the four general aspects of karma?"

"Results reflect the causes," they chanted. "Positive karma brings only positive results. Negative karma brings only negative results."

He nodded, holding up his thumb.

"Karma increases," they continued. He raised his index finger.

Then, as he raised the finger next to it. "There can be no results without first creating causes." Before ending with the fourth general aspect, "Every action brings a definite result."

"Good, good! You all know the *theory*," he chuckled.

And was Bob imagining it, or was Lama Tashi looking directly at him?

Leaning forward in his seat and lowering his voice as he always did when he wished to give special emphasis, Rinpoche said, "Karma is all about *you*. When you understand how it works, you decide on your own future. That's the whole point. Learn to master karma so that you can create the reality that you wish. You might say that karma is the ultimate self-development program. The great paradox is that if we truly wish for transformation, for ultimate fulfilment, we must shift our focus from self to others. In giving, we truly do receive."

His students were silent for a while as they reflected on this powerful message, clearly expressed. Before their teacher told them, "If you ever want to check if you *really* believe in karma, it's very simple," he said. "Just ask yourself this: do you put the needs of other beings before your own?"

6

Wall Street, New York City

AMY THANKED JORDAN AND COLLECTED HER PERSONALIZED CAP-puccino. As she headed to a window table she could hardly believe the message she'd just received. The Orangutan Project was congratulating her for winning an all-expenses fourteen-day South East Asia cruise for two valued at $25,000!

Amy had got plenty of "prize winner" messages in the past. She'd learned to ignore the cruel hoaxes that most of them were. But she sensed this one was different. She could remember buying the single raffle ticket for one dollar on her first day in New York. The guy on ticket sales had urged her to buy a book of ten tickets for nine dollars to increase her chances of winning. Only she'd had almost no money and besides, she wasn't doing it for the prize, but for the orangutans, whose plight had always deeply moved her.

At the window table she read and re-read the message. To make sure, she phoned The Orangutan Project and asked for the person who had sent the email. The promotions executive seemed as excited as she when confirming the message.

After the call, she sat staring unseeing at the traffic on 9th Avenue, thinking about what to do next. In her heart she had already decided.

She had been working at Sharma Funds for less than six months and had no vacation leave. Besides, she didn't have anyone to go with. The boyfriend she'd had back in Aubrey was ancient history. She had close girlfriends at home, but choosing only one to go with would invite no end of complications. Amy's instinct, the moment she'd got the message, was the one she went with now. Opening the email, she pressed Forward, and texted, "Dear Momma, I have just won a prize I'd like you and Dad to have. There's only one hitch—you'll both have to get passports!"

For her mom and dad, the cruise would be the holiday of a lifetime. Her dad had been with Aubrey City Parks and Recreation his whole working life. Her momma was a nurse. There hadn't been much money growing up.

Recently her dad had been diagnosed with Parkinson's Disease and become withdrawn and depressed. Her mom, ever the community fixer, spent her life trying to cheer him up, while also taking care of their elderly neighbors and juggling shifts at the local hospital. A luxury cruise was just the circuit breaker they needed.

Amy felt a glow as she imagined her mom getting the message, and telling her dad, and the two of them, for the first time in a very long while, having something wonderful to look forward to. An all-expenses, luxury cruise from Singapore to Penang and Rangoon and many other exotic places besides. It was more than she'd ever thought possible. But it had happened. And giving it to her parents felt like a gift in itself. Finishing her coffee, Amy felt ready to burst with joy. And she couldn't wait to hear from her momma!

She walked up the street and into the building where she worked on the 25th floor. Although her mom checked her phone regularly, she'd only recently have come off night shift.

Getting out the elevator, instead of the usual hallowed hush that pre-vailed in the wood-paneled reception area of Sharma Fund Management Inc, there was a strangely euphoric buzz, with raucous laughter sounding down the corridor.

She met the eyes of the receptionist.

"Just won the Colgard account," Jaye told her with a smile.

"That's great!" Amy feigned enthusiasm. She knew the institutional investing team had been working for a long time to get that deal over the line. She also knew it would mean a lot more work for her, and she wondered if she was really up to it. In recent weeks, Mr. Black, boss of the accounting team, had called her into his office several times to go through spreadsheets she'd prepared. It wasn't so much that they were wrong, he told her. It was simply that they were old-fashioned.

Not for the first time, she'd felt like a hick. A small-town girl who wasn't up to the speed and sophistication of New York. Especially seeing that she'd never wanted to be an analyst in the first place. She'd only trained as an accountant because she was good with numbers and her dad used to say that she'd always find work because every company needed number crunchers.

She had been at her desk a matter of minutes when she heard her name called. Looking up she found her boss's Personal Assistant beside her work station.

"Mr. Black wants to see you," she said.

Amy tried to keep her composure. This wasn't good. It was a Friday during her very first month at Sharma Funds when she'd seen a colleague walk through reception carrying a cardboard box containing a jumble of items, including a succulent plant she had admired on his desk.

She'd immediately sensed something ominous.

"What's with the box?" she had whispered to Jaye at reception.

"Let go," Jaye had mouthed the words. Before adding meaningfully, "Friday."

Later, Jaye had explained that it was Sharma policy to fire staff on a Friday. The thinking was that everyone else in the firm would have the weekend to process what had happened. To move on. To put the now ex-member of staff out of their minds. When they returned on Monday, it was like the fired person had never existed.

Mr. Black was on the phone when she was shown into his office. He gestured for her to shut the door—not a good sign. And held up his hand when she stepped towards a chair opposite—even worse. She wasn't to sit! Evidently he wanted her out of his office as soon as he'd said his piece.

"Peter Sharp. Lawyer. D'you know him?" He asked, as soon as he'd finished his call.

Amy was confused. Was he a client of Sharma Funds? Had she made an error on his tax return? She shook her head.

"He just called for you. Found you on the online staff directory. Said he'd tried to reach you at a number in Aubrey. That's home in Texas, right?"

"Yes."

Lifting a piece of paper off his desk, which had a phone number written on it, he handed it to her.

"We're guessing this is a personal matter," as he met her eyes, she noted his expression had softened to one of sympathy. "Feel free to use a meeting room instead of making the call at your desk."

"Thank you," she said, eyes widening.

SHE FELT SELF-CONSCIOUS CLOSING A MEETING ROOM DOOR BEHIND her. Usually only senior executives were afforded such privacy. She worried this had something to do with her parents. Or brother.

But when she reached Peter Sharp, in his gravelly, smoker's voice he told her that he had been wanting to contact her in his capacity as executor of Gerald Carson's estate.

The name was ringing bells, but it was taking her a few moments to place.

"You'll be aware that he passed in New Orleans two months ago."

Uncle Gerry! She was with him now.

Gerald Carson wasn't technically an uncle. He was mom's cousin. Six years ago, after high school graduation, Amy had gone to look after him. In his mid-eighties, he had been suffering from a variety of medical complaints, most notably a weak heart, poor blood circulation and secondary diabetes. On top of that, he'd recently had a fall and hurt his back. It was because he had trouble moving that he needed help. Amy, kind and obliging, said she'd go.

At first, she thought she was going to hate living in the dilapidated house with its gloomy rooms, rank odors and elderly resident. But she had quickly got to know Gerry, and to their mutual surprise the two of them found that they enjoyed each other's company.

She had also opened the curtains, redecorated his home and got a plumber to fix the septic tank. She'd brought together the flower pots scattered about his yard to make his formerly stark porch lush and inviting. The two of them would sit for hours there talking and watching the sun go down. There had been several visits to a jazz club at the end of his street. She'd cook for him and they'd drink beer and sometimes just sit in companionable silence. He'd declared her visit the best vacation he'd had in years.

Since then, she'd spoken to him twice on the phone. Being broke, he'd ended up in a state nursing home. She hadn't wanted to think too much about what that was like.

Now on the phone, Amy was surprised. "Uncle Gerry had an estate?"

"In the very last weeks of his life he did," responded the lawyer.

"How d'you mean?"

"His good friend, my client Mr. Larry Denis, died three months earlier and left his entire estate to Mr. Carson. I contacted Mr. Carson, as I'm contacting you now, and he asked me to draw up a will. He knew he didn't have long to live. When he thought about the next generation, you were the only one who'd ever visited him. Which was why he left you everything."

"Everything?" Amy was suddenly light-headed.

"There are two components," Peter Sharp explained. "The estate itself. And royalties from a song Mr. Denis composed, now payable to you."

"Ballantyne Blue?" Uncle Gerry had told her about it.

"Exactly. Worth about fifty thousand a year."

That was much more than she earned at Sharma Funds!

"Mr. Denis's estate is liquidated and in my firm's Client Trust Account. I'll need to pass through some final expenses, but you're looking at just over $1.8 million."

Amy was in such a state of shock she found it hard to speak. "What happens, I mean …"

"It's a simple transfer," said Peter Sharp. "I'll need photo ID and proof of your address. Once you get that to me and sign the paperwork, we'll have the funds to you within days."

Amy left the meeting room in a daze. In no condition to return to her desk, she went to the only place in the office that she would find any privacy. The Ladies restroom, all marble, subdued lighting, and sandalwood air freshener was thankfully deserted. She stepped into a cubicle, locking the door behind her and had no sooner put down the seat, when her phone rang. It was her momma, who had got home from her shift, found her message and had shared the news with her dad. The two of them were overjoyed. Momma was fighting—and failing—to hold back the tears. Even Amy's dad, rarely given to sentiment, was telling her how deeply they appreciated her gift. How it would truly be the most exciting vacation they'd ever had.

"Your mother and I are so proud of you, darling," he told her. Something he'd never said to her before. Something, she knew, he would have struggled to say out loud, even though he might feel it. Which had her bawling too.

It was one of the most emotional and magical conversations the three of them had ever had, her sitting in a restroom in New York, and them hunched over a phone on the kitchen table in Aubrey.

Towards the end of the call, she told them about the conversation she'd just had with the lawyer. How Uncle Gerry had inherited the estate of a good friend only weeks before dying and had left it to her.

Her parents marveled at the news, her mom saying how relieved she was that Amy wouldn't have to worry about money. Her dad noting the extraordinary coincidence that, within such a short time of her giving them a generous and unexpected gift, she herself had received the same. Which had Amy sobbing again.

It wasn't even nine in the morning when Amy emerged from the cubicle but she already knew this was the very best day of her life. Dabbing at her face in the bathroom mirror, she didn't really care if she looked like she'd been crying. The happiness she felt was so heartfelt, went so deep, she was at risk of hugging the very next person she saw.

Which just happened to be Mr. Sharma himself!

1

Omni, Colorado

Bob was shocked to see Margarita's SUV when the garage door began opening. What time had she got back? How was he to account for his absence so early in the morning?

A phrase instantly arose in his mind from the most recent class he'd attended at the Lone Pine Meditation Center. "Take special care in the days ahead," Lama Tashi had said. "Your actions may have consequences way beyond what you expect."

Where had that come from, he wondered, turning his car into the garage and parking with customary precision directly parallel to Margarita's. Lama Tashi had a way of getting into your head that could be irksome. In the past few months in particular Bob had come to resent how stray phrases he'd heard in class would well up into his consciousness at the most inopportune moments. Like now.

Stepping through the internal garage door into the house, he paused to remove the jungle green jacket he'd been wearing and to check his appearance in the full-length mirror. Always careful about the way he looked, Bob scanned from his brown hair—not so neatly parted as usual—his unshaven chin and cheeks, the buttoned-down collar of his crumpled twill shirt. A pleasant-faced man with hazel eyes and a tan face, he wondered about the evidence of where he'd been and what he'd been doing. Just how obvious was it?

His second shock was emerging into the kitchen of their Hamptons-style house to find Margarita sitting at the island bench facing him directly, raw-eyed. Before her on the gleaming, granite surface, untouched, a cardboard tray of two, large Americanos.

She didn't have to say anything. The silence of their house was so overwhelming that he knew she knew. How, he had no idea.

"How long has the affair been going on?" her voice was choked.

Ironically, that wasn't a question for which he was in any way prepared. During the past few months, he'd invented all manner of plausible explanations to account for visits into town, but he'd never had to use any of them. He had come to believe that he and Beth existed in their own private bubble. A parallel universe, the very existence of which was secret. Besides, he didn't think of what was happening as "an affair." That gave it a sordid quality which wasn't how it felt.

It had started by accident. A mistake. The kind of one-off episode that might happen to just about any middle-aged man who'd had too much to drink and found himself alone and in the company of a much younger and attractive woman, similarly intoxicated, whose physical interest in him was undisguised. He couldn't even recall what had happened in very much detail, except that she had been highly articulate about what she'd wanted him to do—verbiage he had attributed to the alcohol.

He'd gone back to Beth the very next day to apologize. He had wanted to make sure she was all right with things. He was acutely aware how badly episodes like this could spiral out of control leaving a reputation in ruins, and a man exposed to blackmail, or potential legal action. Most of all, he wanted to square things away so it wouldn't get back to Margarita.

Beth had been closing the shop when he'd arrived and her response hadn't been among any of the possibilities he had expected. Instead, in a short while he'd found himself naked with her again, this time sober. And most certainly able to remember every last thing that happened. Recollecting vivid details of that late-afternoon encounter in the Paige Turner stock room had reignited his dormant libido in ways he would scarcely have believed possible.

There had been plenty of torrid encounters since then. And a burgeoning friendship. Beth was simply unlike anyone he'd ever met. Even so—an affair?

As he stood, goldfish-like, so shocked he could hardly think, his wife answered her own question, "The night of the book-launch, right?"

His looking down, embarrassed, was confirmation enough.

The launch of Margarita's new children's series, illustrated in her distinctive, vivid style, had been the fun, local start to a much more important program. No sooner had the event finished than she and her publicist were taxiing to Denver for a late night TV show before heading to New York the following morning for a busy round of interviews and appearances. They had discussed Bob joining the tour but had agreed that there didn't seem much to be gained. He would only be a spare part. He had his own business to attend to. And he really didn't like flying. So he'd stayed behind to help Beth clean up after the launch party.

"Here I was thinking your flame had been lit by my absence, and single origin Huila beans," Margarita glanced at the coffees. "Meantime ..."

"I'm sorry," he blurted out, hating to see her so upset.

She was shaking her head. "It's past the "sorry" stage, Bob" she said.

"How d'you mean?"

"You can't have it both ways. Either we're married—" her voice cracked, "—or we're not."

It felt surreal, to Bob, to be standing at the center of their meticulously ordered home as Margarita gave voice to what she regarded as the wreckage of their marriage. What felt even more surreal, however, was that he sensed no instant response. He was struggling to think, much less speak, but there was no instinct to beg for her forgiveness. To dismiss what had happened as a mid-life aberration. To struggle to hold on to all that they'd created together.

"I know a lot of marriages go through ... this," she was trying to stay reasonable. "I'm just surprised you went for Beaky."

"It wasn't like that!" he reacted.

Over a year earlier, when he'd gone into order a book for their daughter, he'd sent them a message to confirm, with an impish reference to the bookstore manager. A reference that now stung.

"Wasn't like what?"

"Wasn't like I decided to, you know, have some fling and then decided who to have it with."

"Or you would have chosen someone with a less prominent nose? Is that what you're saying?" Margarita's voice was arctic.

He stepped around the island bench to the passage beyond. There was nothing to be gained from staying here. Margarita was betrayed and upset, he got that. He knew he deserved her anger. But he wasn't going to be tricked into saying things he didn't mean, or playing emotional war games he couldn't possibly win.

"It's up to you, Bob!" her voice followed him. "*You* decide!"

His footsteps led automatically to the top of the house and the room across the hallway from where they slept. They had converted it into an office after his bike accident four years ago, and it had become his place of refuge during the lengthy rehabilitation that followed. There had been month upon month of repeat surgeries, physical therapists, rehabilitative Pilates and, more than anything, time spent lying on the office recliner able to do not very much except read.

He'd sold the accounting business to a junior partner, for a sum that would see Margarita and him through in comfort, leaving only a handful of his longest-standing clients to service. He'd helped both of their kids through their final years at high school, following Matias through his marine biology degree at Seattle and more recently coaching Gabby through school, until her recent departure for Otis College of Art in Los Angeles.

Prompted by a Pilates instructor to explore meditation as an aid to holistic healing, he'd found himself at Lone Pine Meditation Center. There, Lama Tashi had convinced him that the moose that had been the cause of his bike accident may have forced him off the road—but it had put him back on the right path: he had a developed aptitude for meditation. Meantime, Margarita's career as a book illustrator had taken off like a rocket.

Time weighing heavily on his hands, over the years he'd overseen all those modifications to the house, large and small, that most people never get around to doing. The cabinetry in the kitchen and bathroom were showroom standard. The living areas felt like stepping into the pages of a design magazine. Even his shed was meticulously arranged, every tool in its perfectly appointed place.

When he finally emerged to full health and vigor, it was as a different person from the one who had been thrown from his bicycle. He seemed to have become a quieter, more reflective version of his former self. All Lama Tashi's teachings about the importance of focusing on inner transformation, of such value to him when he'd been feeling frail and vulnerable, seemed to fade in relevance. The teachings about impermanence and the certainty of death began to feel unduly bleak. He tried to curate his thoughts, like his home, to scrupulous perfection. Only it wasn't enough.

It had taken Beth to blast his world open, to let the light in. Spontaneous, chaotic, voluptuous Beth. It wasn't only about the sex, he assured himself, though that was like nothing he'd ever had before. It thrilled him that a woman of thirty-five could find a man of fifty-three—yes, perfect, inverse reflections—so consummately desirable. But there was no end of noisy, messy, exhorting evidence that she did.

From that very first afternoon in the stockroom, she had also impressed him with her creativity, her shrewdness, her irrepressible *joie de vivre*.

"Who would have thought the earnest manager of Paige Turner Books could turn into this!" He'd been exultant, propping himself up on his elbow and watching her panting subside as she recovered against a cardboard box labelled *The Complete Book of Veg*.

"By day, book mouse. By night," she'd grinned. "Venusian goddess!"

He took in the generous, upturned breasts, the fleshy thighs and the dark, unkempt garden, and in that moment it really did seem to him that sensual rapture was the ultimate self-expression for Beth Owen. He marveled that the plain-faced girl with the mousy hair and aquiline nose, a young woman at whom he had never looked twice, could have transformed into a being so alluring, so raunchy, so sexually articulate.

"When I met you before, I'd never have dreamed …" he shook his head.

"What happens on Venus, stays on Venus," she replied, tracing a moist forefinger from his lips to his crotch. "We wouldn't want to blow it, would we?" She grinned, "Excuse the metaphor."

"No, we would not," he'd held her eyes meaningfully.

Since that second encounter—or first sober one—Beth had confirmed her life-shifting liberality in countless, gratifying ways. Whether it was the box of adult toys she produced on his first visit to her apartment, or the way she talked about sex with such zesty, entertaining fluency quite beyond anything he'd ever experienced. She peppered him with questions—what he liked and how he liked it—and set about fulfilling his every whim. She shared stories from her very much more audacious adventures which he did his best to reciprocate, recounting the anecdotes of others when running out of his own more humdrum confessions.

She even gave him a nickname.

"Why Endless Love?" he had asked, after one torrid session.

"Not Love. Luuhv," she corrected, adopting a sultry, Southern accent, "It's because you keep on turnin' baby, and I keep on burnin'. I've never known a man with such stamina."

He'd smiled at the compliment. "You're so creative—it's amazing! Where d'you come up with it all?"

"Oh, I don't come up with anything, Endless Love! My angels do."

"Angels?"

"My Venusian angels." She held her hands up to her face and fluttered them, wing-like.

Like other enigmatic pronouncement of hers—she was an artist, after all, in thrall to her muse—Bob was unsure how to take this, so he said nothing.

They talked about plenty of other things too. She shared her heart and dreams with him, confiding that she'd been drawn to the book trade because, like so many others, she was an aspiring writer herself. They'd been sitting at the kitchen table in her apartment, one evening when Margarita was in New York, and it had taken every ounce of self-control for him to resist clearing it and cleaning it, and dealing with the chaos of used crockery in the kitchen sink some of which, he knew for a fact, had been there over a week.

"Have you had anything published?" he'd asked, sipping wine from a glass that still bore a trace of her lipstick.

She'd pulled a face. "Unless you write genre fiction, it's just about impossible getting anything accepted by traditional publishers these days."

He'd heard the same thing from Margarita.

"What about self-publishing?"

"You have to build your tribe first," she'd nodded. "That's not easy either. And keep on writing. Honing the craft."

"You do that? Keep on writing?"

"At least an hour a day," her eyes hardened with resolve. "Two or three if I can manage."

He'd reached out to give her hand a reassuring squeeze. "Clever girl." Persistence, he thought. There was no substitute.

Standing in his office, Bob had to make a decision. And what he thought of, most of all, was how vividly Beth reminded him of himself when he was younger. When there seemed like everything to play for. When the world felt like it was bursting with possibilities—you just needed to work out how to be in the right place at the right time.

If there was any benefit to being older, he reflected, it had to be experience. Learning from your own mistakes and the mistakes of others. In the past few weeks he'd increasingly felt the urge to scoop Beth off her feet and take her away from all this. To give her the time she needed to write. To introduce her to the kinds of people—editors, distributors and the like—who could help turn her dream into reality.

He could fast track things for her. He could set her up—they could set up—somewhere like San Francisco or New York. He wouldn't be hugely rich after a divorce, but he could afford a home. He could go to work again. Hell, why not? It would be a lot better than death by atrophy if he stayed at home.

It would be Life 2.0 for him and for Margarita. She had her own life now, he reckoned. Her work as an illustrator had become all-consuming. As for the kids, as he looked at the only item on his empty desk, a photo of the two of them from several summers ago, he was sure they'd understand. They'd want him to be happy, wouldn't they? They would continue to be as much a part of his life as they were right now. Especially when he had become a much more engaged and youthful father.

He glanced from the rows of books, perfectly lined up behind the glass panels of the shelving units, across the gleaming sweep of the desk with its wooden drawers, the white shuttered windows, and black-and-white photographs and, not for the first time it seemed to him that he might as well be living in a mausoleum. Everything here was perfect. Resolved. Complete.

Enough already! Margarita had delivered her ultimatum. It was time for him to respond.

"Take special care in the days ahead," said Lama Tashi. "Your actions could have consequences way beyond what you expect." There was that instruction again. What if it was to be interpreted in a positive way? Like, despite whatever hardships awaited him, despite the awfulness of having to break the news to Margarita, the results would be more wonderful than he could imagine?

Turning, Bob went to the cupboard between his office and their bedroom to retrieve a large suitcase. He stepped into the dressing room and began to pack.

He had no idea what the future held. Only that it wasn't going to be here. He was choosing life and love in all its untidy, ardent glory, he told himself. He was turning away from a past of suffering and diminution, to a future that was ablaze with possibility. Never before had he felt so sure of himself. And now that he'd decided, nothing was going to get in his way.

8

"Tom!" General Alexander Hickman answered the incoming call from his former comrade. "Been a while?"

On his balcony, Tom Jackson straightened reflexively as he heard the voice of the most senior officer in the U.S. Army. "I know how busy it gets," he replied. "I haven't wanted to disturb you."

The two of them had known each other for decades and were good friends. It helped that early on in their careers they had discovered a shared regard for Sun Tzu's, *The Art of War,* which they both held to be a pre-eminent guide to military strategy. It had become something of ritual, when they encountered one another, to quote a relevant line from it, as General Hickman did now, "In the midst of chaos there is also opportunity." That's what I try to remind myself."

Tom grunted appreciatively. And because he really did understand how busy the General must be, he cut directly to the chase. "Look, I have a favor to ask. Post Traumatic Stress Disorder. The local branch of Veterans Affairs has programs to support the guys with PTSD. One of the programs involves hiking. I know the mountains round here and I want to volunteer my services."

General Hickman recalled the last time he'd seen Tom, four or five months back. It had been at the funeral of Major General Greg Travis, who along with Tom and Harry Dralke had been one of the self-styled "three musketeers" sent to Kigali, Rwanda, as part of a peacekeeping mission after the 1994 massacres. Travis's funeral had been a particularly somber business. The word put out was that Major General Travis had died of heart disease, for which he'd been on meds for years. But people in the loop knew the story about how his daughter had found him dangling on his belt from a garage beam. Just like they knew that Harry Dralke had overdosed on prescription meds shortly after getting back from Africa.

Standing on the other side of the open grave at Travis's funeral, General Hickman had watched the expression on Tom's face. The same expression he'd once observed when he'd caught him unawares, stepping out onto the Jackson's balcony towards the end of a typically riotous party, and finding him alone and staring so intently into the darkness he'd had to call his name to bring him back to the present. When he'd turned towards him, Tom's face had been ashen.

Now he was volunteering to help on a PTSD program. In a heartbeat General Hickman knew what that meant. Which is why he responded with feeling, "If there's anything I can do to make that happen, just let me know."

"Well, there is something," said Tom.

"Uh-huh?"

"I was advised to initiate something today. It's all in the timing. You know, Sun Tzu: "He will win who knows when to fight and when not to fight.""

"Indeed," the General paused. Before asking, genuinely curious, "There's something particular about today?"

"I was told it's a day—" Tom remembered being held by the commanding force of Lama Tashi's gaze, "—when the impact of taking action would powerful. Instant. Unexpected."

Although he didn't know it, at the other end his words had a special resonance for General Hickman. In the early hours of that morning he had green-lighted two actions in the Middle East. One involving military support for a civilian convoy passing through hostile territory which had the potential to go badly wrong. The other, a strike to take out an insurgent base, which he expected to be executed with surgical precision.

Only, that wasn't what had happened. In both cases, crazy things had unraveled. Enemy combatants seemed to have abandoned the formerly hostile territory, leaving the place wide open to the US alliance. And the surgical strike had gone awry when a helicopter was shot down. The general was still trying to find out what had happened to his men.

"You were advised?" repeated General Hickman.

"Uh-huh."

"Interesting advisor."

He was fishing. If asked directly, Tom would give him Lama Tashi's name. But for the moment, he felt more comfortable keeping quiet on that point. "He's ... unorthodox," he agreed, after a pause. "But I trust him."

"You want my office to contact Veterans Affairs in Boulder to see you today?" confirmed the General.

"That would be appreciated, Alex."

"Leave it with me."

9

Montpelier, Vermont

D R. ROBERTS'S DOOR EVENTUALLY OPENED AND HER ONCOLOGIST stepped out.

"Mrs. Arlingham," he greeted her, evenly professional.

Grace was sure she wasn't the only patient who searched for the slightest micro-expression on the face, the subtlest nuance in tone of voice that might hint at the results of her latest scan.

There had never been a clue in the past. Today, as she followed her specialist into his office and he closed the door behind her, apologizing for the very lengthy delay, she thought she did sense something: perplexity. Agitation. Something seeming to confirm that this morning's appointment wasn't going to be straightforward.

"I had to speak to the radiologist about this morning's scan," he said. Instead of sitting behind his desk, he stepped towards his computer screen. "In a moment, I'll show you for yourself," he ran a hand through his hair. A strangely, nervous gesture, observed Grace. She couldn't remember him ever having done that before.

"Before I do, I need to ask, and this is very important: since your last scan, what have you been doing that's different?"

Grace shook her head right away. Well-meaning friends would sometimes visit with pamphlets for some miracle treatment involving paw-paws or alkaline water, or information about a healing center in Guatemala, or news of a promising experimental trial looking for human guinea pigs. But she had come to terms with what was happening. Made peace with it.

She planned living out whatever remained of her life with the ones who most needed her, undistracted by last-ditch survival attempts.

"No dietary changes?" he probed. "Trips away? Unusual experiences?"

As he went through the motions of double-checking, she could tell from his face that he knew full well that the prosaic routine of her life was unlikely to have changed.

He swiveled his computer screen in her direction, he came to sit on the chair beside her.

"You can see my dilemma for yourself," he pointed towards it.

It took her a while to register what she was looking at. Two scans of her abdomen. The left hand one, from her previous visit, blighted with the dark shadows she so vividly remembered. The one on the right showing no shadows at all.

She peered closer. Checking the time and date stamp at the top of the two images. Looking back and forth from one to the other several times.

Finally, she turned to Dr. Roberts. "Where have they gone?" she asked.

"That's what I had to check," he met her eyes. For the first time, the glimpse of a smile played across his face. "I needed to be sure there wasn't some … false reporting. Or mislabeling. But look, you can see where you cracked your rib, years ago" he pointed to the same mark on a bone that appeared on both images. "This is definitely you. And the very healthy blood sample you provided earlier corroborates what we're seeing."

It was taking a while for the news to sink in. "You mean," she could scarcely believe she was actually about to say these words. "I'm completely free of cancer?"

"So the scans are showing."

"But how could that happen? I thought it was terminal?"

"I wish I had answers, Mrs. Arlingham," Dr. Roberts was apologetic in a curiously triumphant way. "All I can tell you for sure is that this is a *most* unusual development. I personally have only seen this happen only once, at much earlier stage of the disease. This seems like a case of spontaneous remission."

As he held her eyes, it felt to Grace Arlingham like a timeless moment. Her oncologist. A man in a white coat. Facing her directly and speaking the dispassionate terminology of medical science. Using the two most wonderful words a person like her could possibly hear. *Spontaneous remission*!

"Which is medical-speak," he was beaming, "for "we have absolutely no idea what just happened, but it's spectacularly good news!""

Her pace home was much brisker than when she'd set out that morning. She could hardly wait to get home to share her exultation!

Her two elderly sister cats had been joined several years ago by the little West Highland Terrier she had promised to look after when Sara, from the cancer-support group, had to go into a hospice. Over the years, other group members had turned to her, one by one, to take care of their cherished fur babies: Gwen's poodle, Terry's elderly Jack Russell, Belinda's skittish greyhound. Each one of her little ones had lost their loved ones and homes.

Now, she was all they had.

Walking along the picket fence of her home, she looked at her front window. Six, whiskered faces were following her movements intently. At the gate she glanced at the birdbath and the stone nearby, recalling the bee she'd rescued that morning. Struggling in the water, fighting for its life. As she remembered, she felt as if she, herself, had just been rescued from certain death and given a fresh chance. It would probably take her a short while to recover from her ordeal. To recharge her energies, like the bee on the stone. But she had no doubt that she would.

Which was when a strange put powerful thought occurred to her, one she dismissed as quickly as it arose. Her euphoria was making her silly, she told herself. Nevertheless, as she stood there, the notion wouldn't go away.

Instead of opening the gate and heading towards the welcoming committee, she glanced at her watch, made up her mind, and continued swiftly along the pavement. A most determined expression appearing on her face.

9:00 am (Eastern Standard Time)
7:00 am (Mountain Standard Time)
6:00 am (Pacific Standard Time)

10

Galaxy Television
Galaxy City, Los Angeles

EVEN IN THE TIME IT HAD TAKEN DAN KAVANA TO TRAVEL THE short distance from Beverly Hills to Galaxy City, the contagion had dramatically gathered pace. There had been phone calls from the news team on the way, and he'd made many more attempts to speak to one of Maddie's caregivers. By the time he'd gone through make-up and hair, Galaxy reporter Kim Dayton was at the scene of the outbreak. Times Square looked like a sci-fi horror movie. The whole place was in lockdown with streets shut and sidewalks deserted. Bio-security agents in full protection suits, boots and helmets were disembarking from vehicles like something from the pandemic. Kim herself was similarly attired. The visor of her helmet was flipped open, but she was speaking through a half-face respirator.

"Good-morning Kim. Please update us," Dan crossed as soon as he was at the news desk, opposite where Nick Nalder and the newsroom team were working the phones.

"What we've heard is that over twenty people became violently ill when dining at the Golden Drumsticks outlet behind me this morning. Ambulances have taken the victims to hospital. Emergency services are urging anyone else who may have visited this branch of Golden Drumsticks this morning to contact them immediately."

"There's talk of a bacterial contagion, is that correct?" Dan wanted to get the words in early.

"That's what people are saying," Kim was nodding. "As you can see, Federal investigators are taking no chances."

"Can you give us more detail about how the diners were affected?" asked Dan.

"Seems it was quick," Kim was grave. "They were only part way through their meals when they began vomiting. Spasms were so violent that, in some cases, customers fell from their chairs to the floor. Along with the vomiting was acute diarrhea. Diners have reported severe abdominal cramps and serious pain."

The scenario she was describing could hardly have been more graphic. "If this *is* bacterial infection," Dan pressed, "how could it have happened?"

"The usual suspect is Staphylococcus bacteria, which is spread during meal preparation by someone who is infected, or who has unclean hands. Food may not look or smell bad, but the bacteria gets passed on. If that turns out to be the case, then the fall-out from this morning is containable. Customers who came here are unlikely to pose a threat to the broader community.

"The fear—" on cue, the camera zoomed into her anxious expression above the half-face respirator, "—is that we're looking at something different. Something more contagious. If it was a customer who infected other diners, there's no telling how widely this could go—and may already have spread."

"You're talking about a new pandemic?"

"That's not a word they're using, even if it feels that way."

"What's the response from authorities been so far?"

"They've acted swiftly," she nodded. "Times Square is in lockdown. No traffic for several blocks each way. As you can imagine, it's chaos out here right now."

Dan nodded grimly.

"Golden Drumsticks boasts of selling more chicken to Americans than any other food chain," Kim continued. "And Times Square is its busiest restaurant in the whole country. Disease control scientists from the FDA are already testing. We're expecting an official statement as soon as they can confirm the cause."

"And we'll be bringing that to you, live, as soon as it happens," Dan assured viewers. "The fact that this has happened in the heart of our biggest city will be the authorities' main fear."

"We don't know how many potentially infected people already travelled out of the area before the lockdown," Kim ran with the ball. "If this turns out to be a contagion, given the location of the outlet, we could be looking at a massive disruption not only to New York City but beyond."

The teleprompter was signaling an urgent cross to a new, related story. Registering the instruction, Dan segued effortlessly, "On the subject of disruption, we're going now to John F. Kennedy Airport where another Golden Drumsticks outlet is being similarly affected."

Just like at Times Square, images from JFK were bleak. Contagious disease scientists, suited and booted, moving through an eerily deserted terminal like Martians. Over thirty diners at the airport Golden Drumsticks had become suddenly and violently ill, collapsing to the floor racked in pain and losing all control of their bodily functions. The restaurant had been closed down. The terminal was shutting. As flights were re-routed to other terminals, pandemonium had ensued.

A Galaxy TV reporter told Dan and his morning TV audience how the whole airport may have to be closed down. About concerns for passengers, currently boarding their flights, who may have dined at Golden Drumsticks and the risk they may present to other passengers.

What were the connections, Dan wanted to know, between the Golden Drumstick outlets at Times Square and JFK? The franchises had different owners and appeared to have nothing in common except where they got their product. If that was the source of contamination, what did it say about the risk of dining at other Golden Drumstick outlets? It was unprecedented for two of the biggest outlets of the same fast food chain to be affected at exactly the same time. Was the risk about to spread a lot wider?

In the newsroom, Nick Nalder scanned the wall of TV screens showing competitor channels. Wall-to-wall coverage of the two unfolding dramas. In his fifties, ascetic-looking and wearing spectacles with large, black rims, Nalder's job was to direct the news agenda. To see where things were headed and to get there before his competitors.

Working off a variety of news-tips and journalist-feeds, there was one source he trusted more than any other: his gut. Surveying the pattern of what was happening that morning, he had already told several of his top reporters to drop what they were doing and dig deeper into the Golden Drumsticks story. Where was the product sourced? Who else was being supplied? What was happening in other Golden Drumstick outlets? And what about competitor chicken fast-food chains? Go after them—hard!

Nalder might be Head of News, a journalist through and through, but he'd also been around the block a few times. Golden Drumsticks was one of Galaxy TV's major advertisers. Galaxy couldn't be seen to be taking down the reputation the company had spent millions of advertising dollars building up. Nor could they risk ratings by downplaying the news of the hour. But if the story could be spun into a bigger one, affecting other rival chains like Crowing Hen, that was Nalder's out.

He phoned his boss, the CEO of Galaxy. "I think we should call Harvey."

"About food poisoning?" Several steps distant from the news cycle, his boss sounded skeptical.

"About air traffic disruption," he returned.

They both knew Harvey O'Sullivan, owner of Galaxy, practically lived on his private jet. He also liked to be in the newsroom when a major story was breaking. It had happened a few times in the past. It unsettled some of the staff. But Nalder got that about Harvey. He might be an eighty-year-old billionaire, but it was times like these that took him back to his heyday, running his media empire. To the rush of breaking big stories, when it felt like the whole nation was transfixed by the real-life drama taking place and which you, the news team, were telling in your own particular way.

"This is already a massive story and it's only getting bigger," said Nalder.

His boss sighed. "Okay, I'll make the call." Then after a moment, "You'll find the ashtray?"

Harvey O'Sullivan had been a smoker his whole life and, in his own, colorful Irish vernacular couldn't be arsed with political correctness. He was the only person who smoked anywhere in the building. It was his building, as far as he was concerned. His TV station and he'd do what he liked when he was there.

"I know where it is," Nalder was already reaching inside his cupboard.

On air, Dan was announcing a cross to the Mayo clinic where Medical correspondent Sheldon Goldstein was with infectious diseases expert Professor Theo Koudounaris.

In moments, the considerable bulk of Prof Koudounaris had filled the screen. "I can't tell you what's happening in Times Square and at JFK Airport," he spoke with slow but authoritative precision. "But I can tell you this: what we are witnessing is *not* Staphylococcal food poisoning. The symptoms described sound the same, but Staph food poisoning symptoms take at least thirty minutes to develop and sometimes up to eight hours."

"Could this be a mutation, perhaps, of the Staph bacteria?"

"That's not a possibility I've ever heard of," Prof Koudounaris was firm.

"Experts are trying to work out if there's a connection between Times Square and JFK airport. Right now, there doesn't seem to be one besides food source."

"If that hypothesis proves correct," intoned Professor Koudounaris. "Then unless two, unrelated individuals have simultaneously begun passing on the same infectious disease in completely different locations at the same time, we can only conclude that the food source itself is contaminated."

"In which case," Goldstein spelled it out. "Other food outlets supplied from the same source would be at risk."

"Obviously," the professor nodded.

"If we're not looking at Staph food poisoning, Professor, are you willing to offer any suggestion about what might be happening?"

"More than fifty normal, healthy people arrived at various food outlets this morning and, within minutes of starting their meals, they succumbed to severe food poisoning. This is *not* caused by the usual bacterial infections like Salmonella, Clostridium or Staphylococcus. I'm afraid to say, this is very much worse."

"People are of course talking about the coronavirus pandemic. Wondering if what we're seeing today is the start of some new, gastro pandemic. Is this your view?"

The camera came in close on the Professor's grave and brooding features. "It's far too early to put a label on it. To be truthful, it's like nothing we've seen in our lives before."

IN THE NEWSROOM, NICK NALDER'S HUNCH HAD EVOLVED RAPIDLY from pure speculation to a gathering tsunami as his reporters, drawing on all the resources they could, calling in every favor, confirmed that Times Square and JFK were only the start. The same phenomenon was playing out in places as far apart as Buffalo, Pittsburgh, Jackson, Phoenix and San Francisco. And not only in Golden Drumstick outlets. Arch-rival Crowing Hen had been affected in exactly the same way. Not to mention other chicken fast-food outlets. In some cases, contagious disease scientists were still arriving on site and not even the local media had been alerted yet.

Suppliers of chickens to these varying outlets were multiple. What was happening, it soon became apparent, went beyond any individual outlet, chain or even state. Instant, severe food poisoning was now a nationwide phenomenon.

Even Dan Kavana, inured to breaking the most gruesome of stories looked visibly shaken as he reported on developments which was seeing airports shutting down, including all six terminals at JFK. Air traffic was being severely disrupted—railway and subway activities similarly, with people reacting in horror then fear as fellow commuters suddenly collapsed to the ground amid a welter of vomiting and diarrhea. What if the victims were contagious? Was the disease fatal? How to get away from all this as fast as possible?

Such was the avalanche of news that Galaxy staff had never been so stretched in their attempts to keep up with what was happening and to direct resources at the biggest stories. Dan found himself interviewing a medical freelancer who was a recognizable face from rival Channel 60. During the course of their conversation, the reporter referred by name both to Channel 60 and specifically to Dan's arch-rival, anchor Bart Bracking, a direct breach of a protocol, in which competitors must never be mentioned.

But so weird were the times in which they found themselves, that Dan heard himself confirm on live TV that Bart Bracking was, indeed, a highly reliable news anchor. Which happened to be a truth, if an inconvenient one. And there was no rebuke on the teleprompter. Zilch from Nick Nalder. On the other side of the glass, the news boss had more pressing concerns.

There was a cross to Kim Dayton for a major update. "We have an important public announcement just in from the Food and Drug Administration, the FDA," she had a document in her hand. "They're telling the public this morning, for precautionary reasons, *to consume no poultry products* until there's been a thorough investigation of all poultry supplies. That's no chicken products or by-products of any kind."

"Chicken is off the menu, nationally, with immediate effect?" confirmed Dan.

"As well as ducks and turkey. All poultry."

"Is the FDA in a position to tell us the cause of the food poisoning we've seen?"

She shook her head. "All they'll say is that testing is still underway. Independent specialists are confirming that this is unlikely to be any of the usual bacterial problems associated with food preparation. Its action is too swift."

"So presumably we have no idea about the source of the poisoning either?"

Kim was shaking her head. "As a precautionary measure, the FDA has closed down all poultry slaughterhouses."

"That will have a massive impact on the chicken industry."

"On average, around 25-million chickens are processed every day."

"And what about the *big* question everyone wants answered Kim?" Dan repeated the question he knew she couldn't possibly answer, because it was the one that every single viewer would be wondering. "Just how contagious is this thing?"

At that moment, right next to where Kim was standing, two bio-security agents in full protection suits hurried a groaning child on a stretcher towards a waiting ambulance. Unable to suppress her emotion, Kim's eyes welled up. "I don't know, Dan," her voice caught. "No one can say. As a mom, I suggest people stay home today."

The first break he got, Dan pushed back from his desk and headed into the newsroom.

His assistant, Julieta Rodrigo, saw him coming and rose to her feet.

"Did you get hold of anyone?" he'd left his phone with her—and instructions to keep calling Maddie's care-givers. The knowledge that his daughter was lying paralyzed and alone in the darkness had been on his mind the whole news broadcast.

"Jacinda's got it covered," she said, handing back his phone. "She sent me a text to confirm. She was at your home before Maddie even woke."

Dan let out a long breath.

"You're a great Dad, Dan," she reached out, touching his arm reassuringly. "You shouldn't beat yourself up so much."

Like everyone else in the newsroom, Julieta remembered Maddie from the time before the accident. How she used to come in, the vivacious and hard-working intern during school vacations.

"Thanks," he acknowledged. But he didn't return her smile.

If he really was a great Dad, he often thought, Maddie wouldn't have been anywhere near the accident that broke her neck.

||

Hey, peeps!

There's only one thing going down online right now. It's already trending big time and I am predicting that in the coming hours it's going to be the biggest thing we've seen this month. This year. Dang, maybe even ever.

Just five letters—and remember, you heard them from Digital Dave first: K A R M A.

The digital algorithm is showing mentions of KARMA surging 5,000 percent since midnight. Distribution rate is even across all social media channels and demographics. And listen up—because here's where it gets really interesting: so far there has been almost *no virality*. Very few shares and retweets. What does this mean? These are unconnected individuals, going online about what's happening today—and using the K-word.

There's nothing new about KARMA. What *is* new is the way it seems to be ramping up in speed.

Strap on your seatbelts, peeps, we're in for a wild ride!

12

M EGAN MITCHELL, LAMA TASHI'S FRONT ROW STUDENT, HAD rarely felt such excitement as she scrolled through her news feed that morning. Having risen early to meditate, pack school lunches and make breakfast for her husband, Keith, and two kids, Hayden and Shelley, it was only after waving them all off down the driveway that she had time to sit with a cup of coffee and check in with the world.

All the major news channels were covering the national food poisoning and the massive disruption it had caused. Most airports and travel networks were now closed. The FDA had banned the sale of all poultry and recommending against all poultry consumption.

Meanwhile, social media was filled with a myriad of startling stories that day. Acts of generosity being followed by sudden riches. Small gestures of grace towards other people—and even pets or other animals—being rewarded in random ways. Megan took in the faces of people, thrilled and bewildered by the dramatic turn of events.

From a different perspective, she reflected, everything that was happening, including all the bad stuff, was far from random. The speed at which things were occurring this morning seemed to have accelerated dramatically. But none without cause.

She kept remembering how much Rinpoche had been emphasizing teachings on karma in recent months. Had it been to prepare his students? She had no doubt he possessed qualities enabling him to see what was obscured to others, including the future. This morning, she'd had a strong

71

feeling that she should contact him—and not only because she was curious by what he had to say.

After reading Digital Dave's blog about karma, she *knew* she must contact him. This was much bigger than just her, or even Lama Tashi. It could turn out to be the most momentous turning point anyone had ever experienced. And if so—who better than Lama Tashi to explain to people what was happening?

She picked up her cell phone and tapped on contacts.

Although she had been attending classes at Lone Pine Meditation Center for over fifteen years, including numberless retreats, and had sat at Lama Tashi's feet for thousands of teaching hours, they had only ever spoken via computer once, to confirm a travel matter. Megan respected Lama Tashi far too much to intrude into his life, to pester him with questions that could always wait until the next class, or to turn to him for guidance every time she needed to make a decision. "Be your own therapist," Lama Tashi would echo the words of the other much-loved Lama Yeshe, seeking to give his students the tools they needed to attain enduring inner peace.

Which was why she'd been surprised, eighteen months before, when Lama Tashi, hearing that she was about to set up a recording studio, had paid her a personal visit. Apart from being his student, Megan was also a podcaster, blogger and all-round digital savant, whose *Flourish* website attracted thousands of visitors each day. *Flourish* had been a side-hustle when she'd worked as a digital marketing consultant. By the time she'd left employment to have her second child, Shelley, *Flourish* had become a hungry monster, demanding ever-increasing volumes of content. Her frustration had been monetizing all this traffic. She had always been very particular about who she allowed to run promotions on her site, unwilling to let *Flourish* become just another, low-grade purveyor of wellness baloney.

Rinpoche had come round to inspect the home office above her garage. She was in the process of having it subdivided, with a soundproofed booth, so that she could conduct radio interviews to professional broadcast standard.

"Good, good," Lama Tashi had looked around the place, as though already familiar with the layout. "But you need a window there," he'd pointed to the back wall. "So people can see the valley. It's a good background, yes?"

"This is for radio," puzzled lines had appeared on her forehead.

"*And* television."

"But I don't do TV."

"When you do, it will be very good. People like nature. And make sure you put your brand on the glass."

"You mean *Flourish*?" she confirmed, surprised by the commerciality of his advice.

He nodded. "They have to know the name if you are going to be famous."

"You think I should be famous?" she was incredulous.

"Of course!" he was emphatic. "Being famous is *most* useful when you have something important to say!"

At great expense, she'd had a branded, triple-glazed window installed. And a camera.

The forested mountain falling away to a distant valley made for a gorgeous backdrop. Lama Tashi had been right about that. There was something timeless and peaceful about the setting that instilled calm just looking at it. The thing was, she'd never used it. All these months later, she still wasn't doing TV. Beautiful as her studio was, she sometimes wondered if she hadn't hugely over-capitalized.

Pressing the "Call" button, Megan heard the ring tone from the other end. Despite the news that morning, she still felt somewhat improper making this call. Lama Tashi didn't have a phone as such. What he did have was an app on a computer, the details of which he'd shared with only a handful of people. She hoped he wouldn't think she was just being impulsive or attention-seeking.

"Lama Tashi, it's Megan," she announced herself when he answered.

He chuckled, as if they were already sharing an inside joke.

"What's going on today?!" she exclaimed. "Is this why you've been teaching so much about karma in the past few weeks?"

"I think you already know," he said.

"Is it really, like, instant karma?"

"Instant?" he mused. "Generally, the karma we experience in this lifetime, we created in our last."

"Exactly." This was Megan's understanding of the traditional Buddhist teachings.

"But something is happening today. Tell me, my dear, what does karma need to ripen?"

"Conditions," she replied with such familiarity she didn't even have to think about it. Karma was often likened to a seed. If it was to germinate it required soil, moisture and heat: conditions.

"I think perhaps conditions have changed causing some aspects of karma to ripen more quickly."

"So people are experiencing karma *as though* it is instant?" she confirmed.

"Exactly."

Megan took a moment to absorb this, before she said. "Rinpoche, I think people need to know this."

"Of course."

"The reason I called is because I wondered if you'd be willing to explain karma on my podcast."

"Yes, yes," he said, as if this was already a given. "I'll come to your studio."

His suggestion took her aback. Lama Tashi lived an hour's drive from her. "We could do it down-the-line, so you don't have to travel all this way."

"Your TV camera is working?"

"Yes. But the podcast is for online radio."

"Make it TV," Rinpoche told her. "People like to see who is talking to them. I'll be there soon."

13

Wall Street, New York

KAREL SHARMA RARELY DESCENDED FROM THE TRADING FLOOR, where his office was situated, to the land of tax, compliance and HR, one floor below. The administration of Sharma Funds on the 25th floor was of little, personal interest. He had bean counters and management types to take care of that sort of thing. So it was unusual for him to decide, on impulse, to pay a visit to his accountants with a tax query. And even more unexpected when he'd encountered Amy Robbins, eyes glistening with tears of joy.

Karel wasn't good with people. Almost painfully introverted, he was the very shyest of Wall Street wolves. Thirty-something and immensely successful, no number of dollars in the bank had ever made him feel any easier in the presence of people he didn't know—which was just about everybody. He went to sometimes extreme lengths to avoid strangers. He was awkward with staff—especially the young and female, in whose presence he still felt like a stammering adolescent.

"Good-morning Mr. Sharma!" The young woman radiated such heartfelt elation, it was impossible to be unaffected.

"Hello!" he smiled, something he did rarely, and almost never on the 25th floor. The two of them hadn't met, he was sure of it. But such was her self-evident happiness, even he felt obliged to ask, "Having a good day?"

"The best of my life!" she said.

Unprompted, she had told him about how she'd won a luxury cruise which she'd given her parents before getting news of an unexpected inheritance only minutes later. She was so effusive in sharing her story, and so natural, he couldn't fail to be affected.

He was still thinking about it when he got back to his office upstairs. There he discovered the latest blog from Digital Dave that he read in a few moments, before walking to the window and gazing at the familiar vista of high rises in the financial district.

For the first time in a long while he felt a stirring. The sense of a new wave to ride.

Although the world of high finance seemed incomprehensible to many people, to Karel all the jargon and technicalities were simply a layer of complexity that obscured a more simple truth. Which was that if you wanted to be rich, seriously rich, you had to be first in the game. Whatever the game was.

He'd done it with hedge funds in his early twenties. He'd done it with cryptocurrencies five years later. Long after words like "Bitcoin" came into common usage, he had already cashed out and left the party. Of course, he still had his trading floor, buying and selling and keeping the show on the road for client investors. Now in his early thirties, Karel's job, as he saw it, was to be like a scout ant on behalf of the colony, to keep his antennae raised, his senses fine-tuned, constantly on the look-out for the next big thing. Whatever shape or form it may take.

And this morning, for the first time in years, he thought he'd picked up on something. And if it was anything like it seemed, within hours it was going to be the financial markets equivalent of a tsunami.

The blog he'd just read by Digital Dave confirmed Amy's story downstairs.

He had also been following that morning's news. The food poisoning among diners at Golden Drumsticks and other chains. There seemed to be connections to him. Somewhere, somehow, a wave was emerging from the ocean. A monster wave offering the ride of a lifetime. Why wouldn't he want to surf it?

At his desk, he tapped the word "Karma" into a search engine, before adding the word "Buddhist." Despite his Indian surname, Karel had been brought up by a chemistry-teaching father, with little interest in his Hindu heritage, and a Czech mother, who had given him his first name. He was as ignorant about the workings of karma as most other people. But he'd had Buddhist friends who seemed to know about karma and in a few key strokes he'd established that Sera Monastery in Mysore, India was one of the most highly regarded places of higher learning in Tibetan Buddhism. It was only a matter of minutes before Karel was speaking to a guy with a Geshe degree, which he knew was a big deal.

Along with his philosophy that you had to be first in the game, Karel had another simple conviction: always consult an expert. Don't go jumping into a new venture feet first. There was invariably someone who knew a whole lot more about the area you were headed than you did. Someone who'd be willing to share their knowledge if you asked the right questions.

"Karma," he came right to the point with the Geshe guy. "Am I right in thinking that karma says cause and effect are directly related?"

"Exactly," came the reply, with a Tibetan accent.

"So, to create the effect of receiving wealth, the cause is to give wealth."

"Yes."

"The more you give, the more you get?"

There was a pause. "There's more to it than that. It depends, for example, on who you are giving to. Your motivation for giving. Plus other factors."

"Uh-huh," Karel's rollerball was poised over an empty page of his notebook. "So how do I, as the giver, maximize my returns?"

Fifteen minutes later, Karel had summoned three of his most seasoned traders. Around the office they'd acquired the nickname "The Three Gekkos" after the Wall Street movie.

"I've got an idea for Algobrite," he told them from behind his desk.

There was some eye-rolling. Algobrite Infrastructure was a dog of a fund. They'd inherited it, as part of a broader acquisition and its assets were things like a port in South America that couldn't be sold, and power stations in Africa which never delivered hard currency income. They'd been trying to come up with ways to dump Algobrite, but hadn't been able to.

"You're going to think what I ask you to do is crazy, but just do it, okay?"

They nodded. In their volatile world, they understood the importance of discipline and keeping focused.

"I want to donate a hundred and twenty thousand from the fund's cash account to twelve charities. Ten thousand per charity. I've emailed you the links. That's four charities each."

If the gekkos were surprised they weren't showing it. The transactions were so small they were probably wondering why he'd bothered calling them in.

"I want you to make the transfers asap."

They were already stepping towards his door.

"Also in the email is something you must say before and as you are pressing the "Send" button for each donation."

"Quality control?" queried Gekko One.

"It's like an affirmation. A motivation. I don't care what you think of it. Just keep an open mind and do it."

There were puzzled expressions, but nothing more.

"And guys, under the radar with this, okay?"

Along with being first in the game, and always consult an expert, Karel Sharma had another self-imposed rule: put your toe in the water first. The hundred and twenty grand was the toe. And The Three Gekkos had that money out the door within minutes, motivations murmured on the way.

Caught up on a lengthy tele-conference, when Karel turned back to his computer it was to find an email from Monomatapa Bank—a Swiss-based investment firm focusing on sub-Sahara Africa. They wanted to buy all of Algobrite's African assets and were offering an amount based on the book valuation plus ten percent. In one, fell swoop, Sharma could exit a whole bunch of underperforming assets at a price for at least ten million dollars more than they could have dreamed.

Karel looked down at his hands, stretching his fingers out against the shiny, mahogany of his desk. They were trembling. In a good way. He hadn't felt this excited in years!

When he had The Three Gekkos back for the news, they could hardly believe their ears either. It wasn't the money so much. Or even the turn-around in Algobrite's fortunes.

No, it was the principle: you could earn untold riches instantly by giving away money. To the right people. In the right way.

"Before we go wider," Karel adopted his confidential voice. "One more test run, okay? Two million from Algobrite and the same from our private trading account."

"Same charities. Same motivations?" confirmed Gekko Two.

Karel nodded.

Half an hour later, the Venezuelan Government announced the nationalization of two ports owned by Algobrite. This was an eventuality against which the company was specifically and fully insured, with a generous listed valuation. Within minutes, Karel arranged for a claim to be lodged at Lloyds of London. Algobrite would soon be rid of all its poorly-performing assets.

Meantime, a start-up tech company invested in by the firm's private trading account became the subject of a bidding war between two Silicon Valley giants. Valuations were going crazy—twenty, thirty times the true value of the company as executive egos took over.

By nine fifty in the morning, Sharma had made more money than in the previous two weeks combined.

Karel picked up his desk phone and pressed "0" for Reception.

"That girl I was speaking to earlier near your desk," he queried, when Jaye replied.

"Amy Robbins."

"From Texas?"

"Yes."

"Send her up."

14

Princeton, New Jersey

I N A COFFEE SHOP BEHIND HIS LAPTOP, ANOTHER SELF-STYLED TRAIL-
blazer was following the morning's events with interest. Lanky, bespec-
tacled, with an unruly mop of dark hair, there was little in Stan Smugg's
appearance that betrayed the intensity of his excitement. A social psychologist, always on the look-out for new trends that revealed the credu-
lousness of his fellow humans, their tendency to allow rationality to be
hobbled by baseless belief, this morning it seemed like all his Christmases
had come at once.

There was no question the whole country was going through upheaval.
But it was the human reaction that got his attention. On social media, as
people reported the dramatic ups and downs of their lives that day, there
were no end of references to karma. Interviewees were spontaneously pro-
posing it on TV as a possible explanation for the fast-food poisoning. He
was startled when even one of the most prominent member of Princeton's
physics faculty, a Nobel prize laureate no less, referred to "instant karma"
in an email that morning. It was time to bring an end to such mystical
thinking.

Stan had had his first taste of fame when the subject of his PhD the-
sis, a study of the wellness industry in New York, was publicized after
a chance meeting with an enterprising journalist. Too much positive
thinking made you miserable, had been the unexpected upshot of his
investigations. Stan had suddenly found himself on the receiving end of
innumerable interview requests, faculty offers and his very first book deal.

A quick study, Stan's next project was the one that made him famous. He meticulously constructed a large-scale, longitudinal research program to show that patients who were the beneficiaries of prayer recovered no more quickly than those who weren't prayed for. The book that followed, "Pointless Prayer," was serialized in major newspapers, ruffled establishment feathers, and provoked such furious diatribes from fundamentalist church leaders, in particular the Reverend Jeremiah Bellow, that for a few glorious weeks his book had been propelled onto the New York Times best-seller charts.

Exactly as he had hoped.

That had been eight years ago, and it had been slim pickings since then. Planning to ride the crest of the yoga wave, the findings of a survey showing that yoga students were more easily upset than people who stayed on the sofa, never went anywhere. There had been insufficient outrage from the yoga sector.

An attempt to prove that too much time in nature made you depressed backfired when his findings went the other way.

No, what he needed was a bubble he knew he could pop. A cow held sacred by many people. In particular, a subject of the highest possible relevance. "Instant karma," he recognized, offered what he needed to make a meteoric return. But he'd have to act fast.

Hammering away on his keyboard that morning, he soon established a research test, putting in place the protocols and oversights needed to provide methodological rigor. He lined up approvals, participants and methodology. The experiment he had devised had an elegant simplicity to it, the kind he could already imagine himself explaining on prime time television, perhaps even later today: 100 participants would be asked to give away $10 as they wished within half an hour. If instant karma really existed along the lines that was being reported, money would soon be raining down on the heads of every single participant in equal measure.

Of course that wasn't going to happen. Stan Smugg was sure of it. Having taken a Comparative Religions course in his undergraduate years he had made a brief study of karma. The notion that cause led to effect would have been eminently reasonable had the process played out during a specific period. But that was never the claim. The fruit of karmic causes was said to ripen in your next lifetime—or a thousand lifetimes later. And therein lay the flaw. No one had any memory of having lived more than once. There was not a shred of evidence to support the idea. The whole notion of karma was therefore fanciful. Magical nonsense. The kind of errant claptrap he had devoted his career to rebutting.

Ten minutes before he was about to deliver his first lecture of the day, he finished what he was doing, snapped his laptop shut, and strode gawkily outside. His first year psych students were in for a treat this morning, he thought. Soon they'd also be learning at the feet of the master. Today Stanley Montgomery Smugg PhD, New York Times Best-Selling Author, Digital Disruptor and Influencer was about to make the mother of all come-backs!

15

Paige Turner Books
Omni, Colorado

Endless Love was in Fantasy, pretending to browse. Beth had seen him step in from the sidewalk as she was helping another customer. For the second time in the past few days she heard warning bells. The knowledge that she needed to cool it with him. Take things down a few notches. Maybe more.

Like most Friday mornings, today was busy. Many older residents, especially those who lived along the mountain, came into town to meet friends for coffee or lunch or to do their groceries at the end of the week. Sometimes they'd stop at Paige Turner Books, as they had in the days when Paige herself had presided over the emporium, to ask for reading recommendations.

Beth didn't have time for distractions. She'd thought it was clear from the outset that what she and E.L. had was strictly outside working hours. A discrete arrangement between the two of them. As a professional man, not to mention a married one, she thought he'd respect that. Which he had initially. Lately, however, he'd begun to change and she recognized the signals. She'd seen them before.

One of her regulars stepped into the shop. An elderly matriarch prim and correct in her velvet jacket and pearls, Babs was the epitome of the well-mannered grandmother. Beth approached her, eyes gleaming. "You'll never guess what arrived just yesterday," she whispered sotto voce. "The new Lukas Lukassön!"

Babs's face lit up as Beth led her to a shelf, handing her a copy of the new book by the Scandinavian noir author. It was four hundred pages of frenzied violence perpetrated by a diabolical psychopath.

"Oh—thank you, my dear!" said Babs, picking up the book and holding it to her heart. "You've just made my weekend!"

Beth smiled. She had a genuine interest in what her customers read—and why they read it. In her first weeks as a bookstore manager, she'd been surprised how many older women were fans of books depicting the grisliest of crimes, before coming to realize that this didn't signify anything about them except for a wish to escape. To be voyeurs. To enter another reality that was the polar opposite of their own, as a way perhaps of pepping up an otherwise humdrum life. It didn't make them somehow suppressed deviants or criminally-minded. Most of them, she had no doubt, were very clear about the difference between fantasy and reality. Perhaps all consumers of fiction—whether as books or movies—were the same, she sometimes reflected. They all wished to experience another reality. The only difference between them was what kind of alternative appealed.

Endless Love approached the counter as soon as she'd seen her customer off. By now there were several others in the shop, gray heads moving along the aisles. They had come in as she'd been chatting to Babs and she needed to attend to them.

"Back already?" she raised her eyebrows.

Bob glanced about, conscious that he was trespassing. He also noted the absence of warmth. "Wondered if I could see you tonight?" he murmured.

"I thought you were playing "Happy Families'?"

"Change of plan."

"Yeah, well, it's Friday. I'm busy."

She was irritated that he was here with more demands only hours after his sleepover which had, itself, been a concession. Two days ago he'd proposed it on the basis that his wife was getting home and he wouldn't be visiting her for some time. She hadn't been keen. She wasn't a staying-over-the-night person. More importantly, she'd noted a creeping expectation on his part, a possessiveness she wouldn't tolerate.

He arranged his features, now, in an attempt at stoic acceptance. But he couldn't conceal the hurt. The same pained disbelief he'd been unable to hide on that first afternoon when he'd visited her to apologize for stepping over the line on the night of the launch party. No doubt he'd been desperate to make sure that his tedious, imitative little wife didn't find out. Beth had had no intentions for him at the time. But seeing how vulnerable he looked, like a schoolboy who'd just been caught with his hand in the cookie jar, had been too much for her.

"I'm very sorry about last night," he had said, standing on the pavement, looking her directly in the eyes. "I was very drunk."

Beth had been closing the shop for the day. The last customer had left. The day's takings reconciled. She had been bolting one side of the door to the street, top and bottom, and had been about to lock the other. "What are you sorry about?" she'd decided to have some fun. "Being drunk, or what we did?"

"Both, really. I can't remember much about it."

"Then it's not an apology," she shrugged. "How can you be truly sorry for something you don't remember doing?"

He hadn't known how to take her. It was a while before he replied, "Apologizing just seems ... the right thing to do." He'd been all little-boy-lost.

"We could repeat what we did last night, but sober," she'd teased, enjoying the sport of it, and not really caring how he answered. "If you still want to apologize afterwards, be my guest."

She'd practically felt the heat of his gaze descend to her cleavage.

The truth was that she had the upper hand. Last night hadn't been entirely spontaneous. She'd engineered things so that they were alone at the end of the party. For some time her angels had been pushing her in the direction of an older man. A really old man. Daddy-love seemed an archetypal fantasy, the sexual equivalent of one of Lukas Lukassön's gruesome rampages. And while Bob fit the profile—the oldest guy she'd ever been with, up till then, had been forty—he was right about having had too much to drink to remember.

Which was why, after he'd stepped inside and she'd locked the door of Paige Turner Books behind them, that afternoon in the storeroom had been a very pleasant surprise. She knew all the stories about older guys flagging. Or being too limp to do much. Even falling asleep on the job. Bob, however, had been magnificent and unstoppable, working his way methodically through just about every available position before delivering a triumphant finale.

He had also endeared himself to her in a way few men ever did. Lying together on a flattened out cardboard box, bathed in afterglow, when she'd made some self-deprecating remark about her nose getting in the way, he had immediately replied, "But I *love* your nose!"

"How can you?" The idea itself seemed crazy.

Beth's nose was more than a facial landmark. It had dominated her self-image ever since she could remember.

"The lines of an ancient aristocrat," he had told her. "You have a Roman nose."

"Roman nose!" she had sniggered, but was delighted. "Makes it sound special."

"It is special!" Leaning over, he had kissed it.

When he was lying down again, beside her, her expression turned mock-serious. "Now," she regarded him severely. "Being of sound mind and sober judgement, and able to remember what has happened, are you ready to apologize for what you just did?"

He'd held her gaze for a moment, before grinning. "Not really."

"Just as well," she chortled. "Or that would be the last time you karma'd my sutra!"

Beth observed two more Friday-morning customers come into the store, ladies of a certain age who she must help. Endless Love was still facing her across the counter. She had to get him out of here before things got really busy. Perhaps she needed to get him out altogether. She'd tried the older man thing, she thought, regarding him dispassionately. Which was when a new idea occurred to her.

"How open-minded are you, E.L.?" she asked.

"I think you know the answer to that," he chuckled self-consciously.

"Then you can see me later."

"Okay."

"I'm busy tonight, but I have the afternoon off."

He nodded.

"Three o'clock. Upstairs."

"Great!"

From behind the New Literary Fiction shelves, a white-haired man in trademark navy blazer, crisp cotton shirt and white handkerchief in his pocket, was observing the interaction between manager and customer. Ian Turner had known Margarita and Bob Martin forever. His late wife, Paige, had sold them books when they were a couple and through the years they'd had a growing family. After Paige had died he'd retired to Arizona on account of the warm winters being better for his arthritis, and he had put the shop in the hands of a succession of managers. He'd return several times a year to visit the friends he'd known for most of his life. Margarita was one of those. They'd been at school together and, although most folk had forgotten, he'd had a bit of a crush on the gorgeous Latina girl in their teens. In a different, more mature way he still appreciated her company, the way they just seemed to click. It had been at his invitation that Margarita had held her most recent book launch at Paige Turner Books.

Ian may be heading towards seventy, with a variety of physical ailments, but he was nobody's fool. Nor was he one to rush to judgment about how other people conducted their personal lives. But he did feel a pang for Margarita, wondering if she knew about her husband's affair. And he was surprised by Bob, whom he'd always taken to be an astute businessman. The kind of person who didn't need to have explained to him the importance of undertaking due diligence when venturing into the unknown.

Because if Bob had been as clueless about Beth as he had when getting involved with her, thought Ian, he was in for a very rude awakening.

Ridicule

10:00 am (Eastern Standard Time)
8:00 am (Mountain Standard Time)
7:00 am (Pacific Standard Time)

A human being experiences himself, his thoughts and feelings as something separated from the rest—a kind of optical illusion of his consciousness. This delusion is a kind of prison for us, restricting us to our personal desires and to affection for a few persons nearest to us. Our task must be to free ourselves from this prison by widening our circle of understanding and compassion to embrace all living creatures and the whole of nature in its beauty.

—ALBERT EINSTEIN (Theoretical Physicist 1879—1955)

16

Galaxy Television
Galaxy City, Los Angeles

Los Angeles awoke to discover contagion fears taking grip of the rest of the country. All air traffic was suspended. Railways, subways and bus services had stopped running. Those public buildings in more eastern states that had opened were promptly shutting, and most big businesses were telling staff to work from home.

The flood of violent gastro-intestinal episodes was choking every hospital and clinic.

At Galaxy Television, the news team was assembling for the morning briefing in the conference room, next to the studio. On a Friday, they'd usually be seated at the large, oval table engaged in light banter about that weekend's sports games as they waited for Nick Nalder to arrive. Today, they were standing, tense and reluctant to be there at all. There was just too much going on for a meeting.

"Now it's Piper's!" Nick Nalder looked up from his tablet as he strode in.

Piper's was the biggest and most famous burger chain, not only in USA, but in the world. A Piper's burger was the same unit of highly-processed, artificially-flavored dregs served up in an over-sugared bun, with a side of over-salted fries, whether you bought it in Chicago or Shanghai.

"Same thing's happening with meat patties."

Galaxy's four researchers, three reporters, the ratings guy, and two news anchors, including Dan Kavana, looked stunned. The researchers were tapping and scrolling on their tablets, like they always did—the only ones officially allowed such a liberty during the meeting.

"Who's reporting-?"

"Takes longer to act than the chicken," Nalder was reading from his screen. Same symptoms, only worse. The pain is acute. Stand by for the next wave." He glanced round the grim faces, doing a mental check, before asking, "Where's Hedley?"

"Delayed," said Bec, a business reporter. "National Weather Service is running an emergency briefing."

Nalder pulled a face. Emergency briefings only happened when extreme weather events were expected, like hurricanes.

"Obviously we don't have time for this," he addressed the group. Usually they'd chart out the stories they planned running that day, working out the different angles. "We can hardly keep up with what's happening. And, by the way, Mr. O'Sullivan is coming in so it's going to get even busier in here."

His team shuffled. Mr. O'Sullivan, God of Galaxy, was only ever referred to in hallowed tones. He wasn't someone people ever saw unless they'd been invited to an upscale celebrity event where they might spot him in the distance. The fact he was choosing to hang in the newsroom today spoke volumes.

"Where's this story going?" Nalder addressed the researchers—all twenty-somethings glued to their devices.

"Pipers isn't the only burger chain affected," one barely looked up from where he was reading from a social media feed. "Buzz Burgers has had to close three branches in Boston."

"The FDA—" another interjected, "is expected to put out a statement soon."

"What about?" asked Dan.

"Doesn't say."

"My White House guy is telling me that pressure's growing for an announcement," a reporter chipped in. "The Chief of Staff is freeing up space in the President's schedule. Stand by for a media call."

"Is Blake in position?" Nalder wanted to know.

The other nodded.

"What's going on with ratings, Trent?" Nalder wanted to know.

Trent Garvey, roly-poly, geeky and mid-thirties, usually headed up the morning briefing, outlining the all-important viewership figures for the early morning news report.

"Three times the usual viewing figures," confirmed Trent. "Same as the other channels."

"Any points of difference?" asked Dan.

It was the perennial question. How to report the same story as competitors in a more compelling way.

Trent delivered a sheepish glance. "A brief surge, 30 percent up, during your interview with that medical freelancer."

"What were they talking about?" pressed Nalder.

"Bart Bracking at Channel 60," said Trent. "What an influential news source he is."

"30 percent up!" Dan was incredulous.

In normal circumstances, the incident would have demanded explanation and almost certain censure. Today, Nalder just shook his head.

"We wouldn't be talking to freelancers unless we were desperate." Fixing a steely gaze on his reporting team he demanded, "You've called every journalist, every half-decent intern we ever had?"

"All accounted for," said one.

"The networks are chasing the same tiny pool," said another.

"Too much happening. Too few people."

Nalder was chewing his lip as they confirmed his worst fears. Maybe having Harvey in here wouldn't be such a bad thing. He would see, first hand, the impossibility of trying to run a major news organization with the head count of a suburban newspaper.

"What about the advertisers?" queried Dan, acutely aware of the relationship between ad-spend and editorial foot-soldiers. "I'm guessing we've lost all the fast food clients?"

Trent from ratings was shaking his head. "Ad-spend is way up. The fast food chains have pulled all their chicken ads. They're heavily promoting their non-meat options. We're seeing ads go out that have never been shown before with massive expenditure."

The multi-screen display at the end of the room, with live network feeds, showed bio-security agents carrying stretchers, over-crowded hospital Emergency departments and people on the ground outside food outlets, hugging themselves, wracked with pain.

Which was when researcher Tracey Kramer said, "You should know, Nick, that there's also some crazy, positive stories today."

His eyes blinked heavily behind his glasses. He felt his cheek flinch. It always irked him the way the millennial girl called him "Nick" in that wry, familiar way. "Like?"

"Surprise inheritances. Breakthroughs. Prizes," said Tracey. "Like the $2.1 billion Powerball this morning. The biggest ever winner and it's a charity syndicate."

Usually, such a massive, feel-good win would be a headline story.

"Make sure we follow up on that," Nalder commanded.

"The American College of Radiology just put out a release about a spike in spontaneous cancer remissions today," observed Julieta Lopez, Dan's assistant. "Spontaneous remissions are usually rare—like, a few a month. There are twenty known remissions this morning alone—most of them previously terminal cases."

Nalder pointed at Dan. "Do that story, too. Speak to one of the death row people whose come good."

"Stuff going on out there is just off the spectrum," continued Julieta. "It's like there's as much insanely positive stuff as negative stuff."

The newsroom chief was shaking his head. "Where's it all suddenly coming from?" he mused, aloud.

"Good question," chimed Dan. Scrolling through his news feed immediately before this meeting he'd felt overwhelmed by sheer volume of it. It was like their ten most dramatic news days were happening at once.

"Lots of online commentary about karma," replied Chieko, the Japanese researcher who had a social media brief.

Nalder's eyebrows twitched upwards.

"Cause and effect," she explained.

"I know what karma is," Nalder shoved the thick, black frames of his glasses up his nose, his cheek twitching again. "How could it be the cause of national food-poisoning?"

Chieko, whose natural inclination was to avoid all confrontation, bowed her head. Tracey Kramer, on the other hand, who knew her rights, was only too glad to get stuck in. "Some are saying, it's the exploitation of animals through intensive farming methods," she explained. "What goes around, comes around. Only those who created the demand for animal products are sick."

"Where's the mechanism?" Nalder didn't contain his irritation, his face flushing. Along with the reddening, another thing was happening that soon had everyone in the room mesmerized. A mole on his right cheek, just above the corner of his mouth, began to darken. And grow. Moment by moment, as he regarded Tracey testily, what had been a minor blemish, a familiar imperfection, was growing and spreading into a much larger, more observable disfigurement.

Cool under fire, Tracey nevertheless wanted to respond.

"The phrase being used is "instant karma,"" she said. "If it turned out to be true it would account for *all* the dramatic events, negative and positive."

Under Nalder's withering gaze something seemed to be happening to Tracey. There had always been something clunky and inelegant about the girl. Smart, yes. Attractive, no. But in this moment, her face was somehow rearranging itself into more attractive proportions, her blue eyes becoming more doe-like and alluring as she kept her cool.

"The whole idea of instant karma is just ridiculous!" he burst out. "How can people even think that for a second. I mean, where's the logic? Like, why is it just starting up today?" On his right cheek, the mole was expanding to a pronounced black mark the size of a nickel.

"I'm not an expert in karma," Tracey shrugged.

When faced with a topic no one in the newsroom understood, the usual response was the one Julieta proposed now. "Should I track someone down? A karma guy?"

"No!" Nalder was quite certain. "This is no time for hocus pocus! We need authoritative experts with credible explanations."

At that moment, weatherman Hedley Tracer rushed through the door, distraught.

"What's going on, Hedley?" Nalder was brusque.

"Completely weird shit," Hedley was shaking his head. "Outbreaks of severe, micro weather events and seismic activity."

"Micro?" frowned Nalder.

"Highly localized. Like tornados appearing from nowhere and destroying two houses in Harrodsburg, Kentucky. Sinkholes just appearing in places they've never been before."

"If the events are micro," Nalder searched for a benchmark by which to gauge today's unprecedented activity. "They're not that big a deal."

"Depends where they are!" protested Hedley. "And they're happening all over the place!"

At that instant, a massive explosion jolted the newsroom. As the whole room rocked, a plasma screen, mounted high, tumbled from the wall, smashing loudly on the floor.

"Earthquake!" yelled Hedley.

"Under the table!" Dan ordered, dropping onto all fours.

In moments, everyone was on their hands and knees under the conference table, petrified by the deep roar and menacing shudder.

As it continued, on the floor next to his hand, Dan's tablet vibrated to life. His screen was displaying an email he'd opened moments before stepping into the morning briefing—that morning's community notices. On a quiet news day they might run a report on some local worthy cause.

For obvious reasons Dan hadn't so much as skimmed through the notices. Now, as he looked away from his colleague's fearful expressions, an image on the screen caught his attention. It was a seabird, covered in thick, crude oil. "Little bird paralyzed," ran the caption underneath. The headline above was in crude capitals: "VOLUNTEERS NEEDED URGENTLY!"

17

Boulder, Colorado

LAMA TASHI WASN'T ALONE, AS HIS LIME-GREEN VOLVO APPEARED IN the distance. Megan lived at the end of a long driveway, and it was only as the car came much closer that she could make out the other occupant. It was Anton, the cameraman with the dark pony tail and pale face who attended the same Tuesday night class as her. Someone she had been thinking about ever since calling Lama Tashi, wondering if she should ask him to come too. Rinpoche had already got there.

"This is amazing!" enthused Anton, as he stepped out the passenger door to where her home and separate studio were built in a cathedral-like space among the trees.

Megan had been fretting over her appearance that morning since Lama Tashi announced he wanted to do TV. She had changed into this outfit and that, all the time worrying how the camera would add ten pounds to her already maternal bulk, before settling on a black jacket over a grey blouse, with a red pendant for color.

It felt somehow incongruous to be so formally attired, hair coiffed and wearing full make-up, while standing under the towering Douglas firs, with her golden retriever Rusty, snuffling in the undergrowth.

"Ready-made for TV!" Lama Tashi held his hands wide as he approached her, smiling.

"I always thought I had the perfect face for radio," she replied.

"Nonsense!"

It was just as well Anton had come along. Within minutes he was setting up his own camera in the studio and changing the lighting. Megan was to perform the role of interviewer, mostly off-camera, with Lama Tashi in front of that spectacular, tranquil valley.

As Anton took charge of the set-up, Megan and Lama Tashi talked about the questions she wanted to ask, and the sequence in which she should ask them. Despite having been his student for so many years, he still had the capacity to surprise her, as he did now, with his lightness about the interview. It was as if the content of what he was about to say was of secondary importance to the simple fact that he was there. And when Anton showed them the red-robed Lama Tashi such a warm and reassuring presence in the midst of boundless splendor she knew why this was true. It was as if he was the human manifestation of his surroundings.

Seeing Anton take charge of the lighting and camera, and Lama Tashi perfect against the backdrop he himself had ordained years earlier, Megan had the strangest sensation that all the work she'd done with *Flourish* over the years had been leading to this particular day. Going to Lone Pine Meditation Center, becoming Lama Tashi's student, asking his advice about *Flourish*—it was as if she had been led, step by step, to this point without realizing fully the part she was to perform. Yet she was amazingly relaxed about it. Playful even. Lama Tashi's radically different perspective, his benevolent focus and lightness of being communicated powerfully to everyone around him.

"Tell us, Lama Tashi," she began after introducing him to a live, online audience. "We're experiencing a lot of extraordinary things today. Mass food poisoning and disruption to travel networks. Stories of instant wealth and sudden loss. Some people are saying this is instant karma. Is that true?"

"Usually the karma we create in one lifetime only ripens in the next one," Lama Tashi explained. "But I think the conditions may have changed, causing certain aspects of karma to ripen more quickly."

"So it feels like instant karma?" she confirmed.

He nodded.

"Most people know the phrase "what goes around comes around." But there is more to karma than that, isn't there?"

"Karma is an important and complex subject," he said. "But there are a few overall guidelines that are easy to understand. In general, whatever we choose to focus our attention on, increasingly becomes our reality. Buddha himself said, "Mind is the forerunner of all actions." Our thoughts lead to what we say and do, and as thoughts and actions become habitual, they become who we are. Karma isn't just about the big events, the major ups and downs in our lives, which is when people pay attention. It is about every mind moment we have, as we constantly create our future reality.

"So, for example, if a person chooses to practice generosity, wishing for the wellbeing of others, that person is creating the causes to experience a reality of abundance and kindness.

"By contrast, the person who focuses on a lack of money, never seeming to have enough for themselves let alone to share with anyone else, that person creates a poverty mentality. Their reality will increasingly become one of scarcity and hardship, whether or not other people think of them as poor at all."

"What you are saying is that effects relate directly to causes?" confirmed Megan.

"Yes. And there are limitless possibilities. If you wish for long life, help preserve the lives of others. If you wish to avoid betrayal, don't cheat on friends and loved ones. If it's fame you seek, cultivate respect towards influential people worthy of admiration."

"So there's nothing hit or miss about what we experience?"

"Not at all. The specific causes of specific effects have been documented for millennia."

"Earlier you said that karma is a complex subject. Why so?"

"Because at any one moment each one of us has a multiplicity of different karmas, like seeds in a vast storehouse, which may germinate. The way we behave sets up the conditions for which of those seeds, positive or negative, develop. For example, a person may feel his employer takes advantage of him financially, so he feels justified in stealing things from the company to even the score. But being taken advantage of is the effect of a previously-created cause. And by stealing, he has now set himself up to experience even greater loss."

"You talk about the effects of karma in terms of personal experience. How people *experience* loss, or *experience* abundance."

"Of course!" A humorous twinkle appeared in Lama Tashi's eyes, "Reality *is* a subjective experience! It's the creation of our minds. And it's important to recognize that this is where karma operates. Not outside of us. There is no celestial mainframe which allocates happy experiences to this person and misery to that one. No deity figure, no army of devils, moving around behind the scenes and pulling strings. We create our own reality through our thoughts, speech and actions."

"But wealth is more than just some subjective feeling," Megan put across an opposing viewpoint. "It's also about things that can be objectively measured, like dollars in the bank."

"I see," Lama Tashi tilted his head. "So, how many dollars does it take to be wealthy?"

Megan shrugged. "One million. Maybe two?"

"There are many people who, if they discovered they were worth only two million dollars, would feel broke. Despairing. Like they'd lost everything. And there are very many others who, if by some miracle found they had ten thousand dollars in the bank, would feel magnificently rich. So," he shrugged. "Who is right?"

"Everyone's experience of abundance is subjective?" confirmed Megan.

"Everyone's experience of *everything* is subjective," he chuckled. "One of our greatest misperceptions is that the world outside us is completely independent of our minds. That there is some kind of objective reality out there. The truth is much more interesting. You see, you create your own reality. Two people can be in the same room, participating in exactly the same event, and for one it is an occasion of tedium, yet another may enter a state of transcendental bliss. All depends on mind."

"On this very auspicious day," Megan returned to the moment. "What advice would you give to people wanting to make the most of instant karma?"

"Be clear about what you want and create the causes for it. In general, other people, other beings, provide the opportunity for you to experience whatever you wish for. What we do for them, we will experience ourselves. Our future happiness depends on them. And, if I may offer some advice, don't think small!"

Lama Tashi's presence was one of profound kindheartedness as he faced the camera. "Don't focus solely on acquiring wealth, status or relationships. These are useful, of course. They are of benefit in providing security and well-being. But you can do so much better than these tiny, limited objectives. Your mind is capable of much more than mundane concerns. Cultivate the causes to develop your innate capacity for limitless love, limitless compassion—which are the true causes of enduring happiness beyond anything you may imagine. You possess Buddha nature. You have the capacity to be a fully enlightened being. Don't sell yourself short!"

As always when he spoke, words were only a fraction of his communication. Even more powerful was the way he embodied his message, conveying what he said in a palpable way. One felt by whoever was in his presence. It was exactly this effect which had led Pauline Taylor to declare that she had never felt such unconditional love as with Lama Tashi in the Household Detergents aisle. Which had unexpectedly liberated the deeply lapsed Maria Flavio. Which had connected to Darius Styles from the heart.

And now Lama Tashi was sharing it with whoever cared to tune in.

"There'll be many people who don't really believe in karma," said Megan, knowing it was time to wrap the interview. "What would you say to them?"

"That's okay," Lama Tashi shrugged. "Whether you believe or don't believe doesn't matter. Just keep an open mind. Try it. Check up for yourself."

18

Montpelier, Vermont

"KRISTINA? IT'S GRACE. HAVE YOU LEFT HOME YET?" GRACE Arlingham was standing near her friend's house, on a part of the sidewalk known as "Snail Cemetery."

"We're leaving in the next few minutes. Are you still at the clinic?" Kristina was a member of the support group. She remembered that Grace was going in for a scan shortly before she did that morning. Appointments with significant consequences that had been looming large in their minds for weeks.

"No," Grace was trying to keep her voice as neutral as possible. "I got the results."

"And?"

"And I know what I'm about to say may sound strange, but I need you to trust me on this," her voice quavered with emotion. "Before you leave I want you to come where I am, right now, at Snail Cemetery."

"That does sound strange."

"You said "we". Who are you with?"

"Charlie and Hen came round. Charlie's giving me a lift."

"Even better!" The other two, also going through cancer treatment, were members of the same group. "Bring them with you."

The three women appeared less than one minute later from Kristina's front gate. Along with Grace, they were all cancer war veterans, women who hadn't known each other before their diagnoses but who had quickly

105

bonded as their separate journeys evoked similar emotions. Kristina's cancer, like her own, had metastasized throughout her body. Late sixties and stout, like Grace, her biggest fear was not her own death, but what it would mean to her Swedish American family. Henrietta, a decade older and a crabby intellectual, had Stage Four colorectal cancer and was raging against the dying of the light. Her own next scan was later that afternoon. Charlie, forty-something, blonde and willowy, had discovered a lump in her breast. It had been surgically removed only recently, and she was undergoing chemotherapy as a precaution.

Despite herself, Grace couldn't hide her smile of relief when her friends came closer.

"Good news?" Hen had always been the most outspoken of the three.

Grace nodded. "I still can't believe it. Nor could Dr. Roberts. I've had a spontaneous remission."

"Grace that's wonderful!" Kristina was the first to embrace her. Soon followed by the others. For a moment they had a group hug.

"So—the cancer's going?" Charlie confirmed.

"Gone!" Grace corrected her. "Dr. Roberts had to check with radiology that there hadn't been a mix up. All the tumors have completely disappeared."

"Did he say how?" Kristina wanted to know.

"That's the thing. It's why I'm here."

Grace told them about Dr. Roberts wanting to know if there was any way to account for the miracle. How, on getting home, she had remembered the bee she had rescued from drowning that morning.

"It may just be coincidence," she said. "But I have the strongest feeling here," she placed her fingers on her heart. "That there *was* a connection. Which is why I wanted to reach you before you go in, Kristina." She was looking at the snails on the path beside them who were almost certain, if they were left, to be crushed under the wheels of schoolchildren's bicycles, mothers' strollers and indifferent pedestrians.

"We should rescue these."

Still taking in Grace's extraordinary news, Kristina looked taken aback by the suggestion.

Glancing at the snails Charlie wrinkled her nose. "But snails are disgusting!"

"Not really," countered Grace. "The shells are a bit muddy, but they're harmless really."

Hen shook her head in defiance. "This is nonsense! I am thrilled for you about the scan, Grace, really I am. But how can it have anything to do with rescuing bees? Or snails?"

"Well, it's worth a go," Kristina was already lowering herself to the ground, leaning on Grace's arm as she planted first one knee, then the other, on the sidewalk.

"I've got a magazine," Grace offered a rolled copy of Health Matters from her handbag. "You can put them on here and then maybe in your garden."

"This is credulous thinking!" Hen wasn't backing down. "You're connecting two unrelated events. That's the *definition* of superstition." Henrietta had been a physics teacher most of her life and had little tolerance for anything she deemed irrational.

"What if it works?" countered Grace, as Kristina carefully placed a snail on the magazine cover.

"But what's the hypothesis?" Hen's hands were trembling as she observed her friends engaged in blatantly illogical behavior.

"I don't have one," Grace shook her head, avoiding eye contact.

"So how can it work?"

"Well, *something* worked," Grace pointed out a kamikaze snail who had just appeared from the verge next to Kristina's left hand.

"I'm shocked you can even think like this. There's just no science!"

Kristina sighed softly, unused to spending time on her hands and knees. "Didn't we used to learn something in physics about for every action there's an equal and opposite reaction?" she asked, picking up the snail.

"Newton's Third Law of Motion," confirmed Hen. "It has nothing to do with snails and scans. Besides, physics moved on from Newton a century ago."

Despite Hen's protestations, Charlie was squatting and had picked up a snail between her right forefinger and thumb, in an elaborate show of distaste, depositing it on the magazine.

"Perhaps what we're doing is an experiment in itself," Grace shot a glance at Hen. "Let's see what happens when the girls get their results."

"That still wouldn't prove anything, don't you see?" Hen's voice rose in frustration. "You can correlate two sets of anything you like, but that doesn't mean they're connected. There has to be a link between the two. A way that "A" leads to "B"."

"Saving life," Kristina grunted from the sidewalk. "That seems a strong link to me."

"Kristina, I don't know what to say," harrumphed Hen, about-turning to go home. "To think you used to be a logician!"

The other three women snickered once Hen was out of earshot.

"To think you used to be a logician," repeated Kristina to more laughter, pulling herself to her feet with a helping hand from Grace, as Charlie held the magazine horizontal. They were all used to Hen and her crochety ways. She meant well—she just wasn't always the most tactful.

They returned to Kristina's garden and a bed overgrown through neglect. Kneeling around the magazine cover, crawling with snails, Grace told them, "I always like to say something, in situations like this. "May all beings be free from suffering.""

They repeated the phrase out loud as they placed the snails on moist stones.

Afterwards they stood observing the moving mollusks. "Whatever happens at the clinic, at least I did something nice today," said Kristina.

19

Galaxy Television
Galaxy City, Los Angeles

T HE EARTHQUAKE, WHILE TERRIFYING, HAD BEEN AT THE LOWER END
of the scale. Emerging, shell-shocked from beneath the news room
table when weatherman Hedley Tracer gave them the all clear, Galaxy
news staff returned to their posts. The next on-the-hour news bulletin was
less than fifteen minutes away. And the news feeds were crazier than ever.

Contagion fears still dominated the agenda, but there was so much
other breaking news that what had been a headline item, even an hour ago,
now merited only brief mention for the sheer volume of the stories pouring in. National fast-food chains were closing down until further notice.
Entire Midwest cities were shutting their transport networks. Micro hurricanes and tornadoes were sweeping through states they'd never been
seen in before, gathering up individual homes and buildings and those
who occupied them, leaving mounds of smashed debris in their wake.

Even if he hadn't been preoccupied, the news deluge would have seemed
overwhelming. But as he stepped into makeup, Dan Kavana was still
thinking about the community notice he'd seen under the newsroom
table. The volunteer call-out from the bird rescue group in Santa Monica.
The image of the Western Gull, so choked by oil it could barely move.
"Little bird paralyzed."

The moment he'd seen the image, his thoughts had gone to his daughter,
lying in the darkness of her bedroom. Yes, Jacinda would be there for her,
as she had been for months. Maddie's days had been reduced to an endless

round of physical therapy classes and rehabilitation exercises. Hours and hours getting through the most basic tasks like eating and showering.

It had been such a thrill when she'd been able to get movement back into her fingers. When she'd shown she could move her whole hands too, even rotating them from the wrist. The family would celebrate every milestone—every subtle, small improvement was a hard-won struggle. For all the up-beat encouragement about the next mountain to be climbed, the brave talk about what the future might hold, Dan often struggled to conceal his despair. Compared to what she'd had until eight months before, this was no life for his girl. Overnight she'd gone from a beautiful and smart graduate with the world at her feet, to a quadriplegic patient needing round-the-clock care. If it was possible, he would have willingly swapped places. He would have taken on her paralysis so that she'd have the chance to be young and free and have a future. That way he would at least have been able to let go of the self-recrimination. The knowledge that it had all been his fault.

With Alice, his makeup artist, dabbing his face with a cloth, he felt a chill as he relived that night in the back seat of his chauffeured limo when the call came in. As soon as he saw Maddie's ID on his phone, he'd felt terrible.

"Dad, where are you?"

She'd been partying with friends in Westwood. He had been on the late shift and had agreed to give her a lift home. Only he'd forgotten. After the late night news, he'd got into his car as he always did, leaned against the headrest and closed his eyes. His driver was taking the usual route home.

"I'm so sorry," he'd apologized. "Laurel Way. I let it slip. We'll come back for you."

"It's okay." He'd heard her disappointment. But her pragmatism too. "There's a couple of others who live nearby. They'll be leaving soon."

"We can come back."

"You're nearly home!"

It was true. In less than two minutes they'd pull up at the gates.

"Let me call you a taxi."

"It's okay."

"What's the address?"

"I said it's okay." She hung up, terse. Disappointed in him as he'd been disappointed in himself.

It wasn't often they spent time together, just the two of them. When he'd offered her the ride home, early that morning, he'd looked forward to sitting in the backseat, cruising by the brightly-lit billboards and familiar streetscape of Sunset Boulevard, sharing the closeness of the night with his little girl. Now it seemed like he didn't care.

The Police had shown up at the front door less than an hour later. He and Tammy had been in bed when the gate buzzer went. His immediate thought had been that Maddie had mislaid her keys. Instead, they were told about the accident. How the car in which his daughter was a passenger, had run a red light, and been T-boned by a delivery truck. How Maddie in the front passenger seat had borne the brunt of the collision.

"You're thinking about it again, aren't you?" It was the most sympathetic of rebukes.

He was brought back to his make-up lady. "Did I just go cold?"

"Uh-huh." Alice was scanning his face in professional appraisal, before dusting patches. "You said—"

"I know. I know."

"I wouldn't otherwise—"

"It's okay," he reassured her. "I asked you to."

In the early weeks when he'd struggled to think of anything else, he'd asked Alice to say something if she saw him sinking into his thoughts. She'd seemed to have a preternatural ability to mind read, to sense the moment his thoughts shifted from work to home. Once, when he'd asked her how she could tell, she'd explained that it was all in his skin tone. In this most curiously intimate of professional relationships, Alice was closely familiar with the contours of his face, each single line, every subtle shift in expression. He often thought that she could read him better even than Tammy.

Having been his makeup artist for nearly a decade, she also knew a lot more about his inner landscape than most people. In the hours they spent together each week, over the years there were few subjects they hadn't discussed. Little about each other they didn't know. Dan had formed the view that Alice Mangwana, a hardworking African American, Baptist and mother of two was someone who could be relied upon to provide a helpful reality check when everyone else in the newsroom was over-thinking or getting over-excited in the hype of whatever was going on.

"Tell me, Alice, what d'you think of karma?"

Responding to the seriousness in his tone, or perhaps the question which had come out of nowhere, her eyes flicked to his for a moment.

"Never thought much about it," she replied. "Least not until today."

He raised his eyebrows.

"They were talking about it on the car radio."

"What were they saying?"

"Well," she shrugged her shoulders. "You know. What goes around, comes around. 'cept that today everything seems to have speeded up."

"It made sense to you?"

"It would explain some things."

"And you're not worried there's some kind of clash with your beliefs?"

"There's no clash, Danny." It was her special term, and she was the only one who called him that. "If you live a good life and do the right thing by people, whether it's the Bible or karma, you're going to be okay."

"I guess." He was struck by the pragmatism of her reply.

"What about doing something very particular—" he reached to the heart of his preoccupation, "—hoping for a karmic outcome. Would that be all right?"

She delivered one of her withering looks, as though disbelieving he could ask such a dumb question. "Why wouldn't it? So long as no-one's getting hurt."

"Yeah," he agreed, checking the time on his phone—two minutes to the hour—before tapping on contacts.

"Jacinda," he announced, when she answered the phone. "There's somewhere I want you to take Maddie. As soon as you can!"

20

D R. RALPH SHARP'S IMMEDIATE REACTION WAS THAT HE WAS THE victim of a practical joke. And not an especially funny one at that. When the voice on his phone announced himself to be General Alexander Hickman, Dr. Sharp involuntarily rose to his feet. But as soon as he was standing, he readied himself to dismiss the prank. Whoever it was at the other end was a good impersonator. Dr. Sharp had seen enough of the General on internal bulletins and TV to know exactly what he sounded like. The authenticity of the voice gave him pause.

"I'm hoping you can help," the voice at the other end was saying. "There's a veteran, a colonel, who lives in your area. Distinguished service. I know him personally. He wants to volunteer to help run one of your PTSD programs. Hiking."

"I see," said Dr. Sharp.

"I attended your presentation at the Pentagon last year. So we both know what his offer really means."

Dr. Sharp was beginning to review the idea that the call was a hoax. And he was taken aback to hear that the General of the U.S. Army himself had been sitting in the auditorium when he'd spoken about that scourge of military services throughout the developed world. Post Traumatic Stress Disorder was, perhaps, an inevitable consequence of taking servicemen and women out of societies that were increasingly sensitized to the most nuanced forms of negativity, and sending them to places where they experienced the most barbaric violence of which humans are capable. PTSD had been around since ancient times, but it was the extent that had risen so greatly in recent decades. And as Dr. Sharp had told his audience, one of the greatest challenges facing the US Army was persuading those who suffered from it to ask for help.

Some perceived such a thing as an admission of weakness. A lack of resilience. They were warriors, were they not? This was what they'd signed up for. It was their job to hold it together, to follow their training, to obey orders.

For others, it went even deeper. The sheer horror to which they had been exposed affected them in such a profound way that they couldn't articulate, even to themselves, how it affected them. But it did. Years, sometimes even decades later, especially when there was more time for reflection, they found they were living on the side of a volcano, the evil of the deep past erupting from their own, personal subterranean depths like a flow of molten, all-engulfing torment that became unstoppable.

It was one of the paradoxes of the condition, Dr. Sharp had observed, that those who suffered most acutely were often among those who volunteered to help others. The point to which General Hickman had just alluded. People would phone to offer their assistance at the most inopportune times of the day, or night. On such occasions, he had told his audience, what was really going on was a cry for help. One which should be responded to without delay.

"Colonel Jackson called me earlier, wanting to make contact with someone from Veteran Affairs today. Something about it being an auspicious moment."

"Okay."

"There's something else you should know. All on record. The US peacekeeping mission to Rwanda after the 1994 massacres was led by three men. Colonel Jackson was one of them. Both the others, well, they're no longer with us."

Dr. Sharp knew something about Rwanda. The suicide of Major General Travis was the reason he'd been invited to present to the Pentagon.

"I hear what you're saying, sir. Leave it with me."

21

AMY HAD BEEN SITTING AT HER DESK FOR HALF AN HOUR, PRETEND-ing to work, but she just couldn't focus. After what had just happened, who could?

She spent a few surreptitious moments looking at her social media pages. Which was where she discovered that life-changing events were happening to other people. Unexpected upheavals and major break-throughs. Everyone seemed to be talking about instant karma. Which got her thinking about the connection Dad had made between her gift to them and the inheritance she had received from Uncle Gerry. It made a kind of sense. But how had she won the holiday to begin with? What had she done to cause that?

Suddenly, she was pushing back her chair, grabbing a receipt off her desk and crossing to the coat stand, slinging her purse over her right shoulder. Then she was heading towards the elevators. Collecting her boss's suits from the cleaner wasn't in Amy's job description, but it was a regular chore she'd voluntarily taken on. Right now, one that provided a cover.

On the way down, she checked the contents of her bag. There was a twenty dollar bill and eight singles. She folded the singles and slipped them in her coat pocket. Turning left from the building entrance, she continued walking for a while before crossing the street, returning in the direction of Brew Ha and walking past its entrance.

It didn't take long to reach her homeless guy. As usual, he was sitting, head lowered, staring at the concrete in front of him. She bent to put the eight dollars in his cap.

Instead of the usual response as she straightened, he said something different.

"You've already given."

She paused, surprised.

"Same shoes," he offered by way of explanation. "Every Friday." As he glanced up, beneath the disheveled fringe of dark hair she found herself looking into a pair of startling green eyes. Eyes that were the windows to an unexpected perceptiveness.

"Twice today."

"Well, here's the thing," she said, after a pause. "After I gave to you this morning, I won a prize. Then I donated the prize to my parents and got something even better. I think that maybe karma has gone instant."

"You do?!" His face brightened.

"Not only me. A lot of people are saying the same thing."

"So this," he nodded towards the cap. "Is another spin of the wheel for you?"

"Call it an experiment," she confirmed, stepping away.

"God bless!"

The dry cleaner Mr. Black used was only a hundred yards further on. It didn't take her long to exchange his receipt for two suits.

As she headed back towards the office, balancing the suits over her left arm, she felt a tug of anticipation. If the instant karma thing was true, at any moment her phone might ring with some surprise message. The eight dollars she'd just given would be the cause for some amazing windfall, possibly from a source she could never guess.

What she encountered soon jolted her out of such thoughts. Ahead of her, a man was putting two bills into a can held out by a beggar. The man making the donation was wearing a loose jacket and had a blanket draped round his shoulders. Removed from his usual context, it took her a moment to work out that it was her homeless guy! He had just given away some of the bills that she had donated to him.

As he continued on his way, ambling along the street, from above there came a flurry of paper. Money. Amy looked up to see two men at an open window on the first floor, laughing as they tossed handfuls of ten dollar bills into the street. Seemed like they were conducting some kind of experiment of their own.

Several of the bills brushed the homeless guy on the face before he realized he had walked into a vortex of cascading bills. He was reaching out in all directions, bellowing with joy as he grabbed them by the fistful, stuffing them into his jacket.

"It works!" he cried as he caught sight of Amy. "Like you said!"

Some of the money had been blown in Amy's direction. She caught at least five bills as she continued walking.

"Here," she held them out to him.

"No—they're for you!" he replied, laughing as he scooped notes off the pavement as the aerial flurry came to an end. "Commission!"

There were two more homeless men between her and the office entrance. Reaching the first, Amy dropped a couple of bills into his lap.

"Today instant karma is happening," she told him. "Give these away and you'll get back many times over."

The beggar responded with a grunt.

"Today instant karma is happening," she told the second man. "Give these away and you'll get back many times over."

A blackened claw immediately thrust the bills out of sight before he looked up, eyes red and expression resentful.

"Ridiculous!" he spat.

Only a few yards from the office entrance, she was shoved so roughly on the left shoulder that she dropped Mr. Black's suits. They slipped onto the sidewalk in their plastic sleeves. Amy's first instinct was to pick them up as fast as possible. There was heavy footfall on the pavement as the man who'd bumped her continued running down the street. Straightening again, shaken, it took her a few moments to realize he was carrying something. Instinctively she reached for her handbag. Gone.

11:00 am (Eastern Standard Time)
9:00 am (Mountain Standard Time)
8:00 am (Pacific Standard Time)

22

WHEN PRESIDENT TRENT GREY WOKE THAT MORNING, HE WAS preoccupied by one thing more than any other. The preoccupation of most Presidents in the third year of their first term of office: re-election. Which was why a group of the nation's most influential Evangelists had been invited to a Breakfast and Prayer Meeting at The White House that morning. They had helped him win power three years ago. He needed them if he was to win again in a years' time.

One such supporter, the huge, bearded African American, the Reverend Jeremiah Bellow of *Tongues of Praise Churches* in Nashville, was famous for hour-long diatribes against Satan, same-sex marriage, abortion clinics and online psychics. A preacher who was swift to chide and slow to bless, his fire and brimstone sermons attracted an impassioned following. Another, billionaire Marvin Swankler, Chief Executive Officer of Prosperity Ministries, had flown into the capital overnight on his own personal Boeing Dreamliner. "Pray-for-a-Porsche" Swankler taught that God wanted to shower us with riches in this lifetime as well as the next, a truth for which the car park of any Prosperity Ministry Temple appeared to offer gleaming, extravagant evidence.

President Trent's feelings about men like these was ambivalent, to say the least. Plus he had little personal interest in prayer meetings. He was wary of discussing godly matters over waffles and syrup with pious folk who may come to decide that he loved Jesus with insufficient zeal.

Which was where the carefully choreographed White House show came in. Having earlier welcomed his overawed guests into the Oval Office, embodying gravitas, charm and the mystery of power, he personally led them on a ten-minute tour of the West Wing before ushering them into an elegant dining salon. Minutes into breakfast, he'd been called away to attend to urgent business, leaving senior members of his team—people who got the whole Jesus thing—to make his guests feel special.

It was a routine that had served him well with the oil and gas sector, the pro-Israel movement and the telecoms lobby in recent weeks. His role was to be Presidential—charismatic. Enigmatic. Less-is-more. Daylight must not be allowed upon his magic. His staff could deal with the detail.

This morning he returned towards the end of breakfast to be prayed over, before giving his visitors what they really wanted—individual photo-ops to be shared with exuberant incontinence on social media feeds, church emails and fridge doors. Today, as with previous groups, he also gave them a surprise. Looking round the room, meeting eyes and being, at once, right there in their midst, as well as POTUS himself, he told them not only how very grateful he was for their support in the last election, but how inspired he was by all the great work their churches did to uplift the poor of Africa. Which was why he had personally just allocated additional food support worth $10 million to the communities in which they worked.

The room erupted in a rapture of praising-of-the-Lord, Glory Hallelujahs and Amens! The Reverend Jeremiah Bellow proclaimed President Trent to be a true child of Africa as well as of Christ. Marvin Swankler, not to be outdone, immediately pledged $10 million from Prosperity Ministries, lifting euphoria to ever more exalted heights. Never had the kingdom of heaven seemed so close as in those lofty chambers at that particular moment.

Then President Grey was showing them out, just like any of them might show departing guests to the front door of their own homes. Only, they reached a point in this particular home where there was public access. Ornate cordons divided one side of a marble hall where they were emerging, from the other side, where a small group of visitors had gathered for a guided tour.

Standing with the President, for a few moments the evangelists felt even more like insiders, not mere, paying tourists, but members of an inner circle who had just sat down and eaten breakfast with the President and been privy to his innermost thoughts.

"Mr. President!" One of the tourists shouted across the hallway, scarcely able to believe they were looking at the man himself, just yards away.

Obligingly, President Grey waved at them with a smile.

"Heard about all the food poisoning?" called someone else.

"Contagion!" clamored another.

"Pandemic!" yelled a third.

Such was the sudden ruckus of raised voices, President Grey could disregard them all as he bade farewell to his guests.

The calling out died down as quickly as it had erupted, at which point a female voice sounded, in a diction so clear and with a question so compelling he couldn't ignore it.

"They're saying it's instant karma, Mr. President. Do you agree?"

President Grey had never been more conscious that he was standing among a group of evangelical Christians than at that moment. Flanked by the Reverend Jeremiah Bellow and Marvin Swankler, CEO, his visitors' eagerness to hear his reply was not to be ignored.

There was only one answer that was possibly to be given. Turning, he looked across the hall towards the woman. "This is the United States of America," he reminded her in his commanding voice. "We don't do karma!"

23

Omni, Colorado

FOR THE LONGEST TIME MARGARITA SAT, TOO NUMB TO MOVE. Struggling to make sense of what was happening. Fragments of that morning loomed up in her consciousness, mundane but at the same time unbelievable. Seeing Bob climb the stairs to that woman's apartment. The emptiness of home as she arrived with the two large Americanos. Bob appearing in the doorway carrying a packed case. Could a marriage of twenty four years end with so little fanfare? Hearing him reverse his car from the garage and the door close behind him, it was like he was doing nothing more than going into town on some routine errand. Instead, he was driving out of her life.

Sitting at the kitchen bench, she felt foolish. Dumb to have imagined, only hours ago, that she and Bob had never been closer. That their rekindled passion was like some kind of barometer of their love, when their intimate couplings had turned out to be nothing to do with her.

She also felt used. Not just as a proxy for the woman who had really aroused him—though that felt degrading enough. It went very much bigger. The simple truth was that most of their years together had been all about Bob. What Bob wanted. What was best for Bob's career. All the many months he'd been in rehab after the accident she'd been his nurse, his cook, his care-giver, roles she'd taken on willingly because that's what a wife was supposed to do. And this was her reward!

She got up from the table and walked through the house, hugging herself. She picked up a remote, switched on the TV and saw all the news about food poisoning and airport closures. How travel networks were closing down across the whole country. The whole world seemed to be going mad. She turned off the TV. She had no interest. Just like she had no interest in unpacking her work bag from the car and taking it to her studio.

In New York she'd been commissioned to do a new book series to be launched by a major publisher, the biggest creative assignment of her life. It was something she had been longing to share with Bob. Something she would normally have been really excited about. She'd also been asked to undertake a very different assignment—one which had been in her thoughts almost as much as the new series. Only, right now she just felt like a bomb had gone off inside, leaving her wrecked and sad.

Wandering through the house, on the hall table was a photograph of Bob on his bike, taken the day he was finally well enough to resume cycling. His moment of triumph after years in rehab. She'd chosen the gold frame especially for him.

Picking up the photograph she took it to the kitchen, placed it inside a dishtowel, took the meat tenderizer out of a drawer and firmly smashed it. Several times. She heard the glass and frame shatter. She dumped the lot in the trash.

It didn't make her feel any better. She didn't imagine that anything would. Her whole life suddenly felt pointless. Hollow.

The phone rang in her handbag. She didn't need to look to know who was calling. She'd already called once this morning and there had been two message alerts. Her daughter Gabby, who thought she was still in New York, was probably calling to find out how her meetings with the publisher had gone. She knew what a big deal the visit had been to her mom.

Staring out the kitchen window, unseeing, she let the call go to voice mail. When the phone rang again, a short while after, a different thought occurred to her. The images she'd seen on TV. The news about flights being grounded. Maybe Gabby was anxious for her.

She fetched the phone from her bag.

"Are you okay?" Gabby sounded fearful. "I'm seeing all the stuff about New York—"

"I'm not in New York. Flew out last night."

"You're at home?"

"Yes."

There was a pause before Gabby responded to her tone. "Mom—are you all right?"

Margarita dissolved into tears.

ENDING THE CALL HALF AN HOUR LATER, GABBY'S FOREHEAD WAS HEAVily furrowed and mouth tight. An attractive young woman with an athletic figure, dark hair cut in pageboy style and smooth features, the usual congeniality of her sparkling brown eyes had given way to cold fury. How dare he treat Mom this way? And, by extension, how dare he treat Matias and her like this too, walking out of their family like they counted for nothing? Did they really mean so little to him?

As soon as her mom had begun telling her, she knew it to be true. It explained something about her last visit home. She returned from college every few months, and just six weeks ago, it had been for her best-friend-growing-up, Sofia's, twenty-first party. Gabby had spent a few days preceding it with her parents and it had been a happy homecoming. On the Saturday, Mom had been called to Denver to visit an ailing aunt. Sofia's twenty-first was that night. Another friend, Dee, was due to collect Gabby at 6:45 pm. Dee was always late, so it was no surprise when she still hadn't shown up at 7 pm. At 7:10 pm, Dee sent a text saying she was running behind. She didn't specify how much by.

Gabby had been with Dad in the den. On the sofa, he'd told her that he was all set for a TV dinner and an early night. But he'd been twitchy. Even twitchier when she'd got the text from Dee.

"She was supposed to be here half an hour ago!" he'd protested.

"You know what Dee's like," she'd shrugged. The party would probably last into the early hours. It didn't bother her if they only got there closer to 8 pm.

Over the next few minutes her dad had looked at his watch several times like he was on some kind of schedule.

"What does it matter?" she'd said to him. "You're not going anywhere?"

"It doesn't matter to me," was what he'd said out loud. But his expression had communicated something different. Barely concealed impatience. Gabby had been taken aback by a sudden feeling, the first time she could ever remember experiencing with her father that she was somehow in the way. Now she knew why.

She wondered what it was about Beaky that was so utterly irresistible he was willing to walk away from his family. Gabby had never paid much attention to the bookstore manager and had only seen her a handful of times.

Sitting on her bed in the Westchester house she shared with other students, she grabbed her laptop and keyed in "Paige Turner Books'. There was an old-fashioned website that looked like it dated from the days when Mrs. Turner herself had presided over the shop. The "About" section made no reference to the bookstore manager. The "Blog" had last been updated eight years ago. The "Buy Online" button was unexpected for an independent store. Clicking, Gabby found a page listing new releases with some familiar covers and author names—but many more unfamiliar ones. All of which had overtly sexual images of muscled, shirtless men or women in lingerie and choker chains, with words like "captive," "forbidden," and "taboo" in their title. Was this how readers in Omni were spared their blushes while buying such books?

Gabby clicked on one cover and scrolled down the page. The book had dozens of reviews. "How thrilling! Thanks, VG, for the recommendation." "Right on the button, VG!" read another, with a row of winking emoticons. "Would never have discovered this author if it hadn't been for our Venusian Goddess!" said a third.

Venusian Goddess? Why all the references to the exotic sounding creature?

Opening a search engine, Gabby soon found her way to a website which had a home page revealing Beaky as she would never have conceived of her—a seductress in the skimpiest, black leather lingerie, wearing a top hat and brandishing a whip. Venusian Goddess was, it seemed, not only an authority on female erotica. She was a writer of it too. Visitors to the site could click for a free sample of *Journals of a Venusian Goddess*. Many had. With over 15,000 followers, feeds on every major social media site, by the looks of things she never stopped posting.

What were these *Journals* she was promoting so relentlessly? Gabby clicked, opening the link to the most recent entry.

"Dear Venusian Angels, you know there's no pain I wouldn't endure, no quiver of excitement I wouldn't describe for your gratification. That's why I embarked on the Daddy adventure. You were gasping for it, darlings! At fifty-three years he really is old enough to be my father. But the stamina of Endless Love! He's like a steam train: he may be old fashioned, but he knows how to stoke a fire."

Gabby slammed the laptop shut, shoving it away. Revolted by her father. Disgusted at Beaky. Horrified by the thought that people in Omni, people who knew her parents, might hear about the website and read the squalid details of the sexual encounters and figure out that Endless Love was none other than their own Bob Martin.

It was when mulling over exactly this possibility that the thought suddenly struck her: did Bob Martin himself know he was Endless Love? A character in a storyline concocted by Beaky to gratify her digital tribe? A cipher whose value to her was whatever lurid account she could provide of his sexual performance?

Up on the wall-mounted, muted TV screen of her room, grim-looking people in white coats were talking about the food contamination which had spread to meat. According to the news ticker, every fast food chain in the country was closing down, or serving only vegetarian options. There was a local story about how some guy drove into a parking space another man was waiting for and verbally abused him. Minutes later he arrived for his job interview—with the man he'd just abused.

Gabby recalled something she'd seen on social media earlier that day about instant karma. It was being suggested as an explanation for the unprecedented turbulence affecting so many people in different ways.

Was that what was happening, here and now to her family? Her dad being caught out by her mom? Then choosing to walk out on them?

If so, what had Mom done to deserve it? How had she been so terrible, this morning, to lose a husband to whom she had devoted the best years of her life?

And what had *she* done to deserve not having her dad any more—at least, not a man she could genuinely look up to, not the person she had always imagined would be there for her when the time came for her to have her own family?

Hot tears welled up in her eyes. Rolling into a fetal position, she felt utterly miserable. As she wept silently, instant karma didn't seem, at that moment, to account for very much of anything. The person doing the bad stuff was doing okay while everyone else, her mom and Matias and her, would just have to put up with it.

But as her eyes refocused on the laptop on her bed, she wondered about her father. It seemed like Beaky was just using him and he didn't even know it. What if the bad karma he had created came back to hit him with sudden, unforgiving force?

And was it wrong to hope that it would?

24

Boulder, Colorado

A FTER THE INTERVIEW WITH LAMA TASHI UPLOADED, MEGAN HAD quickly highlighted it on a dozen social media feeds, encouraging her many *Flourish* followers to check it out—and share it with others. Lama Tashi had been short, simple and—importantly—clear in explaining the basics of karma. Exactly what people needed right now. With social media feeds going into meltdown as people shared the crazy highs and lows of what was happening, the timing of her teacher's coherent explanation could not have been more perfect.

Plus there was the "X factor': how Lama Tashi conveyed an ineffable lightness, a profoundly reassuring sense that, despite the extreme vicissitudes of the day's events, they would all emerge into a kinder, calmer reality. Megan sometimes reflected that she would be happy even to sit and listen to Lama Tashi recite a dictionary out loud, so uplifting was his presence. She hoped this, too, would be felt by people watching the interview.

Usually, when she had just posted a podcast on *Flourish*, she would stay glued to her screen monitoring what was happening, responding to comments, doing her best to get the material out there into the world. But her anticipation about how people would respond to her very first TV interview was interrupted by Lama Tashi.

"You've been working hard. You need a break," he said before she could manage so much as a sneak peek to check on the most immediate response.

He had been following her, with interest, as she explained what she was doing to get the interview out into the world. He had a genuine curiosity about the process, as well as a nonchalance about its outcome she wished she, too, could share.

"Let's go outside," he suggested, rising from his seat. "It's a beautiful morning."

"I just want to make sure—" her fingers hovered over the keyboard.

"I know," as their eyes met he surmised her thoughts and feelings at a glance. "But you can't," he said.

"Can't?" She got up, slipping her phone in her jacket pocket and followed him out of the room.

"You can only try your best. Put it out with the right intention. And then," he shrugged.

They stepped outside into the late morning. Rusty had been dozing in the sunshine outside the studio. As soon as he saw them emerge, he got up, came towards them, wagging his tail.

"Such a happy sem-chen!" Lama Tashi patted him affectionately. "Sem-chen" were the Tibetan words for "mind haver."

"Always!" agreed Megan.

The air stirred with intimations of the warmer months to come and was sweet with the lilacs that grew along the valley. As they looked out across the verdant panorama—Anton was already some way ahead of them, taking close-ups of bees moving among some hyacinth—Megan knew she should be just taking in the scene, having a break, as Lama Tashi suggested. But what he had just said touched on what challenged her more than anything and, at times, was the source of sometimes great heartache.

She had launched *Flourish*, not as a money-making venture, but from a genuine wish to help others. And while it had initially struck a chord in a way she hadn't anticipated, there had been times more recently when she had wished it would flourish more. She would follow what other people in the self-development space did online, people whom, it seemed to her, had little of the authenticity and rigor that Lama Tashi demanded of his students. Often these self-styled wellness gurus and mindfulness experts seemed flaky, inauthentic and blatantly self-promotional. Yet they kept attracting more and more fans. Some of them seemed to come from nowhere and, overnight, went stratospheric. What was all that about? Why were so many people drawn to people who, to her, were self-evident frauds?

She hadn't gone bleating about this to Lama Tashi. She knew he gave his students all they needed in class to work things out for themselves. Besides, he constantly reminded them that reality was their own creation.

All the same, she couldn't resist picking up on what he'd just said. "I guess when I put stuff out there, whatever happens next will be limited by my own karma," she suggested, voicing the conclusion she had reached after some reflection.

Lama Tashi looked doubtful. "More, the karma of everyone else," he said.

Disconcerted, she realized that she had made this all about herself, when the truth was quite different.

"Remember the stories of Devadatta."

"Buddha's cousin?"

"He had his own following and resented the Buddha. Thought he was a charlatan. The point being—" as Lama Tashi held her gaze, the truth of what he said could hardly have been more striking, "—you can't control what other people think of you. The ideas you have about yourself are *your* ideas. They have *their* ideas arising from their own karmas which compels them to see everything, including you, the way they do. You can't control their reality. You can only control your own."

"Not everyone has the karma to accept karma?" she confirmed.

"Exactly."

She understood what he was saying—it accorded with the teachings he had been giving for all these years. Deep down she knew that the frustration she sometimes felt about *Flourish*, her wish to see important messages shared more widely, arose from her own attachment. Her desire for things to be a particular way.

"If *Flourish* had another 200,000 followers, would that be a true cause of happiness?" he asked her, teasing.

She grinned. What was, or was not, a "true cause of happiness," was one of Lama Tashi's most constant teachings. A true cause, by his definition, was something which always worked, in the same way that heat applied to water always produced steam, no matter where it was applied, who applied it, or how many times it had already been applied. When seeking a true cause of happiness in the external, material world, such a thing could never be found. It was a favorite challenge Lama Tashi liked to set in class. "Find a true cause of happiness and tell us about it next week so that we can all enjoy it!"

No one ever had found a true cause out there in the world. Only a contingent cause. Something which may, or may not, deliver happiness depending on other circumstances.

Megan already understood this. Following the pathway of countless millions before her, she had spent exhaustive hours contemplating exactly this point, only to determine that such a thing was a myth. Any given number of podcast followers was certainly no true cause of happiness because within weeks, if not days, she would become accustomed to the bigger numbers. Habituated. They would be her new normal.

In her pocket, she felt her phone vibrate with incoming messages.

When she'd invited Lama Tashi earlier, her only expectations had been that they'd do an interview. She hadn't thought any further than that. As they stood in the sunshine, her guru was in no apparent hurry to leave.

"Can I make you a coffee?" she gestured towards the house.

"Thank you!" he smiled, picking up a stick that Rusty had dropped expectantly at his feet, and throwing it into the distance. "Hayden and Shelley—are they at school?"

She nodded. "Back this afternoon."

"Good! Perhaps I may see them."

Some minutes later she returned with a tray bearing three coffees and a bowl of cookies. While in the kitchen, she'd checked her phone. The interview with Lama Tashi was more than simply resonating. It had gone viral! She'd never experienced so many likes, comments and shares. The traffic heading to her site was already thirty, or forty times the usual figure. And among the countless messages streaming in via every imaginable channel, was one from Denver's leading radio station with an interview request for Lama Tashi.

"Great news!" she returned to where he was standing next to Anton a few minutes later. "108 FM wants to interview you!"

"Biggest audience in Colorado," observed Anton.

Lama Tashi met her expectant expression with a smile.

"Shall I set that up for you?" she asked.

He looked at the tray of coffees she was extending towards him. "First, let's enjoy our coffee," he said, unexcited by a media request which would usually have had Megan rushing to confirm. He helped himself to a coffee and picked up a chocolate chip cookie between forefinger and thumb. "And here we have, if not a true cause of happiness then the closest thing to it!" he said, face crinkling as he chuckled.

As always with Lama Tashi, reflected Megan, simply being here and now was all he needed to feel a lightness at any particular moment. It really didn't matter to him what kind of impact his interview was having out there in the world, or which radio host wanted to speak to him. It was the simple things in which he found contentment.

Nevertheless, as they sat on a couple of smooth boulders, a short distance from the studio, there was something she had to ask following on from their previous conversation.

"Rinpoche, we know that achieving worldly ambitions doesn't bring enduring contentment," she said, glancing at Anton, seeking to include him in the conversation. "Does that mean we shouldn't set ourselves goals?"

He was shaking his head. "I never said that."

"What I don't understand," her shoulders were hunched. "Is the point? If achieving a particular ambition is not a true cause of happiness, why bother with it? It seems to me sometimes that having goals can be a cause of unhappiness, if you keep failing to achieve them."

"Goals are useful to provide clarity. To give purpose to what we do. In this way, they are helpful. The problem comes if you think your happiness depends on achieving them."

"Once you've set your sights on something," said Anton, "and do all you can to make it happen, it's very hard not to be attached to the outcome."

Lama Tashi was nodding. "Exactly. So you see, the goal itself is not the problem. It is our attachment to it. Our desire. We move from thinking "having this would bring me some fulfilment" to "I can't be fulfilled unless I have it." We turn the goal from something useful into the enemy of our own happiness."

"So, what *is* the way to think about goals?" asked Megan.

Lama Tashi looked up from his mug of coffee to the distant valley, as he inhaled the fragrance of the crisp air. "I am already fulfilled," he said, giving voice to what seemed obvious. "I already possess the true causes of happiness. If I achieve this goal or that aspiration, how wonderful! But it is not necessary to the inner peace which I already enjoy. *That* is how to think about goals. Without attachment."

Looking from one to the other of them, he asked. "And shall I tell you the great secret of non-attachment to goals?"

As they both leaned closer, he continued. "The less attachment you have to outcomes, the more likely they are to happen. It is when you crave things and grasp most tightly that you drive them away."

In Lama Tashi's presence beneath the whispering Douglas firs, with Rusty lying beside them and magpies fluting through the canopy, it felt as though everything was already complete. There *was* already peace in this moment as well as a spacious sense of openness and wellbeing. Why, Megan wondered now, as she so often did sitting in at Lone Pine Meditation Center, did she have to complicate things by spending so much time in her head?

"I wish you could come and do an interview like this every week," she mused.

Lama Tashi chuckled. "Is that a question?"

She was about to answer, when her expression turned rueful. "The wrong question," she admitted.

"You already know a more useful question," his eyes were twinkling.

"I do."

By now, the phone in her pocket was vibrating constantly. No sooner had one message come in than another followed it. Never had she been on the receiving end of such frenetic response to a posting. Nor, paradoxically, had she ever cared so little. Lama Tashi was right. It wasn't just about her karma that made a podcast fly or falter. Rather, it was the karma of the people who saw it and whether or not they perceived it to be of value.

After finishing his coffee, Lama Tashi got up and put his mug on the tray before turning to Megan.

"Now," he nodded towards her pocket. "Shall we see who is next?"

In a moment she had the phone out and was scrolling through page after page of messages. As she did, however, one in particular caught her attention. She looked up as she saw it. "It's the newsroom at Galaxy TV!" she told her teacher, eyes glistening with excitement. "A researcher wants to speak to you."

25

Wall Street, New York

As soon as she walked into reception, Jaye told Amy that Karel Sharma wanted to see her on the 26th floor.

Amy was startled by what had happened downstairs. The twenty-five-year-old had never been robbed before, let alone in broad daylight one Friday morning. If instant karma was the explanation for today's unprecedented events, what had she done to deserve that? She wasn't a thief.

Still, it would take more than a moment's unpleasantness to unsettle a country girl from Aubrey, Texas. She had left her phone on her desk when she went out, so that was safe. She had only lost twenty dollars, her handbag and a few other items—all of them replaceable. What had happened was an inconvenience, a disappointment, but she wasn't going to let it get to her. She was still lined up for a life-changing inheritance.

"Take a seat," the big boss himself gestured towards one of the high-end sofas in his office, when she arrived upstairs a short while later. A coffee table between the two was strewn with an assortment of finance newsletters and glossy photo books.

"When we met downstairs earlier, what you said about giving away the luxury cruise, then getting surprise news soon after about an inheritance?"

Amy nodded, trying to take in as much of her surroundings as possible without seeming too nosy.

139

"The way you told me," he met her bright eyes. "It made quite an impact."

She smiled. Karel Sharma wasn't simply the guy who the business was named after. He was a Wall Street identity. The subject of newspaper articles and magazine profiles. And here was little, old her, from Aubrey, Texas, only six months after arriving in New York City, making an impact on him.

Perhaps it was the way Karel Sharma was holding himself on the sofa, clasping his hands somewhat self-consciously round his right knee. Perhaps it was the surreal tumble of events that was shifting the way she saw things. But in that moment he reminded her of one of the boys from her school, Bashful Byron, very smart and a little geeky, who came from a mixed-up family and had taught her how to play chess. Byron had seemed to live in his own world and it had only been after she'd left school and was about to leave Aubrey that she'd found out all the afternoons he'd sat on her porch, teaching her chess, he'd wanted to tell her he had feelings for her, only he'd been too shy to say so.

"The giving. The receiving. It had me wondering," Karel said. He glanced over, and perhaps it was the way that she seemed so comfortable, so open in his presence that he was able to look her directly in the eyes.

"Had me wondering too," she knew exactly what he was saying.

"Really? What conclusion did you reach?"

"More a theory than a conclusion," she sat forward.

He nodded for her to continue.

"I don't know if instant karma is really a term, but I'm thinking it might be that. Whatever you give, comes back to you, like, dramatically increased."

Karel Sharma focused on the girl opposite. She had surprised him earlier with her unaffected vivacity. Her openness. The power with which she'd told her story. And she was surprising him again now with her candor.

She also seemed smart. "Have you done anything to test the … theory?" he asked.

Amy paused. Employees of Sharma Trading Inc weren't supposed to ramble down Wall Street during office hours handing out cash to beggars. Even if it was under the cover of collecting Mr. Black's dry cleaning.

But instinct told her that Karel Sharma didn't concern himself with such pedantry.

"I've just tested it."

"How?"

"I was wondering how I'd won the cruise in the first place. Then I remembered giving a homeless guy a few coins this morning. So I went downstairs a short while ago. I had eight dollars in bills. I gave them to the same homeless guy."

"Anything happen?"

"It was only a few minutes ago," she said. "But something strange did happen."

He gestured to the table in front of her. For the first time she noticed the cream envelope. Her name typed on the front. "Look inside," he said.

Amy opened the envelope and took out a single sheet of paper. Similar to the monthly pay she received, it was a remittance notice. Eighty thousand dollars had been transferred to her account.

"What's this?" she looked up, astonished.

"A bonus," Karel Sharma shrugged. "I also tested out the theory on the trading floor. We've made good money this morning. A lot of good money." He nodded towards the envelope, "This is a token of my thanks."

"I don't know what to say," Amy felt gratitude explode within her. Tears welling, she just had to get up. To step over to where Karel Sharma was sitting. To give him a hug.

It turned out not so awkward as it might have been. He reciprocated with a brief but warm embrace.

Shifting away on his sofa afterwards, Amy waved the remittance notice that was still in her hand. "I hope you're not just using me to make more money," she sobbed, grateful and mischievous at the same time.

He chuckled. "That's inevitable, I'm afraid. The more I give, the more it just keeps coming back!" Expression turning serious he murmured, "Something strange, you said?"

She told him about the mugging. What had happened and also how little she had lost. That she wasn't going to allow her shock at what had happened get in the way of the bigger picture.

"Market noise," he nodded, in Wall Street speak.

142 — David Michie

"I guess you could call it that."

"At any given hour on any day there will be a thousand people jumping up and down trying to persuade you that the opposite of what's happening is happening. Vested interests. Poor information. Sheer stupidity. Don't let them distract you from testing the theory."

"It wasn't just me who tested it," she said. "I told my homeless guy about instant karma. Then I went to get Mr. Black's dry cleaning. When I came out, I saw him handing over four dollars to another homeless guy. Next thing, this swirl of ten dollar bills literally fell out of the sky around him."

Karel Sharma watched her, intrigued.

"A couple blew in my direction. I ended up giving them to two others who were begging. I told them about instant karma. But one of them," she shook her head at the memory, "he seemed, like, really pissed that I even mentioned it. Why is that, do you think? You're trying to help someone? You're giving them the most precious information they could ever hear, but instead of taking it in, they just get angry?"

Karel Sharma was nodding. "It's called 'confirmation bias,'" he said. "It's one of the biggest problems in trading."

"Confirmation bias?" her brow wrinkled.

"When you look for or give importance to information that confirms what you already think, and ignore or doubt information that questions what you think."

Absorbing this, she nodded. "I can see why that would be a problem," she agreed. "Especially if you're playing according to an old set of rules when the game has moved on."

"Exactly," he met her eyes, approvingly. "Anyone who understands today's rules of engagement should be a millionaire by lunchtime. A multi-millionaire, even. But there'll be plenty of people out there who aren't only failing to get ahead. They will be seriously behind. Some of that will be about confirmation bias."

"Uh-huh."

"So I suggest you go downstairs and give away as much money as you can. And it's important that, when you give it, you remember a particular motivation. I'll email it to you. And also a list of recommended charities."

A smile suddenly appeared on her face.

"What?" he asked.

"I was thinking about Bluegrass Horse Sanctuary, near where I grew up. They can always use some extra cash."

He was nodding. "You'd like to spend more time with horses?"

She knew he was asking her what she really wanted from life, just like she knew she could be straight with him.

"Actually, I always wanted to get into interior design."

"Really?" his eyes widened.

She nodded. "I have an eye for it, but I need to do a course."

Raising his chin, he gestured around his office. "Reckon you could do something to smarten up this place?" he asked.

Fully sanctioned to take in Karel Sharma's inner sanctum, Amy took her time as she gazed from the classic, gilt-framed painting behind Karel Sharma's desk to the art deco lamp to the modern sofas to the large, gilded statue of Ganesh in the corner. The heavy, dated blinds on the windows.

She'd love to give his office the treatment. A corner office high above Wall Street? She could make it look like a million dollars. Was he really offering to become her first client?

26

Miami, Florida

"IT'S FENG WANG, RIGHT?" HE HEARD THE VOICE OF DAN KAVANA, the famous Galaxy news anchor, in his earpiece. And felt a rush of excitement.

"Yes."

"Congratulations, Feng! Two point one billion?!"

"Yes!" he grinned.

"My producer will count us in."

"Okay."

Feng was standing opposite a guy with a camera in the gardens of his apartment complex. It was the first time he'd ever been on TV and he already felt like a natural. Like this was where he was meant to be. Twenty eight years of age, chubby cheeked and smiling, a larger than life guy who laughed from the belly, this was just another episode in the most surreal of days. A day that, deep down inside, he'd always hoped would come. A day that made all the struggles of the past months seem worthwhile.

"Three, two, one," he heard a woman's voice in the background, before Dan Kavana was saying, "We're crossing now to Feng Wang in Miami, whose charity syndicate, The Blue Caps, has just won the biggest Powerball jackpot in US history—an incredible $2.1 billion dollars. Feng, tell us about the moment you found you'd won?"

Feng's face lit up, emoting triumph and joy in equal measure. "It was incredible to see all the numbers line up!" he exclaimed. "I was so shocked I had to send a photo of the ticket to my friends, so they could confirm."

"Those would be your fellow syndicate members?" asked Dan.

"Park Chen and Hu Yang," confirmed Feng.

"And your syndicate raises funds exclusively for charities, is that right?"

"Correct. The three of us were at school together. A couple of years back we decided we wanted to give something back. So we set up The Blue Caps to fund-raise."

"Buying Powerball tickets?" Dan's voice was quizzical. "An unusual method of fund-raising?"

"You could say that," grinned Feng. "Just one of several methods. Mostly we've been doing online crowd-funding. But today's win changes everything!" he looked ready to burst with joy.

"Can you tell us what causes will benefit?"

"We have three main areas. Cancer research. Wildlife conservation. And the Arts."

"Are you aware that the win will instantly make you one of the largest charitable foundations in the country?"

Feng took a moment to absorb this. "I didn't," he was shaking his head.

"A lot of dramatic things are going on today. Including your win. Do you think it's pure luck that the biggest ever Powerball jackpot has been won by a charity syndicate? Or do you think there could be another explanation?"

The camera panned in close as Feng considered the question before responding in a way the Galaxy anchor hadn't expected. "You know, I think you make your own luck," he nodded. "You've just got to keep going, keep believing in yourself, and never give up."

Feng had been told it would be a short interview, what with all the tempestuous news. And as soon as it was over, he got ready to undertake the most momentous task of the day—of his whole life, probably. Stowing the winning $2.1 billion ticket and his driver license in his wallet, a few minutes later he was behind the steering wheel of his BMW on his way to Powerball headquarters in downtown Miami.

"Unusual method of fund-raising," he recalled Dan Kavana's observation as he drove. Much the same comment made by Park and Hu when he'd first suggested it—only without the tact. They'd been outright derisive.

"Powerball? D'you know what the odds are of winning?" Park, ever the numbers man, had sneered. "It's like 300 million to one!"

Feng had shrugged. "Maybe. But someone's got to win it. Even when it keeps rolling over, someone gets the money eventually."

"It would discourage donors if they thought we were using their funds essentially to gamble," Hu had been typically legal—looking for problems which didn't exist.

"Guys, it's just a Powerball ticket! Once a month. We can pay for it ourselves."

They had agreed with him eventually, only to humor him. But they never stopped ribbing him about his Powerball Master Plan every time they tore up another ticket. In the three years since they'd set up The Blue Caps, they'd raised nearly forty thousand dollars. They told themselves this was pretty good going. How many other trios of twenty-somethings had raised as much money for good causes?

There'd be no more derision now, thought Feng.

In the early days, especially, they'd used to fantasize about what they called "the magic number." How a fund totaling somewhere between ten and twenty million dollars would be enough to justify full time jobs for all three of them. Park would take care of all accounting. Hu would do the legal work. And Feng would head up investments—he was, after all, the venture capitalist.

Raising ten to twenty million had never seemed so much a possibility as a bar-time dream. But here they were. Not just ten million. Not even a hundred, or five hundred or a thousand million. But two point one billion!

Park and Hu had been at their respective places of work when he'd sent through the ticket shot. Park was doing grunt work in an accountancy practice. Hu was putting in sixty-hour weeks as a junior corporate lawyer, charging his time in six minute time periods. After a frenzy of messages, the three had agreed to meet after he'd gone to Powerball House to arrange the transfer. The other two had confirmed they were happy for him to do the media. He had always been the front man, after all.

As soon as the transfer had been set up they'd rendezvous in the city for the celebratory lunch of a lifetime.

"Winning a jackpot of this size can be a surprising challenge," the Powerball guy told Feng, after ID had been confirmed and congratulations offered.

They were sitting in a light-filled meeting room, fifty levels up, with floor to ceiling windows offering a panoramic sweep of the ocean. Opposite Feng, and sitting next to Mr. Powerball was a woman he introduced as a counselor.

On the table in front of him, his winning ticket, Driver License, and a printout with an incomprehensibly long number in large font: $2,179,983,968.25

"It will probably take some time to sink in," the man was saying. "But if you have any questions at all about how to deal with your win, feel free to reach out."

Feng nodded.

"We can put you in touch with independent wealth managers on the investment side. Also with counselors if you need support navigating the interpersonal maze."

The woman slid her card across the desk to him. "A lot of people you know may suddenly feel entitled," she said.

"Okay."

"That can put you under immense pressure. We see it all the time."

He looked at her card, thinking how that wouldn't be the case for The Blue Caps. They were a syndicate, after all. They had a proper structure, constitution and all that jazz. Hu had made sure of it.

"As to the jackpot," Mr. Powerball was opening his leather-bound notebook. "We need to take your instructions on what you'd like done with the money. You have a range of options. You are entitled to take the money in cash, check, or have it transferred. Or any combination of these."

"Combination?" Up until that moment, Feng had been thinking along the lines of a single transfer.

"Some people like to take a portion of their winnings in cash, to treat themselves," he explained. "The rest being transferred."

Feng was staring at the number. Yes, it was $2.1 billion, the figure everyone in Miami had seen splashed over billboards over the past few days. But on top of that, it was also $79 million. And on top of that again it was $983,968. And 25 cents.

Anything over $2,1 billion would be more than Park or Hu were expecting.

"This number," he pointed to the print-out. "Who else knows what it is?"

"The first four digits are published on our website," Mr. Powerball regarded him carefully. "The full number is available only to the ticketholder."

Feng picked up the ticket from the table in front, holding it up to them between forefinger and thumb.

Across the table, the other nodded.

Feng was staring back at the printout, a whole new set of considerations racing through his mind.

The past few years had been good to Park and Hu. Sure, they worked hard, but they'd also been earning steady wages. By contrast, he lived from one deal to the next—and for the past eighteen months it had been increasingly tough. On the one hand, he had to project himself as a successful venture capitalist if he was to engender confidence among investors and portfolio companies. On the other, he'd had to bail out a cornerstone investor in a project that went badly wrong with money he didn't have. He'd applied for half a dozen credit cards and maxed them to the limit—the dumbest form of debt. The guitar playing weekend gigs he did in bars "just for fun" had, of late, been the only way he could feed himself. A cash flow injection would solve everything. Paying down his debt would leave him free to focus on The Blue Caps.

It wouldn't be like he was taking money from anyone, would it? Even if he decided to treat himself, like the guy had said, to what, half a million, when the transfer went through to The Blue Caps, it would still be for more money than anyone was expecting.

He thought about the disparagement. The years of mockery, taunting and smirks. And the single, over-riding fact that it had been his idea. $2.1 billion compared to their $40,000. If that wasn't justification then what possibly could be? What he'd pulled off was so massive it was going to change all of their lifestyles forever. He'd won them all a get-out-of-jail card for life. What was a paltry fraction of a percentage compared with that?

"Do you think it's pure luck that a charity syndicate has just won the biggest ever Powerball jackpot?" For some reason he recollected Dan Kavana asking him. "Or do you think there could be another explanation?"

He'd been surprised by the question. It had seemed to come out of nowhere. And after the interview, removing the microphone from his collar, he'd asked the cameraman what he thought it had been about.

"You know about all the food poisoning and stuff on social media," the cameraman had told him. "Today has been so freaky that people are looking for some kind of explanation. There's a lot saying that it's instant karma."

"Oh that!" Feng hadn't made the connection, until that moment.

"Not a fan of the theory?"

"Don't know," he shrugged. So far as he was concerned, only the feeble-minded really believed in stuff like karma, kismet and astrology. Like he'd told Dan Kavana, he believed you make your own luck. If good karma came to those who had unfailing self-belief, who kept on picking themselves up when they were knocked down, who recognized opportunities when they were available and seized them with both hands then yes, maybe what was happening had come about because of karma.

Glancing back at Mr. Powerball he told him, "I'd like a split."

The other sat, pen poised, ready for instruction.

"Five hundred thousand in cash. The rest as a transfer."

"Very good, sir."

"How long will it all take?"

The other nodded. "Both cash and transfer should be done within the hour."

12:00 noon (Eastern Standard Time)
10:00 am (Mountain Standard Time)
9:00 am (Pacific Standard Time)

27

Food & Drug Administration
White Oak, Maryland

COMMISSIONER SAUL APPLEBAUM, M.D. LOOKED OVER THE TOP OF his glasses as Teagan Chase, his Chief of Staff, knocked on the door and stepped into his office.

"They're ready," she told him. "But are you quite sure—"

"Definitely," he said, an edge to his voice.

He had already donned his jacket, checked his hair, and cleaned his horn-rimmed spectacles. Now he rose from his chair. Commissioner Applebaum was introverted by nature and almost certainly on the spectrum. Slight, pale, with a large, shiny, completely bald head that seemed out of all proportion to the rest of his body, he was an intellectual, a man of science. His preferred method of communication was through technical language, leaving it to those above him, on the political level, to deal with the public. At the same time he was not someone who shirked his responsibilities. And the announcement he had planned was, he believed, fairly and squarely his to make. He handed his phone to Ms. Chase—as he always properly referred to her—all the while hoping an incoming call from the Chief Scientist might offer a reprieve, he followed her out his office, along the corridor to the Media Briefing room.

His day from hell had begun before seven that morning, with a group text message about a suspected food poisoning incident at the Times Square outlet of Golden Drumsticks. Incidents of this kind were not unusual—it had been the severity of the symptoms that made this particular case atypical. As well as the rapidity of onset.

By the time he'd got to the office, reports were flooding in, not only from JFK, but from up and down the entire Eastern Seaboard as his fellow citizens woke up that morning and ordered fast food breakfasts.

They had crisis management scenarios at the FDA, naturally. These covered every disaster that could be conceived. Contagions, viruses, pandemics. You name it, the FDA had meticulously considered it, planned for it and drilled their preparations so that, if it occurred, a well-rehearsed and correctly calibrated response would swing into action.

And lo, the time had come. Their crisis response had been initiated promptly. Scientists had been deployed across multiple sites with meticulous efficiency. Samples had been collected and tested. Stringent restrictions in event of a biological contagion were ready to be implemented.

Everything had gone precisely to plan. Then, from his Chief Scientist, nothing. Contagious disease experts soon ruled out all the usual suspects. It wasn't Staphylococcal, Salmonella, or Clostridium. Batteries of increasingly exotic bacterial and viral infections were investigated—and came out blank.

Every sample from the abattoirs, closed as a precautionary measure, reported clean.

None of this was supposed to happen. In every disaster scenario they'd prepared for, there had always been a *reason* why people got sick. One scenario the agency hadn't contemplated was spontaneous, nationwide outbreaks of severe food-poisoning for no apparent reason at all.

Applebaum's political masters hadn't been happy. No sooner had reports of food poisoning at JFK airport come in than he'd had a call from General Hickman's office at the Pentagon, demanding to know the national security implications. Were they looking at a contagion which spread rapidly throughout the population?

Commissioner Applebaum couldn't say.

When airports, then whole transport systems had been closed down, he'd even come into the crosshairs of President Grey's Chief of Staff, Will Salt, who had been pressuring him for an explanation.

Commissioner Applebaum had none.

Until the precise mechanism causing the widespread sickness was identified, all else was speculation. But Applebaum decided that he couldn't keep saying nothing. In an information vacuum, speculation ran rife. Even if he couldn't yet tell people why what was happening was happening, it was his duty, as the nation's ultimate upholder of food safety, to reassure them about what was being done.

Teegan Chase had disagreed sharply. Not about talking to the media, but about who should do it. His loyal Chief of Staff of over five years, she'd had plenty of time to watch Saul Applebaum in action and knew that putting him front of a frenzied media pack would be a disaster. He was brilliant when addressing conferences of eminent scientists on epidemiology. Highly respected at gatherings of public health professionals or talking to World Health Organization specialists. Research he'd recently undertaken into nanoparticle drug delivery was widely regarded as a game-changing study that bordered on genius.

The problem was that Commissioner Applebaum just wasn't street smart. He looked and sounded like a dweeb. That great, shiny dome of his perspired under pressure. And no matter how hard she'd tried over the years, she hadn't been able to train him to stay on message. When it came to the media, Commissioner Applebaum was the most foolish genius she had ever encountered.

But she hadn't been able to dissuade him. And ultimately he was the boss. Like it or not, the media conference was happening.

The Commissioner knew they had a full house today. All the same, nothing quite prepared him for the lightning strikes of cameras, the wall-to-wall barrage of TV crews as he made his way to a lectern at the front of the room and retrieved the folded one page briefing note from his inside jacket pocket.

In formal, measured language, he began with a summary of the food poisoning incidents across America that morning. He confirmed that while it had seemed only poultry-based food outlets were affected, other outlets serving meat-based meals, such as burgers, were now experiencing the same problems. Importantly, the phenomenon wasn't confined only to fast food restaurants. During the past hour the FDA had received a rapidly growing volume of calls about people suffering from severe food poisoning as a result of eating meat, not only in restaurants, but in their own homes.

Scientists working for the FDA had yet to confirm the cause of the food poisoning. Until they did, the possibility that this was some kind of contagion could not be ruled out.

"The advice of the FDA at this time—and it is critical advice," Commissioner Applebaum paused, looking up at the sea of journalists in front of him. "Is that it is not safe to consume any meat, wherever or whenever you purchased it."

A fresh flurry of flashlights and camera whirring accompanied the momentous announcement.

"The FDA advises you eat protein from other sources. We are monitoring the situation around the clock, and as soon as we have more information, we will tell you."

That was it. As he folded the briefing note and put it back in his pocket, there was a shouting contest from the assembled media crews.

"Are we now a vegetarian nation?!"

"How long will this last?!"

"What's the number of fatalities so far?"

A more seasoned performer would have been unmoved by the clamor. He would have done exactly what he had agreed with his Chief of Staff and, having delivered the statement, would about turn and leave. But Commissioner Applebaum didn't recognize the traps set by journalists with apparently innocuous questions. Nor was he one to suffer fools.

"No fatalities," he confirmed to the baying reporters. Then, "Of course I'm advocating vegetarian." Before, unable to help himself, "I've no idea how long this will last."

"Is the cause instant karma?!" a reporter from a green news channel shouted at him.

Commissioner Applebaum didn't respond. He never got the chance. Reaching her hand under his arm, his Chief of Staff guided him firmly from the lectern, reminding him, "No questions," as she did.

When they returned to his office, he walked towards the tank on top of his filing cabinet, inhabited by his pet Mexican axolotl, Miguel.

"I thought that went okay," he mused, as though conferring with the ethereal creature.

Teegan Chase looked from the pink blur on one side of the glass to the large, pulsing forehead of the Commissioner on the other. Not for the first time, she wondered which was the more otherworldly of the two.

"The "no idea" line is what they'll run with," Teegan Chase was blunt.

"No idea?"

"What you said at the end."

"Did I?" He was thinking back. "It wasn't in the message I read."

"It's the message they'll take," she looked at him pointedly, as she placed his phone back on his desk, before stepping from the room.

Commissioner Applebaum stared at the axolotl. The bellowing journalists. The formidable officers who'd phoned him during the morning. They all wanted the same question answered. One he had been scientifically trained to answer. Only, science wasn't delivering the goods.

"Is the cause instant karma?" that reporter had shouted.

He'd been taken aback. It wasn't within the scope of the FDA to determine such a thing. Karma didn't form a part of any epidemiological framework he'd ever heard of. But nor could he ignore the fact that intensively-farmed chickens reached maturation aged six weeks, compared to twenty weeks if they hadn't been pumped full of hormones. That hormonal manipulation also applied to cattle and pigs. That the relentless pursuit to profit from rearing and slaughtering of animal units of production, without any regard to their sentience, was one that made him increasingly queasy the older he got. And that 80 percent of the world's agricultural land yielded only 20 percent of its food, thanks to the spectacularly extravagant requirements of meat production. Not for the first time he wondered what would happen when Mother Nature responded, as she always did when pushed to the limit, by unleashing some untold cataclysm, bringing the whole damned horror show to an end?

What if today, was that day? If karma was a dynamic, like any other, that could be studied and tested? Could causes and their effects be subjected to scrutiny that was observable, measurable and repeatable? If so, how might such an investigation be conducted?

Eyes running over the piles of paperwork on his desk, his attention was drawn to a particular folder containing staff awards and commendations. Recognitions of outstanding service which had been awaiting his signature before they were announced. The kind of task he had kept putting off because there was always something more urgent demanding his attention.

Seizing the folder, he opened it, took a pen from his desk drawer, and got signing.

28

Montpelier, Vermont

G RACE ARLINGHAM'S GLORIOUS DAY JUST KEPT GETTING MORE extraordinary!

She was amazed how transformed she felt putting the finishing touches to her lipstick, stepping back from the bathroom mirror, adjusting the scarf over her bald head. She had gone from frail, weary, and old before her time, to vibrant with conviction and purpose. Not that she had much time for contemplation. In a day when massive new breakthroughs were occurring by the hour, she had to get ready for her visitors. At sixty two years of age, she was about to undertake what she now felt to be the most important mission of her life. And she was about to appear on national TV!

After visiting the support group women, and rescuing the lives of many snails, she had waved goodbye to Kristina and Charlie, who were driving to the same medical center from which she had just returned, with every heartfelt wish that Kristina would have the same scan experience that she had. Before returning home to her wagging-tailed welcoming committee of six.

It had been an especially joyful homecoming, all the sadness she had felt this morning completely lifted. She wondered if her dogs were able to sense that her death-sentence had been removed? Not permanently, of course. She got that. But she'd have time, at least, to see them through to the ends of their own days. Time for many more walks witnessing the changing of seasons in her beautiful Vermont forests. Grace had always had an intuition that pets didn't just come into your life by chance. They only arrived because of some previous connection. If karma was true, wouldn't that help explain what such a previous connection might be?

Out of habit, she had turned on the TV in her kitchen as she made herself a coffee. And for the first time she'd seen all the news about the food poisoning. How the FDA had already banned all poultry products and there was talk of the ban extending to all forms of meat. Her thoughts turned immediately to John.

John Caruso, a pig farmer, and she, had been friends for a very long time. John and Grace's late-husband, Teddy, had known each other at school, so she'd met him even before she and Teddy got married. They'd remained friends as they'd settled down and raised families. And friends as she grieved the loss of Teddy, and John had mourned the passing of his wife. John's farm near Manchester was a two hour drive away—not so far that they didn't sometimes visit, if they were in the neighborhood, but too far to be convenient. When they did see each other, they enjoyed the easy rapport that came from lifelong kinship.

John had inherited the farm from his father, and had expanded it considerably in his heyday, buying the farm next door and diversifying into apples and greenhouse-grown vegetables. The piggery had always been the economic mainstay of the operation and, even though John had been successful at it, Grace knew his feelings about what he did were conflicted. Years ago, standing in rubber boots overlooking a pen in which pigs were feeding, she had asked him why.

"We do our best to take care of them here," he'd told her. "But when we load them up onto the back of the truck, they know exactly where they're going. I've never doubted it."

Grace had seen the distress in his eyes—the recognition that the life he had so enthusiastically given himself to as a young man turned out to have moral consequences he hadn't even contemplated. He was responsible for the creation of thousands, probably tens of thousands of beings, brought into existence only to be killed in the prime of their lives. It was a responsibility lightly worn only so long as you didn't believe the beings were conscious, or that they wished to be happy, to live, to be free. It was a responsibility you could accept only if you believed the creatures with whom you played God were morally irrelevant or inferior. She knew that John no longer believed that. Not fully.

John was one of the good farmers. There were many others who kept their pigs in stalls that were so small they weren't able even to turn around—including those of sows who were denied the simple instinct of being able to comfort their babies with their snouts.

Seeing the news on TV, she picked up the phone.

"John, it's Grace," she said, when he answered her call. "I've just been watching the news. Is it affecting the farm?"

It was most definitely affecting the farm, he soon told her, voice rising in frustration. The delivery of pigs he was due to make the next day had been put on hold, along with the one in two weeks' time. Indefinitely. No one could say when the slaughterhouses would be open again. Until the authorities could work out what the hell was going on, the whole supply chain had shuddered to a halt.

"We're not doing any more breeding," he sounded exasperated.

"What about the pigs that are staying?" she wanted to know. "Do you have space for them?"

"Space isn't the problem," he told her. "It's cost. Do you have any idea how much it costs to feed a fully-grown pig?"

"Tell me," she said. "Because I have an idea."

Grace's dogs went crazy at the window as a large, white van pulled up outside her house. "Galaxy TV—Always First" was emblazoned in orange letters down the sides of it. Shushing the dogs, Grace led them to the enclosed back veranda where they would be quiet. She was returning when her phone buzzed with the message she had been waiting for. It was Kristina. She had been given the all-clear too!

Grace called her immediately. The two of them were ecstatic. But they couldn't speak for long. Several more cars had parked on the road outside her house and reporter Tilly Hendricks was striding towards the front door. Grace made Kristina promise to come around too—and to prepare herself for a television appearance.

Grace opened the door to Tilly. She had spoken to her already that morning, and she knew her from the TV. In real life, thought Grace, she was shorter and more playful than the persona she portrayed on the news.

As Tilly was followed by a camera crew, and a lighting team who were soon rearranging the furniture in the lounge, Tilly told her, "This will be a live cross. You know what that means?"

"No second chance if I fluff my lines?" smiled Grace.

"Exactly," Tilly grinned, nodding. "But I have a feeling you're not going to."

They had already spoken that morning, after Grace returned from her snail-gathering mission. Galaxy TV wanted to do a story on the sudden increase in spontaneous remissions reported that day. Would Grace mind describing how it felt?

Grace, who had only just put the phone down from John Caruso, told her about the plan she had hatched. A plan Tilly Hendricks said she could mention on live TV.

As the two of them walked to the lounge, Grace told Tilly about Kristina's news. How she, too had just been given the all clear—and was on her way. Galaxy TV was in the running not for just one spontaneous remission story—but two!

Grace's lounge hadn't been so filled with people since one of the Christmas parties she and Teddy used to throw. Everywhere you looked there were TV people getting set up. The camera crew trying to decide on the best setting. Lighting people fussing with the curtains, lamps and reflectors. Sound people wearing headphones, hunched over meters. When Kristina arrived, there was a fresh wave of euphoria as the two women hugged—even some of the Galaxy crew applauded.

Soon they were sitting, Tilly facing the two friends, having cameras and lights adjusted. In the background a TV set was streaming live from the Galaxy newsroom in Los Angeles. They had covered the FDA announcement banning the sale of all meat and were now exploring the implications by interviewing farmers, economists and nutritional experts.

Tilly signaled that a cross was imminent. The mood in Grace's lounge suddenly became very focused.

"The unprecedented news stories today haven't all been negative," Dan Kavana was saying. "To counterbalance the food poisoning, travel disruptions and freak weather events, there have also been some extraordinarily positive stories. A short while ago the American College of Radiology announced a huge spike in the number of spontaneous remissions being recorded today. Typically, a spontaneous remission is what happens when a cancer patient is scanned and found to no longer have any tumors present. One such patient is Grace Arlingham. My colleague, Tilly Hendricks is with her right now in Montpelier, Vermont."

"Thank you, Dan," Grace watched Tilly morph into the earnest reporter with whom she was familiar. She outlined how Grace had been diagnosed with Stage 4 cancer some months earlier, how the tumors in her abdomen had failed to respond to chemotherapy, and how she had been fearful of the results of her most recent scan that morning. "Instead of the confirmation you dreaded, something completely different happened this morning, didn't it Grace?" she prompted.

"That's right!" Grace's eyes twinkled. "And it's still sinking in. You see, the scan came out completely clear. It was such a surprise, my oncologist had to check with the radiologist to make sure there hadn't been some kind of mistake. It was just so unexpected. So total."

"Your cancer went into spontaneous remission?" confirmed Tilly.

Grace nodded. "That's the phrase my oncologist used. But," Grace leaned towards Tilly, as though sharing a secret. "He said that's the term used by medical people when they have no idea what causes cancer to disappear." Then before her interviewer could respond. "And I wasn't the only one in our small town to experience this today. So did Kristina!" The cameras panned out to include Kristina, sitting on the sofa beside Grace in denim jeans and a sweater with an elated expression.

Tilly questioned Kristina about her own journey, observing how the unlikeliness of the two cases supported the announcement from the American College of Radiology.

"What I think is important," Grace was not to be deterred from guiding this interview in a particular direction, "is that any viewers watching who are ill, understand that the *real* reason Kristina and I had our lives saved is because we saved the lives of others. I rescued a bee which would otherwise have drowned in my birdbath. Kristina rescued a number of snails. Something strange is happening today, so that the actions you take have an immediate effect, and on a scale you would find hard to believe."

Grace was in such full flow that Tilly did nothing to interject, leaving it to Los Angeles to issue her orders through her earpiece.

In the newsroom, Dan Kavana was transfixed.

Nick Nalder was staring at the screen. "Where the hell is the woman going with this?!" he shouted, the mole on his right cheek seeming to swell.

"Quiet, Nalder, I'm interested," countered a gravelly voice. The only one that carried more weight than his in the newsroom. Galaxy owner, Harvey O'Sullivan, was stationed behind him, drawing on a cigarette.

"We have a wonderful opportunity today which ties in exactly with what your Mr. Kavana was just saying," she told Tilly. "There are many people who are desperately ill, like I was, who can benefit by taking action to save the lives of others. And there are many farmers with animals they didn't expect still to have, whose lives are there to be saved. This is why I have set up The Arlingham Foundation, in partnership with a local farmer. A seriously ill person can become well by sponsoring an animal that would otherwise be killed. A pig or a sheep gets to live a natural, happy life. A farming family can stay on the land, doing what they love. Everyone benefits!"

"Thank you, Grace. This is … an unprecedented idea." Tilly was surprised to have received no instructions from her producers on where to take the interview, so was winging it. "How can people get in touch with you?"

29

Galaxy Television
Galaxy City, Los Angeles

DAN KAVANA HANDED OVER TO AL GREENBERG FOR MARKETS Update, tugged off his earphone and rolled back from his desk. There had been times in the past when he'd felt the whole world was going crazy. But this broadcast was, without question, the craziest ever.

He'd no sooner made it out of the studio than Julieta was approaching him.

"What's it like in there?" he gestured the briefing room.

She rolled her eyes. "Thank God for Harvey."

The presence of their proprietor would, they both knew, act as a brake on Nick Nalder.

"First thing he said when he came in," Julieta told him, under breath, "What's happened to your face, Nicky?"

"The mole?"

"It's got huge! Every time he loses it with someone it seems to get bigger. But hey—" her expression quickly changed. "You've got to see this."

She held up his phone. "Message just in from Maddie."

It was a video clip with the message, "Look at me, Dad!" He pressed Play. There she was sitting next to a sink at the Pacific Seabird Rescue, beaming as she raised both arms to shoulder height before stretching them fully, flicking her gloved hands playfully. In the background Jacinda was saying, "She's made more progress this morning alone than in the past twelve months!"

165

Dan shook his head as his eyes welled up. "Incredible!" He took the phone and was soon calling his daughter.

"The Vermont cross," Nalder barked, as he stepped into the newsroom a few minutes later. "What the hell was that about?"

"The remissions story?" Dan acknowledged Harvey with a nod. Harvey liked playing the invisible observer. Fly on the wall, he'd say. In reality, more like elephant in the room.

"Woman turned it into a promo for her foundation."

"I was treating it as a public service announcement," replied Dan.

"Don't tell me you buy that story—"

"Like the rest of the country, I'm trying to make sense of what's happening," Dan didn't back down. Especially with what was happening to Maddie. "Right now, what goes around, comes around is making a lot of sense."

"We've been through the whole karma thing already!" Nalder's voice rose. Around the newsroom, researchers and reporters were looking up from their desks. The clashing of alpha male antlers happened from time to time. But in front of God himself?

Nalder's tone had a real edge to it. "The whole thing is ridiculous!" he continued. "How can fishing a bee out of a birdbath eradicate a whole bunch of tumors?"

"*Something* made it happen," countered Dan.

"There's no way we're going there!" Nalder was emphatic. Was it Dan's imagination, or was the mole expanding across his boss's right cheek even further? "There's zero evidence."

"Except for just about everything we've reported today, which points in the same direction."

Dan wondered about mentioning what had happened to Maddie, but decided not to. Nalder would only complain that he'd lost all objectivity.

"It's toxic. You heard the President."

They'd seen the grainy video clip of President Grey doing the rounds on social media. Along with his sweeping declaration that "This is the United States of America. We don't do karma."

"Since when did we defer to the towering intellect of President Grey?" Dan was scathing.

"None of the other channels are going near it, and that's for a reason: they'll lose their audience." Nalder turned, as though appealing directly to Harvey.

Tracey, one of the researchers was waving a print-out at her desk. "There's something you should see!" she called out. Nalder ignored her.

"I'm not saying we need to push a line here," argued Dan. "I'm just saying we should explore it."

Julieta, never backward about coming forward, had taken one look at Tracey's document before seizing it and handing it directly to Harvey. He glanced at the headline before laughing mirthlessly. "Science proves karma doesn't exist," he read aloud. "Research conducted this morning by Stanley Smugg, PhD, New York Times Best-Selling Author, Digital Disruptor and Influencer. Well, whaddayaknow?!" he waved the paper in the direction of the two men. "Maybe this is the way in."

"Interview Smugg?" asked Nalder.

"Nah! Something more ... combative," proposed Harvey.

"Head-to-head?" asked Dan.

The God of Galaxy was nodding.

"We'd have to find an expert on karma."

Researcher Chieko, who focused on social media, intervened without hesitation. "Lama Tashi!" she told them.

They all turned to where the studious young woman, who seldom said boo to a goose, was sitting at her screen.

"Never heard of him," snapped Nalder, mole darkening. "Aren't there any famous Buddhists?"

"Yes," said Chieko. "But Lama Tashi did a social media piece this morning that's gone viral. Everyone online is talking about him."

"How many is everyone?" Nalder retained an old news world skepticism about digital channels.

"Over one hundred million views."

"A few more than were watching our news," O'Sullivan looked at Nalder sardonically.

Next to the researchers' desks, ratings executive Trent Garvey was shaking his head, incredulous.

"D'you think he could handle himself in a debate situation, this lama?" asked Nalder.

Chieko was nodding. "It's not only what he says. He has, like, this effect. He's mesmerizing."

"Mesmerizing is good," grunted Harvey.

"We'll set it up" said Dan.

"Before anyone else gets to him," Harvey, whose commercial instincts ran deep, gave Nalder a pointed look. "Always first," he quoted the Galaxy slogan.

30

Veteran Affairs
Boulder, Colorado

D R. RALPH SHARP WATCHED AS COLONEL THOMAS JACKSON STEPPED out of his large, black, pick-up truck in the parking lot, and headed towards the front door. Normally, a receptionist would be on duty, Ralph would be in his consulting room down the corridor and the whole place would be buzzing with people.

With all the disruption, Ralph had no staff on duty and no clients to meet today. None, that is, except the one he had been asked to see by General Hickman.

Colonel Jackson was uneasy about being here. That was what his body language was saying. Ralph observed the way his visitor made a sur-reptitious sweep of the area to check if he was being observed. How he assumed a closed, head-down posture as he crossed the parking lot. It all fit the model he had explained to his audience at the Pentagon. The same model to which the General had referred during their earlier conversation.

"Colonel?" he stepped forward, as his visitor entered reception. "Dr. Ralph Sharp. Head of VA for Colorado."

Tom's handshake was brisk. Ralph sensed a reflexive need for deference and tried to put his visitor at ease. "We meet in unusual circumstances. I'm the only one in today."

There was no need for him to elaborate.

"Your time is appreciated," said Tom.

"*We* appreciate your offer to help," Ralph replied, supporting Tom's chosen narrative. "Come this way," he ushered him down the corridor.

Ralph's office was designed to put men such as Tom at ease. With baize green walls, framed academic certificates, Chesterfield furniture, wooden library shelves and gleaming trophies, it was expressly masculine while avoiding any military reference.

"I am sure you could make a great contribution to our program," Ralph told his visitor, once they were sitting across the coffee table from each other in facing wingback chairs, a glass of water apiece. "Did you have something particular in mind?"

"Hiking," Tom replied immediately. "I've always spent time in the mountains. I could help take groups."

"You've heard about our outdoor program?"

"Saw it on your website."

Post-Traumatic Stress Disorder was heavily referenced on the outdoor program page. Ralph's visitor was sending a helpful signal.

"It's valuable if volunteer leaders—which is what you would be—have some understanding of PTSD."

"Read about it."

"Excellent!" he said encouragingly. Before guiding Tom down a conversational path with which he was long familiar. One which could lead to a moment of self-revelation and even a willingness to engage on the part of his clients.

"Many of us experience some of the symptoms of PTSD at different times of our lives, even though we may not have been diagnosed as having the condition. A diagnosis only occurs when a number of symptoms are present simultaneously."

Tom nodded.

"It can help us empathize with those we're leading when we've experienced some of the same things they have." He deliberately paused for an unhurried sip of water.

"What kind of things?" Tom took up the invitation.

"Persistent flashbacks of a traumatic incident, sometimes in the form of nightmares. Or when fully awake. Or both."

Tom inclined his head.

"Insomnia," he met Tom's guarded expression.

"Uh-huh."

"Which often leads to excessive alcohol consumption."

"That's something a lot of us know about!" Tom's use of humor to distract, noted Ralph, seemed reflexive, revealing an inner conflict between the wish to get his own situation out in the open and what was probably a life-long habit of concealment.

"What other symptoms?" asked Tom.

"There can be persistent fears. Horror. Shame. Negative beliefs about oneself and an inability to think or feel positive emotions. PTSD can make one feel increasingly detached from others—"

"I get all that!" It wasn't clear whether Tom was more irked by Ralph's continuing list, or by having his own symptoms so clearly itemized. Either way, it came to the same thing. "What I don't get is why hiking?" he demanded.

Ralph regarded him evenly. "The outdoor program—where you'd come in—takes participants into nature. It's well established that when we're in outdoor settings, we are easily drawn away from our thoughts. Out of what neuroscientists call narrative mode and into direct mode, when we pay direct attention to what we see, hear, smell and so on. You see, the way we deal with negative thoughts and feelings is not to suppress them. Suppression is never a permanent fix."

"No?"

Ralph knew he had Colonel Jackson's undivided attention. "It only holds things at bay. And once the energy to suppress is weakened, what may have seemed dormant turns out to be dynamic. If anything, more powerful for being kept down."

"But I can't spend my whole life in the mountains!" objected Tom. "At least, no person could."

And there it was! The moment of acknowledgement. Admission by his visitor of the beast that had emerged from his own personal darkness.

"Agreed. No person can," said Ralph, not making a thing of it. "The outdoor program is only part of a treatment plan, involving one to one sessions to address the underlying causes. And offering tools to help clients better manage their own thoughts. All parts—" Ralph gestured a broad circle, "—of a holistic package."

Tom stared at his glass of water for a long while. He knew he'd outed himself although he hadn't intended to. When Lama Tashi told him that the cause to be free of the horror that visited him, night after night, was to help free others from the same thing, he had immediately thought about the PTSD program. He'd known about it for years. At some level he'd recognized that he should be attending it himself as a client, only he hadn't been able to bring himself to that point. Not even after Greg's funeral last year, when it was just him left. The last of the three musketeers not to take his own life.

Tom hadn't planned for things to unfold the way they had. But the psych was showing no surprise and he supposed it was for the best to have it in the open.

When he looked at the psychologist he asked, "No silver bullet, then?"

Ralph shook his head, reflecting Tom's own wry smile. "And the next program only begins in six weeks."

As he saw Tom's expression cloud, he was thinking about the most important principle of all his therapeutic interventions. The one element he believed to be the most important he could confer to any of his clients, especially those battling with depression: it was the renewal of hope.

"I have no doubt that you will find the program a significant turning point," he told Tom. "We have outstanding responses from clients. You know, Colonel, when you are able to use personal pain to fuel growth, the more pain, the more growth. The outcomes can be extraordinary!"

Tom was following him intently, thinking how the message he conveyed was like something Lama Tashi might say.

"In the meantime, I am sure we can find something to help you through to the start of the next program."

Tom raised his eyebrows.

"If you'll indulge me," Ralph sat back in his own wing-back chair. "Relax in your seat. Take a few deep breaths. Exhale slowly."

In other circumstances Tom might have bridled at such a suggestion. But the game playing was over. And besides, he wasn't going to return home to the guru without a positive report. So he did as he was told.

"Do you suffer from a fear of heights?" Ralph asked.

He shook his head.

"Then I'd like you to close your eyes and imagine you're in a hot air balloon traveling above the landscape. A different landscape than usual. Actually, it's the landscape of your life, and you're floating back in time, able to see everything that happened as it unfolded. Back through retirement, your sixties. Your fifties. You're looking down and seeing it all laid out there, like an impartial observer from above. All the major milestones. The ups and the downs. And as you do, you're feeling perfectly calm. You are impartial. Objective."

Tom had never attempted this exercise before. The idea had not been suggested to him. If it had, he would probably have dismissed it as some kind of head-shrink psycho-babble. But leaning back in the wingback, it came surprisingly easy. He found he was able to recall milestones as Ralph Sharp counted down through each of the decades, until they arrived at the time he had enlisted in the army at the age of eighteen.

"Now look back further. Your teenage years and childhood. Is there any activity that required your single-minded focus?" Ralph urged him. "Anything you did which completely absorbed you?"

It took some looking. The answer didn't come up immediately. But when it came, it was obvious and effortless. He remembered his mother's initial encouragement. Once he'd proved himself, his father's too. All the hours of practice. Rehearsals at school. Examinations and performances. It had been a big part of his life, so much a part of him that leaving it behind had been his only regret when he'd entered the military.

"The piano," he said.

"You play the piano?"

Tom thought of the Steinway upright in the living room. The same piano he'd played through his childhood, and which he'd inherited when the time had come to sell his parents' home. From an early age he'd been drawn to the structure and rules of music. How every single piece of music emerged from the same 12 tones and 24 keys. How the longer you practiced, the more accomplished you became. Scales and studies were disciplines he'd found nurturing until they had been replaced by an entirely different set of disciplines.

"I haven't played for half a century," he said.

"Then it's time you did again," Ralph told him.

31

Omni, Colorado

MARGARITA WAS GLAD SHE'D ANSWERED THE TELEPHONE CALL from her daughter. Speaking to Gabby had helped her process the initial shock of her discovery and had also reassured her that this wasn't all about her. Ever her staunch defender, Gabby had been outraged by her father's actions, not that she'd seemed quite as blindsided by the news as Margarita had expected.

Gabby had called back half an hour later to say that she'd been doing some investigating on "the bitch." She had no doubt that her father was being used—not that that excused what he'd done. In no time at all, Gabby told her, her father would be on her doorstep, begging for forgiveness. What Mom had to decide was whether or not she'd have him back.

Gabby's loyalty gave Margarita courage. And after speaking to her daughter, that second time, she decided she must *do* something. Not about Bob, who had made his choice. Nor was she in any state for creative work. But she had to get out. Sitting around the house all day wasn't going to help her state of mind. She was already picturing the small parcel in her briefcase which she'd been asked to deliver. That most unexpected commission she'd accepted the evening of her recent book-signing in New York.

Three days earlier, at the end of the afternoon session in a flagship 5th Avenue book store, the line of autograph seekers had come to an end. Her publicist was wrapping up ahead of a celebratory drink with the whole publishing team back at her hotel. Margarita had been aware of a couple, hanging about near the desk where she was doing the signing. They didn't fit the profile of her usual fans—Moms with kids. Instead, the man looked like he was her own vintage, the woman somewhat younger. It was only when she'd got up from behind the desk, hitched the strap of her handbag around her shoulder, and was about to leave that they approached.

"Margarita!" The man called her name. Was it something about the voice or the face that had some ancient familiarity? She had searched his features for a clue of what was triggering a memory, but although she sensed an echo during that timeless moment that their eyes met, she was unable to place its origin.

"Norman Manderson. Isabella's brother."

She stared at him. The Manderson family had moved to Omni when she was in high school, and Izzy and she had become firm friends. She'd often see Norman, three years their senior and the eldest of the three siblings, at the Manderson house when she'd gone round to play with Izzy, the youngest. At the age of seventeen, Norman had won a scholarship to college in San Francisco and had left home. For reasons no one ever fully understood, not only had he never returned, he had cut himself off completely from his family.

Margarita remembered the pain the Mandersons had felt at the estrangement. Norman had been their brightest star, the family luminary, and when he stopped speaking to them so inexplicably and completely, it was as though he had taken his light with him and cast them into the darkness. There had been endless conferences round the Manderson kitchen table for months afterwards. On-going efforts to reach out to him on birthdays, Thanksgivings and Christmases in the years that followed. Messages passed through intermediaries in the hope of reconnection. But Norman had never come home, not even when Mrs. Manderson had fallen ill with cancer and died. Not even when Mr. Manderson was diagnosed with dementia and had to be moved into care.

In time the family came to accept there was nothing to be done. Rob and Izzy had grown up, found spouses, and had families of their own. Margarita had continued to be friends with Izzy, now a grandmother twice over. Taking in the man before her, over forty years since she'd seen him, she tried to remember when Izzy had last mentioned his name.

It must be at least a decade ago, maybe even two. Norman Manderson, the New York-based architect, had won some award for energy efficient building. Izzy had come across an article with a photograph of him on an online news site and had pointed it out to her. When she'd read it, Izzy told Margarita, she'd experienced a strange ambivalence, feeling the tug of recognition, at the same time as a renewed shove of rejection, reading a few scant details about a life Norman had deliberately chosen not to share. The two of them hadn't spoken of Norman since.

"I saw a poster about your appearance," Norman was saying, taking something out of his pocket. "I wonder if you'd mind taking something home for Izzy."

Margarita's expression had hardened. "Why don't you send it yourself?"

"She might not accept it from me, if I went direct," said Norman evenly. "I couldn't be sure she even got it."

Margarita was suddenly back in the Mandelson family home, remembering Izzy's efforts to get word to Norman that their mother was dangerously ill. Surely he'd come to visit his own dying mother? Later, Izzy's eyes filling with tears at her mother's funeral, when she'd turned to Margarita to say, "You know the worst part about this whole thing?"

Margarita had squeezed her hand. "You don't have to say."

In the 5th Avenue book store, Margarita held Norman's eyes. A being who had inflicted immeasurable pain on a dear friend and her family. Someone so emotionally damaged he didn't even seem to possess any filial instincts?

"Why now, Norman?" she demanded.

"Things have changed. I need to make amends." He was looking at the woman beside him.

Her face was serious, but she nodded encouragingly. Glancing down, Margarita noticed a wedding ring.

Norman held a small, gift-wrapped box and card in his hand.

Margarita's publicist was looking over, queryingly.

"I don't want Izzy to have to go through more heartache," said Margarita, nodding towards what Norman had in is hand.

"That's definitely not my intention," said Norman. He seemed sincere.

Now, Margarita picked up her phone, opened her contact list and found a name among her favorites. A short while later, the number was ringing.

"Izzy, it's me," she said, when her friend answered. "Yes, I'm back. Are you going to be at home this afternoon? I have something to drop off for you."

32

Back seat of The Beast
Washington, D.C.

PRESIDENT TRENT GREY WAS ON HIS WAY TO DELIVER A LUNCHTIME
speech to one of the most powerful lobbying organizations in the
country. Re-election was why he had agreed to address the National Gun
Association at their Annual General Meeting. The NGA had helped him
win power three years ago. He needed them if he was to win again in a
year's time.

President Grey had little personal interest in guns. He was also wary
of discussing semi-automatic firearms over macho meals with leathery
men who may come to decide that his attitude towards preserving the
Second Amendment was insufficiently unwavering.

So it was to be another carefully choreographed appearance. He'd
sweep into the Grand Ballroom of The Piccard, one of the capital's most
lavish hotels, after lunch had been eaten. He'd do what he did best—
provide a compelling manifestation of that ultimate of all powers, the
Commander in Chief, an authority which the martially-minded held in
deep reverence. He would deliver a twenty-minute speech invoking patrio-
tism, liberty and personal freedom. He had long since come to realize that
it hardly mattered what he said—long after everyone in the room had
forgotten every word he'd uttered, they would still remember the way he
made them feel. Which was privileged. Awe-inspired. In the presence of
a power they didn't fully understand.

Then he'd leave, off to whatever formidable responsibilities awaited him.

Devoid of all illusions about what those formidable responsibilities actually entailed, in the back of the Beast his Chief of Staff, William Salt, knew that it was rare windows like these that gave him his best chance of getting his boss's attention.

"Great set of GDP figures to be released later," he told the president, opening a folder. "Nearly a full percentage point above forecast."

President Grey looked nonplussed.

"We'll have you say something about an endorsement of your growth strategy—"

"Reducing taxes."

Salt was writing margin notes. "Reducing taxes," he repeated. "Boosting employment."

"Blah blah," the president twirled his hand. "What d'you think *really* did it?" he turned to eyeball Salt. "Only last night Rose Mulrooney was talking falling GDP."

Rose Mulrooney was the Chairperson of the Federal Reserve Bank.

Salt nodded. "It *is* a big turnaround from what all the forecasters have been saying."

"Caused by?"

"D'you want me to get a view from our economics unit?"

The President had already moved on, staring at the empty sidewalks, the closed restaurants. It was one thing seeing what the food poisoning thing was doing on TV. Another out here, traveling through an empty city. "What's going on is ..." he was shaking his head.

The multiple debriefs this morning from the FDA, the Department of Transportation, the police had been on such a scale and intensity there'd been vigorous debate about whether the President should even do the NGA thing.

Salt studied his boss closely. He'd long-since learned that his job was to join dots. To listen with care to the fragmentary, apparently random comments the president made, and reflect them back as coherent policy. His boss was capable of moments of great insight. He could also be maddeningly contradictory.

"What's the pattern, Will. You tell me?" he asked.

Pattern? Cause of the turn-around? President Grey was being high level.

The obvious response, the one that had been trending massively on social media, the one which Salt had watched Lama Tashi explain, along with over 100 million of his fellow Americans, was also the one the president had specifically ruled-out. Although he had done so in the company of that formidable thundercloud, the Reverend Jeremiah Bellow and the expensively tailored Marvin "Pray for a Porsche" Swankler. Salt decided to chance it. "Instant karma," he replied.

"Exactly."

"Occam's razor," Salt referred to the principle that, when trying to understand any given situation, the explanation requiring the fewest assumptions was usually the correct one.

"I like it." The President nodded before explaining himself. "You know I authorized $10 million dollars in food aid this morning. It's a modest amount but ...."

Seeing where his boss was heading with this, connecting his donation to the newly-released GDP figure, Salt recalled what Lama Tashi had said about karma increasing. "One of the general aspects of karma," he was authoritative with his new-found knowledge, "—is that karma increases, sometimes dramatically."

For the first time in a long while, Will Salt felt he had the President's undivided attention. There was an intensity about his scrutiny, a forcefulness that was almost palpable.

"You know about karma?" asked the President.

"Only what I've learned from Lama Tashi," said Salt.

"Who is Lama Tashi?"

"He's a Buddhist teacher trending massively online. Hundred million views this morning already. Everyone's trying to make sense of what's happening and he's become, like, the go-to guy."

"Karma can increase dramatically?"

"Just like a single acorn can turn into an oak tree, is the example he used. This one, small seed ultimately leads to a huge tree which, for year after year keeps bearing thousands of seeds. Something that seems out of all proportion to the original cause."

"So, ten million in food aid turns into a 1 percent GDP uptick?"

"If that's what's going on."

"Occam's razor," the President reminded him. "What's the next data release?"

"Employment figures later today."

"If we want to boost our own employment figures, we boost someone else's, is that the idea?" The Presidential brow furrowed as he worked through options. "There's that new trade deal with India, but even if I sign off on it now it'll be days before we hear back. We need a quicker fix."

"Government call centers!" exclaimed Salt, swiftly scrolling through emails on his tablet. "There was a proposal we base part of the rolling, 24-hour team in Swaziland."

"Switzerland?"

"Swaziland."

President Grey was bewildered. "Is that even a place?"

"Small country in Africa. Less than two million population. Placing a call center there would have a massively disproportionate impact on their employment levels. Which would result in a massively disproportionate impact on ours."

"You see!" the President jabbed him with his index finger. "That's why I hired you. You're smart. Make it happen."

"Right away."

They were already approaching The Piccard Hotel, the Presidential motorcade slowing as they drew nearer the soaring columns and fluttering flags.

Seized by a new thought the president suddenly looked at him with a ferocious intensity. "Ratings," he said. Followed by "Instant karma."

Of all the data sets President Grey followed, the ones on which he was most fixated were his personal ratings. In public, his stated position was that polls were mere polls, and the only vote that mattered was what people decided on election day. Like most politicians, however, the truth was that he was obsessed by survey figures, with every subtle shift in numbers being the cause for exhaustive analysis.

"Whose credibility can I boost?" demanded the president. "Who can I make untouchable?"

The motorcade had come to a halt and secret service agents were fanning out around the presidential state car in a state of high alert, entries and exits being times of greatest vulnerability.

Will Salt was opening a file. "There are so many awards and endorsements put forward by committees. The question is which one will have the biggest impact?"

A secret serviceman was signaling to open the door of the vehicle.

"In a moment," snapped Salt, holding up his phone. "We're busy."

As he scrolled down a list, the President said impatiently, "Pick one."

He jabbed the screen at random with his index finger. "Dr. Saul Applebaum, Director of the Food and Drug Administration for his work on nanoparticle drug delivery."

"Nano what?" Queried the President, before waving aside his own question, and preparing to exit the vehicle. "Oh forget it."

"You don't think we should hold off given all that's happening today with the FDA?"

"No time, Will," the door on President Grey's side was being opened. "Go with Applebaum. Make it happen right now."

"Will do, sir."

33

Galaxy Television, Los Angeles
Princeton, New Jersey
Boulder, Colorado

"JOINING US TODAY FROM PRINCETON, NEW JERSEY, IS ASSOCIATE Professor Stanley Smugg, PhD, the best-selling author of *Pointless Prayer*, and from Boulder, Colorado, Tibetan Buddhist Lama Tashi." Dan Kavana introduced his two guests.

Stan Smugg looked studiously clever against a backdrop of leather-bound books. In the *Flourish* studio, Lama Tashi emanated a benevolence as panoramic as the sweeping vista behind him.

"With all the events today, there's huge speculation about instant karma." Dan set up the debate. "Part of the challenge we face is that most of us don't know much about karma apart from "what goes around comes around." But there's at least one person who is convinced there's no such thing as karma. Earlier today, Stan Smugg conducted what he has described as a rigorous test of the concept and says he found no evidence to support it at all. Tell us about your study, Professor Smugg?"

"Well, Dan, the research involved 100 participants, each of whom was asked to give away ten dollars within half an hour. If instant karma really existed, you would expect that, soon after giving the ten dollars away, each of the participants would receive a financial gain. But that didn't happen. 36 participants got something but 39 got nothing at all and 20 actually lost money. What's more, the windfalls of the fortunate 36 varied greatly. So—" a condescending smile playing on his lips, Stan Smugg told viewers, "—if there *is* such a thing as "instant karma" I found no evidence of it in our study this morning."

Slam, dunk was the impression he conveyed. Case closed. He'd tested the concept and numbers never lied.

In Colorado, Lama Tashi's face was bright with humor, his shoulders shaking as he chuckled.

"Too funny!" were his first words on the subject. Behind his spectacles, Professor Smugg's eyes narrowed.

"You find the results humorous, Lama Tashi?" Dan confirmed.

"The whole thing!" he was shaking his head. "The whole concept. But it's useful that researchers are starting to take an interest."

"You mean in instant karma?"

"Karma, more generally," recovering himself, Lama Tashi resumed the kind-hearted presence that had so endeared him to the townsfolk of Omni over the years—and, earlier that morning, to many millions of people online.

"You know, this idea of "instant karma" is not something we have in Buddhism. Usually, causes created in one lifetime only ripen in a lifetime that follows, when they meet the right conditions. But we have to keep an open mind, yes? Perhaps conditions are suddenly heating up today so causes ripen more quickly. Karma climate-change yes?"

Instantly, thousands of social media feeds were quoting the line. The most memorable so far. Karma climate change. Could there be a more apt descriptor?

"You're saying there *may* be such a thing as more instant karma?" Dan wanted to clarify.

"What we are experiencing today," Lama Tashi tilted his head. "It seems that way."

"But the study conducted by Professor Smugg—"

"It's based on a flawed understanding. A mistaken idea about what karma is. Quite a common misconception," Lama Tashi seemed to be directing this at Stanley Smugg himself. "So, no problem. I am grateful the study was done so that we have this chance to discuss an important subject. Plus there are some technical problems with the research."

"Technical?" The smile had gone from Professor Smugg's face, but the condescension remained.

"May I ask if you took into account the four factors affecting the impact of karma?"

"We took into account dollars out and dollars in," Professor Smugg said smugly.

"In any action there are four factors which affect the strength of the karma created. The subject—the person carrying out the action. The intention—what that person intends to happen. The action itself. And the object—the person to whom the action is being done. Straightforward, yes?"

Dan was nodding.

"Depending on what these factors are, the impact will be different." When Professor Smugg didn't respond, he continued, "For example: intention. The intention of someone who gives ten dollars to someone to repay a debt is different, for example, from someone who gives ten dollars to a charity collector, and different again to someone who gives ten dollars, or a gift worth ten dollars, to someone who he hopes may do him a favor.

"It's the same with negative karmas. Someone who transfers money from a business to a personal bank account by mistake is different from someone who does so deliberately. The ordinary law recognizes this distinction," he shrugged. "For example, murder versus manslaughter. The same act but different intention makes for a different karmic outcome too."

Once explained, the significance of intention seemed so self-evident that when Dan Kavana turned to Professor Smugg it was with a certain expectation, "You took intention into account, Professor Smugg?"

"Not directly," he replied, not allowing the newly-exposed flaw in his research to affect his composure. "It may account for some of the variation in results." His tone suggested that such variations would be of little consequence, despite the implications just revealed.

"You mentioned *four* factors, Lama Tashi?" returned Dan.

"Yes. The *object* of your actions is another one. If one of your students had spent dollars taking a friend out for coffee and cake—"

"Were the participants your students?" interjected Dan, wanting to confirm.

Professor Smugg nodded. Though it didn't escape him that nowhere in his report had this fact been mentioned.

"If the student bought coffee and cake for a friend, that's different from taking his mother out for coffee and cake. Parents are more powerful objects, karmically speaking, because without them we wouldn't exist."

"The power of the object, Professor Smugg?" Dan once again referred to the New Jersey studio. "Is that something—"

"Not directly," he repeated, struggling to maintain his lofty demeanor.

"The power of the *subject*," continued Lama Tashi. "Refers to the one who takes the action. A gift offered by someone who knows exactly what they are doing is different from the same gift given, say, by a toddler. It's probably not so relevant to this study. But the power arising from the substance of the action itself would be. A person can spend ten dollars buying a bunch of flowers at a gas station on his way to visit someone. Or, thinking about the person he is about to visit and remembering how they mentioned really liking a beautiful notebook they have seen in a particular shop, he could go out of his way to buy the notebook instead. In both cases he has spent ten dollars. But the substance of the action and the happiness it delivers is a different order of magnitude. Therefore, the karmic impact is different too."

"Useful explanation," Dan didn't bother reverting to Professor Smugg for a further, embarrassing confirmation that he had taken none of them into account. "Karma is a more involved subject than most people think."

"I have one question about the research," asked Lama Tashi, his peace-ability somehow transmuting what had been set up as a confrontation into something that was more congenial.

"Go ahead," prompted Dan.

"The ten dollars your students gave away. Where did the money come from?"

It was the question that Professor Smugg had most dreaded before coming on national TV. Because even he had begun to harbor doubts about his hastily arranged research—only after it had gone out into the field.

"I gave it to them," he replied.

"So the students weren't actually giving away their own money?"

"No."

"More like, passing on ten dollars as part of a research project?"

"Conditions weren't perfect," conceded Professor Smugg. Despite his initial intentions to kick down the sandcastle of karma and trample it firmly underfoot, in the same way he had made a name for himself out of demolishing prayer and positive thinking, he was smart enough to realize that wasn't going to happen. Not today, at least. Lama Tashi had called him out. In the gentlest possible way the guru had shown his research to be fundamentally defective.

"Lama Tashi," Dan wasn't even bothering with Professor Smugg now. "You said earlier that most people have a misconception about what karma actually is. What do you mean by that?"

Once again, Lama Tashi was bright with humor. "This idea that giving ten dollars here will result in receiving twenty dollars there," he chuckled at the absurdity of it, but with so total an absence of malice, and so engaging a sense of inclusion that even Professor Smugg had a lightness about him.

"It is based on the idea that karma concerns some kind of objective reality. But as we have seen, not all ten dollar gifts are the same. Their impact on the mind of the giver and the receiver varies greatly. It's like that with all actions, positive or negative. The same act may have very different effects depending on intention, object, subject and substance of the action."

"You're saying that karma happens in a person's mind?" confirmed Dan.

"Of course! We need to get away from thinking of what is going on out there as the whole story. At all times, our experience of reality is subjective. Take this discussion, for example. There's the TV man, the professor and the monk talking together nicely. Lots of people watching. We all agree on what is happening. But the way we are experiencing what is happening, probably very different. Same appearance, different reality for each one of us."

As so often when Lama Tashi spoke, but now, for the first time, on national television, he conveyed the truth of what he was saying with an energy, a force that was somehow tangible.

"We create our own reality. Every experience we have is unique to ourselves. Two people may do the same thing, watch the same event unfold, but what they feel about it may be different—sometimes subtly, sometimes greatly. This is because our karma is different. We experience things in a particular way because of the causes we have created in the past.

"One thing very precious about our lives as humans is that we have such freedom and power in the karma we can create. If we choose to focus on weapons, conflict and violence, we are creating the causes to experience more of this in the future. If we want to focus on supporting the life and well-being of others, we are creating the causes to experience this instead. In simple terms, as we think, so we become."

Like many viewers, Dan Kavana listened to what Lama Tashi was saying in a way that was very personal, a way that went to the heart of what mattered to him most. He was thinking of Maddie, paralyzed by the car accident, but whose most recent video showed her capable of new-found freedom, after she had focused her attention on helping seabirds to fly again.

In Montpelier, Vermont, Grace Arlingham agreed out loud as Lama Tashi stated the transformative truth she had discovered for herself earlier that day: that in saving the life of another, she herself had been saved.

Amy Robbins watched Lama Tashi with a sense of profound gratitude as he explained what she had experienced that day. In giving the cruise to her parents, she had been focusing only on her parents' well-being. What a wonderful paradox that, in so doing, she had created the causes for her own dreams to come true.

Although there was one niggle that disturbed her: the mugging. There she'd been, offering donations to the homeless, passing on the glad tidings about instant karma and, next minute, she had her bag stolen. What was *that* all about?

In White Oak, Maryland, Commissioner of the Food & Drug Administration Saul Applebaum, M.D., stood watching Lama Tashi, transfixed. Could this lama be the key to delivering on the question everyone wanted answered: the cause of food poisoning?

Across the nation, hundreds of thousands of others were nodding their heads in agreement as Lama Tashi explained the mechanics of why their generosity that day had resulted in windfalls, transfers, bequests, prizes. A multitude of life-changing events which they had soon told others about, and asked questions about and, like Amy, tested. And which had soon resulted in yet more riches as the news spread faster than any pandemic from coast to coast.

Other viewers, however, had very different feelings.

In his Omni Springs motel room, Bob Martin didn't know how to interpret the words of his teacher, now a national TV guest. We create our own reality. Yeah, sure, he agreed with that—it was what Lama Tashi had always said. We have the freedom and power to create the reality we wish. Wasn't that exactly what he was doing, leaving home to be with Beth? He wanted to believe it was absolutely the right thing. But something deep down, something he was finding it hard to pinpoint, was unsettling him. Even though he had been attending the Lone Pine Meditation Center for several years, right now he was finding it hard even to think straight.

In a waiting suite just off the Grand Ballroom of The Piccard Hotel in Washington, D.C., Mick Mackenzie, Chief Executive Officer of the National Gun Association was poised for the encounter of his life: his first meeting with the President of the United States, who was now less than one minute away.

Mackenzie had slipped out of the lunch to greet President Grey and lead him personally into the NGA gathering. A short walk, but his most awesome duty ever.

A muted TV screen in the hotel waiting room adjacent to the Grand Ballroom, showed Lama Tashi answering Dan Kavana's questions. Glancing up, Mackenzie glowered. A choleric man who despised anything he perceived as foreign, and a staunch advocate of a shoot-to-kill policy when it came to illegal immigrants, he jabbed his finger at the TV screen furiously. "God-damned immigrant, and probably illegal. Turn the fucking thing off!"

"Yes, sir!" Sven Persson the Piccard Hotel Manager, who was, himself, a God-damned immigrant, quickly obliged.

They had been warned that Mackenzie was irascible. The warnings hadn't been wrong.

"Before you go, Lama Tashi," Dan prepared to wrap up. "There's a lot of talk about instant karma explaining today's food poisoning pandemic. Would you like to comment?"

"The FDA has said no to meat products?" confirmed Lama Tashi.

"Correct."

"Well," shrugged the other. "That seems clear." As so often with Lama Tashi, the lightness with which he answered the question was in marked contrast to the previous deluge of anxiety-ridden coverage.

"What many people are struggling to understand," probed Dan, "is—why? If we are, in fact, experiencing karma climate change, what is the cause for people becoming ill because they eat meat?"

"If we force other beings to suffer and die, we create the cause to experience it ourselves."

"But people who buy burgers aren't causing suffering and death. Not personally. That's happening at the slaughterhouse."

Lama Tashi paused, the simple force of his presence seeming to reflect the inanity of what had just been suggested. "Every barcode for a meat product scanned at the checkout; every beef burger ordered; every chicken, lamb or fish meal eaten triggers an order for more animals to be killed. Just because the killing happens away from our eyes, doesn't mean we haven't caused it."

"Some would argue," Dan tried asking the questions he felt people wanted answered, "that these animals are only bred to be eaten. They wouldn't exist if we didn't need them. What's the problem with that?"

"Every chicken, every lamb, every calf is sentient. It has consciousness. Just like you and me, he or she wishes to experience happiness and to avoid suffering. Many of the ways in which we seek happiness is the same, all of us sentient beings. We want tasty and nourishing food and shelter. We seek physical comfort. Most beings also seek emotional bonding and support with our mothers, families, others of our kind. And most importantly, we place the highest value of all on our life. We do not wish to die. We only wish to live and be happy. When we take the life of another sentient being we are saying that my wish to eat a burger is more important than your wish to live. This has an impact on our mind, a causal imprint."

"Karma is a big subject," Dan needed to cut to a commercial break. "Many different dimensions."

"Yes," agreed Lama Tashi, smiling gently. "But in another way quite simple too. If you ever find yourself wondering if an action is positive or negative, just ask yourself: "What if everybody else did this too? Would the world be a happier place or not?""

"Thank you, Lama Tashi," said Dan. He was about to thank Professor Smugg, but when he looked at the New Jersey studio feed, the desk where his other guest had been sitting was now empty. Associate Professor Stanley Montgomery Smugg, PhD, New York Times Best-Selling Author, Digital Disruptor and Influencer, had left the building.

In the newsroom, Trent Garvey, the geeky ratings guy, was emoting.

"We've never seen ratings like this!" he was reporting on the Lama Tashi interview. "We hit double our previous all-time high! Up 60 percent on our nearest rival. People are crazy for this guy!" he was gesturing towards a screen where the feed from *Flourish*, in Boulder Colorado was still live, and Lama Tashi, relaxed and beneficent, looked like he was about to remove his microphone.

"Let me speak to him!" In the rarest of interventions, Harvey O'Sullivan wasn't so much asking as demanding access to the lama.

Moments later, he was talking. "Lama Tashi, I'm Harvey O'Sullivan, owner of Galaxy Television," he announced himself.

Lama Tashi nodded, a twinkle in his eyes, "Very good!" he said. "Hello Harvey!"

"I just watched your interview. Terrific! People are hungry for what you can teach us." Most of the Galaxy team, having never seen Harvey in charm mode, were surprised at what an immensely agreeable and humble man he could become. "I have a question I am hoping you can help me with," he said, with that faint, Irish lilt. "What is the karmic cause for Galaxy to attract more viewers?"

Lama Tashi chuckled. "In general, whatever you wish for, give to others."

"I should promote my rivals?" he confirmed after a pause.

"Would you like them to do that for you?"

"Christ, yes!" While Galaxy was one of the most powerful networks, there was no telling where it could be with the collective clout of all the others channels, plus the public broadcasters behind it. "A bit ... counter-intuitive, this strategy?" he said.

"Whether you believe or don't believe really doesn't matter," Lama Tashi repeated his oft-used line. "Just keep an open mind. Try it. Find out for yourself."

"Oh, er, and lama," Harvey flicked ash off his cigarette onto the studio floor. "I smoke cigarettes. Is that a karmic cause to get cancer."

"No," the other shook his head immediately. "It's a condition. But if you already possess the karmic cause for cancer, smoking creates a condition for that karma to ripen."

Harvey was soon briefing Nalder to organize prime time promotions for all their rivals. Nalder, apoplectic at the mere idea, was forced to control his outrage on account of who was giving orders. And was it everyone's imagination, or was the mole on his right cheek, the one that had extended and darkened during his earlier fit of ill-temper, somehow retreating and fading as he found himself compelled to exercise patience?

"We already have some evidence this strategy will work," Trent Garvey was eager to impress the God of Galaxy.

Harvey turned to scrutinize him.

"Earlier today, Dan Kavana said something positive on air about Bart Bracking at Channel 60. We saw a spike in ratings."

Harvey grunted.

"Even so, this is unprecedented. High risk," said Nalder. "Are you abso-lutely sure you want to do it?"

Harvey fixed him with a beady stare. "Always first," he reminded him. "Okay."

"And I want you to hire Lama Tashi."

"*Hire* him?"

"Commentator. Expert. Whatever. Pay him whatever he wants. He's ratings gold!" Harvey took a long drag of his cigarette before stubbing it out decisively in the ashtray. "And that's the last of these fuckers I'll ever smoke."

Violent Opposition

1:00 pm (Eastern Standard Time)
11:00 am (Central Standard Time)
10:00 am (Pacific Standard Time)

Physical concepts are free creations of the human mind, and are not, however it may seem, uniquely determined by the external world.

—ALBERT EINSTEIN (Theoretical Physicist 1879—1955)

34

The Piccard Hotel
Washington, D.C.

THE FIRST GUNSHOTS STARTLED WORKERS AT THE PICCARD HOTEL—
but did not alarm them. The noise was expected. Every year the NGA
held its annual meeting at the hotel. Most years featured some new firearm in a demonstration video. Beyond the large, swing doors of the Grand
Ballroom, in soft-lit reception rooms and in the kitchens, staff continued
preparing for the delegates' next coffee break.

The shooting continued in rapid sprays. Raised voices were heard. Even
that caused no consternation. It was only when a gaggle of figures burst
from a side door, one clearly injured, that the alarm was raised.

Four large men in suits were moving at high speed towards an escape
exit. Someone was shouting—to whom wasn't at first clear. As they went
by it became evident that the injured man, no longer able to move, was
being carried by the other three. One on each side of him, another behind.
His shirt and jacket were blood-stained. He was trying to speak, but what
came out of his mouth was an incoherent gurgle. The entire right side

197

of his face was awash with blood. But despite his injuries and contorted voice, there was no disguising who he was.

The President of the United States had just been shot.

In those first few moments, after the President was hurried out by secret servicemen, and before anything else happened, for the few staff witnesses, time seemed to hang, suspended, as the enormity of what had just happened sank in.

Was this an assassination attempt? Would President Grey survive? What other horror was going on inside the Grand Ballroom?

Live gunfire continued in further bursts. Then suddenly it was silenced. Next thing, a hotel waiter, Juan Garcia, raced from the main entrance. "Shooting!" he cried out, distraught, pointing behind him.

Closely following came the first few NGA guests, dazed and disheveled. Some ranting in garbled language. Others seemed sightless as if sleepwalking.

For Piccard Hotel Manager, Sven Persson, who had been in the Grand Ballroom until a visiting sheik on the 5th floor demanded his personal attention, what he encountered on returning was a sight of horrifying carnage. There were bodies on the floor. Blood-flecked guests crouching under tables, some of them moaning, unable to move.

Persson instantly had his phone out and was calling emergency services. Scarcely able to believe he was saying the words "mass shooting" and "Piccard Hotel" in the same breath.

From outside came the wail of approaching sirens, emergency services having been summoned by the President's bodyguards. In the Grand Ballroom some guests were helping others splayed on the floor or under the table. Journalists, having broken through the lobby cordon, were interviewing guests. Great, suited men were on their knees, sobbing.

Approaching the head table, Persson searched for his lead contact at the NGA.

"Have you seen Mick Mackenzie?" he asked a female guest, who was limping for the exit.

"Bastard's dead," she jerked her head behind her. "Least, he deserves to be."

Persson turned to survey the space behind the head table. Several male bodies lay on the floor. Motionless—except for the one he recognized as his client—but only just. Mick Mackenzie was lying face up and unconscious, his face having broken out in what looked like a spontaneous rash of boils. Beside him on the carpet, a gold-plated, semi-automatic rifle. And a metal serving tray.

35

G RACE ARLINGHAM'S DAY JUST KEPT GETTING BETTER! WHILE Grace was many things—sentimental, old-fashioned, set in her ways—she wasn't naïve. She was very well aware that Galaxy's only interest in her was on account of her remission, and that she was unlikely to be allowed air time to talk about her new idea, The Arlingham Foundation. She'd been surprised when they let her pitch the concept on live TV. Even more astonished when they prompted for her phone number. The contagion fears had even the newsrooms asking the kinds of questions they usually avoided. Opening to possibilities they would, in normal circumstances, have immediately shut down.

Her phone hadn't stopped ringing since. All the while she spoke to someone, she could hear other callers trying to get through. Hanging up, she'd be told that she had ten, twenty, fifty new messages.

Which was where Scott came in. Her nephew ran a telecommunications business. A bright young entrepreneur, within a short while of her speaking to him, he'd re-routed her phone to a call center where dozens of trained staff would answer, "The Arlingham Foundation, how may I help you?"

He'd also set up Arlingham Foundation sites on major social media channels, featuring a scanned photo of Grace, with the line, "May all beings be free from suffering." Her TV segment was the first posting on them all.

Kristina and Charlie had stayed with her during this time. After the

Galaxy interview, they'd toasted their scan results with glasses of champagne—only one glass for Grace, as she hadn't drunk any alcohol for
months on medical advice and didn't want to get too light-headed to speak
to callers. They took it in turns to take pledges, writing down names and
email addresses and giving the details of an Arlingham Paypal account
Grace already had from her days offering private music lessons.

When Grace had conceived of the plan, only a short while before, she'd
had in mind something local, a way that ill people in Vermont could help
John Caruso take care of his pigs for the rest of their natural lives. She
hadn't thought there would be very much interest. Most people, she knew,
didn't like to think of farm animals as fully conscious beings who just
wanted to be happy and free. They preferred keeping their gaze firmly
averted on that subject. Persuading them that there was a connection
between helping others—especially non-humans—and being helped
themselves, seemed an even bigger stretch.

And yet her phone still didn't stop ringing—even after Scott's company
took over call management, routing only the most important calls to her.
People weren't just interested. Her idea was resonating across the country
in ways she could never have imagined.

Very soon she had farmers' associations calling to ask if their members
could be considered for the scheme. Which was just as well. John Caruso's
pigs were accounted for within fifteen minutes of her TV appearance.

Patient support groups, cancer charities, even medical practices were
phoning to make lifetime pledges, ensure that animals were freed from
intensive farming pens, and allowed to live out their days in contentment.
And with every moment that this was happening, Grace was feeling more
and more energized. Fitter, stronger, more youthful. She began to feel that
the idea she had conceived was no longer only her idea—if it ever had been.
She had merely been the initiator, the one who first caught the spark and
breathed it into flame. Now it had become a fully-fledged fire with a life
of its own. The conditions were perfect for it, and what a joy to behold!

Grace had never been greatly interested in the world of investment
banking, but even she recognized the name of the caller put through to
her by Scott's team. If Warwick Bates wasn't America's richest man he
certainly was one of them. He was also as famous for his lifestyle as he

was for his wealth—he and his wife still lived in the same, modest family home they had bought when starting out, forty years before.

"I think you're onto something, Mrs. Arlingham," he sounded normal and unassuming when she took the call. "You see, my wife and I went for our morning walk today. There's an older couple we pass who take their dog out. The elderly man hasn't been around lately. Today the woman was looking upset. My wife—she's the talkative one—asked if she was okay. She said she wasn't. Her husband had gone into a nursing home some weeks ago and she had just been diagnosed with Alzheimer's. She's going to have to move into the nursing home too. She'd been unable to find a home for her dog. So this would be his final walk. Today she was having to take him into the vet to be put to sleep.

"My wife and I looked at each other. We didn't even need to have the conversation. We've always admired that little dog—Harry, his name is. Maltese poodle. We offered to give him a home. We took him, then and there.

"Later, I went for a blood test. Not many people know, but I've had prostate cancer for a while. PSA level spiking sharply. But today's reading came back: three point zero."

"That's normal," said Grace, who'd been through the whole prostate cancer journey with her late husband, Teddy.

"Exactly. I'd been wondering about things, you know, thinking along the same lines as you. Then someone sent me a link to your Galaxy interview."

"Seems like we've both been granted a reprieve," observed Grace.

"And we should make the most of it," said the billionaire with feeling. "I'd like to help you with The Arlingham Foundation. I believe it's an idea whose time has come. This thing will go crazy and you'll need a whole management team to take care of donors and beneficiaries, to invest the donations you receive, to market the cause, to take care of admin and tax—the not-for-profit sector is complex. In the long term it could swallow you up whole.

"But I have people who can do that all for you. Professional people. Good people. They can organize structure and staffing and management, leaving you free to be the figurehead. And live your life."

As he'd spoken, Grace had recognized the truth in what he said. Right now, at this moment, it was thrilling to see what a huge effect she was having. But she could see how she may have unwittingly created a monster.

"I hear what you're saying, Mr. Bates," said Grace. "But that all sounds very expensive."

"Not to you," he was quick to assure her. "Not to The Arlingham Foundation. This would be a gift, from my organization to yours. You may like to think of it as a kind of partnership."

"I ... I don't know what to say!"

At the other end, Warwick Bates chuckled. "Yes" is the word I'm after."

36

The Piccard Hotel
Washington, D.C.

OUTSIDE THE ENTRANCE SOON BECAME A CHAOS OF EMERGENCY vehicles. Police were sealing every street within two blocks. Along with the wail of sirens was the deafening clatter of helicopters. Survivors were being airlifted to the hospital from a small park across the street.

The Police, and operatives from Homeland Security were doing their best to take charge. They were behind the eight ball from the start. Journalists had been present both outside The Piccard and within. Many NGA delegates were celebrities, pin up boys—and a few girls—of the Second Amendment lobby. Now the lucky ones were emerging, bloodied and broken. The less fortunate were being identified and photographed *in situ*, before being placed in body-bags and ferried downstairs into mortuary vehicles.

Despite security efforts to control the news flow, some of the delegates themselves had recorded fragments of what had happened on their phones. Photos and videos were being uploaded and shared as news of the Washington horror spread quickly across the nation. The world.

President Grey was undergoing surgery to remove a bullet. His condition was described as serious. He'd also received a superficial wound to the forehead. His deputy, Vice President Jane Nelson was temporarily the acting President.

Everyone was trying to make sense of exactly what had happened. In particular—who had done this? Was it a terrorist attack? Had shooters infiltrated the convention while the President of the United States himself was speaking? Where were the murderers now?

What quickly became apparent was that at least one NGA member was responsible for killing. Mick Mackenzie's name kept coming up—CEO of the National Gun Association. Who had he been trying to eliminate? Had he succeeded? How much of the damage had been collateral?

Juan Garcia was the other person survivors mentioned—although not by name. By all accounts, the Piccard Hotel waiter had been the hero of the day. The one who had brought the terror to an end only to vanish minutes later. Who was he exactly?

So many questions in the fog of the immediate aftermath. So few answers. But as the body count passed the sixty-eight mark, Washington, D.C. Police chief Hans Ziegler knew he was going to have to make the announcement that every policeman dreaded: on his turf and under his watch the United States had just experienced its worst mass shooting ever.

37

Omni, Colorado

IAN TURNER CHECKED HIS APPEARANCE IN THE RESTROOM MIRROR OF the Early Settler Coffee House. Hair, blazer, handkerchief. Taking a deep breath in, he drew himself up to full height, rolled back his shoulders and steeled himself for what lay ahead.

He had spent very little time with lawyers during his life. "Keep clear of hospitals and courts and you'll do well" had been his father's advice. Words he'd always heeded.

But he felt he'd had no alternative but seek legal counsel when he'd made the discovery. It had come as a real shock. The biggest in his life since he'd moved from Colorado to Arizona. He hadn't wanted to go the legal route. Confrontations and unpleasantness were things he tried to sidestep. But some things were so important that a showdown could no longer be avoided.

When he'd put the bookstore into the hands of a manager, he hadn't expected to make much money out of it. He'd done the Paige Turner accounts for over thirty years and had a keen grasp of the economics. If he made an income of $1,000 a month, net of all expenses including the manager's salary, he'd be doing well.

The main reason he was continuing the business was because of the building. He and Paige had bought it when they'd first got married, and in the past forty years it had risen considerably in value. He didn't have much else to leave their sons when he died, but the building would be

208 — David Michie

a very nice windfall for the two of them. So long as the store continued paying its way, he was happy.

After the first two managers came and went, he'd hired a third, Beth Owens. On the surface of things, everything seemed to be business as usual. Beth was good with the customers and Ian had even seen a modest increase in income.

He hadn't paid too much attention to analyzing the detail of the e-book statements that came in. He was aware that while print sales were in decline, the shop was generating more income from e-books sold via the company website, a subject that held little interest to him. In his view, there was no substitute for a printed book, ideally a hardback with a satisfying aroma of paper, ink, and binder's glue.

A month ago when his eight year old grandson, Jasper, came visiting, he'd found the laptop Ian used for his emails and banking. As a game, Jasper had keyed the names of his parents, aunts and uncles into a search engine to see what came up. They'd chuckled at some of the photos and references to events in the past. Then Jasper had put in the name "Paige Turner." Ian had expected references to the shop, but nothing like the kind that appeared. What came up was row upon row of books, and not with the sorts of covers that graced the shelves of the store. These were all of semi-naked women in raunchy poses, and highly suggestive titles. Quickly, he had seized the laptop from his grandson. Not before Jasper had asked,

"Pappa—what is B&D?"

"B&B it said," he answered, quick as a flash. "B&B. It means bed and breakfast. Time for a chocolate chip cookie, what do you think?"

Later, after Jasper had gone, he repeated the exercise, wondering how he'd found his way to such a page. Which was when he'd discovered that, under the direction of Beth Owens, Paige Turner Books had become a highly active digital emporium of erotica. In a state of shaken disbelief he found himself scrolling down page after page of lurid listings.

Wondering if he'd been trapped in some digital alley, he returned to the Home page. Which confirmed that only a smattering of mainstream new titles was to be found. Most of the Paige Turner Books website was devoted to filth!

Ian was bewildered. There had never been a calling for that sort of thing in the past. Retrieving his most recent quarterly statement, to his chagrin he recognized just how much of the total business income was being derived from the sale of soft porn. He thought of Omni townsfolk and found it hard to imagine them buying books like *Slave to Desire* and *Daddy Love* in such prodigious quantities. The more he looked into it, the more he realized that the old Paige Turner Books was nothing more than a literal shopfront, a fig leaf, for a digital business that was a grotesque aberration of the edifying salon his late wife had originally set out to create. It had been hijacked right under his nose.

Like Gabby Martin before him, Ian soon found his way to the cause of this marked change. Beth Owens as the self-styled Venusian Goddess who was using the bookshop as a way to build a following for her own journals, purportedly real. And quite a following it was too, with over 80,000 regular visitors. All eager to read about the sexual antics of the Venusian Goddess and her current partner, someone named Endless Love.

Unable to sit, Ian had paced the floor of his Scottsdale townhouse. Omni was his home. It was where he and Paige had made their life and brought up their family. The close-knit community was where most of his dearest friends still lived. While he now spent a lot of the year in the next door state, it horrified him to think that his friends might make the same discovery he just had. Even if they realized it had nothing to do with him, it was a disreputable stain on Paige's legacy. He had to bring it to an end. And soon.

Hence the lawyer. After reading the contract between him and Beth Owens, the solemn young man advised him to tread cautiously. In promoting a specific genre of book, even if it was one that he found personally distasteful, his manager had done nothing illegal. If Ms. Owens had benefited financially in other ways from traffic generated by the Paige Turner bookstore—such as through sales of her "journals"—that was a different matter. But how to prove it?

"The laptop," Ian Turner had proposed.

"Laptop?"

"The one I left at the shop, because it has so much business stuff on it. Last time I was there this woman—" he pointed at the contract, unable to bring himself to say the name Beth Owens, "—asked if I could buy a new model."

The lawyer followed him carefully.

"What if the laptop shows that she's channeling visitors from the bookstore site to her own site to sell things?" asked Ian.

"That's precisely the kind of evidence we need to establish breach of contract."

Ian's mission today was simply to retrieve the laptop. He had an IT expert on hand—a friend of his son's—to analyze its contents. He had already authorized him to gain access to the entire Paige Turner Books IT system and website. He had seen the laptop stowed under the counter during his undercover visit earlier.

One of the oddities of the contract between the Manager and him, as the lawyer had pointed out, was that there was no separate rental agreement for the upstairs apartment. It was included under the same contract. As such, Ian Turner was entitled to visit the premises any time he liked during business hours. If, for any reason, the Venusian Goddess had taken her laptop upstairs, Ian had a key to her apartment door. He wouldn't hesitate to use it.

38

Food & Drug Administration
White Oak, Maryland

SINCE HIS DISASTROUS PRESS CONFERENCE, FDA COMMISSIONER
Saul Applebaum had been subject to immense pressure. So much
that he wondered if his position had become untenable.

He'd had the Federal Aviation Authority on his back ever since the
Golden Drumsticks episode at JFK early that morning. Every minute that
airports remained closed was causing untold disruption and costing the
country millions. The FBI and CIA were troubled by the prospect of a
terrorist-related biological warfare. General Hickman demanded to know
about health implications for armed forces personnel, should they need
to be deployed. The President's Chief of Staff himself had become a frequent caller, on behalf of both President Grey, as well as, latterly, Acting
President Jane Nelson.

Like everyone else in the country, they all sought an answer to the most
basic of questions: what was causing the food poisoning?

Applebaum's Chief Scientist and his team took their seats around the
meeting table of his office. They were about to participate in a conference
call set up by Chief of Staff, Teagan Chase.

As Teagan had correctly predicted, the "I've no idea" meme had
become ubiquitous whenever Applebaum's name was mentioned online.
Americans had been ordered to become vegetarian, by the most senior
public health official in the nation, people railed angrily online. When
asked why, the answer was "I have no idea." Such was the vehemence of

211

public outrage that satirical videos, cartoons and even songs, parodying Applebaum's outsized, bald head were all over the internet.

It was always much easier to shoot the messenger, observed Applebaum. What would they have preferred that he do—lie to them?

"We still have no answer," his Chief Scientist, the white-coated Melinda Myers told him. Under unprecedented stress herself, her usually neatly combed dark hair was disheveled and expression was drawn. "Every food sample, human sample, slaughterhouse check has come back clear of all known bacterial and viral infection. We've been focusing our efforts on known unknowns in recent hours. Even that ..."

Commissioner Applebaum fixed his Chief Scientist with a long, hard gaze. They'd been working together for years. Whatever her weaknesses as a professional, Melinda Myers was someone he knew that he could trust. She had thrown absolutely everything at this. Marshalled not only the full resources of the FDA but called in people from the private sector, including some of the most specialist diagnostic technicians in the country. Still there was zilch. Zero. Nada.

"Let's see what this meeting produces," he nodded towards where his phone was set up for a conference call in the middle of the table. "I'm not optimistic."

"I've been in touch with London," his Chief Scientist agreed. "They're in the same place we are."

Food poisoning was a global phenomenon. It wasn't only residents of the United States who were affected—the same thing was happening around the world. In a few moments they were due to hold an emergency conference call, under the auspices of the World Health Organization, with their counterparts from the UK, Europe and several Asian countries.

They were about to initiate the dial-in when the door of the room opened. Applebaum's Executive Assistant was urgently calling her boss. "You need to see this now!"

Applebaum and Chase hurried to the door.

"Just delivered," the EA handed over a large, white envelope addressed to Saul Applebaum with a Private & Confidential stamp and branding that was discrete but unmissable: The White House.

Applebaum braced himself for the worst. Nodding to his EA to open it, he watched her draw a letter opener deftly up the full length of the envelope before handing him the one page letter within.

It was from the President's office and a single paragraph in length. In recognition of Dr. Applebaum's contribution to health, in particular his breakthrough study on nanoparticle drug delivery, the President was pleased to be awarding him the National Medal of Science. An invitation to an award ceremony at The White House would follow soon.

Applebaum showed the letter to his Chief of Staff.

"Congratulations, sir!" she offered her hand.

He was immediately recalling the staff awards and commendations he had signed off that morning. His personal test. As he'd handed the folder to his Chief of Staff he'd asked her to expedite the delivery of all the commendations. Given everything else that was happening today, she'd been surprised. He wondered if she'd made the link.

They returned next door, joining a conference call which had been already been going for several minutes. Chaired by the WHO Director in Geneva, with Teutonic efficiency, every country spokesperson was required to provide an update of in their own country lasting no more than two minutes.

As it happened, the status update required less time than that: they were all in the same boat. Major episodes of public food poisoning leading to the closure of restaurants, fears of contagion, mass stayaways, transport systems coming to a halt, the banning of meat product sales—and despite their very best efforts, they could find no evidence, whatsoever, of any bacterial or viral cause.

"We're under extreme pressure from the Chancellor," said Berlin.

"None of our scientists can offer a cause," said Rome.

"What if the cause is not a scientific one?" asked New Delhi.

The WHO asked him to clarify.

"What if the cause is karma?"

The call went silent. After a pause the WHO said, "But who would be willing to go public with such a statement?"

In Berlin, the Director of the Federal Ministry of Food and Agriculture recollected the delightful and quite unexpected arrival of a spare part needed to restore his classic Mercedes Benz that morning, after he had helped the next door neighbor's boy attach a brake pad to his bicycle.

In London, the Secretary of the Department of Food recollected a road rage incident, witnessed just a few moments ago from his Whitehall office window, where an angry driver, getting out of his car and intending to punch the face of the motorist in front of him had raised his fist with such force that he'd thrown himself off balance, knocking himself unconscious on the tarmac.

In Maryland, Commissioner Applebaum glanced at the letter from the White House on his desk.

"I would," he said. "Because I happen to believe it is true."

"As do I, personally," said Berlin, in a tone that made it clear this was an individual opinion.

"We *invented* karma," said India, eager to claim credit.

"It would be easier to sell to our public," Britain tried to build an international consensus, "If the United States said it first."

A short while later, agreement was reached.

2:00 pm (Eastern Standard Time)
12 noon (Mountain Standard Time)
11:00 am (Pacific Standard Time)

39

Miami, Florida

Feng Wang's heart was pounding in his chest. His hands felt clammy on the steering wheel. It was a twenty-minute drive from Powerball House to The Atlantic Bar & Grill where he was to meet Park and Hu for the celebration of a lifetime.

Everything about today still felt surreal, like he was acting out a part in a movie or a lucid dream, except he knew that he wasn't. He told himself the reason he was feeling this way was to be expected. How many people went from the situations that Park and Hu and he were in, to controllers of a $2.1 billion charity foundation in the course of a single morning?

He tried to persuade himself that this was the reason he was feeling edgy, just like anybody in his situation might, but he didn't believe his own lies. Never had been able to. No, if it wasn't for the half a million dollars in the zip bag stashed under the passenger seat, he'd be going to meet his friends in a state of unbridled euphoria. Instead he felt guilty as all hell.

He told himself he shouldn't. He didn't regret the decision. If he could replay the scene, giving a different answer to the Powerball guy, he wouldn't. The Blue Caps were still getting $2.1 billion weren't they? He wasn't taking from the total amount everyone had in their minds? The winning ticket which *he* had bought, and which had been *his* idea, was still going to create a foundation that would deliver untold benefits to their chosen causes, along with lucrative jobs for the three of them.

In the meantime, all he was really doing was squaring things up.

Tidying away his own financial affairs before embarking on the next chapter.

He'd pay off the credit card debt right away. Later today, or realistically tomorrow, he'd go to the bank, deposit the cash and arrange transfers to clear his credit cards and other debts. He'd relish the novel sensation of being debt-free. He'd quit his bar gigs. Take things easy. He wouldn't splash the cash, at least not in an obvious way. Maybe he'd take a discreet vacation somewhere. Invite that cute waitress Caley, where he did his bar gig, to the Caribbean.

You shouldn't have taken the money! a voice inside him kept saying.

Well, he hadn't taken it—not finally. Not irreversibly. He could show up at the bar with the bag of cash and tell the guys he had been advised by Powerball to do so. That it had been Powerball's idea that they should have some liquidity. Not that he could see either lawyerly Hu or accounting Park being happy with $500,000 in cash. $500 maybe.

No, that was a dumb idea. Besides he didn't want to hand it over. Unlike them, with their steady income streams, he'd had to do the hard yards for years and years. Taking risks and sometimes heavily on the chin. But also, from time to time, taking advantages of the opportunities he had created. Like this one.

He pulled into a space in the nearly empty parking lot across the road from the bar. He decided to leave the bag under the passenger seat. Normally he wouldn't have dreamed of leaving half a million bucks in the car. But there was no time to go to the bank. He reminded himself that his car had never been broken into before. This was as safe a suburb as you could get.

Get a grip, Feng! He took a few, deep breaths before emerging from the driver's seat, shutting the door behind him and making sure the car was locked when he pressed his remote. He strode across the car park, puffing himself up in preparation for his encounter with his partners. He glanced at his watch. Park and Hu would be in the bar by now, ready for a lunch like no other. Would they even go back to their jobs afterwards?

As he neared the door of The Atlantic Bar and Grill, which overlooked the sea, he was suddenly flung against the restaurant wall. And slid against it, winded. Had he been attacked? A deafening clamor sounded as a collection of garbage bins, upturned by powerful gust of wind, rained down nearby. Startled, he saw them falling. Before his attention was caught by something much more horrifying.

His car had been collected by a micro-tornado. Like a garment in a washing machine, the vehicle spun around within the sinister dark vortex which was heading swiftly out to sea. Peeling himself off the ground and getting to his feet, he took a few steps back from the restaurant entrance, to see his car, at the center of the moving column, heading well out from the coastline to heaven-knows-where.

Shaken, for some time he stood there watching after it. Before stumbling towards the entrance and going inside.

Park and Hu were at one of the premium tables on the balcony overlooking the ocean. Approaching them he gestured towards the sinister vortex moving rapidly into the distance.

"My car just got picked up in a micro-tornado," he pointed.

Observing his distress, they followed his gaze to the rapidly dwindling column. Their expressions seemed pretty low key. Hu picked up his phone and took a few photos. "Might help with insurance," he said.

Feng nodded. Ever the lawyer, he was thinking.

He noticed they were both having their usual Mexican Standoff beers— not the celebratory shots or champagne he had envisaged. He thought about the half a million dollars that was about to disappear forever. It seemed to eclipse all the joy of the lottery win. Its loss meant he still faced all his financial dramas—and now he didn't even have a car.

As he stood there, looking utterly bereft, Hu asked, "You came straight here from Powerball?"

"Uh-huh."

"Was there something valuable in the car?"

Feng realized that both Hu and Park were looking at him closely. "No. I mean …. no," he shook his head miserably.

His two partners exchanged a glance before Park lifted his phone and displayed a screenshot of The Blue Caps bank account. "It's just that when the transfer came through, it was missing half a million dollars. I checked, you see, against the details you sent earlier. Joint ticket holder. We wondered if you'd taken some in cash?"

"And why?" added Hu.

"Yes," agreed Park, expression sour. "And why."

40

Omni, Colorado

S INCE HIS APPEARANCE ON GALAXY TV, *EVERYONE* WANTED A PIECE
of Lama Tashi. Which surprised Megan not one bit. Now it wasn't
only Nick Nalder wanting to hire him for some ill-defined but lucrative
role as "Karma Correspondent." It was every other major network too.

Emails and text messages were flooding into *Flourish*. Major Hollywood
talent agencies were vying to get him onto their books. Online gurus were
reaching out, hoping some of his magic would rub off. Major business
tycoons wanted him as their advisor.

It wasn't like there weren't any other Buddhist teachers and monks
making appearances in the media. Not to mention plenty of self-styled
karma gurus jumping on the bandwagon. But Lama Tashi was the pos-
sessor of something that was priceless beyond measure, something palpable to anyone who watched him for even less than a minute—he was
the real deal. Authentic. He didn't simply understand the subject—he was
the embodiment of it.

Megan found that she, too, was becoming famous by association. When
she'd put on a black jacket that morning, and red pendant, when she'd
brushed her straight, shoulder-length hair the way she always did, and
spent no more than five minutes on make-up, she had never dreamed her
appearance would evoke such a response.

By virtue of becoming known as Lama Tashi's student and founder
of *Flourish*, however, she had acquired an entirely unexpected celebrity
of her own. She found herself being referred to in comments as "Lama
Megan." A cartoon image of her in her black jacket and dazzling blue eyes

221

appeared alongside that of Lama Tashi. Suddenly she was said to embody all kinds of transcendent qualities.

What Lama Tashi had told her earlier about other people's minds, other people's karma was made suddenly and powerfully apparent. *She* hadn't changed during the course of the morning. Not fundamentally. She was still the same Megan Mitchell she had been before with her strengths and her failings. It was other people who were seeing her differently. They were creating their own whole different reality about her.

Not that she had any time to dwell on it. Lama Tashi, Anton, and she paused to take in the latest news images live from Washington, D.C. Wounded men and women were being hurried into ambulances and rushed to hospital. Two large mortuary vans were filmed driving into the underground parking lot of The Piccard Hotel. The President was said to be out of surgery, but still unconscious. A row of TV reporters outside the hotel lobby were talking to the cameras of national and international media. All of them trying to make sense of what had happened.

Not that what was happening in Washington was a priority for Megan right now, nor even the spectacular developments with *Flourish*. It was past one o'clock and she had guests. When she offered them something to eat they had accepted with alacrity.

She led them back to the house where they sat around the kitchen table drinking fruit juice as she prepared toasted sandwiches and salad. As they waited, her kids Hayden and Shelley got back from school and were thrilled to discover their visitor. Lama Tashi was an almost mythical figure in their home, a Magic Uncle who they usually had to visit but who, today, was here in their midst. Eight year old Shelley immediately went to sit on his lap. Sixteen year old Hayden sidled up beside him for a hug.

Sandwiches made, they stepped out of the kitchen door with their plates and drinks. The back porch overlooked a small back yard that led to the forest. It had turned into a warm and cloudless day, the air vibrant with spring flowers wafting up from garden. Dipping the ring finger of his left hand into his drink, Lama Tashi flicked tiny droplets of water in front of him, then in the three other cardinal directions, a ritual he undertook before drinking anything, symbolizing the wish for all beings throughout the universe also to enjoy good drink, food, and freedom from suffering. For all beings to be well.

They sat following Lama Tashi's example, absorbed by the beauty of the moment, the sun on their skin, the deliciousness of their meal. In the distance, Rusty the retriever snuffled through the undergrowth. What could be more worthwhile paying attention to than what was here and now? Megan glanced at her kids, both unfamiliarly quiet and content just to sit. As she smiled, Lama Tashi caught her expression, and looked over at Hayden and Shelley, and soon they weren't just smiling, they were giggling too, as if sharing a private joke about how much contentment there was simply in being.

After they'd eaten, Lama Tashi asked Hayden if he could do him a favor. He wanted him to write a summary of all the messages that had been left on his mother's phone, as well as answer the phone and take the details of new callers that afternoon. With a strong sense of purpose, Hayden sat at the kitchen table and began his list.

Megan asked Rinpoche what he would like to do next. It was clear to her by now that the *Flourish* TV studio Lama Tashi had originally proposed had been to prepare for today. That he'd known exactly what was going to come up, even to the point of bringing Anton with him. How were things to play out next?

"A lot of these are people who saw you on Galaxy and have their own questions about karma," Megan glanced down the list.

"There are many questions?"

"Dozens," she confirmed, glancing down Hayden's list as he continued to listen and write. "Oh, and all the major TV networks are asking for you—along with everyone else. They're in a hurry. You can do whatever you like, right now, Rinpoche. Accept any offer. They're offering chartered planes. They all want to relocate you."

Lama Tashi was shaking his head. "No. We're staying here. Hayden can answer the phone. The three of us can go back to the studio to answer those questions."

Megan was surprised. "Don't you think one of the big networks can give you more exposure to get your message across than a studio in a forest?"

Lama Tashi recognized her generosity of spirit and smiled sweetly. "If I choose one network, the others will not want me," he said.

"True."

"If I choose *Flourish*, they will all cover it."

Megan raised her eyebrows. Even though Lama Tashi had no TV of his own, he seemed to have an intuitive grasp of exactly how the networks operated. What's more, his idea was more audacious than she would ever come up with on her own.

"All of them?" she confirmed.

He shrugged. "We'll see."

Which was how they came to be back in the *Flourish* studio, against that transcendent backdrop, as Megan pointed all her social media feeds at another live Lama Tashi broadcast.

"This morning, I explained the general aspects of karma," he told a fast-growing audience across the nation. "How karmic effects reflect karmic causes. You can only get positive effects from positive causes, and similarly negative effects from negative causes. I explained how karma increases. How even small causes will have effects, but you should never expect effects without causes. This is simple, no? Easy to understand?"

She was nodding.

"Recently I talked about the four factors that give karma its power. Its weight. How depending on subject, object, action, and intention, all these will affect the result."

"That's right," said Megan, before illustrating with the examples he had used during his Galaxy interview. Lama Tashi, she noted, was speaking as though he was delivering a seminar on karma, completely unconcerned about whether people had seen it online or via a news channel.

"Now I am happy to take some questions. Karma is a complex subject. There are so many dimensions to it. So many implications. Perhaps I can help clarify some of these?"

Megan was nodding. "I'd like to start with a very specific one—but it keeps coming up on all our social media feeds. One, you might say, that reflects the concerns of many viewers."

"OK?" Lama Tashi looked serene.

"If generosity is the karmic cause of wealth, what is the karmic cause to be good-looking?"

Lama Tashi gave a shoulder-shuddering laugh, before answering, "Patience. Of course! When we cultivate self-restraint, understanding, we are not only helping matters in the here and now. We are creating the causes to be attractive in the future."

"Some people might not see the connection," Megan was saying. "In giving, you receive, people get that. But what's the connection between patience and beauty?"

"Probably easier to illustrate with its opposite—anger. When someone is angry, do you find them attractive or do you want to get as far away from them as possible? If you wish for someone to like you, is it better to show them a red, scowling mouth and furious expression, or a happy, open expression?" Lama Tashi paused to allow viewers to process this.

"Anger is the most destructive of delusions," he continued. "The person experiencing the anger can have no peace, no well-being. Nor the person they are angry with. Much better to cultivate patience. If there is anyone watching who has anger management issues—" he chuckled, "— you may find it useful to think about the situations and people that make you mad. And when you have your list of aggravating people, reframe them all as "Precious Treasures." Why Precious Treasures? Because unlike our dear friends and loved ones, unlike everyone else we usually come across in our lives, *they* are the ones offering us the opportunity to cultivate patience now—and to be very good looking in the future. You may even like to think of them as your personal beauty therapists!"

"Much food for thought," Megan had been scanning the Flourish social media feed as more and more viewers around the country followed them. Although there'd been no forward planning, no build up to this broadcast, the volume of viewers was rapidly rising through the tens of thousands. And the number of questions filling her screen was unprecedented.

With a few key strokes, she clicked through to a screen showing feeds from all the major networks. She had to look twice. Channel 60 was streaming them. Live! Flying on their coat-tails! There was Lama Tashi center screen, the *Flourish* logo unmissable to the left of him. And as

Anton pulled back to include her, out the corner of her eye she noted the Channel 60 coverage do likewise.

At the same time it *felt* just like it did before. Rinpoche and she enjoying the warmth, the spontaneity of this time together, talking about things that mattered.

"I have a question from Amy in New York City," she said, reading from her screen. "This morning Amy donated money to a few homeless people. Soon afterwards, she got a major bonus from work. But another thing also happened. She was mugged. Amy wants to know, if only positive results come from positive causes, how come this happened?"

"A very good question," Lama Tashi nodded. "As I said, karma is complex. In any one moment we are not creating only one karmic cause, or experiencing only one karma to ripen. Each one of us has created limitless karmic causes, for both positive and negative effects, to ripen. All we need is for certain causes to meet with certain conditions and—" he snapped his fingers. "We experience the effects.

"Now what happens when the conditions are there for a negative effect to occur? Perhaps for something very damaging, even life-changing. But do something positive just before that karma ripens. Virtue has ten times the power of non-virtue. The impact of that virtuous act of generosity will be to lessen the experience of negative karma. We may still have a harmful experience, but reduced. More bearable. Something negative, yes, but perhaps a fraction as bad as what may have happened otherwise. Negative events cannot arise from positive causes. But they may be diminished by them."

Galaxy and a national, public broadcaster was, by now using the *Flourish* feed, Megan noted. Not that she had time to do anything but be aware of what was happening. Because the rapidly growing audience, not just from across the nation but from around the world, hungry for advice from Lama Tashi, was bombarding her with questions. A great many of them feeding on what he had just been saying.

"Lama Tashi, viewers are asking lots of questions about negative karma. What you've been saying about us having potentially created the causes for innumerable bad things to happen. This is worrying people. I'm getting lots of anxious questions here asking if we are condemned to experience the effects of things we may not even remember doing?"

Lama Tashi nodded, serious but compassionate. "It is useful to be aware of this negative potential. Ignorance doesn't serve us well. But the idea that karma is like fate and there is nothing we can do to stop it—this is a misunderstanding. As I was saying earlier, a positive action can greatly reduce our experience of a negative effect. Karma is dynamic. It's happening in our minds. Our minds are constantly active. So to answer your questions," he looked directly into the camera, "one of the most important things we can do with our precious, human lives is to purify our karma."

"Is there any practice you would recommend?" Megan knew exactly where he was going with this.

"Cultivate bodhichitta," said Lama Tashi. "Bodhichitta is, for the sake of others, the wish to attain enlightenment. Every one of us wishes to be permanently free from dissatisfaction and pain and to enjoy only enduring wellbeing. This is something we share with all sentient beings, human or non-human. Do you know what the number one cause of our unhappiness is?" he asked rhetorically.

Still looking directly into the camera, for everyone watching it was as if Lama Tashi was speaking to them personally. That way he had of reaching people out of their usual preoccupations. Surprising them with a recognition about themselves they would never have guessed at. They held onto his every word as he said, "We think too much about "me." "Myself." "I." How *I* have been hurt by others. Why it's unfair that *my* actions haven't been rewarded. All the problems facing *me*.

We have all these thoughts about our self, and instead of treating them as mere thoughts, we start to believe in them as facts. To buy into them as if they are true. We keep telling ourselves the same, often negative things until we create our own unhappy reality.

"Think of the times you've been at your unhappiest: who was the focus of your thoughts then? Was it not "me?"" He nodded, touching his heart. "Think of the times when you've really been able to help some other person, or perhaps maybe a pet or even a wild animal. How good did that feel here?" he was still touching his heart.

Lowering his voice to impart a special truth, there was something both self-evident as well as profoundly uplifting in the words he spoke. Made even more special by the knowledge that so many millions of people around the whole country were, at this very moment, being uplifted too.

"When we practice bodhichitta we deliberately train our minds to focus on the wellbeing of others. Not just their temporary happiness, but their permanent wellbeing and freedom. And not only some beings we happen to know, but *all* living beings—ourselves included, of course. By self-consciously thinking bigger, by deliberately widening the circle of our attention and compassion, we open our minds. We let in the light. We create the possibility of freedom.

"The truth is that when we focus our attention on helping others, we are also helping ourselves. The idea that their wellbeing is somehow separate from ours is like an illusion because we are all interconnected. When we learn to think this way, and loosen the grip of "self" versus "other" our actions are those of enlightened self-interest." He smiled. "We become wisely selfish."

Megan nodded thoughtfully absorbing this. "Bodhichitta is such powerful psychology," she observed. "But what makes it powerful in terms of karma?"

"The strength of karma is affected by several factors," said Lama Tashi. "Intention being one. There is no more powerful intention than wishing for the enlightenment of every living being. Have you ever come across a more ambitious idea? A more altruistic purpose?

"Object is another factor. There is no greater object than every sentient being in universal space. We are not focusing on only a few beings to whom we are partial. Bring these two factors together," he drew together his index finger and middle finger. "What you have is the most powerful karmic purifier ever conceived. The most powerful force to propel your own happiness, both now and in the future."

The number of viewers displayed on Megan's screen had grown so large that she could no longer, at a glance, take it in—it was just too long. But she did note that Lama Tashi's daring prediction had come true: *all* the national TV networks were now feeding off *Flourish*.

"In practical terms," she asked her teacher. "How should we practice bodhichitta?"

"Our main job is to make bodhichitta our normal way of thinking," he said. "We are trying to cultivate compassion for ourselves and for others as our default mode. So, when you wake up, train that the first thing you think is: "May my every action of body, speech, and mind today be a cause for me to become enlightened, so that I may help all other beings attain this same state." Much better," his eyes twinkled, "than, 'Another day, another dollar!'"

"Every time you do something nice for someone—make them a coffee or meal, open a packet of cat food, support and protect a life, recollect bodhichitta, "May this act of generosity be a cause for me to become enlightened, so that I may help all other beings attain this same state." Going to the toilet, having a shower, washing the dishes or the car—"may this act of purification, and so on." Every drink you have or meal you eat, "may this nourishment." We need to be mindful for opportunities. Keep recollecting."

"This may seem contrived to some people watching," said Megan. "Like you're trying to apply a motivation to something you would have done anyway."

"Artificial? To some extent when we begin. But this is subtle mind-training. Step by step we are learning a new way of thinking. A bigger outlook. We are self-consciously starting to broaden the way we think, which creates our reality. Keep on recollecting bodhichitta, day and night, and after a while it is no longer contrived. It is who we have become. No longer something we need to think about, but spontaneous and heartfelt. When compassion-based bodhichitta becomes our real motivator, we are propelled by the most powerful virtuous karma there is."

As always, with Lama Tashi, the truth of what he was saying was evidenced by his presence. For a few moments, around the world, everyone who was watching felt themselves to be the focus of his own panoramic benevolence. In a way they may have been unable to express, they discovered that whatever suffering they felt referred to a view of themselves that was hopelessly limited and fleeting. Lama Tashi had revealed a much deeper reality, as all-embracing as it was benevolent. And the confident expectation in his eyes, the warm reassurance that this was a state in which they could continue to abide, was so wholehearted, so unexpected, that many were moved to tears.

"Bodhichitta," Lama Tashi summarized. "Is the ultimate manifestation of our pure, great love and pure, great compassion. You might say it is our true nature."

41

The Piccard Hotel
Washington, D.C.

S OME SURVIVORS OF THE NGA SHOOTING BLAMED IT ON THE WAGYU beef. By contravening FDA orders to avoid meat, the lunch of dry-aged, marbled Texas steak had proved fatal, they declared. Others were quick to debunk that theory, saying the truth was a lot more prosaic: in all the turmoil earlier that morning, Mick Mackenzie had forgotten to take his meds.

Whatever the truth of the matter, after Police Chief Hans Ziegler had been briefed by his tenth eye-witness, and received his tenth, identical report, he had no doubt what had happened. It was just that he was struggling to believe it.

The pertinent events were as follows. The annual convention had been disrupted from the get go. Massive transport problems that morning had delegates running late. Instead of the scheduled 9 am start, it was closer to 10 am before they had a quorum.

There was the formal business to attend to. The re-election of seventy-five directors and confirmation of the NGA executive. Survivors described Mackenzie's mood as "tense." He insisted on running a tight ship. Keeping things on schedule. And that day, nothing was going to plan.

Much time had been taken up with a lengthy, unscheduled debate about whether meat should be served for lunch. Members who felt it important to stay within FDA guidelines were contested vigorously by those who believed that NGA members should be free to eat what they

231

damned well liked. Mackenzie tried to close the debate down. His ire had been provoked by references to karma. As a God-fearing nation, there was no place for subversive alien ideas he thundered, citing the President's own comments that morning.

But NGA delegates were an unruly bunch. They didn't like being told what to do or how to think. The dispute about meat continued along with protest references to karma. Mackenzie became visibly furious. Someone suggested a simple show of hands for a vegetarian option. A revised lunch order was sent to the kitchen. But the CEO was struggling to hold it together. And a curious thing starting happening to his face. His skin tone didn't simply deepen with anger. It broke out in what looked like blisters.

They raced to clear the agenda before the President's appearance at lunch. Motions were voted up, down or postponed at unprecedented pace. In the past, a pre-lunch highlight had always been the showcasing of a new firearm. Arms manufacturers around the world would do just about anything to have a new product shown at the NGA annual meeting. And Mackenzie had promised to play a video of today's semi-automatic rifle, one with a full twenty-five rounds per magazine, in exchange for a sum of money that significantly boosted NGA coffers. The weapon itself, decorated in real gold trim especially for the occasion, was mounted in pride of place on a black, velveteen podium beside him, having been scrutinized by the President's security team.

After a rushed meal, the President's appearance had been accompanied by the usual stately protocols. If President Grey had been aware of the harried undercurrents in the room before his arrival, or perturbed by the CEO's erupted countenance, he gave no sign of it during his pause-perfect presentation. Ending fifteen minutes later, he was granted the standing ovation befitting the patron saint of all those who lived and breathed their right to bear arms.

Mackenzie formally thanked him on behalf of the NGA. Responding to the applause that followed he confirmed, as per the script, that the President had no time for questions.

President Grey, taking in the abnormally boisterous gathering, and wanting to show willing, glanced at his watch before saying he'd be glad to take just one.

It had been a sallow-skinned delegate from California who had put it to him plainly, "Are today's unprecedented events the result of karma?"

President Grey never got to answer the question.

"Don't even say that word!" Mackenzie hadn't so much ordered, as screamed. "I forbid it!"

"It's alright, Mick," President Grey had projected his usual unperturbed persona.

But his words had been lost in the uproar as NGA members reacted angrily to their CEO. How dare he disrespect the President, or a delegate, they bawled! He had no right to forbid anything.

Something in Mackenzie snapped. A brain seizure. A red rage. Who could say? All that was for sure was how, face suppurating, he seized that day's glistening semi-automatic weapon from its velveteen podium, together with a magazine that he had concealed. With ease of practice he'd swiftly clipped the magazine into place and began firing.

There were disbelieving screams. The President's bodyguards tackled their boss to the floor. Their only purpose—to get him the hell out of here. More bursts of gunfire as the NGA boss skillfully mowed down his own directors. The NGA Treasurer standing nearby, a huge, former Delta Force man, made a run for him. Mackenzie downed him at close range. He swept in a wide arc—a bullet passing directly through a table and into the President's shoulder.

When Mackenzie ran out of rounds, he produced a second magazine. It was during this momentary hiatus that the President's security had rushed him out the door.

Mackenzie's demeanor all this time wasn't one of frenzied hysteria. More like he was in a trance. Even though most delegates were now under the tables, he was spraying gunfire on all who remained. The terror had only ended when a young waiter from Mexico, Juan Garcia, came up behind him, armed only with a steel serving tray. Forcefully striking him over his head, he felled him to the floor.

"The biggest mass-shooting in our history was carried out today by a lone shooter," Police Chief Hans Ziegler's statement was issued a short while later. "The Chief Executive Officer of the National Gun Association, Mick Mackenzie, killed 68 delegates at their annual conference this afternoon. He also shot and wounded the President. Mackenzie is currently in police custody."

Meanwhile the hero of the day, Juan Garcia, was nowhere to be found. Hotel staff had searched the building and tried calling on his phone. He had vanished without trace.

42

Wall Street, New York

AMY HAD TAKEN KAREL SHARMA'S ADVICE TO HEART.
Returning to her desk after her visit upstairs, she took out her phone and checked the bank balance: just over two thousand dollars in her account. Karel's extraordinary $80,000 "thank you" bonus would appear later. The money from Uncle Gerry would take another week. As of this moment, she didn't have much money to play with. But euphoric from the day's events, and having proven to herself that instant karma really was a thing, she was determined to make the most of it.

She wrote a list in her office notebook. She gave herself a donation budget of $1,500 until the bonus arrived. Her instinct was to make Bluegrass Horse Sanctuary the major beneficiary, not only because of all the time she'd spent growing up there, and the kindness Mr. Deal had shown her, but also because she knew that every dollar they received would be both valued and wisely spent. She knew how valuable Bluegrass was, not only as a safe haven for horses—but also for people. Before Equine Assisted Therapy had become more mainstream, Mr. Deal had instinctively understood what the ancient Greeks had also known—that for people who had difficulty communicating with other humans, looking after a horse could be amazing therapy. Several autistic kids and a number of Vietnam vets were regulars at Bluegrass and had had their lives turned around.

Within minutes, $1,000 was on its way to the sanctuary bank account, accompanied by a message to Mr. Deal. The other $500, Amy split between other worthy causes, including the one that had started her off on this whole journey—The Orangutan Project. There was also the Parkinson's charity that supported her Dad. And the care-givers who used to come to visit Uncle Gerry before he had to move into a home.

With each transfer, she made a point of reciting the motivation that Karel had received from a karma expert and written down for her: "May this generosity be a cause for me to attain enlightenment, for the sake of all living beings." For a moment she would pause, imagining every horse being as well cared for as those at Bluegrass, every orangutan roaming through the pristine forests far away from the devastation caused by palm oil planters. In her heart she had a special place for people like her Dad, who suffered from Parkinson's, and Uncle Gerry who, like the retired racehorses at Bluegrass, were so stoic in facing a future of physical decline from which there could be no return. Her compassion went out to them and all others like them.

She didn't have long to wait until an email came through from Akara Foon, one of the cryptocurrency traders who'd set up a staff fund to which she'd contributed $100 back in her first week of work. As a result of that day's trades, he was pleased to announce, her holding was now valued at $3,215.89. Would she like the cash, by transfer, or did she want to continue trading?

Better still was the email she got from Mr. Deal, who happened to be at his desk when her donation came through. He told her how moved he was by her kindness, and how much he valued her donation. Bluegrass was facing an uncertain future because their landlord had decided to sell, and it would be tough trying to find an equally large property for the same low rent. He and the folks at Bluegrass thought about her often, he said, and he was pretty sure that Flash did too. She could be sure they'd all give her a warm welcome whenever she returned home from the Big Apple.

Amy teared up, reading his words. For a while she sat staring at her screen, pressing her fingers into her cheeks, fighting the urge to sob. She couldn't help contrasting the struggles faced by Mr. Deal and Bluegrass Horse Sanctuary, with her own extraordinary windfalls today. Comparing her immense good fortune to be in the right place at the right time, with what might have happened if she'd made different choices or had been somewhere else.

She glanced around at her colleagues. Jaye on reception, filling in the time between calls playing Sudoku. Other accounting staff working away at their Excel spreadsheets, or in the kitchen taking a break.

She was struck by a sudden, imperative urge. She needed to see Karel Sharma. Rising from her desk, she walked down the corridor to the stairwell.

Upstairs, the Sharma Funds boss had overseen the most spectacular progress his firm had seen in all the years it had been trading—and within the space of just a few hours. The initial trial runs he'd directed with his top traders, "The Three Gekkos', had laid the groundwork for all that followed. Having shown spectacular results with Algobright Infrastructure fund, he had briefed every one of his traders to follow exactly the same model with every single client account.

Initially, ten percent of holdings were to be donated. With instant karma returns running at anything from 100 percent to 1,000 percent, once a client account was back at the total at which it had started the day, all funds in excess were to be gifted. And gifted again.

Using the same list of charities, the same motivation he had received from the lama, it hadn't been long before Sharma funds, both retail and wholesale, were up by hundreds, then thousands of percent.

Unless he'd been at his desk, presiding over the whole thing, he wouldn't have believed it possible. There was something fantastical about the way it was playing out. But following what was happening on the trading floor, as well as on the outside world through the newswires streaming through his desktop screens, when viewed through the prism of instant karma, all of it was totally predictable.

Of course giving was the direct cause of receiving. Of course those who saved the lives of others would have their own lives saved. Of course those who ignored the suffering they caused others, would suffer. Where else would the biggest mass shooting in the nation's history happen but among those who most vigorously demanded that they be free to shoot?

He'd viewed resistance to the new paradigm. The strident calls of the Reverend Bellow to reject ungodly beliefs. The pseudo-science of Stan

Smugg. The violent reaction of Mick Mackenzie. Confirmation bias. Plus a variety of other encumbrances, habits and beliefs. All that would soon go. How could they possibly hold in the face of experience?

In the meantime, while the rest of the world was coming to terms with the new reality, early adopters like him were making the most of it. In a single day, Sharma Funds had grown a hundredfold. His own net worth had risen even more. Even if he parked all his money in the bank at 3 percent and lived a life of prodigious excess, there was no way he was ever going to burn through all his cash. Which begged the question: what next?

There was a movement at his open door. Amy Robbins. He gestured for her to come in.

"Good results from your donations?" he queried.

She nodded, smiling. "And you?"

"Very."

"I have a suggestion."

"Shoot."

"What you said earlier about how there's no reason anyone shouldn't become a millionaire very quickly. I was thinking how lucky I am to know that. I kind of stumbled on something myself. I tried it out with those homeless people, like you know. But hearing you say it straight out like that, it made me realize what an amazing time of opportunity this is. Everyone should know!"

"Yes they should."

"A thousand candles can be lit from one without the original being diminished, isn't that so?"

"Sounds like Gandhi."

She nodded. "Why don't you start right here, at Sharma Funds?"

"The traders are all wise to it, by now," he returned. "I've never seen them look so happy. Winners are grinners."

"What about everyone else? All the people on the 25th floor. The admin people. The accountants. The support team."

He was nodding.

"And you should tell them," she met him in the eye.

She saw the apprehension on his face—and was reminded again of Bashful Byron.

"I'll send out a group message."

"It would be better if you tell them yourself. Hearing it is a lot different from reading it."

He was shaking his head. "I'm no good at that sort of thing. Public speaking."

"They're not the public. They're your staff!"

He twisted awkwardly in his chair. She knew that he agreed with her. That his staff deserved to be told.

"They respect what you say, Karel," she tried another tack. "You have an authority—it's your name on the building," she pointed upwards. "They think the world of you."

"They do?"

She detected a shift. "You're like this mysterious figure they hardly ever see" she wiggled her fingers, making him smile. "Nobody knows where you're from, or what you do, but somehow you make magic happen."

He chuckled.

"And now you have the chance to show them how to make magic happen for themselves. Come on!" Stepping to his desk, she reached out, took his hand, and tugged him to his feet.

Before today she wouldn't have dreamed of taking such liberties. But in their earlier conversations she felt she'd pretty much figured out Karel Sharma. He might be brilliant at making money, but when it came to people, there were certain things he wanted to do, but didn't, because he was shy. Like Bashful Byron, whose hand she had similarly once taken when he'd been sitting on the sidelines instead of joining the more gregarious kids on an outing to Holey Moley Mini Golf. Once he'd got there he'd had a wonderful time, bashfulness being no impediment to putting a ball with some precision.

And just as she'd been surprised how willing Byron was to be guided onto the bus once she'd taken his hand, Karel was obedience itself as she led him to his office door and into the corridor. They headed towards the stairs and she made small talk to keep his mind off the idea of public speaking.

She told him about her $1,500 budget and the donation she'd made to Bluegrass Horse Sanctuary. How quickly she'd got the email from Akara

Foon—and the grateful message from Mr. Deal. She told Karel about the challenges Mr. Deal was facing having to find a new home for the sanctuary, and how that made her feel about her own incredibly good fortune today. How important she believed it was for *everyone* to know about instant karma.

Despite the distraction, Karel Sharma was still uncertain. "I don't know about this," he said as they arrived in Reception.

"You're great at explaining things!" she enthused. "Like the way you told me about Confirmation Bias. A lightbulb went on when you said that. I'll stand right in front of you. Imagine you're talking only to me. Just be yourself."

Then as he hesitated, she told Jaye that Mr. Sharma was holding an impromptu staff briefing immediately and to summon everyone on the 25th Floor. Before walking to her desk and beckoning her nearby colleagues. So unusual was the event, that within minutes the lobby had filled with staff. Amy collected a sturdy plastic filing box from the stationery cupboard which she placed, upside down on the floor, to provide a platform.

Karel glanced at her with an intense, inscrutable expression, before stepping onto the box.

As she'd promised, she stood directly in front of him, just a few yards away, and gave him a warm smile and encouraging nod.

He began speaking, somewhat hesitantly at first, about the unusual patterns of behavior he'd noticed earlier that day. And a lot of weird stuff on TV. How he'd carried out some market testing, with the firm's most experienced traders to confirm what was going on.

Initially glancing to her for support, as he began describing what had happened it was as though he had lift-off. There were gasps as he told his team they should have no doubt about the phenomenon of instant karma—including how that applied to money. Employees of Sharma Funds knew their ultimate boss was not prone to exaggeration. Quite the opposite. They were absorbed as he said that there was no reason any of them couldn't become extremely rich, extremely quickly.

Karel Sharma picked up on the dynamics of the group and it boosted his confidence even more. Suddenly, everyone was seeing a different side to their boss—including Karel himself. He became positively ebullient as he gave them the specific instructions on how to maximize the impact of instant karma. He explained the power of the object—the causes to which they should donate. And the power of intention. He had them recite into their phones the precise wording of the bodhichitta motivation to be used.

As he stood there on the stationery box, holding his staff in the palm of his hand—and loving it—it was as though he was channeling a new energy, a fresh purpose. And when he finished there was a round of hearty applause, before he told everyone, "Go back to your desks now and make some money—for yourselves. Or go home if you like. It *is* Friday afternoon."

When he got down from the box, Amy beamed. "That was wonderful! *You* were wonderful!"

He smiled, shy once more, before heading to the stairs.

43

Pacific Seabird Rescue
Santa Monica

MADDIE HAD NO IDEA WHY HER FATHER WANTED HER TO SKIP physical therapy that day and go to Pacific Seabird Rescue. Jacinda told her he'd been insistent. For her own part, she could do with a change in routine. It felt like every day since the accident had turned into a grueling marathon of rehabilitation classes and exercise routines, PT appointments and response testing. Her medical team were always supportive but cautious. They referred frequently to managing her expectations. Yes, there was a chance that, with enormous effort and training, she may regain some control of her upper body—her hands and perhaps more movement in her arms. That, they told her, would be an outstanding result.

As for walking unsupported, or getting in or out of a chair –it just wasn't going to happen. Her brain wasn't able to communicate with muscles in the lower part of her body any more. No patient with an injury like hers had ever managed to stand up on their own. Best for her own peace of mind, doctors advised, to come to a place of acceptance that it wasn't ever going to happen. This was the new normal.

The volunteer coordinators had been surprised when they arrived, Jacinda pushing her in a wheelchair. But they needed all the hands they could get. And with the crazy things going on in the world today, trying to get the attention of volunteers was proving a challenge.

The two of them had been given training on how to hold a Western Gull, especially the importance of keeping them warm while washing so that they didn't go into shock. Then they were outfitted in rubber gloves, boots, protective overalls and goggles and led to the clean-up room. They'd soon taken their place among the grid of shallow sinks, Maddie on one side, Jacinda on the other. Tentatively at first, but with increasing confidence, they had begun to help with the clean-up.

Maddie had always been an animal lover. Seeing the poor birds unable to move, they were so congealed in thick oil, would have been heartbreaking if she'd been unable to help. But for the first time since the accident she felt useful. She was actively doing something to improve the life of another being.

Watching her patient closely, as she had since first starting to work for the Kavanas, Jacinda observed Maddie's heartfelt response to the sea birds, the outpouring of her natural compassion. She had never seen Maddie so purposeful. Even though she was relying on Jacinda to hold the gulls steady, it was she who was removing the black grease from their faces, beaks and wings, she who spoke to them tenderly all the while she was doing it.

It was intense work, but so rewarding, thought Maddie! To take a miserable, immobilized gull and return it to pristine, orange-beaked, clear-eyed beauty—what could be better than that? She saw herself in each one of them, of course. Her empathy was effortless. She knew how they felt.

So absorbed in what she was doing, for a while any idea of herself as volunteer and bird as sufferer seemed to dissolve. There was no self, no other, nor any boundaries between. Only cleaning, healing, making whole again. An awareness of what was happening in which time and self fell away.

Such was her focus that she didn't notice, at first, the change in her own movements. The increased flexibility in her own hands and wrists. How she was working with greater agility and confidence. When she stretched out her right arm, before folding it at the elbow, she shot a look of exhilarated surprise to where Jacinda was holding a gull.

They didn't speak then. Nor even, between birds, when she deliberately stretched both arms parallel, shooting out her fingers before balling them into fists, rolling them this way then that. Instead, the two continued cleaning and, an hour and a half after starting, Maddie felt a warmth in her shoulders as energy flowed into them. She elaborately rolled back her shoulders, as Jacinda watched her, beaming.

"Give and it will be given to you," Jacinda quoted from the Bible, eyes welling up. Standing, she leaned over the sink to hug Maddie.

Maddie was shaking her head. "Amazing!" she said. The improvement she'd just experienced was the equivalent of endless hours in rehab. It was a personal milestone she'd set herself for eighteen months down the line.

"You tired, honey?" asked Jacinda, seeing a group of volunteers head through swing doors to an office where snacks and drinks were being served.

"Only just getting started!" Maddie shook her head emphatically. "But let's do a video for Mom and Dad."

That had been the short clip Dan had received earlier.

Because they hadn't seen the news that day—like most TV executives, Dan enforced a strict TV ban in their house outside the media room—and hadn't spent any time on social media, Maddie and Jacinda had heard little about what was happening. Not that it mattered. The wonderful, unassailable truth was that the more Maddie helped free Western Gulls, the freer she became herself.

Half an hour later, she was able to turn on her chair, twisting her whole torso to each side. An hour later she felt a soft, electric tingling, like lightning strikes through her legs. These were followed by waves of heat, the first sensation she'd felt in her lower body since the crash.

She held her focus on the gulls. There were so many in need of help. And despite being in the middle of a miracle herself, she knew the only miracle for them would be delivered by her own hands, as well as the hands of other volunteers. No time to lose.

She and Jacinda were taking it in turns to hold the gulls and clean them. She was strong enough, now, to do either. As time went by, she began shifting on her seat. Feeling a faint but unmistakable twinge in her knees, her calves, her ankles.

Part of rehab was about stimulating the very muscles in her legs doctors had explained she would never be able to use again for walking, but which mustn't be allowed to waste away. She was beginning to feel them. Deliberately, she wiggled her toes in her boots, scarcely able to believe she

246 — David Michie

could sense what was happening. She tapped her heel on the floor. Under the sink she lifted and swung first one foot, then the other.

She did all of this without Jacinda knowing. All the while, they kept cleaning more gulls. Till eventually Jacinda said, "I don't know about you but I need a break. Just for a few minutes. Perhaps something to eat?"

"Okay." Maddie glanced round at where other volunteers were coming and going from their sinks.

Standing, Jacinda was about to step behind her wheelchair when Maddie held up her hand.

"Uh, uh! Want to try something," she said, pushing her chair away from the sink before locking it in place, lifting one foot to the floor then the other, and shifting her thighs to the edge of the seat, before grasping the arms of the chair in each hand and pushing herself upwards.

She didn't quite have the strength. But she raised herself off the chair, momentarily, before falling back again. The second time, she let Jacinda help her.

Other volunteers, knowing nothing of Maddie's circumstances, may have wondered why both women were smiling through tears as they stood, holding each other, wordless at the unfolding miracle.

"Standing," sobbed Maddie.

"You are!" affirmed Jacinda, both knowing that what she'd just done was medically impossible.

"Next time, I'll do it on my own!"

3:00 pm (Eastern Standard Time)
1:00 pm (Mountain Standard Time)
12 noon (Pacific Standard Time)

44

The Pentagon
Washington, D.C.

G ENERAL ALEXANDER HICKMAN HAD BEEN FOLLOWING THE DAY'S unfolding events with growing incredulity and concern. From all the intel coming into his office that day he was now certain that in some dramatic way he had yet to define, the rules of engagement had changed. The words of Sun Tzu, from The Art of War, chimed clarion-like in his mind: "If both ignorant of yourself and your enemy, you are in peril."

Throughout the day he'd been struggling to make sense of a torrent of divergent news. Peace keeping troops winning the hearts and minds of groups who had, hitherto, been sworn enemies. Routine patrols in occupied territories being ambushed, resulting in serious injuries. Everything was heightened, disproportionate, inconsistent.

Meantime at home his Commander in Chief was in hospital, undergoing surgery. The nation has just endured its worst mass shooting. Transport networks were frozen. The public was paralyzed by food contagion fears. This was precisely the moment when America's enemies would strike.

At the back of the General's mind was one of the earliest conversations he'd had that day with his old friend, Tom Jackson. "I was told it's a day when the impact of taking action would be powerful. Instant. Unexpected." Whoever Tom's mysterious advisor was, thought General Hickman, his were the only words making sense.

Or perhaps not the only one. Like anyone else following the news, the

General had seen Lama Tashi being interviewed. The man had a mesmerizing presence, no doubting it. There was something about him that made you want to stop everything and give him your undivided attention.

General Hickman wouldn't pretend to understand the full workings of karma. But he'd heard enough to absorb some of the key principles. And he recognized that, while the disparate intelligence he was having to grapple with was bewildering on an ordinary level, when viewed through the framework of karma it made a certain sense. In fact, it could hardly be more predictable. Attack a target, any target, and you come off second best. Give aid, assistance, relief, and the world is yours.

But what US Army General was going to come out and say that the age of war was over? That all forms of aggression would instantly be rendered counter-productive? That the military should be deployed only to support relief missions and peacekeeping activities?

Those were the implications of karma, as General Hickman understood them. And if they were so he, for one, could not be more pleased. He'd seen enough of martial conflict to despise it. He'd attended enough funerals, like those of Major General Greg Travis, to know that for many years after battles were waged on the ground, the war continued in the minds of those who fought in them. He understood the ravages of military intervention like few others and how rarely, if ever, it brought about enduring peace.

But if it was true that instant karma had come into play today, he had a very serious concern. And he could think of only one person who could help.

45

Omni, Colorado

O*PEN MINDED.* THE PHRASE HAD BEEN RUNNING THROUGH BOB Martin's thoughts in the hours since Beth proposed his visit that afternoon.

The past few weeks of their sexual escapades had already been any-thing-goes, so far as he was concerned. He'd never been with a woman so unfeigned in expressing her desire, so intensely curious about his every sexual predilection and so willing to explore it—the more whacko the better. What, exactly, was *open minded* going to entail?

His ascent up the stairs to her apartment was even brisker than usual. He was aroused before he'd even knocked on the door. It opened wide enough for him to step through. Inside, behind it, she was naked and waiting.

It wasn't the first time this had happened. Words were unnecessary. There was no pretense what this was about. No wish to distract from the single-minded pursuit of gratification. As he shed his jacket and undid the buttons of his shirt, she was tugging his belt until she'd freed the buckle. She pulled off his shoes and socks and was dragging his pants down his legs. Soon, he was naked too.

In his stripped state he sensed that something was different. Not about her appearance, nor the apartment—as chaotic as ever—nor how she'd drawn the curtains close enough to cast the living room in semi-shadow. It was some other shift he couldn't place, something signaled—he realized only afterwards—by her expression as she glanced down with an ironic

251

detachment. A transmutation in the way she led him towards the thick-pile shag rug in the middle of the room and gestured that he get down on it first. Not so much in eager anticipation, as had been the case in the past. But more like an emcee at a show introducing the support act, while the source of true delirium waited in the wings.

She stood astride him and he looked up, taking in her firm, voluptuous figure. Despite the whisper of intuition that things were somehow awry, he craved her more than anything. All he wanted was for her to lower herself down towards him. For their bodies to meet.

When Ian Turner stepped into his shop, the assistant behind the cash register instantly recognized him.

"Mr. Turner!" Sally Seddon smiled broadly. "We weren't expecting you."

The Turner and Seddon families went way back, and Ian had known Sally since she was a baby. He thought of her as a good kid, even though she was a mother herself now.

"I must be going senile," Ian used a line he had prepared earlier. "I didn't copy some tax file details from the laptop when I moved to Arizona, and now the bank is asking for them. It will only take a couple of minutes."

"Haven't seen the laptop today," Sally was glancing under the counter to confirm. "Beth sometimes takes it upstairs to do internet stuff."

Ian nodded. "D'you know if she's in," he pointed upwards.

Sally shrugged. "I'm sure she won't mind you visiting."

"Thank you Sally. And how's the family?"

As Ian and Sally exchanged news, upstairs Bob was having his most immediate wish fulfilled as Beth enveloped him. But even in this intimacy there was an evasiveness about her. She seemed to be goading him at the same time as being, in some uncertain way, removed.

Until she leaned down to murmur in his ear, "Are you ready for fantasy, Endless Love?"

"Uh-huh," he grunted, wondering what came next.

She arched back up before turning, "Come in Hot Rod!" she beckoned over her shoulder.

Out of the bedroom stepped a young man, naked except for a towel around his waist. Shocked by this unwelcome and disagreeable development, even in that first glance Bob recognized the boy from somewhere. It took him a few moments to place him as the plumber's apprentice.

The summer before, Bob had arranged the garden taps to be moved, and in the heat of the day he had taken out a tray of cold water for the workers. At the time he had noted how the apprentice, stripped to the waist, had a fine, ripped physique. Later, Margarita had told him the boy was Rodney Turner, Ian's nephew.

"No need to be shy." Straddling Bob, Beth had Endless Love exactly where she wanted. "Lose the towel!"

He could have forced her off him, Bob thought later. As soon as Rod Turner made his unwanted appearance, he should have shoved her away. He didn't even try because as she was turned, looking at the boy, he was experiencing an epiphany. About the undercurrents that day, of course— but much bigger than that, about his whole relationship with Beth. Or rather, hers with him. Because the expression on her face, as she gazed upon the young man, was one he had never seen before. It was a look of such ardent desire. Of untrammeled adoration. Of an affinity he knew she'd never come close to feeling for him, nor ever would.

In that moment, all of his ideas about taking her away from all this, of the two of them setting up home in New York or San Francisco, were exposed for the absurd fantasies they evidently had been—make-believe that had no basis in reality.

What did he have to offer Beth compared to a young man her own age with a body like that, and a self-evident connection? How could he have ever imagined he was anything more than a passing fancy, a plaything to such a sexually voracious woman?

If he'd known about the young man, he would never have made his way up the steps to her apartment today—as, in fact, Ian Turner was doing right now. Bob found the whole idea of a threesome with another man perverse and degrading. He had no wish to take things any further. He probably wasn't even capable.

Rod Turner took the towel from around his waist and tossed it over the back of the sofa. As he stepped in their direction, Beth reached out, drawing him to her.

There was a knocking at the door—three, sharp raps.

Both men looked at her.

She raised a finger to her lips. "Wait for them to go!" she whispered.

The three formed a surreal tableau on the shag rug, aroused and watchful.

More door knocking. Then, unexpectedly, the turning of key in lock. Ian Turner stepped into his former home. He took in the scenario at a single glance.

"Sorry to interrupt," he was looking around, before his gaze fell on the laptop, wedged on the kitchen table between a stack of used plates and a large Vaseline dispenser. "Just need to borrow this," he seized the laptop before stepping back.

"Things looking up for you, Rod," he observed, before closing the door behind him.

"Well, that's just wonderful!" exclaimed Beth bitterly, getting off Bob and storming to her bedroom.

"What's going on?" Rod wanted to know.

"I'm busted! That's what!"

Bob scrambled to his feet and was quickly dressing.

"Busted? How?" Rod began to flag.

"Your uncle is going to find all the Venus Goddess stuff, isn't he? He's going to throw me out."

Disappointed, Rod pointed towards his genitals, "Aren't you going to ..?"

"Can't, honey." She was donning her panties. "Not now."

Bob, recognizing he was completely out of his depth, stopped in the bedroom door. "I didn't want this," he said.

"Me neither."

"Any of it," he gestured towards Rod.

"That's the thing about storylines," Beth didn't even look at him as she clicked the bra-strap behind her back. "They end up in places you never imagined."

46

Food & Drug Administration
White Oak, Maryland

T HE FDA COMMISSIONER WHO SHOWED UP IN THE MEDIA BRIEFING
Room was a very different person from the wooden performer who
had made his earlier, reluctant appearance. And despite the fact that, in
the intervening hours, President Grey had been shot and the United States
had just endured its worst mass shooting ever, there was still a pack of
vociferous journalists, right there, in the FDA media room. Demanding
an answer to one simple but far-reaching question: was the nation in the
grip of a contagious disease? And there was only one man who could
credibly answer it.

Commissioner Saul Applebaum was free from doubt now. Already
emboldened as recipient of the President's Medal, the newsflash he'd
just caught in in his office before coming here only confirmed it all.
Investigations by Police Chief Hans Ziegler at The Picard Hotel had determined that the man who had brought the horror to an end by knocking
out "Mad" Mick Mackenzie, advocate of the shoot-to-kill policy on illegal
immigrants, was himself an illegal immigrant. It was the kind of thing
you couldn't make up.

He strode to the lectern, unfazed by the mob of agitated reporters
before him. He didn't have his reading glasses with him, nor even a statement to read. His Chief of Staff, Ms. Chase, had no idea what the nation's
most foolish genius was about to say. Since the WHO teleconference she
had given up trying to influence her boss. Instead, she stood at the side

of the room, holding his phone and trying to conceal her discomfiture beneath a blank expression. She now regarded it as inevitable that the two of them would be fired by close of business.

"I am sorry for the delay it has taken before making this announcement," Applebaum cut straight to the chase, as the room fell silent. "My job is to advise on the food safety of our nation. I'd rather err on the side of caution than get things wrong."

Flash lights were whirring all the while, one by one, the major networks began streaming him live.

"Our scientists have undertaken comprehensive testing of samples from people affected by food poisoning and from the entire food supply chain. We have conferred with peers in other countries, who are experiencing the same phenomenon, under the auspices of the World Health Organization in Geneva."

Applebaum paused, surveying the packed rows of seats before saying, "The findings of multiple diagnostic teams around the world is unanimous: this is *not* a contagion. We have identified no bacterial or viral cause for the food poisoning. There have been no reported cases of human-to-human or animal-to-human transmission. Accordingly, we are advising transport authorities, and public and private organizations, that it is safe to return to business as usual."

"So it's okay to eat meat, again?" a Channel 60 reporter shouted.

"No." Applebaum's expression was stern. "People must remain on a plant-based diet."

For a while there was an eerie and unprecedented silence from the media crews as they absorbed what he had just said. Until they erupted with questions, demands, repudiations.

Holding up his hands for silence, and bowing his head, Applebaum waited for the furor to die down before he pointed to the Galaxy TV reporter. Her question captured the volley that had just been launched. "Are you saying, Commissioner," she chose her words deliberately. "That you have no idea what's causing the food poisoning?"

"I'm saying," the Commissioner knew exactly the game she was playing. "That there is no *scientific* explanation for the food poisoning." Then amid a tumult of further questions, "The FDA is responsible for food safety. I can reconfirm that meat products are no longer safe to eat. I am also saying that our scientists can find no *biological* basis for this danger. But that doesn't detract from the fact that it is a danger, and people should follow FDA advice."

"If there's no scientific explanation—" called out a network journalist, "what explanation *can* you offer?"

"I am a medical doctor, scientifically-trained," said Applebaum.

At the side of the room, it was all Ms. Chase could do not to cringe.

"As FDA Commissioner, my job is to advise the public on evidenced-based findings. As I have already said, there is currently no empirical evidence to explain what we are experiencing.

"Quite apart from being FDA Commissioner, I closely watch intensive animal farming. I find the practices profoundly disturbing from the perspectives of both ethics as well as climate change."

Something about Saul Applebaum had shifted, reflecting the fact that he was no longer addressing them as a senior bureaucrat only, but as a fellow human, albeit one with a particularly large and shiny head. It was a subtle transition and, far from detracting from his credibility, seemed only to add to it. Here he was revealing, at some personal risk, what he believed. And was his Chief of Staff imagining it, or had the mood in the room somehow changed?

"Can we continue to escalate the levels of pain, suffering and death we inflict on so many animals, at every moment, in our relentless craving for meat, without there being any consequences? The vastly disproportionate amounts of land and water required for meat production? Will we forever remain insulated from the rising levels of methane produced by the process? Or at some point will the cost of this have to be paid?"

Although he didn't know it, Commissioner Applebaum was being broadcast live on all the major networks, his words corresponding persuasively with what Lama Tashi had been saying earlier.

"You're saying that this is some kind of retribution of nature?" the science writer from one of the broadsheets wanted to know.

"Speaking personally," Applebaum looked at him directly. "I'm saying that, today, the rules have changed. If you don't want to be hurt, don't cause others to be hurt." There was surprising stillness in the room while the media pack absorbed this. "In a way it's really quite simple." Raising both hands, palms up, he shrugged. "It's karma."

Applebaum needed no guiding hand from Chief of Staff Chase to leave the lectern. At the moment of peak impact, he turned and left the room. The media scrum flared up with dozens of questions, which the Commissioner calmly shrugged off.

"So, there you have it, Ms. Chase," he remarked as they returned down the corridor. "I guess the karma line is what they'll run with."

"I guess it is," she agreed.

"Outside my brief, maybe—"

"But authentic," she said. "They were listening in there."

"You think?" For a fraction of a second, his eyes met hers.

"Definitely."

In his office, he crossed to the filing cabinet behind his desk. "What d'you think, Miguel?" he said, taking in the strange, pink creature who stared back at him.

It was a few moments before they were both aware of a presence. A man was standing, motionless and silent, on the other side of the Commissioner's office. Looking like he'd stepped out of the American Gothic painting, missing only his pitchfork, he was a bleak, balding figure with round, steel-rimmed spectacles, a white collarless shirt and dark jacket.

"You're destroying our livelihoods," his voice was flat.

"How did you get in?" Ms. Chase demanded. Access to the executive floor was strictly card-controlled, with CCTV cameras and security guards a visible presence.

Commissioner Applebaum held his hand up to her while replying to the man, "*I'm* not destroying anything, sir," he said. "It's my job to make sure that Americans are safe. Would you rather I allow people to fall sick?"

The intruder said nothing, responding by lifting his right hand from his jacket pocket. He was holding a revolver, which he pointed directly at Applebaum.

Ms. Chase wanted to scream, but was frozen in shock.

"That will not be a solution," the Commissioner spoke calmly. "So put it down. We have a situation of very rapid karma today. If you try to shoot me, you'll be shot yourself."

"Better than starving to death," replied the other, hands trembling as he gripped the revolver more strongly. He squeezed the trigger. Such was the force of discharge that his hand jolted upwards and he fired over Applebaum's head. In that same, surreal time frame, there was a second shot from the door and the intruder fell to the floor, blood appearing from his shoulder. Two security guards came running in.

The Commissioner turned to his Chief of Staff, gesturing one of the chairs opposite his desk. "Please, sit down, Ms. Chase. You may be in shock."

She did as she was told, all the while staring at her medal-winning, geek of a boss who had remained so calm under fire.

The guards were calling into their radios speculating urgently about how the intruder could have got in.

Applebaum glanced at his computer, quickly drawn back into a cerebral world evidently much more compelling than his immediate circumstances. As the security men picked the man up and began dragging him towards the door, Applebaum turned to his Chief of Staff with an expression of imperative urgency—struck by a flash of insightful lightning. "There's someone I need to speak to," he said.

"Need to speak to," she repeated, still shaken.

"Lama Tashi," he nodded. "From TV."

"Okay."

"It's critical. Can you get hold of him for me?"

47

Galaxy Television
Galaxy City, Los Angeles

T HE REACTION TO COMMISSIONER APPLEBAUM'S KARMA EXPLANA-
tion was instant and vehement. The Reverend Jeremiah Bellow immediately called Galaxy TV demanding airtime to denounce Applebaum's
blasphemous suggestion. *Tongues of Praise* was an important client of
Galaxy, he thundered. Give him a news platform or he'd take his advertising dollars elsewhere.

Commissioner Applebaum was the first senior public servant to use
the "k" word. What's more he was a respected scientist—and the most
recent recipient of the National Medal of Science. It was one thing for a
gazillion social media users to throw around the idea. Or a Tibetan lama.
But when the word came from the lips of someone like Commissioner
Applebaum it had the official ring of endorsement. It was like throwing
fuel on a conflagration already raging out of control.

The Galaxy newsroom had never been so frenzied, one monumental
news event being so rapidly followed by another. Nick Nalder was relieved
he'd called in his ultimate boss because he'd have had to run major decisions by him anyway. And right now, Harvey O'Sullivan was firmly back
in the driver's seat—and in his element.

It had been Harvey who'd taken the decision to live stream the output
from *Flourish* when Lama Tashi did his Qs and As. Just like it had been
Harvey who'd followed through on the lama's advice and had thirty-
second promotions shot for Galaxy's main competitors. He'd had Dan

Kavana look into a camera and speak stirringly about the respect he had for Channel 60 anchor Bart Bracking. Reporter Kim Dayton recorded a poignant, front-line piece about the acclaim with which her NBC rival was held by other reporters. These, and others like them, had gone to air and in a matter of minutes, were taking effect. Ratings man Trent Garvey kept doubling back to where Harvey now held court in the newsroom with the latest record-busting figures showing how more and more people were switching onto Galaxy.

"What I'm getting," he explained. "Is that people out there believe we've turned into some kind of news aggregator. Like, if they watch Galaxy, they'll get the best of *all* the channels."

"What did I tell you!" cheered Harvey. "That Lama Tashi guy knows what's going on. The only one around here who does!"

Told by Nick Nalder of demands for air time from Jeremiah Bellow and, soon after, Marvin Swankler, Harvey's response was immediate, "Sure! We support freedom of speech. Get them on." A devilish glint appeared in his eyes, "Only, let's have some fun with it."

"Invite Lama Tashi too?" Nick Nalder guessed his boss's train of thought. "Another head to head?"

"Lama v. the Religious Right!" chortled Harvey. "Too confrontational. Let's bill it a panel discussion."

"I'll see if the lama's willing." Nalder stepped away, sending a message to Megan Mitchell, before leaving the newsroom to attend to the call of nature.

It was while washing his hands afterwards that he looked in the mirror and saw the mole. He had felt it, of course, during the helter-skelter morning. A burning sensation as if it was expanding during his argument with Tracey Kramer. He'd even put his hand up and felt it seem to grow—but he'd instantly dismissed that idea. Skin moles didn't grow. Not at that rate. He hadn't given the matter any further thought. There hadn't been time. Although the teasing comments Harvey had made about his face had made him wonder, for a few moments.

Facing himself in the mirror, now, there could be no denying what had happened. In a flash he was reminded what Lama Tashi had said about anger being the karmic cause of ugliness—and its opponent, patience, being the cause of beauty. There was no doubting—the once modest mole, hitherto nothing more than a minor feature on his middle-aged countenance, had swelled and engorged, becoming an unsightly blemish. Alarmed, he moved his face closer to the mirror, confirming his worst fears.

What was to be done? Today of all days he was needed at Galaxy. He didn't have time to consult with doctors or dermatologists and besides, the world out there had gone crazy. Any non-urgent medical appointments would have to wait for another day.

As he stepped out of the bathroom he felt unusually self-conscious. Reaching up, he touched the mole with his fingertips. And who should he almost collide with, emerging from the female bathroom, but the vexatious Tracey Kramer.

She instantly surmised what was going on with him. As she so often did. "It got bigger when you were ranting at me," she nodded towards his raised hand.

His heckles rose instantly. But instead of slamming back the ball, he remembered the angry karma thing and held off. He regarded her evenly. As he did, he felt his cheek spasm.

She raised her eyebrows as she observed the twitch. "If the lama is right, I could make it go away completely."

"How so?" He couldn't place her tone.

"I could be your Precious Treasure," she goaded. "I could be wrathful and you'd have to practice patience. For your own good looks."

"You'd love that."

She shrugged. "It would have to be reciprocal."

He remembered that earlier session they'd streamed of Lama Tashi. How he'd said it didn't matter whether or not you believed in karma. You only had to be open-minded enough to give it a try.

"A girl can always use some beauty treatment."

They were approaching the newsroom.

"Okay," he agreed.

"When?"

"Right now," he paused at the B Studio door. "In here."

It was a much smaller studio than the main one. Just a camera facing a desk and no glass wall into the newsroom.

"You first," he directed, propping himself against the desk.

She rubbed her palms together. "In the spirit of being your Precious Treasure," she declared. "You have to be the most arrogant shithead I've ever had the misfortune to work for."

Nalder stood, hands by his sides, unresponsive.

"The way you order everyone about, even your most senior journalists, people who are paid, like, three, four times what you earn. I mean, if anyone out there knew what went on in here, they wouldn't believe it."

Nalder had to strain every sinew not to react to the abuse from the upstart. As she well knew. He had fired subordinates for saying less. It hurt—by God! Which, he supposed, was the point. Instead of reacting in anger, he took a deep breath in.

Tracey Kramer, for her part, hammed it up with relish. Was there a kernel of truth to her accusations? Of course—they had to sting. But she wasn't blustering in anger. She was being wrathful. And as she saw Nalder wince, she knew she was hitting her target.

"More!" he demanded.

Little did the two of them realize, but an automatic trigger from the Studio B camera was already streaming the two of them onto a newsroom screen, attracting the growing interest of their colleagues.

"You're such a right-wing bigot you don't even realize how offensive you are. Journalists are supposed to be curious. Open. You're so narrow minded—I mean look how you reacted this morning even to the suggestion of karma."

Nalder had to grind his teeth to keep his mouth shut. All the while his cheek twitched uncontrollably.

"It was only because Harvey was here that we ever got to see Lama Tashi. And now look where we are with ratings!"

Nalder's hand shot to his cheek to hold it, so violently was it spasming.

"As for misogyny—you treat women like we only exist to do your bidding. Why is it always me, or Julieta or Chieko who have to make the coffee run, and never Guido or Drew? What's it about having a dick that lets you off clearing away the Boardroom?"

So dramatic was the wincing, Nalder was bending double.

Tracey reached into her handbag, drawing out a compact mirror. When he straightened again, she held it out to him. The mole had retreated, back to its usual size, observed Nalder. Maybe smaller. There was a youthful clarity about his eyes. His face seemed somehow less crumpled.

"Shit!" With both hands, he gestured that she should deliver more abuse.

She shook her head.

"Just one more minute."

"My turn," she insisted.

"That's just typical of an entitled millennial," he found himself, curiously, having to manufacture outrage now that he had permission to let her have it with both barrels. "Sauntering in here at nine am every morning, sipping your chai fucking latte, when all of us have been working like dogs since 7:30."

Tracey's eyes widened. Working hours were set out clearly in her contract. In normal circumstances she would have put him straight on work: life balance.

But she'd never been happy with the coarseness of her skin. Blue eyes that were set just a little too wide for her to be really attractive. Her disappearing chin.

"Think you're so "Woke" and "Politically Correct," he affected a sneer. "With all the phrases you use and games you play to make out that you're so damned inclusive and morally superior. Meantime, you mouth off about anyone who's male or a Baby Boomer, like it's open season, like there are certain groups of people it's impossible to be prejudicial about. You're such a hypocrite and the fact you can't even see it would be laughable if it wasn't so goddamn offensive."

It took every ounce of willpower for Tracey to hold her tongue. Cheeks reddening, a curious almost grinding sensation going on in her face, she had never in her life accepted such harsh censure in silence.

"As for wanting to be CEO next week, give me a break! You'd hardly got through probation and you were looking for promotion and a pay rise. You sit there pontificating on this and that, meantime the rest of us in the room have done everything you've suggested—and much smarter, by the way—as you would find out if you just shut the fuck up instead of demanding the right to 'express' yourself."

Like Nalder, Tracey was being physically affected by the verbal tirade. It wasn't pain so much as a curious, preternatural realignment going on that made her raise her hands to her flushed features. And, a short while later, holding her compact mirror to her face to discover her eyes subtly closer than they were before. Her skin somehow finer. She angled herself to check on her profile with an expression of glee.

"We'd better go back in," Nalder jerked his thumb in the direction of the newsroom.

"Just one more insult!" she pleaded.

He paused for a moment before saying, "That frumpy dress last Friday—who did you come as?" He hadn't really disliked the dress. But he knew she'd been pleased with the outfit. He gestured she must reciprocate.

"No one ever suggested you bring anti-perspirant into the office?" she eyeballed him with faux incredulity. "By four pm the B.O. around here is like, whoo!" She pinched her nose theatrically.

"Still living at home in your thirties?" he taunted.

"Still single, Mr. Charmer. How could that be?"

She held up the mirror again and this time he wanted to see too, pushing his head against hers so they could both see the effect.

"Nice work!" observed Nalder.

"Any verbal abuse—I'm up for!" she said.

The invited belligerence between the two had somehow changed the dynamic between them. There was something deliriously cathartic about being able to vent—and even accept—the most exaggerated spite conceivable—and for the consequences to be so entirely pleasing.

When they returned to the newsroom, moments later, they were greeted with a smattering of applause from colleagues. Looking at the wall, they saw the Studio B screen on.

"If only all my staff could be so forthright and mature in airing their grievances," commented Harvey. "I could fire half of Human Resources."

A short while later, Nalder got a message from Megan Mitchell. "Lama Tashi will do a panel discussion," he reported back to Harvey. "But he wants it to be broader than just him and a couple of evangelicals."

"Catholics?" queried Harvey. "Episcopalians?"

"A neuro-psychologist," Nalder read off his phone. "And a quantum physicist."

"Don't know where he's going with this," Harvey looked puzzled. "But make it happen."

48

IN THE SECURELY-PROTECTED PRIVATE WARD, PRESIDENT GREY'S EYES flickered open for a moment. Facing him, a TV was tuned to his favorite channel.

"I'm saying that, today, the rules of the game changed," FDA Commissioner Applebaum was up on the screen. "If you don't want to be hurt, don't cause others to be hurt. In a way it's really quite simple." Raising both hands, palms up, he shrugged. "It's karma."

"sright," the President seemed to mumble.

Standing next to him, Chief of Staff Salt was the first to respond to his boss.

"Are you back with us, Mr. President?" he asked.

"Mouse."

"Oh honey!" First Lady Lucy Grey, on a visitor's chair next to the bed, leaped up to kiss him on the cheek as he blinked again. "We've been so worried!"

"Wazza .... mouse," his voice came from a thousand miles away.

"No, not the White House," she told him. "You're in hospital."

It was taking a while for the President to compute where he was and what was happening. He glanced from his wife, to his Chief of Staff, to the nurse at the foot of his bed. The secret servicemen guarding the door.

"Do you remember what happened?" she asked.

They had been warned that his short term memory may be fuzzy. In some trauma cases, staff said, people couldn't remember anything about what had happened at all.

"That maniac Mackenzie shot me."

Tears welled in the First Lady's eyes and she reached over, brushing his face with her right hand. "He did, my darling" she nodded. "The bullet went in, just under your left shoulder. But no broken bones and no vital organs damaged. Thank heavens for your bodyguards! They saved your life."

"How many killed?" He was recollecting those terrifying moments, pinned to the carpet of the Grand Ballroom while Mackenzie ran amuck.

"More than sixty," Salt was somber. "We're still waiting for the final count. There were a lot of serious injuries. At least a dozen NGA delegates are on life support."

President Grey closed his eyes heavily. "Worst ever mass shooting," he confirmed. "What happened to Mackenzie?"

"Knocked unconscious by a waiter with a serving tray. Juan Garcia. Turns out he was an illegal immigrant. He's disappeared."

"Poetic justice," President Gray grunted.

"That's what folks are saying."

After a pause he continued. "When they find Garcia, I want to meet him. Thank him personally. Find a way to make him legal."

"I'll make sure of it, sir."

"Darling, you should know that Jane Nelson is Acting President," the First Lady told him. "Take as long as you need to rest."

"Uh-huh." President Grey was absorbing all this. Usually he was the very first to assess any given situation, how it had come about and the political implications that followed. Coming out of anesthesia, however, everything had slowed right down. He was processing things step by step.

The First Lady turned to confer with the nurse at the foot of the President's bed.

"Was that the FDA guy on TV?" asked President Grey.

"Yes, sir," replied his Chief of Staff. "He's confirmed there's no contagion. Transport networks are starting up again. Public buildings can open. But no meat products."

It was a moment before the President murmured, "Karma?"

"That's what the Commissioner said."

"Remember what we were talking about in the car?"

"I do, sir. And your decision to award Commissioner Applebaum the National Medal of Science. Which happened immediately."

"How d'you reckon my ratings are doing right now?" President Grey smiled grimly.

"All time high," replied Salt.

They both knew that nothing like an assassination attempt caused the people of the United States to rally around their President. If an election was to be held right now, he'd romp to victory with the widest margin ever.

"So it's true. We're now in instant karma," mused the President. "Not that I could ever say it. I'd lose the support of the religious right."

"If we really are in instant karma, Mr. President, you won't need their support. Or anyone else's. In this environment, the way to win approval is by giving it to others who are worthy of approval—like you did with Commissioner Applebaum."

President Grey's eyes opened fully for the first time, and he lifted his head off the pillow as a thought struck him. "By God, you're right!" he said.

The nurse left the room to fetch his surgeon. First Lady, Lucy Grey, returned to his side. He lifted his right arm from under the sheet to take her hand in his. "Imagine, Lucy, if I didn't have to indulge those bastards at the NGA. Going on about civil liberties the whole time, when they're just gun-crazy. We could put in controls. Bring mass shootings to a halt."

His wife smiled indulgently.

"I wouldn't have to suck up to psychos like Bellow and Swankler. Imagine if I could wake up every day and just do what I thought was right for America."

The First Lady was massaging his left arm as she met Will Salt's gaze. "You've just had a lot of anesthetic, darling," she spoke tenderly. "Let's wait for it to wear off."

"I want a full briefing on karma," the President glanced at his Chief of Staff. "Everything about how it works."

The door to the ward opened and the President's surgeon appeared, accompanied by two nurses and a doctor. The surgeon was a tall, young man with a professional demeanor.

"Great to see you awake, sir!" he approached the President.

President Grey nodded distractedly. Still contemplating karma, he was struck by a sudden and powerful thought. "Lama Tashi—he's the guy you mentioned?" his eyes bore into his Chief of Staff's.

Will Salt nodded.

"Get hold of him! There's something I need to know!"

4:00 pm (Eastern Standard Time)
2:00 pm (Mountain Standard Time)
1:00 pm (Pacific Standard Time)

49

Omni Motor Lodge
Omni, Colorado

B OB RETURNED TO HIS MOTEL ROOM IN A STATE OF SHOCK. HUMBLED to discover how completely he had misjudged his relationship with Beth. Not only had his fantasies about them setting up home in New York or Los Angeles been confections with no basis in reality. She didn't even like him. He'd left his wife of twenty-four years this morning for a woman who couldn't even bring herself to look him in the eye when he left her apartment.

What's more it had been mortifying to be discovered in such sordid circumstances by Ian Turner, a man who had been such an established part of his and Margarita's social circle. Someone for whom he felt genuine warmth and respect. He recollected the expression on his face. The unfailing, dry humor on observing his naked nephew.

Exactly how he could emerge from any of this was too overwhelming to contemplate. Besides, he had a very much more terrifying concern. Something that had only become evident after Ian's departure when Beth made her comments about Venus Goddess, being busted, and storylines. Bob had never been the most imaginative of people but he was no fool either. All the time he'd scrambled into his clothes and driven to Omni Motor Lodge he wondered how he could have been so damned foolish.

In his room, waiting impatiently for his laptop to fire up, he couldn't believe it had taken him all this time to do, as he did now, which was to open a Search engine and key in the words "Venusian Goddess." The site opened, and there was Beth, scantily-clad and seductive in fishnet stockings and a riding crop. It was seeing her journals, and so prominently displayed, that made his heart beat so loud it felt like it was pounding in his head.

He scrolled down through the most recent entries at random. There it all was—details of their sexual encounters described in pornographic relish. Her detached, often belittling response to his love-making that of a self-styled Venusian Goddess to whom men were mere playthings.

Even worse were the comments from all her followers, the so-called Venusian Angels. It was they who had challenged Beth to try out a "really old guy." They who wanted to know every biological detail about his every performance. They who had clamored for a threesome with Endless Love and Hot Rod.

How could he have been so stupefyingly naïve to have been part of a squalid, online sex show without ever realizing? Beth had dropped so many hints, after all. And her sexual articulacy was a part of what had attracted him to her. What would happen if it all came out? *When* it all came out, he corrected his thoughts. The truth always did. What was it that Rinpoche sometimes said? "Three things can never be hidden forever: the sun, the moon and the truth." Not that he wanted to think about Lama Tashi right now. Things were terrible enough without bringing in a whole bunch of moral considerations, which should, of course, have stopped him from going down this road in the first place.

He paced the floor of the small, old-fashioned room with its wood-clad walls, threadbare carpet and depressing aroma—damp mustiness overlaid by pine disinfectant.

What to do? Should he phone Ian and beg him not to tell Margarita—or anyone else for that matter? Should he call one of his lawyer friends and find out if he could shut down the Venusian Goddess website? Was that even possible without revealing his own part in the whole discreditable business? And what exactly had Beth meant when she'd complained of being "busted?"

So many competing thoughts, it felt like his head was about to explode. He felt like a caged tiger, padding up and down, up and down in this hole of a place, wondering how he ever got himself in this fix.

Wanting to give himself a break, to escape the nightmare—if only momentarily—he picked up the TV remote and switched on hoping for some mindless distraction. Only, the first news channel had live coverage from The Piccard Hotel—the first he'd learned of the shooting of President Grey and the biggest mass shooting in U.S. history at the hands of Mick Mackenzie. The next news channel was all about the FDA announcement—the nation wasn't in the grip of a food contagion, reporters were saying. According to Commissioner Applebaum it was in the grip of karma. And, for those who didn't know already, henceforth America was a vegetarian nation.

Having been preoccupied by his own dramas, opening the door to what was going on around him only made his sense of personal overwhelm even greater. Changing channels, hoping to find something more commonplace, who should appear, seeming to address him personally, but Lama Tashi.

"Why do people do harmful things, karmically speaking? That is a good question," the lama was saying. Behind him was the panoramic valley vista Bob recognized—he had even helped Megan put some of the finishing touches to the *Flourish* studio during his convalescence.

"We all experience dissatisfaction. Suffering. Perhaps we believe we need more money, for example, to live in a better home. Or maybe the relationship we have with our loved one has gone stale. Or we wish to achieve some milestone, a contract, say, or achievement of some kind.

"We think how wonderful it would be to have the new home, or lover or job. In our minds, we exaggerate the positives of this desirable thing and we don't even think about the problems that may be associated with it—or we discount the problems if we do. And the more it occupies our thoughts, the more it disturbs our peace of mind. This is called a delusion."

Bob had heard Lama Tashi offer this same explanation, in countless classes over the years. The same steps of logic. Often using the same words. Even so, as he stood there mesmerized, listening to his teacher it was like he was hearing them for the first time. *Really* hearing them.

"Once we are in the grip of a delusion, like attachment and craving, on the one hand, or aversion and hatred on the other, we begin to believe

278 — DAVID MICHIE

that our only choice is to act on it. To possess. To enjoy. To achieve. Or perhaps to destroy. To suppress. To be free from.

"This delusion grows and grows. It starts off as just a thought, an idea. But we begin to believe it is a truth. A definite fact. And when we act on it, we create karma. Karma is action. Cause—and effect. When actions are driven by delusions, they can only have negative outcomes.

"So you see—suffering leads to delusion, which leads to karma, which in turn leads to more suffering. And so the whole cycle keeps repeating. We call this samsara: a mind afflicted by karma and delusion. Its opposite is nirvana: a mind no longer afflicted by karma and delusion."

Bob couldn't bear to watch any more. He turned the TV off and sat on the end of the motel bed, head in his hands. How could he have been such a fool? Dressing up his own motives as somehow less self-serving than they really were? Walking away from the person who'd been his most loyal friend, lover, and mother of his children for someone he didn't even know—someone for whom he was nothing more than a derisory figure in a sordid tale?

Lama Tashi was right. He had just set it all out in simple terms. Bob's dissatisfaction had been boredom. It had made him ripe for the delusion of craving. Lust. There had been plenty of times he could have stepped away. Called it off. Ended things. But, no. Instead he had invented a whole fantasy around what was happening. Created an imaginative fiction about new chapters, youthful vigor, Life 2.0. And the karma that he had created, based on delusion, had become instantly manifest in the form of acute suffering.

Fewer than eight hours had passed since he had left Margarita devastated in the kitchen of their home, carrying the suitcase which now lay unopened on a nearby chair. He wondered what she'd done since then. Had she called the kids—Matias and Gabby? Who else would she have spoken to?

Would she be willing to forgive him if he admitted that he'd made the most terrible mistake?

50

Hey, peeps!

I hope you haven't forgotten where you first heard about karma? Yep. I was the cyber analyst who broke the news about surging karma mentions since midnight.

Since then it's gone mainstream with the worst, nationwide food poisoning in history. The biggest mass-shooting. The President hospitalized. There's a word for it folks: Karmageddon!

In the biggest digital scramble I've ever seen—total traffic up 1,000 percent—*everyone* online is talking about karma. Most of them started the day as "Don't Knows." I'll be honest: me too.

As the hours tick by, people are polarizing. The Early Adopters have had wonderful or terrible things happen. Sometimes both. And they've been taking advantage of instant karma, bigtime. They're following the advice of Lama Tashi—hard to believe no one had ever heard of the guy just six hours ago and now we can't get enough of him. If you don't already know about the main causes and effects, or what gives karma its weight, then I'm sorry to break the news, buddy, but you're not making money, attracting followers, or getting laid. And that's just for starters.

Some of the biggest online early adopter groups, which have come out of nowhere and now have gazillions of followers, include a few unexpected ones like *Karma Climate Change*—a greenie/pro-karma fusion—and *Christians for Karma*—slogan: "By your standard of measure it shall be measured to you; and more shall be given to you besides." Jesus: Mark 4:24

On the other side of the digital tracks are those objecting to karma because of science or religion. Scientists cite lack of evidence-based research. The religious right says that karma is blasphemy. Rare to see these guys in the same camp, and they're taking no prisoners. They're violent in their online attacks—reflecting what we've seen today at The Piccard Hotel.

Time will tell how instant karma plays out. But it's hard to go against personal experience. Like Lama Tashi says, you don't have to believe anything—just try it. I did. I promoted some of my fave digital analysts online and, within two hours I'd been rated one of the U.S.'s "Top 10" Digital Experts by blue-chip consulting firm McIntley. Didn't even know I was on their radar.

What I'm most curious about, in all this, is what happens to Lama Tashi? He came out of nowhere, and now everyone wants him. In just hours he's become the most important person in the country. Many would say the most loved. *Karma Climate Change* say that, although he's a Buddhist lama, he was born in Colorado. Could this mean Lama Tashi for President?

You heard it here first.

51

Wall Street, New York

AMY WAS TAKEN ABACK BY WHAT HAPPENED AFTER KAREL Sharma's rousing staff rally. There was an initial wave of excitement as staff returned to their desks. Donations made by colleagues were followed by rapid returns—just like she'd experienced.

A few donors, following Karel's suggestion, immediately gifted the larger amount they had received. But not all. Many were happy to collect what they had got and leave it at that. Getting up from their desks, they grabbed their personal items and headed for the door, taking up the boss's offer to leave early. Others had left work right away, saying that the public transport crisis meant they'd have a long walk ahead.

Within half an hour, few people remained on the 25th floor of Sharma Funds. Which astounded Amy. How could people be so uninterested in getting rich? Having heard from a man with impeccable credentials on exactly how to do it, and invited to try it out for themselves on company time, how could they be so incurious, so lukewarm about the opportunity of a lifetime? Especially when the process was so easy?

She knew that her own experiences, earlier that day, meant that she'd already been convinced. Even so, she didn't know why everyone wasn't at their desks, just like her, giving away money—and telling everyone they cared about to do the same thing.

Having requested the cryptocurrency dividend from Akara Foon, as soon as the $3,215.89 reached her account, Amy donated it to the charitable causes Karel had suggested—with bodhichitta motivation.

Meantime, she posted messages on all her social media channels, sharing her own direct evidence that in giving, you truly did receive. She wrote emails sharing the same message to the folk back home who weren't on social media.

When she got an email from Peter Sharp, advising her that a life insurance policy he'd uncovered in the name of Larry Denis meant she would be inheriting an additional $35,000, she wasn't greatly surprised. Still, she paused, staring at the screen. First thing this morning, if she'd been told she would soon enjoy a windfall of this amount she would have scarcely been able to believe her luck. As of now, it wasn't only the $35,000 that was on its way to her. It was also the $80,000 bonus from Karel Sharma, the $1.6 million from Uncle Gerry's estate, and ongoing royalties of $50,000 a year.

She knew she shouldn't be greedy. She only wished she had money in the bank now for Bluegrass Horse Sanctuary. Mr. Deal had been touchingly grateful for her earlier donation, but he really needed help on a much bigger scale. The $1,000 she'd given him would help with horse feed for a while, but relocation costs, renting a new property and getting things the way they needed to help his aging, noble dependents like her own, dear Flash, was on an altogether different scale. As soon as the money came in from her bonus, she decided, she was going to transfer a much larger amount to Bluegrass.

Come 4:45 pm, she was the only one left on her side of reception. She could see a few people behind their partitions across the foyer. Copying her email to send to more friends in Aubrey, she was so absorbed by her task that she got a start when she realized someone was standing right next to her.

"Mr. Sharma!"

He glanced round at the deserted workstations. "Home alone?"

"Looks that way." She shook her head. "I can't believe that everyone isn't here giving away all they can. I only wish I had more savings—right now I'm flat out."

"The bonus should hit your account, but maybe not till later, or maybe tomorrow."

She nodded.

"Anyone especially you're planning to help?"

"Bluegrass Horse Sanctuary," she said right away. "Remember I mentioned—"

"Charles Deal. Having to relocate."

Amy took note. She hadn't thought Karel had been paying attention earlier, when she'd been prattling away, trying to distract him from what was about to happen. Charles, Karel said. Had she used his first name? In town they called him "Charlie" but he had always been "Mr." Deal to her.

"He's one of those quiet saints you never get to hear about. His whole life is dedicated to giving racehorses the retirement they deserve."

"Quiet saints," Karel smiled. "Like it. Anyhow, I agree."

Her expression was uncertain. "Agree ..?"

"Agree he needed to be helped. I had one of my property guys get hold of the seller. We've bought the land."

"What?" Amy was finding it hard to keep up with him.

"He can stay as long as he likes."

"Oh, Mr. Sharma, I can't believe you did that for him!" Jumping to her feet, Amy put her arms out, hugging him.

"I didn't do it for him," he said, at her cheek. "I did it for you."

"Me?" she pulled back.

"What you did over there," he leaned towards the foyer. "Forcing me out of my comfort zone."

"Onto the filing box."

"I even enjoyed it!"

"We could see!"

"It made me realize I can do more. Widen my horizons. I don't have to spend the rest of my life sitting alone in an office."

"You can do whatever you like," she beamed. "Tell me about Mr. Deal— he must have been ..." Shaking her head, she was gleeful imagining his reaction.

"I've left it to you to break the news," he replied. "The transaction's been agreed with the seller, but it will take a while to go through legal."

"You haven't told him?"

"More appropriate you should," he said.

She looked at him, questioningly.

"You're the new owner," he grinned. "It's being transferred to your name."

"Oh, Mr. Sharma!" Tears welled up and her face creased with emotion. "That's so beautiful!"

He held her to him. "You're so beautiful!" he said.

52

Eccles Building
Washington, D.C.

Rose Mulrooney, Chair of the Federal Reserve Bank, removed her glasses, placed them on her leather-topped desk and sighed deeply. It had been the most volatile day in U.S. banking history and while the news hadn't been all bad—some had been astonishingly good—she still had no idea what the drivers were. Why the unprecedented transfers of money, both domestic and international? Why were some of the huge bank deposits, rarely used, suddenly circulating? How were she and her colleagues supposed to make important decisions about the financial health of the nation when all the usual norms had been turned on their head?

This morning's GDP figures, almost a full percentage point higher than expected, had been her first inkling that economic ructions, as unexpected as that day's food contagion fears, were sweeping the markets. Economic growth may be a good thing—but *unexpected* growth, figures that came out of nowhere, were unsettling for one simple reason: they meant that the Federal Reserve didn't have a firm grip on things.

Since then, it had been coming at her from all angles. On a day when many people were staying at home, cash flows in and out of bank accounts would normally have been steady. Today, transactions were trending thousands of per cents above average.

The stock market was on a precipitous roller-coaster, with stocks exposed to animal farming losing 90 percent of their value, plant-based protein companies going stratospheric, and a tumult affecting pharmaceutical companies, transport, and other sectors marking a fundamental realignment in company values. Even the media giants were caught up in the mayhem—Galaxy TV shares had spiked 24 percent above their all-time high.

Rose had been braced for a set of hiring figures confirming a grim, downward trend in employment, but the set she had just received showed the very opposite—a leap of nearly 2 percent in hiring intentions despite the current wave of food poisoning. Where in God's name had that come from?

She walked across her office to the window. Usually the view, facing across Constitution Avenue to the Lincoln Memorial Reflecting Pool, was reassuringly constant, altered only by the predictable rhythm of the seasons. Today, however, a large and angry mob surged down the avenue towards the Capitol. The Reverend Jeremiah Bellow had instigated a March Against Karma, and the spontaneous uprising of vocal, placard-waving activists was heading for Congress.

Rose had kept a watch on her TV for most of the day, and knew what everyone else was seeing. She was well aware of the debate around karma. She had been as engaged as anyone else when Lama Tashi had appeared on just about every channel, exposing the self-serving shallowness of Professor Stanley Smugg for what it was, and explaining the different factors that gave karma its weight with a logic that surprised. But instant karma? Really?

She decided to call Will Salt. The President's Chief of Staff and she had a cordial, working relationship given that he'd been an economist earlier in his career. They spoke the same language.

"The hiring intention figures have just come in," she told him.

"And?"

"Up 1.94 percent."

"Uh-huh."

"You don't sound surprised?"

"That'll be Swaziland."

"Swaziland?" She frowned. She couldn't remember ever having said the word out loud before. It was one those places, like Timbuktu and El Dorado that seemed more mythic than real.

"We funded a jobs creation program for them earlier today. Call centers for Federal departments."

"The President believes in instant karma?" she asked, voice raised.

A short while ago, watching Commissioner Applebaum's media conference, she had considered his account for the food poisoning pandemic to be eccentric. Even though he had been clear that his "karma" explanation was a personal opinion rather than a scientific one, it was kind of pronouncement she expected more from metaphysical pundits than a public health official. She certainly hadn't believed any other senior figure, civil or political, was thinking along the same lines.

"The President has an open mind on it."

"But earlier today he said—"

"D'you see who he was with?" Will gave her time to absorb this before continuing, "The Swaziland thing was an experiment. We wanted to test the theory. What you've just said is confirmation."

"Extraordinary!" Rose watched as the furious March Against Karma mob jostled angrily towards the Capitol.

"I'm working on ways to row back from his earlier comment."

"Where is the President getting his advice on karma?"

"The same place as everyone else," he told her.

Ending the call, moments later, she crossed her office to where her Executive Assistants were busy at their desks.

"Margaret," she approached her most senior E.A. "I need to speak to Lama Tashi. Right away."

5:00 pm (Eastern Standard Time)
3:00 pm (Mountain Standard Time)
2:00 pm (Pacific Standard Time)

53

Omni, Colorado

S INCE HIS APPOINTMENT WITH DR. RALPH SHARP, TOM WAS FILLED with a lightness he hadn't felt in years. It was the first glimpse of sun breaking through a dense cover so ominous and unrelenting he'd almost come to believe that the clouds were the sky. For the first time he felt certain that there *was* a way through this. He wasn't the only person in the world to experience PTSD. Others had come through the other end. Why shouldn't he?

Setting out this morning, it hadn't been his intention to lay his cards on the table. He'd planned a reconnaissance mission to Veterans Affairs. But the dynamics of the situation had shifted, no doubt helped along by Dr. Sharp's insight into such matters, and he'd found himself opening up. The weird thing was that he hadn't felt exposed. Instead, the opposite. Even in the telling it was like he'd thrown off the heavy chains which had burdened him for so long. Dr. Sharp had made it possible for him to confide what he'd spent years concealing, and rather than shame or fear, what he felt was release. Liberation. Along with the simple question: why had it taken him so long?

He knew who he owed this all to. If Lama Tashi hadn't scared the daylights out of him yesterday, he would have remained stuck firmly in his rut. His neighbor had been trying for years, subtly to begin with, then more directly. He had spurned all his efforts, resenting the intrusion all the while some part of him recognized he couldn't keep going the way he was. The timing of Lama Tashi's intervention, Tom was coming to realize, had not been random.

On the drive home from the V.A. in Boulder, he'd turned on the car radio and listened to all the craziness going on in the nation. How President Grey had almost been assassinated by the leader of the NGA. The biggest mass shooting in history at the same time that spontaneous remission rates had spiked to unprecedented levels. News that some March Against Karma in Washington, D.C. had self-destructed when home-made firebombs, launched by a group of violent protestors, bounced off windows back into the main body of protestors, creating pandemonium.

As the waves of news washed over Tom, next thing it had been the voice of his neighbor on the car radio. In the decades they had lived next door to each other, Tom had never asked Lama Tashi about his beliefs or practices. He hadn't wanted to go there in case things turned personal. "Live and let live" had been his motto, one which he'd used to absolve him of ever having to give the big questions a moment's thought. Now as he listened to Rinpoche's measured tones as he explained the workings of karma, he wondered how he could have remained so foolishly uninterested.

When he got home, Tina was taking an afternoon nap. He closed the door to the bedroom corridor before returning to the hallway and making his way to the living room. He'd hardly touched the piano since joining the army at the age of eighteen. Which was the polar opposite of his growing-up years, when he used to play for hours every day. He still enjoyed listening to classical music and had been known, during his time in the service, for his eagerness to attend piano recitals especially when the army took him to distant cities. But sit at the piano himself? It had felt that in choosing the army he had forsaken that part of his life. At eighteen he had believed that he didn't have the time for both.

There was no reason he couldn't return to it now. As he pulled out the piano stool, sat down and opened the lid of the keyboard, he felt his hands extend to the sides of the stool to adjust its height. It was an automatic movement. Instinctive. And noticing what he'd just done, he smiled. Was it still there, he wondered, the ability to play?

Tina had encouraged him to believe so. A few years ago she had called in a piano tuner who'd spent the morning adjusting the strings before pronouncing the Steinway to be good as new. Like Dr. Sharp, Tina had no doubt wanted to give him a different place to go, different terrain to explore instead of the ever-narrowing pit to which he'd felt condemned. She hadn't stopped trying to help over the years, Lord knew. Not only getting the piano tuned, but with every manner of suggestion from horse riding and white water rafting at the manly end of the spectrum, to pottery turning and musical appreciation classes at the more artistic. He hadn't done any of those things.

Tina had been the innocent victim. Spending her golden years in the presence of abject misery wasn't something she'd signed up to, but that was the way things had turned out. Inevitably his own darkness had cast its shadow upon her too. She had become increasingly withdrawn, diminished. The high-spirited feistiness that had attracted him to her, had become subdued.

For a while he sat, fingertips trailing up and down the surface of the keys, reacquainting himself with the instrument that had been so much the focus of his life growing up. It felt strange to be here again after half a century's dislocation, back in the presence of an old friend.

What to play? He had no sooner asked himself the question, than the answer arose, not so much as an idea than the upwelling of a sentiment in need of expression. A piece he'd practiced, and technically mastered in the earliest of days, even though the emotion it conveyed was one he had only come to know much later in life. He began the Adagio Cantabile from Beethoven's piano Sonata No. 8. The Pathétique.

His playing was hesitant at first. In a way, disbelieving. Was it really possible he could pick up where he had left off? So ingrained were the movements and the chord progressions, however, and so profoundly etched in his consciousness the urging, ever-forward flow, that it felt like he was being carried by the music. Led along waterways with which he was already familiar, but which he was discovering had an even richer meaning now than when he had first explored them.

He didn't need sheet music. Not for the Beethoven Sonata, nor for any of the pieces that followed. His technique was rusty—he stumbled trying to play anything fast. The muscles in his hands began to hurt. But

294 — DAVID MICHIE

he played on through the afternoon, oblivious to the fact that he was no longer alone. On the living room sofa facing into the dining room, he was being closely followed by two pairs of eyes.

He paused for a break, to find Tina behind him. She was weeping, and seeing her cry made him emotional too. She crossed over to hug him and they held together for the longest time.

"That was beautiful!" she murmured, eventually.

"Things are going to be okay," he said. Then after a pause, "When did she come?"

They both turned to look at Shanti, Lama Tashi's Siamese, lounging comfortably on the sofa as if it were her usual spot rather than the first time she had ever visited.

"A few minutes ago," said Tina.

Tom glanced at his watch, startled. "Is that the time? Lama Tashi asked me to feed her around now."

"Seems like she knew the arrangement—"

"And saved me the bother of going around," said Tom. "Do we have any cans of tuna?"

"In the pantry."

Minutes later, watching Shanti attacking a saucer of food with noisy relish, Tom's phone rang. Alexander Hickman.

"Tom. How did it go?" asked the General.

"Better than expected."

"I've seen Dr. Sharp present. Knows his stuff."

"I agree."

"Look. You may find this strange but I want to ask. You mentioned an advisor earlier. Someone who suggested you act today."

"Yes."

"Do you mind telling me who that is?"

Whatever sensitivities Tom may have felt about this question had well and truly gone by now. "Sure. Lama Tashi."

"You *know* Lama Tashi?" General Hickman's voice was filled with admiration.

"For twenty years."

"You're a dark horse, Colonel Jackson."

"We live next door to each other."

"He's all over the media today."

"He expected to be tied up. Which is why I'm feeding his cat right now." Tom followed where Shanti, determined to get every last morsel of food from the saucer, was licking it across the balcony floor.

"I'm guessing you'll have his phone number?" asked the General.

"He doesn't have one," said Tom.

There was a gasp of frustration at the other end. "He's not getting home tonight?"

"Said he could be away for several days."

"He seems to be based out of a place called *Flourish*?"

"That's a student of his from the Lone Pine Meditation Center. They're probably the best way to get hold of him."

"I'll try. If you get to see him in the meantime, can you ask him to call?"

"Sure," agreed Tom. "Looking for some Buddhist wisdom to complement Sun Tzu?"

""He who uses the same strategy in each battle will ultimately lose the war,"" quoted Hickman.

"Touché, General," responded Tom. "And today's a very different battle."

54

Boulder, Colorado

As soon as the red "On Air" light changed to green outside the *Flourish* studio, there was a knock on the door. It was Hayden in a state of high excitement.

"Rinpoche! Mom! You won't believe who's been calling!" He looked at Lama Tashi, who was removing his headphones, standing up and stretching his arms.

"We've had calls from the FDA and the Federal Reserve and General Hickman's office at the Pentagon!" he was exhilarated as he checked off his list. "Even—" he'd kept the best till last, "—from the White House. President Grey wants to speak to you!"

Megan shot an exhilarated look at Rinpoche. Not only had their Q & A session found its way onto every major news channel, with Lama Tashi interacting with a huge, global audience. The most powerful people in the nation were turning to him.

If Rinpoche was in the least surprised he wasn't showing it. "Let's go outside for some fresh air," he suggested, waiting for Megan to get up from her chair and ushering her towards the door.

They emerged from the studio into the mid-afternoon sunshine. Rusty got up from where he'd been dozing and approached them, tail wagging. After being closeted in the studio, Lama Tashi seemed perfectly content just taking in the peaceful vista, feeling the warmth of the sun on his skin.

Unsure what to make of his apparent indifference to the callers, Hayden looked queryingly at his mother, who in turn, nodded towards where Rinpoche had raised a hand to his eyes and was gazing into the far distance.

It was a few minutes before he returned, bending to give Rusty a hearty neck rub. "Tell me, Hayden," he said. "Did any of these important people call me personally?"

Hayden shook his head. "They had their staff call." He looked at his message log, "It was President Grey's Chief of Staff's office—"

Before he continued with the others, Lama Tashi interjected, "Okay. That's fine," he said, as though relieved. "I guess they don't want to speak that much."

Hayden looked puzzled. "That's just how they operate."

Rinpoche nodded, a mischievous twinkle appearing in his eye, "Tell me, Hayden. If you wanted to invite a girl out on a date, would you get your Mom to call her?"

Seeing the expression of distaste on Hayden's face, they all burst out laughing.

"You also have a ton of messages from other people," Hayden was looking back at his list, afterwards. "Democrats and Republicans wanting you to join their parties as a fast-track candidate."

"Yes, yes," Lama Tashi nodded at the well-worn suggestion.

"A whole bunch of *Fortune* Top 50 companies who want you for their Boards. Charities asking if you'll be their patron. There's a message from Omni City Hall wanting your permission to commission a statue of you to go outside the library!" His eyes gleamed. "Interview requests from just about every news organization. They all want you, Rinpoche. They all have questions."

Lama Tashi met his eyes, the ease and lightness of his presence communicating something to Hayden, who continued, "But they're the wrong questions, aren't they?"

Lama Tashi smiled broadly, stepping over to give Hayden a hug. "My work here is done."

"Ask a useful question if you want a useful answer?" confirmed Hayden.

"Exactly."

The Galaxy panel discussion was lined up for 5:30 pm. Galaxy producers had confirmed both the cognitive neuroscientist and quantum physicist who Lama Tashi has proposed. After that had finished, said Lama Tashi, he would take Anton home, having earlier promised to return him that afternoon in time for his regular squash game.

Megan had had years sitting at the feet of her guru to become thoroughly familiar with him. Through this time she'd watched the way he interacted with people in a variety of situations and come to understand how, no matter what presented itself to him, he was always himself. At ease, untroubled, non-attached.

Even so, she had never seen anyone walk away from the kinds of offers that most people would regard as the pinnacle of a lifetime's achievement. Shrug off requests for advice from the most influential leaders in the nation. He genuinely had no interest at all in the worldly pursuits and distractions that absorbed almost everyone else, in some cases to the point of obsession.

Which was exactly why everyone wanted to be near him. To have access to this living, breathing embodiment of a lighter way of being. To be inspired that a different way was possible.

"Before we do the Galaxy discussion," he said. "I'd like to record a message."

"Okay."

"Not too long. Just a few minutes."

She was nodding.

"For you to use on *Flourish* when you see fit. But *only* from tomorrow," he was emphatic.

"Yes, Rinpoche," Megan assured him. Then, to clarify, "So, some time tomorrow or ..?

"You decide," he said. "Tomorrow, or the next day, or soon afterwards."

"Okay."

"I hope it will help answer their questions," he nodded towards the list in Hayden's hand.

$$55$$

Galaxy Television
Los Angeles

"JOINING US FOR OUR PANEL ROUND-UP ON KARMA TODAY," DAN Kavana announced, "in our Washington, D.C. studios, the Reverend Jeremiah Bellow of Tongues of Praise Churches and Marvin Swankler, CEO of Prosperity Ministries, two of our nation's largest churches. In Boston, clinical neuropsychologist Professor Golda Roth, in San Francisco, quantum physicist Dr. Karl Bohn, and in Boulder, Colorado, Buddhist teacher Lama Tashi. Welcome guests!"

They were an odd assortment. The two men of God looking ill at ease behind their desk, the Reverend Bellow appearing on the brink of eruption. Professor Roth, diminutive and with a shock of grey hair, gave the impression of intelligent joviality. Dr. Karl Bohn, ascetic and European in his steel-rimmed spectacles, fawn jacket and nondescript tie. Lama Tashi, his usual serene presence.

"Reverend Bellow," said Dan. "You contacted us about the suggestion the FDA's Dr. Applebaum made earlier. No scientific cause can be found for the food poisoning across the nation today by people eating meat. Dr. Applebaum suggested the cause was instant karma. You wanted the chance to respond?"

"Yes, I do wish to respond—" the screen filled with the large, bearded, seething face of the Reverend Bellow. "Because it's blasphemy! An offense to the Lord. "Cry aloud, spare not, lift up thy voice like a trumpet, and show my people their transgression, and the house of Jacob their sins,'" his voice rose in indignation.

"Karma has no part in the hearts of God-fearing Americans," rejoined Marvin Swankler in less biblical terms.

"True, brother!" agreed the Reverend Bellow.

"It is a belief of arrogant pride!" Swankler warmed to his theme. "A ploy of Satan to make mere mortals think that *they* are in charge and not the Lord God Almighty."

"Amen!" Reverend Bellow thumped the desk in support.

"Mr. Swankler," Dan proposed one of the questions prepared by his research team. "Prosperity Ministries encourages followers to donate ten per cent of their income to the church, in the expectation of future prosperity. Your church slogan is "Reap as you sow." Isn't this idea karma, pretty much?"

"Not at all," Marvin Swankler's clear blue eyes were unmoved by the suggestion. "You can only prosper if you have accepted the Lord Jesus Christ as your personal savior. Be not deceived. God is not mocked!"

"But if you have the right beliefs—from your perspective," Dan wanted to get this straight. "If you have accepted the Lord as your savior, *then* you reap as you sow?"

"Of course! "One gives freely yet grows all the richer; another withholds what he should give, and only suffers want. Whoever brings blessing will be enriched, and one who waters will himself be watered."

"Lama Tashi, you reap what you sow. This is a standard definition of karma?"

The lightness, as Lama Tashi filled the screen, came as a relief after the intensity of the two men in Washington, D.C. "It's a very good metaphor," he smiled. "It suggests a karmic seed which germinates and grows when it comes into contact with certain conditions—soil, moisture, warmth. So, it is not only about the karmic cause. It also implies conditions. There are many factors at play. All of which help explain why we experience reality the way we do. This is a field in which Professor Roth is a great expert. She can explain how reality is unique to each one of us."

"Professor Roth," Dan looked to the small, lined woman in Galaxy's Boston studio with surprise. Like everyone else in the Galaxy newsroom he hadn't known why Lama Tashi had wanted to introduce a scientific expert as a guest. "There's some connection between neuropsychology and karma?"

The other chuckled, her lined face crinkling with amusement. "I think what Lama Tashi is alluding to is the subjectivity of experience," she spoke with crisp, British diction.

Lama Tashi was nodding.

"Most people still believe in what's known as the direct perception theory, which suggests that we are all passive observers of the outside world. That our brains are mere receptors of sensations channeled to them via our eyes, ears and so on. But this view was abandoned long ago by neuroscience. 80 percent of fibers in the part of the brain that processes visual imagery comes from the cortex—which governs functions like memory—and only 20 percent from the retinas.

"Instead of being passive receptors, all seeing the same thing, in reality we are projecting out onto the world what you might call predictive hypotheses about what's happening. Our own perceptions are what makes things out there attractive or unattractive. It's not coming from them. It's coming from us. Which is why two people can see the same painting, hear the same music, taste the same food, and have two vastly different perceptions."

In the Washington, D.C., studio, the Reverend Bellow was impatient to get this discussion back on track. Not for him having to listen to arcane talk of neuroscience or predictive hypotheses. "All things come from God, through God, and return to God," he butted in. "Romans 11:36!"

Mr. Swankler nodded decisively.

"We Buddhists say just the same thing about sunyata," observed Lama Tashi, relaxed and genial. "There may be interesting parallels there. What we're focusing on now is *how* things come from God—or from sunyata. And why it depends so much on mind."

"That dependence comes as a surprise to most people," confirmed Professor Roth. "But it shouldn't really, because we perceive the same things so very differently."

"Most people can probably relate to that," Dan wanted to ground the discussion. "Sometimes it's hard to believe you're talking about the same movie, or TV show as someone else, they have such a very different take on it. What you're saying, Lama Tashi—" he wanted to clarify, "—is that this difference is accounted for by karma."

"Exactly," agreed Rinpoche.

While a look of bemusement came over the two men of God, in San Francisco Dr. Karl Bohn was suddenly animated.

"Would you care to comment, Dr. Bohn?" Dan invited him.

"From a quantum science perspective, it is even more subtle than this," he spoke with a slight German accent. "The concept of substance, you know, has disappeared from fundamental physics. Even a pen," with a flourish he produced a Montblanc Meisterstuck from his pocket. "Comprises atoms. These atoms are mostly space with only a few, tiny, sub-atomic particles. When we study sub-atomic particles, we discover that the smallest unit of what you might call substance, may also be energy. The particle is also a wave. So where is the pen?" he shrugged. "And what is it? As Einstein said, "Physical concepts are free creations of the human mind and are not, however it may seem, uniquely determined by the external world.""

"We're making it up!" confirmed Lama Tashi. "And this is why we suffer. We believe the outside world has an objective reality which we all perceive accurately and in the same way. We cling to this mistaken view. If something out there really was a true cause of joy, with happiness-giving qualities from its own side, then we'd all agree. We'd all want it. But no such thing, or situation, exists.

"What we believe to be reality is actually the play of our own mind. We create it. So if it is happiness we seek—and we all do—we need to recognize that true happiness doesn't come from out there. It comes from cultivating our own love and compassion. When our actions are based on these qualities, the results can only be happiness and abundance. When they are not, we experience the opposite. If you look at what has happened across the United States today, it fits this pattern."

"As a quantum physicist, would you agree with this, Dr. Bohn?" asked Dan.

"What I would agree with," said the other, "is that every person's world picture is a construct of his own mind. You can't divide the observer from the observed. What we call reality arises from mind itself."

In the Washington, D.C., studio, the two churchmen were becoming visibly fractious.

"You don't accept this explanation, Mr. Swankler?" asked Dan.

"It seems to me that these gentlemen are complicating something that is really quite simple," he declared. "Reality comes from God. God cannot be understood."

"How unsearchable His judgments and untraceable His ways!" rejoined the Reverend Bellow.

"Amen, brother. When you accept the Lord your God as your personal savior, you will know grace."

"What Lama Tashi says about cultivating love and compassion," Dan searched for common ground. "That's part of being a Christian too, right?"

The Reverend Bellow was having none of this. "You must submit to the righteousness of the Lord!" he roared. "Not establish your own righteousness!"

"So the only way to deal with things today-?"

"Give your life to the Lord!" Marvin Swankler answered before Dan had even finished the question. "Accept him as your own, personal savior."

"Lama Tashi, would you say that people need to become Buddhists?" Dan wanted to check if he held an equivalent position.

Lama Tashi chuckled, "Oh no!" he said. "The purpose of Buddhism is not to convert people. It's to give them tools to become happier. Whether that makes you a happier Christian, a happier atheist, a happier whatever-you-are. Labels and what we call ourselves, this is less important than cultivating a good heart."

They were up against the clock. Dan was aware that he had to draw things to a close ahead of the 6 pm news.

"If every person's world picture is a construct of his or her mind, Reverend Bellow, how is the world looking to you today?"

"I'm seeing bitter division and contempt as people turn their backs on salvation!" he fulminated. "I'm seeing the worship of false prophets! We don't make God up. He makes us up!"

"Praise be the Lord!" enjoined Marvin Swankler, thrilled by the rhetorical flourish.

"Mark my words," he raised a heavy index finger to his face. "We are now in the end of days. We are approaching the time of final reckoning. The Last Judgment!"

"Oh yea!"

"Because I have called, and ye refused; I have stretched out my hand, and no man regarded; I also will laugh at your calamity; I will mock when your fear cometh.""

"And Mr. Swankler," Dan turned to his more urbane colleague. "Your world picture?"

"I agree with my brother-in-Christ," he said. "Which is why Prosperity Ministries will withhold finance and endorsements of any media network or political party that seeks to corrupt the soul of our great, Christian nation with alien ideology."

"Amen brother!"

"And Lama Tashi?" asked Dan.

"What we are experiencing today is a rare and precious opportunity," he said. "Although there has been great tragedy and hardship, we've also seen transformation that's truly extraordinary. As people awaken to the law of cause and effect, we will increasingly realize our ultimate nature. Whatever conceptions may appear to divide us, at heart we are all the same. May our innate love and compassion manifest quickly!"

56

Boulder, Colorado

WHILE LAMA TASHI HAD BEEN ON AIR, AT THE KITCHEN TABLE A short distance away, trying to work through a Physics assignment, Hayden had been on the receiving end of calls from the most powerful people in America.

Persistent callers were the chiefs of staff whose bosses needed to speak to Lama Tashi. Yes, Hayden told them, he had passed on their message. No, Lama Tashi wasn't able to speak—he was live on Galaxy TV. Of course, he said, he'd once again pass on their message, but he kind of doubted that Rinpoche would respond. He found himself repeating the story of asking a girl out on a date to each one of them, his confidence growing with each telling.

The result was predictable. Dr. Saul Applebaum, Commissioner of the FDA was the first to call personally. "Will you please tell him that I called?" he beseeched Hayden.

"Of course."

"There's a particular question I need to ask." He recollected the lightning strike moment when it had occurred to him, after the guy in his office had taken a shot—only to fall to the floor, wounded, himself. "I wonder," asked the FDA Commissioner, "if *you've* heard Lama Tashi talk about this?"

He confided in Hayden what had suddenly become so important. Hayden had to tell him that no, that wasn't a subject which had come up so far.

Next it had been Rose Mulrooney, Chair of the Federal Reserve. Then the Director of the FBI. Hayden was only a third of the way through his thermodynamics homework when President Trent Grey was on the line.

"Hayden Mitchell, a pleasure to speak to you," the President made him feel suddenly important and connected—like they'd known each other for a long time. Like they had some kind of understanding. Like all Hayden wanted to do was to be of service.

The President also had a specific question. The same specific question as all the others. Once again, Hayden had to confess than he hadn't heard Lama Tashi discuss that particular point.

Trying to concentrate on his homework was difficult after such an exciting afternoon. But he tried, all the while keeping an eye on the light outside the studio door.

When the Galaxy panel discussion ended and the light came on, it seemed brighter than before. Afternoon sunshine filtered through the canopy of the forest, dappling the plants and ground below in gold. Lama Tashi, Megan and Anton stepped from the studio, rubbing their arms as they emerged into the sun.

Hayden, hurried over to update Rinpoche on the calls. He had written names and phone numbers on a piece of paper which Lama Tashi gratefully acknowledged before folding the paper and tucking it into a concealed pocket in his robe.

"And Rinpoche, there was a particular question they all wanted to ask you."

He smiled. "I think I can guess." Before turning to Anton, for the first time that day conveying a sense of urgency, "We go soon?"

Anton already had a camera in one hand and was carrying a bag of cables in the other. He nodded, walking over to Rinpoche's car briskly.

"I can help carry stuff if you like?"

After a few minutes of carrying, Anton's equipment was stowed, and Lama Tashi was behind the steering wheel. Anton sat in the passenger seat. Megan, flanked by Hayden, Shelley and Rusty were there to farewell them. Megan didn't know what to say at the end of a day which had been unimaginable in almost every respect. She raised her palms to her heart in profound gratitude.

"We'll speak soon," Lama Tashi smiled.

"I'll get your message out tomorrow, Rinpoche."

"I'll be gone," he nodded. "Only a short while. You know the story of the deer being pursued through the forest?"

"Yes, Rinpoche."

It wasn't a parable she had thought about for a while. It explained what to do if you found yourself in a forest and saw a deer rushing through the undergrowth before, some while later, hunters following in hot pursuit. If the predators demanded, "Where did the deer go?"

In such circumstances it was right to shrug and say, "I don't know." Protecting the life of a sentient being trumped the need to tell the whole truth.

"You remember," he instructed her.

"Okay," she smiled.

Then responding to Hayden's anxious expression he said, "Don't worry about your new friend, Mr. President. All is well!"

They watched as the lime-green Volvo made its way up the long driveway and into the afternoon, before rounding the corner out of sight. For a while they stood, even the kids turned silent by the extraordinariness of a day in which their own dear Rinpoche had been propelled from simple monk—the only title he would allow for himself—to the most sought-after celebrity in the nation. While including them in a journey of which he almost certainly had prior knowledge, through it all he had remained his serene and benevolent self.

For Megan, what had happened felt too much to take in. And the reference to the deer in the forest story was typically, inscrutable Rinpoche. What had that been about?

A cool, afternoon breeze gusting through the branches above, causing leaves to rustle, drawing her back to the present. She glanced at her watch. Keith would be home from work soon. And despite all the excitement, it wouldn't be long before the family needed to be fed.

"Homework Hayden, while I sort out dinner," she commanded, leading the way to the house. "Shelley, are you organized for athletics tomorrow?"

In the kitchen she opened the fridge, surveying the contents, before looking in the pantry and freezer. She ran through the options.

Having opted for a quiche, using a pre-made pastry base, about forty minutes later Megan was pouring a mix into the base when she first heard the unusual noise. In the quiet of the countryside, sound travelled far.

Rusty stirred on the veranda and began barking. Hayden evidently heard it too and, always eager for a distraction from thermodynamics, came bounding down the stairs. Megan heard him go outside before scampering back towards her,

"Mum it's the cops!" he cried. "They're at the end of the drive!"

Megan's blood ran cold, her thoughts immediately turning to her husband, driving home.

Outside, Rusty was going crazy.

"Put Rusty in the back room, please." She tugged the knot of the apron around her waist, and hung it on the back of the kitchen door. As Hayden had said, a Police vehicle, emergency lights flashing, was making its way towards the house. And not only one vehicle. Along with Police cars she made out several gleaming, black SUVs. All of them heading inexorably towards them.

They, alone, weren't responsible for the clattering din that was drawing closer. It was only glancing up that Megan saw the helicopter circling lower towards the house. For a moment it seemed to skate perilously close over the tops of the Douglas firs before veering into an empty field next to the drive.

Today's dreamlike surreality hadn't ended. Even as the sun's rays were beginning to lengthen there was more. The police cars at the head of the convoy cut their emergency lights and slowed as they approached the house. Evidently this was no regular visit. And what came behind them drew Megan's attention even more. Because there weren't only a handful of vehicles, but a whole convoy. Large, up-market, and with a road-presence signaling importance, they were following the police vehicles, right up to the house, and gliding to a dignified halt. Doors were being opened. Executives in suits and police officers were getting out. In the nearby field, uniformed army officers were stepping from the helicopter cockpit and, doubling over, hurrying beneath the slowing rotor blades. As they neared the house their strides were brisk. Even before a word had been said, in the hastening of visitors towards her front door, the rivalry was tangible.

"Mrs. Mitchell, I'm the County Sheriff," a man in police uniform was the first to approach. "I'm here at the personal request of the Director of the FBI."

"Bonny Ratcliff, Megan," a woman in immaculate couture and sparkling earrings struck a more informal, woman-to-woman approach. "Rose Mulrooney, Chair of the Federal Reserve asked me to visit."

With more and more people approaching—thank God that Rusty was in the back of the house—Megan had already surmised that the visitors didn't have anything to do with Keith, whose modest car, caught behind all of theirs, had to make a detour off the driveway before pulling into the garage alongside the house.

Out the corner of her eye she saw him appear from the garage, a satchel over his shoulder, and approach the gathering crowd outside his own front door with an expression of bemusement.

A tweed-jacketed man was trying to get her attention on behalf of Commissioner Applebaum whom, he stressed, had been the first public official to mention karma.

Like a group of journalists at a press call, however, it was the loudest who got the attention. This seemed to come in the form of a very tall, suited African American with the build of a professional wrestler, who had climbed out the back of a shiny, black stretch Hummer and was calling, "Mrs. Mitchell, the President of the United States is waiting on a direct line, right here," he gestured behind him. "He needs to speak to Lama Tashi."

What could possibly beat that?

The army officers tried. Arriving, somewhat out of breath, they called out, "Mrs. Mitchell! General Alexander Hickman *must* see Lama Tashi. The security of the United States depends on it!"

"So does our food security!" cried tweedy guy.

"The integrity of our economy is at stake!" Glamor-girl was not to be outdone.

"Ma'am," African American Hummer reminded her. "The President is right here!"

About to explain that Lama Tashi had already gone, just as Megan drew breath what sounded like a lawn trimmer buzzed over the roof of the house before pausing above the group, hovering. It was a drone the size of a lawnmower and instantly commanded the attention of all present, heads turning and necks craning to see what the hell was going on.

The drone, in turn, seemed to be making the same assessment, swinging this way and that, a lens extending beneath its blades. Then from the undercarriage, a screen the size of a television unrolled. On it, the face of Galaxy's boss live-streaming from Los Angeles.

"Megan, we spoke earlier—it's Harvey O'Sullivan from Galaxy," his voice was genial above the racket. "You know, Lama Tashi's first and closest media partner? I see you have a few folks here, no doubt on behalf of their bosses. But I'm here virtually myself. And I really need to speak to Rinpoche, so I do."

"He's not here!" she called out to Harvey and the assembled throng. "He left an hour ago."

"Where?" everyone wanted to know.

"Didn't say," she was shaking her head. "Only that he'd be gone for a while. I'm guessing he's taken himself on retreat for a few days."

The disbelief was palpable. How could the man who had become the nation's most popular guru, the only guy who had all the answers, suddenly absent himself. How could he just vanish? What kind of celebrity did that?

What direction had he travelled in, the police were calling out? Where might he be headed, demanded the FBI? They all knew that Lama Tashi was uncontactable by phone—and therefore untraceable. Harvey O'Sullivan, always first, was offering to sponsor Rinpoche through his retreat. African American Hummer, spur of the moment, offered Camp David as a meditation venue.

Amid the furor, Megan recollected the last instruction Rinpoche had given her—the story of the deer being pursued through the forest. Just as she now knew why he had reminded her of it.

"I truly have no idea where Lama Tashi has gone," she said. "He is my teacher. My guru. He's not accountable to me."

Just as with Hayden earlier, this revelation prompted outpouring of a different kind. There was a particular question the President wanted answered. The same, specific query, he had confided in Hayden earlier—along with the bosses of the Federal Reserve, FBI, FDA, CIA and US Army. Plus a whole lot of other callers with more evident commercial motivations. On the hovering drone, even Harvey O'Sullivan's eyebrows were raised at the unanimity of the crowd gathered outside Megan's front door as they requested, demanded, pleaded to know if Lama Tashi had said anything in connection with this subject.

Megan faced the group in the golden sunshine of that extraordinary day. "He didn't," she said. "So I can't help you. I'm sorry."

They didn't leave immediately. Instead, they paused, struggling to take it in. Wondering what to do next, and how to report back on the fact that not only had they failed to get hold of Lama Tashi, but the imperative question they all wanted answered by him would have to remain unanswered until who knew when?

Keith was the only one to move, walking through the group and up the three steps to the veranda where he hugged his kids and kissed his wife.

"Good day at the office?" he smiled, ironically.

"You're home early?"

"It's been that kind of day."

There were proffers of business cards and pleas to call as soon as Lama Tashi's whereabouts became known. In the dusk, Megan was aware that the police were already on their radios, tracking down Lama Tashi's vehicle registration. The FBI gathered around them, eager to pounce on America's Most Wanted. Harvey O'Sullivan didn't depart without extracting a promise from Megan to consider his personal request to appear on a magazine program next weekend about being a student of Lama Tashi's. And African American Hummer insisted that Hayden come take a look inside the vehicle which had clearly grabbed his attention.

It was ten minutes before Megan finally closed the front door behind her family and, unusually, locked it. "Shelley, let Rusty out the back room, won't you?" she asked, before returning to the kitchen, unhooking the apron from the door, and tying a bow behind her.

Despite all that had happened, she still felt curiously self-possessed. Perhaps the impact of Lama Tashi rubbing off? On the other side of the kitchen table, Hayden was gabbling excitedly about the communications system installed in the Hummer. Shelley wanted to know if the pretty lady who had visited was from The Real Housewives of Key West—she looked exactly like her! Keith, meantime, just looked baffled.

Responding to the wholesome aroma of baking coming from the oven, Megan regarded her family brightly. "Quiche for supper. Sorry it's nothing fancy. Today's been …" she raised her hands, upturned, towards the ceiling, as she searched for the right description. Before giving up.

"There are no words," she said.

ON ONE OF THE SIDE ROADS BETWEEN BOULDER AND OMNI, BEHIND the steering wheel, Lama Tashi slowed and indicated a left turn.

"This will only take two minutes," he told Anton.

His student nodded. It was an unpaved path leading into a forest, a turning Anton must have driven past dozens of times without ever noticing. They continued for only a short distance before coming to an entrance to a property comprising a white, timber cross gate set within an imposing stone wall.

Lama Tashi pulled up the handbrake between them and turned to face Anton.

"You drive yourself the rest of the way, okay?"

"Where are you going-?"

"Friends," Lama gestured the entrance beside him before getting out of the car. "You get going now!" He gestured imperatively.

Anton hurriedly undid his seat belt, climbed from the car, and was soon sitting where Lama Tashi had been. He glanced around. Apart from the impregnable-looking entrance, they seemed to have stopped in the middle of nowhere. "You sure your friends—"

"Yes, yes," Lama Tashi, clapped the roof firmly. "I will let you know about collecting the car."

Self-evident

There are two ways to be fooled.
One is to believe what isn't true;
the other is to refuse to believe what is true.

—SØREN KIERKEGAARD (Existentialist Philosopher 1813-1855)

Later

57

Galaxy Television
Los Angeles

D AN KAVANA AND TARA GREEN WERE BEHIND THEIR NEWS DESKS, as the large, neon timer, counted them down, 3, 2, 1.

"On this, the first day of instant karma in recorded history," Dan opened with words penned by Harvey O'Sullivan himself, "we have an extended edition of the evening news."

They took it in turn to read the headlines, starting with Tara: "The United States endured its worst mass shooting today, when the President of the National Gun Association turned a semi-automatic weapon on his own members at their annual conference in Washington, D.C., killing sixty-eight people and seriously injuring many others. President Trent Grey was injured during the shooting and is currently recovering from surgery at Walter Reed."

"Unprecedented bank movements have seen more millionaires and multi-millionaires created today than at any time since records began. The Chair of the Reserve Bank, Rose Mulrooney attributes the trend to the practice of generosity. Individuals and companies donating money are experiencing instant wealth creation on levels previously unseen."

"Airports are re-opening and transport networks resuming operations after fears of a food virus disrupted the lives of many Americans today. The FDA has assured the public that there is no contagion, but warnings remain in place that eating any meat product leads to serious food poisoning. America is now a vegetarian nation."

"Spontaneous remissions spiked at levels never before reported by the American College of Radiology, with fifty-two terminal cancer patients showing clear scans and numerous other miracle recoveries reported from coast to coast. Grace Arlingham of farm animal rescue organization, The Arlingham Foundation, and one of the first spontaneous remission cases, says that saving the lives of others is the cause for one's own life to be saved."

"The nation's top ten organized crime bosses and dozens of their henchmen died today according to the FBI. An exclusive Galaxy Television analysis shows that all ten of the men, responsible for drugs, racketeering, sex trafficking and money laundering, were killed during severe, micro-weather events including micro-tornados and earthquakes. According to the FBI, the deaths are evidence that the crime syndicates were putting in motion plans to kill others."

"Across the nation, people's personal appearances have been prone to dramatic change. Outbursts of anger have resulted in the significant worsening of facial flaws, blemishes and disfigurements. The opposite has also occurred with deformities disappearing and both facial and physical attractiveness improving in a way never previously witnessed. The American College of Cosmetic Practitioners has announced that anger is the cause of disfigurement and patience the cause of beauty. It will host an emergency summit next week to explore new, non-surgical treatment methods."

"Celebrity Scoop, the controversial gossip magazine, collapsed today. A sink hole in Manhattan swallowed up the twenty-five-floor building from which the magazine operated. The commercial property is believed to have been deserted apart from the magazine team and owner, who were working on the next issue. A spokesperson for Media Monitors International observed that lies, divisive speech and idle gossip are among the ten worst non-virtues."

"Helping us make sense of all these and other developments—" it was back to Dan for the final headline. "We bring you a full report on karma, including an exclusive interview with Lama Tashi."

58

Woodrow Wilson Building, Brooklyn

ON THE THIRD FLOOR OF THE WOODROW WILSON BUILDING, AMY could barely contain her excitement as the superintendent took the key from his jacket pocket and turned it in the lock.

"Ten minutes," he said. "I'll be waiting."

It had been Karel who'd prompted her to call the real estate agent, when she'd told him how she'd dreamed of living in the building from the first time she saw it. In minutes she'd found her way to a website showing apartments for sale. The realtor himself wasn't available for a viewing this evening. But he said he'd speak to the superintendent who had keys to one of the apartments. She could have an initial viewing right away.

"What d'you think?!" she asked, thrilled as she stepped into the main living area, a spacious room with beige walls and a high ceiling. "Isn't this just amazing?!"

Behind her, Karel Sharma looked around him trying to see what she could see. He'd never had much of an eye for aesthetics. But he had an eye for Amy, and he enjoyed her unaffected delight, the enchantment she took just being here. The women he knew socially, mainly through business, worked at being chic and cultivated, and he never really knew where he stood with them. There was a straightforwardness about Amy, a sweetness that put him at ease, and prompted a protective impulse that surprised him.

For a moment he wondered how many of his female friends routinely stopped to give money to the homeless. He had his doubts.

He looked at where Amy was bending, gazing out the window facing Eastern Parkway. Slim, petite, delicately-sculpted features with that cute, up-turned nose.

"The view from here does look pretty amazing," he said.

She half-turned, laughing as she registered his compliment. "I'd paint the whole place white," she turned, gesturing the walls. "Make it feel bigger. Maybe put some geometric panels above the doors and windows. Bright colored glass in the kitchen. It's an art deco building. This place needs to be taken back to its roots!"

She didn't know what to make of his amused expression. Was he wondering how she could get so excited about a two bedroom apartment in Brooklyn that was undeniably in need of attention? "I know it's probably nothing compared to where you live," she said.

It was true that he owned the penthouse of an Upper East side building. But work pressures meant he was rarely there, and when he was, he no longer really saw it, and hardly stepped into half the rooms. The rooftop balcony was a disgrace. It had been lush to begin with, but he'd fired the landscapers and never gotten round to replacing them. The whole place needed the attention of someone who cared.

"What?" she asked, trying to figure out his expression.

He shrugged. "I'm enjoying your enthusiasm."

"Well, okay," she headed along the short corridor to look at the bedrooms, still uncertain what to make of the enigmatic Karel Sharma.

After his most unexpected gift of the Bluegrass Horse Sanctuary property, and even less expected hug, she had wanted to call Mr. Deal immediately to tell him the exciting news. Mr. Deal hadn't been in the best of health for some years and she knew that the stress of trying to rehome all his horses would be the heaviest of burdens.

Before she called, however, she asked Karel's advice. She wanted to tell Mr. Deal he need never worry again about Bluegrass Horse Sanctuary coming under threat. At the same time, there was no avoiding the fact that he was an elderly man running the place with a group of volunteers. What would happen to the horses if he became unwell or died?

Karel had shrugged. "That's easy," he said. "Set up a trust. Put the property in it, and appoint trustees who will enforce terms that it will remain a horse sanctuary in perpetuity."

Amy had stared at him, shaking her head. "Y'see. That's why you're so successful. You know this stuff!"

A short while later she'd called Mr. Deal to tell him what was happening. How he never need worry about the horses, or his life's work again. He'd been mostly silent as she explained it all, expressing his gratitude in only a few, stumbled words. She knew why. Hand over the mouthpiece, he hadn't wanted her to hear him crying.

Now as she took in the rest of the Woodrow Wilson apartment, she scanned the bedrooms—tired and dated. Nothing that couldn't be transformed into "wow" by a couple of coats of paint and some imagination.

Ten minutes was up pretty soon and it was time to leave. Karel and Amy descended to the lobby in the elevator, and as they did, her stomach growled. It was a short bus ride from here to her apartment, or a long walk which went past her favorite grocery store. She was mulling her options when Karel asked, "Can I buy you dinner?"

"Oh!" The idea that he might suggest this had occurred to her earlier. But she'd immediately dismissed it. She imagined he spent his evenings hanging out with the rich and powerful, doing whatever it was that rich and powerful people did in their spare time.

"A meat free dinner?" she confirmed.

"Naturally. Pizza Margherita?" he proposed.

"That would be great!"

"Glass of Syrah?"

"How did you know?"

"Know what?"

"That's my favorite."

The doors slid open. "I didn't," he ushered her out.

Her eyes sparkled. "There's a great place just round the corner," she said.

59

Omni, Colorado

ON HER WAY TO THE FRONT DOOR AFTER THE BELL RANG,
Margarita paused to check her appearance in the sitting room
mirror. Not for the first time. She had no reason to be feeling nervous, she
kept reminding herself. But she was anyway, a curious blend of apprehension and anticipation.

She opened the door and neither of them said anything. They stood,
looking at each other, before he stepped towards her, taking her in his
arms. They held together for the longest time.

Her decision not to spend the whole day moping around the house had
led to unexpected outcomes. When she'd called Izzy, saying she wanted
to give her something, her friend hadn't asked her what it was, nor had
she volunteered. Izzy had probably thought it would be a book, or a plant
cutting, or any of the many, small things they used to share with each
other—the tangible tokens of a lifelong friendship.

Margarita's only hesitation, before visiting, was what to tell Izzy about
Bob. There was no need to say anything. It wasn't like he came up in every
conversation they had. Once she had more of a handle on what was happening, the logical side of her reasoned, *then* she could share the news.

Only, the moment she'd shown up in Izzy's kitchen, a scene of typical
chaos with her friend in the midst of icing two dozen cupcakes, Izzy had
taken one look at her and without preamble asked, "What's happened?"

There'd been no point pretending. Who was she to imagine she could fool her oldest confidante? Anyway, she'd been there for Izzy during the break-up of her first marriage and tortuous relationship with her second husband, who'd dumped her before filing so many lawsuits against her that she now referred to him as The Plaintiff.

She told Izzy what had happened, and Izzy had been ferociously loyal without making any dogmatic judgments. She had shed tears and her friend had hugged her and they'd talked for ages over tea and freshly-iced cupcakes.

It was only after that she'd been able to get to the original purpose of her visit. She told Izzy about the book signing in New York three days earlier. The man approaching who had been familiar in some inexplicable and distant way. How he'd turned out to be Norman Manderson.

Izzy had been surprised by the story. Captivated. The whole saga of Norman leaving the family was so long ago, her own children now the age that Norman would have been when he left, that the wounds had long since healed over. But he was still her brother. And when Margarita handed over the envelope and gift-wrapped box he'd asked her to bring, she eagerly tore open the envelope first to read the card.

"I know I should have done this decades ago. It was complicated. I would love to reconnect if you are willing. You are often in my thoughts. With love, Norman."

Izzy handed Margarita the card to read while she unwrapped the box. It was the size in which a jewelry store might pack a pair of earrings, brown faux leather with a single hinge. When she opened it, inside there was a small, transparent bag inside with what looked, to Margarita, like dull metal filings. Accompanying the bag, a small certificate declared the contents to be pre-solar grains estimated to be over seven billion years old. Part of only a tiny sample sold to the public to pay for Astro geological research. The grains had been retrieved from a meteor site.

Izzy held the packet up to the light, staring at it, before handing it to Margarita.

"Pre-solar grains?" she queried.

"Matter that came into existence before our own solar system," Izzy shook her head with a contemplative smile. "Typical Norman to come up with some obscure thing."

On receiving the box, Margarita had guessed it contained a piece of jewelry. No doubt Izzy had too. "Does it mean something to you?"

Izzy was nodding. "The last summer before Norman went to college, there was one night we sat outside talking after everyone else had gone to bed. I don't know what it was about that night, it was probably the first time we had chatted just like two adults, instead of squabbling kids. Norman was talkative, telling me how excited he was about going away to study architecture. He was explaining architectural theories, all very grown up and important, which went way over my head. I asked him what was his ultimate goal in life, you know, all very *Breakfast Club*, and he told me he wanted to design the most beautiful building in the world.

Then he asked me my own ultimate goal. I had no idea. I'd always done well in science subjects. And it just so happened that this shooting star scooted across the sky behind him. I felt I had to keep up with his impressive architecture theory stuff, so I told him I wanted to be an astrophysicist. The words just came out of my mouth. Don't think I'd even said them before. I definitely hadn't spent time thinking about it." Izzy looked sheepish. "Closest I ever came to being an astrophysicist was making silver stars for the cupcakes."

Margarita tilted her head to one side. Despite her chaotic personal life, Izzy was no fool. Who could tell how far she could have gone if she'd taken that path? "The thing is, he remembered," she gestured towards the box containing pre-solar grains.

"He remembered," agreed Izzy. "Long after I forgot." She held up the card. "I'm going to call him. Today."

Margarita had left Izzy in a very different state of mind than when she'd arrived. It had been a relief being able to share what had happened with Bob. Cathartic. It didn't stop the rawness of it, the hurt. But she no longer felt alone. With friends like Izzy she knew she would come out of it. For the moment, she would accept Izzy's one and only piece of advice: take every moment at a time. Don't think what may or may not happen in the months or years ahead. Especially don't think about Bob and the other woman. Stick to what mattered, here and now.

As it happened, the refrigerator needed a restock, so after Izzy's she drove into town, visited the grocery store, and picked out the things she'd need for the weekend. She returned to her car and was driving slowly towards the parking exit, when an incoming vehicle approached just as cautiously beside her. They were about to pass when, at the same moment, the two of them recognized each other and braked.

"Margarita!"

"Ian! You visiting for long?"

"Only until Sunday. Sorry I haven't called—it's a flying visit. The shop."

Since the time that Ian and Paige Turner had moved to Scottsdale, during their regular visits home they often visited Margarita and Bob, or took them out for a meal, or socialized with mutual friends. This had continued after Paige's death. And although all four of them had got on well, it was the connection shared between Margarita and Ian that was the glue. Something which went right back to their school days. An unexpressed bond, a sense of being on the same wavelength, a shared humor.

Margarita knew that on the last Saturday of a visit, Ian would treat his hosts—his brother and wife with whom he always stayed—to dinner out.

Spur of the moment she said, "If you don't have plans for tonight, you're welcome to come round."

As it happened, Ian didn't have plans. At least, he had, but they'd fallen through. Recalling his very recent encounter with Bob, pinned firmly beneath his naked bookstore manager, the idea of an evening with him and Margarita, trying to act like everything was normal, was an awkwardness he could do without.

"It'll only be me," Margarita said.

"Oh!" said Ian. "I am free, as it happens." A horn tooted behind him. He had to move.

"Come round to the house. Seven-ish."

They both drove off.

And here he was, on her doorstep, with a bouquet of vivid pink tulips and a bottle of Chianti. After they hugged, she showed him in. She'd made them eggplant parmigiana, with a side salad of rocket and pear. Before her visit to see Izzy, she reckoned, she wouldn't have felt able to say what she was about to—she would still have been too overwrought. In truth, if it hadn't been for her visit to Izzy, she almost certainly wouldn't have gone to the supermarket when she did and had the chance encounter with Ian.

Accepting the tulips, she led the way into the kitchen to find a vase. She put it in the sink to fill with water, and handed Ian a corkscrew for the Chianti.

"In the spirit of our long friendship, she began. "I should tell you why Bob's not here." She was looking at him directly. "He left me for your manager."

Ian's shock was genuine. What he'd witnessed earlier wasn't his idea of fun. A threesome with a much younger couple. He'd immediately assumed Bob must be going through a mid-life crisis. The idea that he had walked out on Margarita for that woman was incomprehensible.

"This morning." Margarita surprised herself how calmly she was able to deliver the news. "It's been going on for some months. Since the launch party, apparently." She rolled her eyes.

"Also in the spirit of our long friendship," Ian looked across the benchtop. "I had to go to her apartment this afternoon to get our laptop. Bob was there. If it's any consolation, he didn't seem happy."

She shrugged. "It's his life, now. He's made his choice."

The vase had filled with water. Lifting it from the sink, she toweled it dry before placing it at the front of the bench. Ian twisted the corkscrew and eased the cork out of the bottle, before pouring wine into two glasses Margarita had already taken out.

She stepped round beside him and he handed her a glass. They clinked in a toast.

"To long friendships," proposed Margarita.

"*Vecchi amici*," chimed Ian.

BEFORE SETTING OUT FROM OMNI MOTOR LODGE, BOB HAD CHANGED into a fresh shirt and trousers. He'd showered since that afternoon's encounter, hunching under the showerhead angled above the old-fashioned bath, trying to wet himself without spattering water across the whole of the scarred bathroom floor. Trying to lather up from the motel

330 — David Michie

bar of soap of a size which, had he found it in a soap dish at home, he would have thrown out.

Having gained harsh and stark clarity on what he really meant to Beth, he had come away from her apartment feeling sullied and cheap.

And having been on the receiving end of one of Lama Tashi's lectures on delusions, albeit via television instead of at the Lone Pine Meditation Center, he had no room for high sounding self-justification. If he had learned anything from the guru over the past few years, it had been the urgent importance of being real. Authentic. Of not trying to contrive elaborate fictions to conceal a simple truth.

There was only one course of action open to him now. Having betrayed his wife of twenty-four years that morning, he must return and beg her forgiveness. Ask her to take him back. Accept he must make amends. Reparations. Regain her trust. He must do whatever it took, because the alternative was just a void. A purposeless drift into the future.

After he had dressed, and combed his hair, he wondered what to do about the suitcase. Leave it here, on the basis that the special mission of supplication would fail? Or take it with him, for the opposite reason?

An optimist, by nature, Bob left the motel room with the packed case, placing it on the rear passenger seat. Soon, he was homeward bound.

As he slowed about to turn into their driveway, even in the deepening twilight he noticed the grey BMW parked outside the house. He recognized it immediately as Ian Turner's.

The bastard! *He* hadn't let the grass grow under his feet, had he? He'd no sooner discovered Bob in the most compromising circumstances than he was knocking on Margarita's door to tell her.

Instead of going in, Bob drove past the house and parked on the roadside outside the neighbor's. He approached his own home on foot. He didn't have any specific idea about what he was going to say. Things weren't going to plan.

It was no secret that Margarita and Ian had had some kind of thing going on way back at school. All quite innocent, it seemed. From time to time he and Paige used to tease them about it, all in a good humored way. It had never troubled him that his wife was fond of Ian. He had been fond of Paige—what of it?

In the clutches of full-throttle jealousy, he wondered what Ian Turner's intentions were towards his wife. Was he there simply to gloat over his own spectacular indiscretion? Or did he have plans to relocate Margarita to Scottsdale? How much would he tell her about earlier that afternoon? Even without embellishment, the scene he had encountered was more salacious than even Bob could have dreamed up.

He got closer to the house. The curtains weren't drawn, the lights were on inside, and he was concealed by the darkness. Sensing movement in the kitchen, he stepped behind a garden trellis to a place where he was shielded behind a creeper.

There the two of them were quite visible, Margarita filling a vase containing tulips with water at the sink. Ian pouring red wine out of a bottle into two glasses. Far from the melodrama that had played out in his mind, the two of them were carrying on just like they would have if Paige and he had been sitting in the next room. He wondered if Ian had already told her what he'd seen in Beth's apartment. Was that something he was keeping till later? Or perhaps not planning to tell her, after all?

What about Margarita? How had she explained his absence that evening? Had she told him he'd left her? Or was she not planning to go there?

He watched them clink their glasses together and smile. And as he did, it occurred to him that an unprompted appearance by him right now would not only backfire badly, it was also something to which he wasn't entitled. Frankly, if he walked in there right now, it would make him an even bigger asshole than he already felt himself to be.

He was the one who had absented himself from the scene playing out before him. He had left the house with a spring in his step only hours earlier. Had he been asked, back then, how he'd feel about a visit by Ian Turner that evening, it wouldn't have troubled him in the least.

Tissue paper mind, the words of Lama Tashi returned to haunt him, as they did at the worst possible time. *Up one moment*, he could practically see the guru curling his fingers through the air. *Down the next. Don't allow your delusions to take charge of your mind. You take charge of it!*

Bob retreated to his car and climbed into the driver's seat. And sat, staring into the darkness. He thought of the many times he'd sat in this very seat on his way to the Lone Pine Meditation Center. The countless hours he'd spent listening to Lama Tashi's clear and compelling instructions. How Rinpoche's teachings had focused strongly on karma in recent months. He'd drilled his students in detail on the subject so that they had a strong grasp about the law of causality and all the factors affecting it.

Bob himself had been among the special cohort, he could see now, who the guru had been preparing to make the very most of today's dynamics. To recognize what was going on in order to extract the maximum benefit from an extraordinary opportunity.

But he'd blown it. So caught up in his own cravings and fantasies, it hadn't been till mid-way through the afternoon he was even aware of what was going on. Even then, he'd been unable to focus on anything other than "me," "myself," and "I." Self-absorbed, wrapped up in his own tiny world, his was a textbook case of the futility of knowledge without action.

It didn't matter if you knew everything there was to know about karma—if it didn't change your behavior, your knowledge was pointless. Belief in karma didn't get you anywhere unless it affected what you did. Which in his case, it hadn't.

But it wasn't over yet. Karma didn't stop working just because the sun went down. For the first time he started getting his mind straight. Becoming clear about what he really wanted. Cultivating the heartfelt motivation that, through his actions, he would free all living beings from exactly the kind of misery he was experiencing right now, and lead them to a state beyond pain.

Taking out his phone, he scrolled down his contact list before pressing the dial button. He had met Vlad Zekulic at rehab when recovering from his bike accident. A young man, wheelchair bound and living in social housing, Vlad was isolated not because he didn't want friends, but because he didn't so much talk to people as talk at them. Within a short while of saying hello, he would be off on one of his two main subjects: Star Trek or the Peloponnesian War. Ignoring most efforts to change the conversation, deaf and blind to social cues, Vlad would carry on regardless, never understanding why he wasn't invited out a second time. Once, he had confessed to Bob, on their way home from physical therapy, that his life-long ambition was to dine at Quark's Restaurant. It was a goal that had eluded him as he never had anyone to go with. Bob had tucked away that bit of information as a future opportunity for a turbo-charged session of compassionate acceptance, generosity and patience all rolled into one.

"It's Bob," he announced himself, when Vlad answered the phone after a single ring. "What are you doing tonight?"

60

GOING OUT FOR DINNER TO CELEBRATE THEIR SPONTANEOUS remissions had been Kristina's idea. After a day of miracles Grace was more than ready for it—only she felt badly for Hen. "*I* would love to, darling. But it's always been the four of us," she said when Kristina suggested it, late that afternoon.

"We don't know how Hen's scan came out. And if it's not good ..."

"Mmm." Kristina thought for a moment before saying, "What if I text Hen an invitation? That way she can join us if she wants to, but there's no pressure."

Grace remembered Hen striding away from Snail Cemetery earlier, denouncing karma as illogical. Refusing to pick up even a single snail on the basis that to do so would be credulous. Unscientific.

Grace worried for her friend. If she hadn't created any causes for her life to be preserved, on what basis could anyone expect a favorable outcome?

"Charlie's keen," persisted Kristina.

"Charlie's always keen," observed Grace, and they laughed because it was true. Charlie's kids were young and exhausting. Going to a "cancer support" function was the perfect out to leave them with her own parents, giving Greg and her a night off.

"Blake must be ecstatic?" Grace asked after Kristina's husband.

"He is. You know the toll this has had on him," Kristina didn't need to elaborate. "He's happy for me to have a girl's night out tonight," she said

335

before Grace raised the subject. "We'll have many more nights than we expected, now, to celebrate things ourselves," she sighed.

"We will indeed," agreed Grace. Before saying, "All right. I'm in. The Blue Elephant at 7.30 pm?"

"I'll text Hen an invitation," confirmed Kristina. "See you soon!"

Grace, Kristina and Charlie arrived promptly and were shown to their table. The Blue Elephant had jungle murals on the walls, a wooden, ornamental bridge over a shallow stream, and plastic orchids on the tables. The women had eaten there once before and the Thai food was excellent even if the décor was tacky.

They talked for a while, waiting to see if Hen was coming. She hadn't replied to the invitation, but was probably in the scanner when Kristina sent it. Like Grace and Kristina, Hen was also a patient of Dr. Roberts and by the end of the day he might well be running late. She would be in and out of appointments and may not have a chance to check her messages.

After ten minutes had passed, and still no word, they decided to order a bottle of champagne to celebrate.

"Special occasion?" the *maitre d"* uncorked the bottle at their table with a muted but unmistakable "pop," and was pouring out three champagne flutes.

"It certainly is!" said Kristina. "All three of us are cancer free!"

It probably wasn't the kind of special occasion the *maitre d"* had in mind. He offered them his congratulations nonetheless.

"Even saying it out loud seems somehow impossible," Kristina commented as he walked away.

The other two nodded. It would take time for the reality of their total reversal of fortune to sink in.

They raised their glasses. "To healing!" offered Kristina.

"And to The Arlingham Foundation," Charlie beamed at Grace. "What an amazing thing you have accomplished in just one day!"

It was Grace's turn to propose a toast. "May all beings be free from suffering!" she said.

Ten minutes later, they had ordered starters to share when Kristina's phone bleeped. She read Hen's brief message out loud: "On my way."

Hen arrived shortly afterwards. The three women studied her closely as she was shown over the wooden bridge. When she saw them, she smiled broadly.

"Clear scan!" she punched her hands in the air as she approached.

They leapt to their feet to hug her, as a waiter hurried to fetch another champagne glass.

"I've just come from Dr. Roberts now," she explained excitedly as they sat. "Same thing as with you, Grace. He wanted to check again with me being his third remission of the day. That's why I've been so long—"

"And do you have any idea why it happened?" asked Kristina.

"Instant karma," Hen said with great certainty. "Obviously."

"I thought you didn't believe in karma?" asked Grace.

"I didn't," said Hen. "At least, not until I saw Dr. Bohn on TV."

From their puzzled expressions it was evident that the others had no idea who she was referring to.

"He was on Galaxy when I was waiting for the scan results. He reminded me of some basic quantum scientific principles. You know, how the way we think about matter is fundamentally flawed, because everything exists in dependence on other factors, and when those factors change—including our mind—so does our experience of the thing itself.

Hen's eyes were gleaming with the passion of a convert. "I'd never had karma pitched to me like that before, so I'd never understood the link between cause and effect. But it's all going on in our mind!" she was emphatic. "When you think about it, the only thing that's happening is a constant state of flux, of unfolding, and the causes we create make them unfold in a particular way."

It was a moment before Charlie observed, "Sounds very profound, Hen."

"Not really. Just takes a bit of time to get your head round," she said.

Profound or not, all of their expressions were euphoric. Then Kristina said. "Just one thing, Hen. You said you didn't understand karma till you saw Dr. Bohn on TV."

She nodded.

"After you'd been scanned."

"Yes."

"So what was the karmic cause-?"

Hen sat back in her chair with a rueful smile. "Oh, that!" she said.

"This morning, after leaving you lot picking up snails, when I got home I found Shere Khan on the veranda with a lizard in his mouth."

The women were all familiar with Hen's large and indulged tabby. "I'm no fan of lizards, but I objected to his behavior. It just isn't necessary. I keep telling him to leave them alone, but do you think he ever listens?" she frowned.

Grace wasn't the only one who found it amusing the way Hen would flip from no-nonsense rationalist to giddy sentimentalist when it came to her cat.

"He wouldn't drop the thing, so I took matters into my own hands. Perhaps it was having just watched you rescue those snails. Anyway, I put my finger over his nostrils so he couldn't breathe. He had to open his mouth and he let go. The lizard didn't seem injured. Still even had its tail. As it scrambled away under the deck, I remembered your line Grace, about may all beings be free from suffering. I said it out loud, and picked up my naughty beast and took him inside to distract him. So," she looked back at Kristina. "That was probably the cause."

Evidently, it didn't matter if you knew nothing at all about the workings of karma. Belief in it was completely unnecessary. What mattered was only what you did—your behavior.

Lifting the glass Kristina had just poured, she toasted, "To lizards."

Across the table, Grace winked. "And to naughty beasts for making salvation possible!"

61

"I WANT TRENT HOME AS SOON AS POSSIBLE. OBVIOUSLY." THE FIRST Lady was frowning at the President's Chief of Staff. "But like this?"

The two of them were outside the private ward just after the surgeon had visited for a second, post-operative visit. Six hours had passed since the conclusion of surgery and the specialist said he was very satisfied with the outcome. President Trent had been fortunate where the bullet had entered his body. It had missed major arterial injury by a fraction of an inch, and similarly avoided hitting any bone. Instead, it had passed through muscle and fat. Having cleaned and stitched the wound, all that remained was to let nature take its course and allow the President's body to heal.

He left his patient some strong painkillers, although he didn't think they'd be needed overnight. He'd visit again tomorrow and saw no reason why the President couldn't be discharged first thing.

"Great news!" the President had declared, thanking his medical team.

The First Lady and his Chief of Staff shared his relief. But underneath her smiles, Lucy Grey was worried.

"You heard what he's just been saying," she challenged Will Salt.

"I know," he nodded, seriously.

"It just seems out of control."

"I hear you."

"And it's not even the anesthetic!" she welled up.

339

"Lucy," he eyeballed her. "Clearly you know the President very much better than I do. But politically-speaking, he's not a conviction politician. He's a pragmatist. And that's exactly what this nation needs right now. Someone who can adapt to the new order. Which he is doing wonderfully! You have to trust that. You have to believe in his ability to channel the zeitgeist."

"It's not the zeitgeist that worries me. It's the all the redneck so called "patriots" that will try to kill him."

They both looked into the room where the President, sitting up in bed, was on a conference call via a secure laptop connection. From the moment he came round, it seemed, he had embraced the notion of instant karma with gusto. Friday afternoon or not, he'd demanded heads of key departments get back to him with imaginative, flagship policies appropriate to the new era of instant karma. As the ideas started coming in, neither the First Lady nor his Chief of Staff had ever seen him so excited.

The Department of Health and Human Services suggested universal healthcare funded by tax-free donations. Who *wouldn't* donate to support the healthcare of others, they suggested, if the result was to guarantee one's own health—along with an immediate financial windfall well beyond the size of the donation?

To turbo-charge the US economy as never before, Treasury was recommending a unilateral and immediate write-off of all foreign debt.

The Department of Commerce wanted to drop all trade tariffs in anticipation of immediate global reciprocity—and the dumping of red tape.

The Army suggested a withdrawal from all offensive action and conversion of the military into a peacekeeping and emergency services force.

But it was a proposal from some Congressional leaders that alarmed the First Lady. They were suggesting removing the Second Amendment from the Bill of Rights altogether. If shooting others only created the cause to be shot oneself, they reasoned, what possible motive could there be for buying or keeping the instrument of your own execution?

Further inquiries by Police Chief Hans Ziegler at The Piccard Hotel had resulted in a startling analysis: all the delegates shot dead that lunchtime were part of a hard-core lobby group within the NGA who, only that morning, had been intensively lobbying Congress to ease restrictions on assault weapons.

"What about you?" the First Lady had objected a short while ago, when the President had told her about the proposal. "You weren't out lobbying this morning. You got shot."

"A minor injury," he'd looked at her over the top of his reading glasses. "If I wasn't who I am, they would have discharged me already. And I'm ashamed to say, I was the cause of the injury myself."

Her eyes narrowed.

"This morning in the gym, the window was open and this mouse came in. My personal trainer didn't notice. It was behind him. I told him to do something. He threw a tennis ball at it. It limped away. Never crossed my mind till I was coming round."

"Mouse', the First Lady remembered. She thought he'd been mumbling something about "house."

"Even if that's true," she clutched herself with her arms. "You know what the gun lobby is like." Her lips had started to quiver. Her eyes filled with tears. "They'll crucify you!"

The President ended his conference call. The First Lady and Will Salt returned to the room. He seemed to have some idea what they'd been discussing because he reached out his arm. "I know you're worried about me, hon, but I want to tell you something. I've just been on the phone to Commissioner Applebaum, you know, at the FDA."

She nodded.

"A farmer tried to kill him this afternoon. Somehow got into his office. Took a shot at him from three yards away. He missed. The Commissioner's security shot the farmer—not fatal, just to put him down. You see," he squeezed his hand. "As of today, no one can kill you unless you create the cause to be killed. If they try, they'll only hurt themselves."

Lucy knew her husband well enough to recognize he wasn't going to change his mind. Not now, at any rate. There was nothing to be gained by discussing the subject further.

"In the meantime, what do we do next time Mr. Mouse comes visiting?" she wanted to know.

"Humane mouse trap followed by a visit to the country, over the hills and far away," he said.

"Over the hills and far away," she repeated. "I'm feeling envious."

62

Galaxy Newsroom
Los Angeles

WEIRDNESS CONTINUED AT GALAXY NEWS DEEP INTO THE EVE-
ning. Dan Kavana and Tara Green co-hosted news coverage
that continued late as dramatic events poured in from around the world.
Bosses of the most powerful drugs syndicates in Columbia had been
involved in peace talks gone wrong: during the ensuing shoot-out, they
and their top echelons had been mutually destroyed.

In the Pacific, philanthropists working to save endangered orangutans
were gifted an entire island to be retained, in perpetuity, as a red ape
sanctuary.

Freak weather events saw oppressive dictators on every continent
engulfed by landslides, drowned in floods or burned to death in their
own beds. World history was being rewritten overnight.

With so many people working late, Harvey O'Sullivan had laid on food
and wine from a nearby vegan restaurant. Along with all the hard work
and intensity there was a strangely festive, end-of- an-era atmosphere.
Previously a remote, even God-like figure, now that they'd had the chance
to work with Harvey, the news team had come to appreciate his rapier-
sharp acumen. His willingness to take risks. His considerable charm.

He and roly-poly Trent Garvey had been in constant touch through
the day as Galaxy implemented Lama Tashi's advice to promote their
competitors. When the initial gamble had paid off, Harvey had been reso-
lute. "Promote the bejesus out of them!" had been his command. Much

to the bewilderment of commercial rivals, they were soon the subject of lavish endorsements by Galaxy's most-loved anchors and reporters. And Galaxy's own ratings just continued to rocket.

"They must have worked out what we're doing by now," observed Trent when the mid evening ratings chart went perpendicular. "Why aren't they doing the same thing?"

"Fear," Harvey told him. "They're scared of making idiots of themselves. Once you get over that," he placed an avuncular hand on Trent's shoulder, "the world's your oyster, my friend."

In his element, back in the newsroom, Harvey had been scheming with researcher Chieko, about social media collaboration with *Flourish*: he wanted Megan Mitchell to partner with Galaxy in taking her brand global.

And well into his third drink that evening he pushed a glass of wine into Nick Nalder's hand. "You're a good lad, Nick. Run a tight ship. I appreciate that."

Nalder nodded.

"Let me see about getting you more resources—"

"I'd appreciate that," said Nalder.

"—but there's something I want in return."

Nalder swallowed. "Oh?"

"Your HR approach." He tilted his chin in the direction of Tracey Kramer. "Refreshing."

"That—" Nalder was about to explain how Precious Treasure was just a concept today.

"I want you to unroll it across the whole organization."

"You mean—"

"Two people in a room. Get it all out there. No holds barred. Then—" Harvey, brushed his hands together. "—move on. You should see the money we waste on mediation, conciliation, arbitration. Therapists. Lawyers. And months later they're still feeling bitter and victimized. *You've* got the right idea."

"Well …" Nalder looked down.

"Plus we'll end up with the best-looking TV network ever seen."

"You noticed?"

"Impossible not to. Patience is a cause for beauty. Not so?"

Later, Nalder found himself next to Tracey Kremer, putting a slice of tiramisu in a dessert bowl.

"Harvey wants me to take the Precious Treasure thing around the whole of Galaxy."

Not being a technician, or in front of the cameras, Tracey had consumed several glasses of wine that night and was well on her way. She looked at Nalder, giggling.

"What?"

"By the time you get back from that you'll be so good looking they'll want to cast you as James Bond!"

"Not sure whether to take that as a compliment or an insult."

"Me neither," she shrugged, picking up the bowl. "By the way, my dress last Friday. Did you really think it was frumpy?"

It took him a moment to work out what she was referring to. "Oh that," he shook his head. "I knew you liked it. That's the only reason I was nasty about it. You don't want to listen to me on women's fashion. What do I know?"

She handed him the dessert before getting a slice for herself.

"The B.O. problem." It was his turn to be vulnerable. "How real is that?"

She served herself a slice. "Just wanted to get you worried."

They both laughed before she mused, "Don't know how good I'm going to be at this anymore."

"At what?"

"Being your Precious Treasure."

"You were pretty damned good at it back there," he pointed towards the second studio.

"Yeah but things changed, didn't they?"

He held her gaze. "I guess they did."

"I even kind of … like you now."

"Yeah. Ditto." He looked forlorn before saying, "You need to find me a spoiled brat millennial."

"And you need to find me an arrogant shithead boomer," she replied. They turned to scan the news room. "But where?"

Dan and Tara finally came out of the studio after the late night news. It had been the longest of days and they were both exhausted. Within minutes they were out the door and into the corporate vehicles waiting for them. By then, the whole news team had gone home.

Dan had checked his phone a couple of times during breaks. No more videos from the Pacific Seabird Rescue, but Jacinda said that Maddie was continuing to make progress. Also, that she was refusing to come home till the last gull was clean. There was a whole gang of volunteers similarly committed. It was going to be a late night.

He must have nodded off on the way home, because next thing he knew they were through the gates and up the short, paved driveway. Inside, he found Tammy waiting for him. Although she was in her nightgown, she somehow managed to appear poised and welcoming, not a hair out of place.

"Some day, huh?" she murmured, after they'd kissed. "I'm having Baileys on ice. Like a whisky?"

"Definitely."

It had become their ritual if Dan was on the late shift. Tammy would wait up for him—she was a night owl and there was always work to be done. They'd pour a drink and sit outside if the weather was good, looking out across the twinkling lights of Beverly Hills and beyond. It was their special time together to reflect on the day, make plans, or simply enjoy the night, winding down before bed.

Despite everything that had happened in the world around them, there was only one subject of conversation that night. They were thrilled by Maddie's progress. She'd done things they had been told may take many months to happen, things that she may not even be able to do again. They replayed that video again and again. They couldn't wait to see her, to share her life-changing breakthrough.

Dan explained how the call for volunteers had come to his attention— under the news room table during an earthquake. How he'd talked the thing through with his make-up lady Alice, still uncertain, in those early hours of instant karma, if it would work.

"You look tired," Tammy was sympathetic. "Must have been one hell of a ride today."

"That's no lie," Dan kicked off his shoes, tugged away his tie and undid the top button of his shirt. "But tomorrow's Saturday. Day off. I don't care how long I have to stay up, I want to see my girl."

Tammy was the same. "Every time I call, Jacinda tells me there's just one more bird."

They must have dozed off, because next thing they knew they were waking to the sound of keys in the front door. The echo of Jacinda's footsteps in the hallway.

"Jacinda?" Tammy called from the veranda.

"You awake?" she was surprised.

She appeared across the sitting room. Behind her, the familiar sound of the wheelchair tires as Maddie followed.

"Darling!" Tammy was on her feet, soon followed by Dan, walking inside.

She looked exhausted too, her long-sleeve top and face spattered with oil, her hair drawn back in a pony tail.

"We cleaned every last one!" she was triumphant. Before holding up her hand before they could get any closer, "Stop!"

She flashed a glance at Jacinda who was standing a short distance away.

"D'you want-?" began Jacinda.

"No!" she was insistent.

Putting her hands under her right thigh, she raised it up, while moving her right foot and placing it on the floor. Then she did the same with her left. All movements doctors had said would never be possible again. Then, hands on the arm rests, muscles quivering, she thrust herself upwards, till she was standing. Balancing carefully, she smiled at her incredulous parents, breathing mindfully. Until she was ready to take first one unsteady step, then another, towards where the two of them were watching her through their tears.

Next Day

Do not believe in anything simply because you have heard it. Do not believe in anything simply because it is spoken and rumored by many. Do not believe in anything simply because it is found written in your religious books. Do not believe in anything merely on the authority of your teachers and elders. Do not believe in traditions because they have been handed down for many generations. But after observation and analysis, when you find that anything agrees with reason and is conducive to the good and benefit of one and all, then accept it and live up to it.

—THE BUDDHA (5th century BCE)

63

The Delighted States of America

WAKENING TO A BEAUTIFUL, SPRING SATURDAY, THE GOOD PEOPLE of the United States—and even the not so good ones—recollected the momentous events of the day before. Some turned on their television sets or went online to find out if instant karma was still a thing. Others required no such validation, the reality of it playing out in their own lives within minutes of opening their eyes.

One idea, above all others, soon came to be uppermost. A singular motivation more compelling than any up till then: whatever it was that they most dearly wanted, how best might they give it to others?

Twenty-four hours of instant karma was all it had taken for this most remarkable paradigm shift. For people to place other beings at the heart of their benevolent intentions, knowing that in so doing, they would be the first beneficiaries. To let go, at some level, of the duality between self and other and to practice being wisely selfish with conviction.

The most conscientious citizens had already written down the motivation Lama Tashi had said should be recited at the start of each day: "May my every action of body, speech and mind today be a cause for me to become enlightened, so that I may help all other beings attain this same state." Others were reminded of the words when they went online—the digital world fast becoming a treasure trove on every aspect of karma. It was, after all, the subject *du jour*. Why would you *not* want to understand every element of its workings when your happiness depended on it?

People quickly became expert, not only in the general aspects of karma, but in understanding which causes created which specific effects. If you wanted to be healthy, wealthy and wise, the instructions were clear. Just as, if you aspired to be good-looking, famous and influential. A shortened lifespan, infirmities, ugliness and squalor all had their causes. Of course you should avoid them: get with the program!

Knowing how much the weight of karma was affected by intention, it wasn't long before everyone was practicing bodhichitta—the most powerful motivator. Those who contemplated all the causes for negative experiences they had created in the past, causes that might manifest as greatly increased effects when conditions allowed, were especially diligent. Not just saying the words, but taking the time to understand the meaning of the words. And not that alone either, but *experiencing* the meaning of the words.

As they did, just as Lama Tashi had said, what began as a fabricated exercise became something more profound. "Aha" moments occurred as people's understanding deepened to the point that it changed their behavior: they became as wholehearted and persistent and imaginative at pursuing the happiness of others as they had once pursuing their own. *Self*-development came to be regarded as narrow and ineffectual, founded on a basic misconception. *Other* development was in!

The wish to give material things was universal. You couldn't go anywhere without being so showered with gifts that it took single-minded resolve to be a net donor rather than a net recipient. The result wasn't so much a trickle-down as a flood-down effect, with the world's richest one per cent sharing more of their 45 percent of wealth with the other 99 percent. Not that they were without it for very long. As philanthropists of the past had discovered, no matter how enthusiastic you were about giving your money away, all you did was create the causes to become even richer.

In business, erstwhile competitors did all they could to promote commercial rivals, and were genuinely overjoyed when they got lucrative deals over the line. Celebrities had zero-tolerance for bad-mouthing their peers, seeking only to celebrate their successes. There was plenty of room for everyone to succeed. Only a self-loathing dunderhead would begrudge other people's triumphs.

Kindness and compassion were the order of the day. It wasn't only the lovelorn, the jilted and the betrayed who wanted to feel whole. Everyone did! Which was why when strangers met the eyes of one another, they did so with a smile. When friends encountered each other, they embraced with warm affection. In the new emotional climate, the frozen-hearted thawed, the insecure stirred from their shells and attention-seekers set aside their pretentions in favor of a humbler, more authentic way of being. Enlightened self-interest segued from a fabricated habit to a motive spontaneously felt.

The wish to preserve the life of all sentient beings was embraced with enthusiasm. Never had there been such reverence for living beings, especially the small and vulnerable. The notion that only humans had a monopoly on the high value they placed on their lives, or that *homo sapiens* alone wished for happiness and to avoid pain, was seen as a cruel and self-evident falsity just like historical prejudices along the lines that slavery was okay, or that women shouldn't be allowed to vote.

Elaborate lengths were taken to avoid stepping on sidewalk bugs. Bee-friendly plants appeared on apartment balconies. Garden bird-feeders were stocked with avian delicacies. Every chance to preserve life was welcomed as a special opportunity—even cockroaches were caught and relocated using large matchboxes by rescuers murmuring their bodhichitta motivation as they did.

People had never been so patient. Road rage evaporated—what kind of loser would allow the slipshod driving of someone else to make himself ugly? Instead, that Saturday saw a flurry of messages suggesting social calls with in-laws—the more infuriating the better. Mind-numbingly tedious individuals, usually shunned, became suddenly popular as everyone wanted a chance to cultivate their patience. Few people would pass up the rare opportunity to spend time in the company of someone from the opposite end of the political spectrum, listening to their ignorant gibberish and outrageous provocations, all the while responding only with a gently-expressed query here or there. Religious zealots found themselves explaining their harsh censure of unbelievers to the very people they described, who regarded them with indulgent smiles. The overall attractiveness of the human race was elevated to levels never before seen.

The media, both traditional and social, also took on an altogether different complexion. Given the high price to be paid for lying, divisive comments, harsh speech and idle gossip, gone were the click-bait headlines, the deliberate inuendo, the lengthy, babbling speculation about what celebrities may or may not have thought, said or done, based on the most tenuous evidence. Instead, there was a firm focus on the positive, the uplifting, the useful, so that people came away from what they'd absorbed, uplifted and happy.

There was, of course, no crime. If planning murder, theft or violence resulted only in unspeakable misery for oneself, why would you do it? Especially when the true causes of wealth and happiness were so easily achieved?

Those who had been involved in criminality before, and who'd somehow survived the first day of instant karma, had become understandably anxious. How to avoid the tsunami of horror which would strike as soon as conditions made them possible? Bodhichitta was the go-to method for purification. Heartfelt amends were freely offered. Reparations were made. Hadn't Lama Tashi said that virtue had ten times the power of non-virtue?

Throughout the developing world, warlords became peace-lords, transferring their looted gains from overseas bank accounts to pay for food, schools, and hospitals. African dictators, who had somehow avoided hail, fire, and floods the day before, sold off their luxury hotel portfolios, liquidated off-shore assets, and even dispensed with their Mercedes Benz Maybachs in favor of the chemicals needed to provide clean water to their citizens.

Overseas, politics changed overnight. Dramatic breakthroughs were made to previously irresolvable conflicts. In Jerusalem, the Israeli Government renounced all claims to the city, seeing how significant it was to the Palestinians and Christians. The Palestinians wouldn't hear of it—no, they declared, Jewish and Christian groups should be in charge, given the city's importance to their religions. The Christians were equally adamant that they should have no say. Arms folded around the conference table, it was only when a U.N. negotiator proposed a joint system of government that there were smiles all round. Compromise and goodwill broke out everywhere.

Accompanying the massive karmic reverberations that continued throughout the world, upending century-old enmities, replacing hatred with love, despair with hope and sadness with joy, there was, at the same time, a collective relief about what was happening. A sense of stepping lightly and resting easy. A gradual awakening to the reality that appearances are illusion-like. No essence can be found to anyone or anything because all is a state of flux, of becoming something else. So long as you take part in this ever-changing dance with intentions that are benevolent, then all is well. There is nothing to be too attached to because reality is your projection and yours alone.

And for a very select group of people, students from the Lone Pine Meditation Center, the wisdom their teacher had recently voiced never seemed so obvious. Lama Tashi had posed a question ten days earlier, which felt like a lifetime ago. The answer to it, hopelessly idealistic at the time, was so much more practical in light of the past twenty-four hours' events.

"If you ever want to check if you *really* believe in karma, it's very simple," Lama Tashi had said, his presence as ethereal as a wisp of incense. "Just ask yourself this: do you put the needs of other beings before your own?"

64

Boulder, Colorado

O NE SUCH STUDENT, MEGAN MITCHELL, WOKE EARLY, SLIPPED into her track suit, and while her kids and husband were asleep, crossed from the house to the studio. Rusty was eager to get outside and explore the woods. As he snuffled through the undergrowth, eagerly exploring the herbaceous aromas of dawn, Megan made herself a coffee and sat on the studio step, laptop on her knees.

Flourish had received tens of thousands of emails since her first interview with Lama Tashi yesterday, and she'd glanced through only a fraction of them. Many were questions for Lama Tashi from ordinary people having extraordinary experiences. Many more were the kinds of invitations that had started pouring in for Rinpoche the day before, wanting him to consider being a director, a patron, an expert advisor.

More astute observers, recognizing their slender chances with Lama Tashi, were coming after her. There were invitations to speak at conferences, be interviewed, go on tour.

Hunched on the step, just scrolling through the first page of emails felt overwhelming. She would have to hire someone to go through her mail, she thought. Before wondering what Lama Tashi would do in such a situation. At which point she relaxed her shoulders, placed her laptop on the studio floor, and looked through the trees to the distant valley.

"Rusty!" she called softly. Her golden retriever came over for a hug.

Lama Tashi would laugh, was the truth of it. She could see him, as if he were here now, his face crinkled and head thrown back as he chuckled

357

at the craziness of it. He hadn't felt obliged to reply to every message he had received yesterday. Why should she?

What he had done was make the most of every opportunity to connect with nature and with other beings. When it came to sharing wisdom he had been highly effective, setting his own agenda, not by responding to the countless requests and messages wanting to steer him this way or that.

After a while, Megan pulled back her laptop, closed her emails and opened the message he had recorded the day before, to be released at a time of her discretion. This was all that really mattered today, she decided. The one thing her teacher had asked her to do.

It was only a few minutes long, and she watched it with complete absorption. It anticipated the question that had been so urgently asked the evening before by the nation's most powerful leaders from President Grey down. Not that Lama Tashi's answer would give them much comfort, she reflected. But as always with Rinpoche, there was an added insight, an unexpected offer of special wisdom. Something for people to mull over during the course of the weekend.

No sooner had she finished watching the recording, she knew what to do with it.

That afternoon, Megan sent the file with Rinpoche's message directly to the nation's leaders who had gone to such extraordinary lengths to contact him twenty-four hours earlier. It was labelled strictly confidential—not for distribution to the media.

An hour before the main evening news, she contacted major media outlets, letting them know that Lama Tashi had recorded a special message, now available on the *Flourish* website.

Around the kitchen table with her family that night, she flicked through the TV channels. Every one of them was leading with it.

"I hope that every one of you is taking advantage of the extraordinary opportunities we now enjoy." Megan could imagine a collective tranquility settling over the nation, as Rinpoche appeared against the familiar backdrop.

"Some people will be asking how long will this continue? Have things changed forever, or only for a day or two? Will we revert to the way things were before? If so, will that be permanent, or does karma climate change mean we can expect more waves of instant karma in the future?"

Those were exactly the questions which leaders had wanted answered the previous day. How could strategy be set when the world around them was so volatile?

And not only the leaders. Settling down after the wild events of the day before, many less-than-fulfilled workers were left wondering if they could throw off the shackles of employment on Monday morning and just practice generosity instead? Middle income earners began debating if they should replace health insurance premiums with automatic payments in favor of The Arlingham Foundation. Many a carnivore, munching a lackluster cheese and tomato sandwich that lunchtime, couldn't help sneakily questioning if meat was permanently off the menu.

As always, the ease of Rinpoche's presence took the edge off the intensity of these concerns. There was even a playfulness on his face as he posed the questions.

"I am sorry," he said. "I have no answer. While I have been expecting a big shift in the way that karma manifests, it's not possible to predict how the dynamics will play out."

He paused for a while as the camera came in closer to his face. "In a more important respect," his tone was firm, "it shouldn't make any difference. The law of causality remains unchanged. It always has existed. It always will. All that's different is the timing.

"If you only experience the beneficial effect of a cause you create after six weeks, instead of six minutes, is it no longer worth creating the cause? What about six years or even sixty years later, by which time your small acorn of kindness has perhaps grown into an oak tree—what about then? Or a future experience of reality, completely different from this life? If you have cultivated a mind of warm heartedness and virtue, why would you not experience the results of that?

"The same is true, of course, for negative causes and effects. As we think, so we become. The reality we experience arises from previous causes. No other being is forcing us to have this reality. *We* are in charge.

"Look at the big picture. The panoramic view. Karma is eternal. Don't get too caught up worrying about the speed with which causes ripen.

A human lifetime is like this," holding up his right hand, he snapped his fingers beside his face. "Like a flash of lightning in the night sky. A waterfall rushing down the mountainside. Of course, it usually takes time for causes to meet with conditions to ripen. There is an interval between sowing and reaping.

"So let's look at what we're experiencing now as a call to action. A precious and unprecedented reminder of exactly how reality is created. How lucky are we to be alive, here and now?"

Lama Tashi nodded with a serene smile. Before changing the subject. "There is one other message I'd like to share. Since yesterday morning, I've received many kind requests from people asking me to be their representative, their patron. There is even one group that wants to put up a statue of me!" Bringing palms to his heart, he chuckled at the notion, like a parent regarding a small child's act of generosity. "I sincerely appreciate these. Really, I do. But I am afraid, they are not the best requests to be making. If you want a useful answer to something, it is important to ask a useful question, not so?"

He paused, allowing people to absorb this point, before he continued. "As I always remind students, if there is somebody that maybe you like or respect, somebody you think has worthwhile qualities, the right question is *not* "How can I have or possess this person?" "How can I bring them into my life." Or, "How can I put them on a pedestal and worship them?"

Shaking his head, his pensive expression shifted to one of startling resolve. Eyes alight and expression more compelling than in any moment he'd yet been seen on television, this was a different Lama Tashi, one of extraordinary power.

"The right question to ask is: "How can I *be* like them?" We all possess the same nature, the same basic qualities," his eyes were utterly commanding. "Each one of us has the same, brief, human life. How you choose to use it—that's *your* choice. So, be the best that you can be! Don't just aim to be rich or beautiful or powerful—those are tiny ambitions. You can do better! You have the capacity to become a fully enlightened being of infinite benefit to both self and others. Why settle for anything less?"

That evening

65

Vulture Peak Drive
Omni, Colorado

THE FRONT DOOR WAS OPEN EVEN THOUGH NIGHT HAD FALLEN WHEN he arrived, flashlight in hand, having walked the short distance along Vulture Peak Drive. The entrance hall was a blaze of lights from where Tina, only moments before, had put the finishing touches to a large and extravagant arrangement of spring flowers. Tulips, daffodils, hyacinths, and snap dragons burst, vivid with color, from the midst of curly kale leaves. Even from the front door, the aroma of new life was irrepressible. From deeper inside the house came the sound of lush chords.

He had raised his hand to knock on the door when Tina appeared back in the hall, a watering can in her hand.

"Oh!" She exclaimed in delight, catching sight of him. Placing the can on the table she hurried over.

"Can you hear?" she asked, eyes shining.

"The piano."

"Yes!" Seizing his right hand in both of hers, she led him through the hallway. "This is only thanks to you, you do realize?"

Lama Tashi chuckled.

"I don't know what you said to him. He's been a changed man since he came back from the V.A."

And you a changed woman, Lama Tashi thought, but didn't say. What he did say was, "I wanted to let you both know that I'm home again. And to thank you and Tom for feeding Shanti."

363

"Oh, we loved having her visit."

"She came here?" Rinpoche was surprised.

"Of her own volition. Made herself completely at home," chortled Tina. "Quite a character."

They were in the sitting room next to the sofa. Back towards them, immersed in a Chopin nocturne, Tom didn't know they were there.

Even in the day since he'd returned to the piano stool, his playing had improved immeasurably. It was all flooding back. He had been returned to the forgotten country of his childhood, rediscovering pathways both intensely familiar but long unexplored. Turning the pages of sheet music on the stand, for piece after piece he found he only needed the starting point to be suggested and he was off again, utterly absorbed in the festival of primordial memories and inexpressible sentiment, taken to a time and place much bigger than himself, a state of being transcendent and numinous.

At the end of the nocturne, they both clapped.

Turning towards them, Tom's face was bright.

"Lama Tashi!" he stepped away from the piano to hug his neighbor in a gesture of unprecedented affection. "I don't know how I can ever thank you," he said. "You gave me my life back!"

"Please. No need," said Rinpoche. "I am glad you have rediscovered your music. You are highly accomplished."

They went onto the balcony lined with salvia baskets in prodigious bloom. "The Hanging Gardens of Babylon again," observed Lama Tashi.

"I missed them," said Tina.

"We both did," Tom held her eyes, the significance of the blossoms, like the display in the entrance hall, requiring no explanation.

Tina offered to make tea and when Lama Tashi accepted, she returned indoors, leaving the two men side by side, looking out into where the darkness was lit by stars above and twinkling lights in the valley below.

"I thought you'd be gone for weeks," said Tom. "Seems like everyone wants a piece of you. Even my old mate General Hickman."

Lama Tashi shuffled from one foot to the other.

"Rest assured, if you have any trouble with people, we'll put a barrier across the road right outside my gate. I won't have you being disturbed by unwanted visitors. They'll have *me* to answer to."

"That's reassuring," said Rinpoche. "I'll be protected by the U.S. Army!"

"Least I can do." Tom couldn't avoid glancing over at the balcony chair on which he'd used to sit every night.

Following his look, Lama Tashi said, "The piano stool is a better place, yes?"

"*So* much better," agreed Tom, with feeling. Before turning to face him. "I watched your message today. About not worshipping people but seeking to be like them."

"They showed it?"

"On every channel," Tom couldn't be prouder of his famous neighbor. "Like everyone else, I suppose, it's no surprise that I'd like to be more like you. The thing is, I can't meditate like you. And even if I started, at my age, how far am I going to get with it?"

Lama Tashi met the intense expression in those very clear, blue eyes with a playful twinkle. "What is it, particularly, that you would like to copy?" he asked.

Tom met his eyes, "Exactly this," he gestured towards him. "The way things never get to you. It's like you've let go of the need to be something or someone. Like you've let go of any self at all."

"That's what you want to let go of?" Rinpoche clarified, for Tom's sake rather than his own. "This sense of self?"

Tom's eyes glistened as he nodded.

"Tell me, Tom, where does it go when you play the piano?"

Tom was taken aback. "I don't … I mean … when I'm playing a piece, when I'm really in the flow, there's no feeling of being me." As he spoke, he began to understood what Lama Tashi intended.

"Time falls away?"

"Yes."

"Self falls away?"

He nodded.

"No subject. No object. Just a single experience?"

"That's right," he was smiling.

"There are many ways to non-duality, Tom. The piano is yours. You don't need to start at the beginning. You already know your way there."

Later, before going to bed, Lama Tashi stood on his porch. Above him, the moon and stars were waltzing through a universe of possibilities. The nearby stream murmuring busily as it continued its life-giving purpose. He contemplated how the past two days had been about making manifest what previously had been unmanifest. Bringing to attention what had been there all along, hidden in plain sight.

If outward appearance reflected one's own consciousness, if the world was as we made it and mind the forerunner of actions, what may arise when we discovered ourselves to be the possessors of minds that had no beginning and no end? Hearts that were the wellspring of more uncontrived goodness than we may have even thought possible?

Shanti hopped from the cottage window and came towards him, rubbing herself on his ankles and weaving between his legs with a throaty purr. He picked her up, so the two of them could share the munificent night.

"I'm also very happy to see you," he said.

They were together in watchful contemplation, when something different arose from along the mountain. An evening breeze brought with it the swell and ebb of a piano, arpeggios of rapturous triumph followed by ripples of poignant delicacy, the soaring and the profound in passages of an enthralling drama searching constantly for resolution.

"And that, my dear," said Lama Tashi, "is the sound of a man who is finding his way home."

DEDICATION

Through reading, thinking and meditating
And the actions flowing from these,
May anyone who encounters this book
Purify all negative karmas and accumulate infinite virtue.
Blossoming under the guidance of precious teachers,
May we all have long life, good health and profound wellbeing.
By letting go of our selves,
May we taste the exalted joy of enlightenment.

Then may we, as Buddhas,
Support all sentient beings throughout universal space.
By manifesting spontaneously and effortlessly in myriad forms
May we help those who experience their selves as separate and
suffering
Quickly to realize their own Buddha nature,
So that all may abide in the sublime state
Of radiant compassion and boundless wisdom,
Non-dual, great bliss and sunyata.

Author's Note

NSTANT *KARMA* IS A WORK OF FICTION. KIND OF. I HAVE DONE MY BEST to present traditional Tibetan Buddhist teachings on karma as accurately as possible. These include elements such as the general aspects of karma, the specific causes of certain effects, the factors that give karma its power, and concepts like bodhichitta and the dependent nature of reality.

The scenarios created to illustrate these principles are, of course, my invention. Some readers may feel I have gone too far. Others that I have gone not nearly far enough. Some people may think it would have been useful to have highlighted other cases of negativity about which we humans, on an individual or collective basis, are strangely complacent.

In writing this book what I've tried to do is stimulate thought, start conversations, and open people's minds—and hearts—to the notion that karma may indeed offer a credible explanation for why each of us experiences reality the way we do.

Because if it *is* the case that everything is in an ongoing state of flux, of change, of becoming, and if the causes we create on a moment-by-moment basis really do result in later effects, surely the big question each one of us must resolve is this: how best to use our powerful but finite human lives to create the best possible outcomes for ourselves and for others?

About the Author

DAVID MICHIE IS THE INTERNATIONALLY BEST-SELLING AUTHOR OF *The Dalai Lama's Cat* series, *The Magician of Lhasa*, *The Secret Mantra* and other books including the non-fiction titles *Buddhism for Busy People*, *Buddhism for Pet Lovers*, *Mindfulness is Better than Chocolate* and *Hurry Up and Meditate*.

In 2015 he established Mindful Safaris to Africa, combining wildlife viewing and meditation sessions in journeys to unexplored places, outer and inner.

For more about his work go to: https://davidmichie.com/

Lightning Source UK Ltd.
Milton Keynes UK
UKHW012024161122
412328UK00018B/184/J